INVASIONS

Also by Eugene Izzi

KING OF THE HUSTLERS
THE PRIME ROLL

INVASIONS

Eugene Izzi

BANTAM BOOKS
NEW YORK • TORONTO • LONDON • SYDNEY • AUCKLAND

This novel is a work of ficton. Names, characters, places, and incidents are either the product of the author's imagination or are used fictitiously. Any resemblance to actual events, locales, or persons, living or dead, is entirely coincidental.

INVASIONS
A Bantam Book / May 1990

Library of Congress Cataloging-in-Publication Data

Izzi, Eugene.
   Invasions / Eugene Izzi.
    p.   cm.
   ISBN 0-553-05769-3
   I. Title.
PS3559.Z9I58 1990
813'.54—dc20   89-18670
                      CIP

Published simultaneously in the United States and Canada

Bantam Books are published by Bantam Books, a division of Bantam Doubleday Dell Publishing Group, Inc. Its trademark, consisting of the words "Bantam Books" and the portrayal of a rooster, is Registered in U.S. Patent and Trademark Office and in other countries. Marca Registrada. Bantam Books, 666 Fifth Avenue, New York, New York 10103.

PRINTED IN THE UNITED STATES OF AMERICA

BOMC offers recordings and compact discs, cassettes and records. For information and catalog write to BOMR, Camp Hill, PA 17012.

The war against invasions is a tough and nearly impossible one, yet one still being fought every day by dedicated professionals who fight the daily battles so the rest of us can live safe and secure.

This book is dedicated to one of the true heroes of that war.

For Alice Vachss, who, as chief of the Special Victims Bureau in New York City, brings justice to the abused by courageously staring the invading scum down without flinching, fighting hard and valiantly to put them where they belong, and who, in her *spare* time, works to save the victims.

To this incredible warrior woman I proclaim my admiration and respect.

Chapter

ONE

The tall muscular guy was holding a wee little Mexican Chihuahua on a slim leather leash, the leash attached to a leather collar studded with blue, green, and red rhinestones. It was early October, and there was a chill in the air, but the character wore a purple silk ribbed tank top that ended just above his navel, showing washboard abs. His hair was obviously dyed, bright yellow, combed straight back in a sweeping style. It hung to his shoulders, brushed them as he tossed his head to get the few wisps that fell forward onto his forehead out of his eyes. He had on black spandex pants with the name of a race car written down each leg. He had something stuffed down the front of his pants, making his groin area appear massive, but the casual passerby couldn't make out what it was without being too obvious, and the big guy ignored the few men who did try to see what was down there. He minced as he pranced slowly forward on his Air Jordans. Here on Astor Street, the richest real estate in Chicago, he passed a couple of black nannies dressed in their nurses' uniforms, watched with a bemused and frank expression as they tried to keep from cracking up as they approached, made it, then laughed aloud the second they passed, kidding each other. One of them said, "Lord, what a waste of a fine-bodied man . . ." and the guy smiled.

He passed a huge mansion, stopped so the dog could relieve itself in the gutter. As it squatted, he said, "Really, Foo-foo, couldn't you have waited until we got to the alley?" Giving the house a quick once-over, seeing nothing out of the ordinary. The stop-sign-shaped red sign attached to one of the gate halves said in bold white letters: PREMISES PROTECTED BY ADT TRIPLE-ALARM SYSTEM! TRESPASSERS WILL BE PROSECUTED TO THE FULLEST EXTENT OF THE LAW! The man looked around the property through the gates, his eyes wide, Foo-foo pulling at the leash. He felt the urge to boot it in the ass, but that would be out of character. After a short time he turned away, walked with the dog to the end of the block, around the corner and into the alley.

Here Astor Street looked a lot like Beirut. There was gang graffiti sprayed on the tall privacy fences, most of them topped with barbed wire, curling three or four feet into the air all the way around the edge of the properties. The stone fence surrounding 5258 Astor didn't have the wire, but had razor-sharp arrowheads sticking out of the thing at one-foot intervals. The man knew that broken glass was embedded between the iron heads. Someone had posted a bill in the middle of the wall, the little poster mimeographed, hung crookedly. It had a picture of a rat in a circle, with a line drawn through the rodent. It said: TO CONTROL PESTS, PLEASE SECURE THE LID ON YOUR GARBAGE CANS! To Foo-foo, the man said, "Quaint," then minced out of the alley, setting his face in a mask of open invitation, ready to take the ridicule he would have to face farther south, down State, as he headed back to the parking lot where he'd left the stolen car.

The mob guy's name was Tonce DiLeonardo, and they called him the Lion. He had a full head of hair that he dyed black and had styled every week at a place called The Gentleman's Shoppe. He liked the *Shoppe* part; it showed that the fuckers who owned the joint had class. He was sitting across the desk from a guy he considered to be a punk, but a guy he needed right now, so he fought the urge to climb over the desk and slap the son of a bitch, the way he was sitting there grinning at him. He'd be giving up maybe twenty-five years, the punk was maybe thirty, thirty-one, but they were both big and weighed about the same and the Lion figured that experience was on his side.

They sat in the office of the Lion's South Side home, in what he called the Lion's Den. There were bodyguards outside in the hall and in the living room, the muscle belonging to both of them. He didn't like the fact that this kid had brought in some of his toughs, like they had a chance against his men if he decided to get hard. Still, he didn't say anything. Yet. He'd poured the kid a drink personally, watched him sip it, saw the surprise on the kid's face because this was seventy-five-year-old Royal Salute, top-shelf stuff, better than anything the kid had ever put down his throat before. Tonce figured if this guy had ever had a shot of this stuff before, it was after stealing it in a liquor store robbery; he pictured this slob behind an alley somewhere, drinking Royal Salute out of the bottle, maybe after mixing it with Kool-Aid or Boone's Farm. The kid made a face, lifted the glass in a mock salute, then drank the rest of the scotch down in one gulp, with a flick of his wrist. He slapped the glass down on the desk, burped, and said, "Good shit, Mr. D," smirking still.

"Thank you, Tommy," the Lion said, then made up his mind. The second the deal was done, he'd suffocate the life out of this kid, teach him a lesson.

But for now he smiled, sipped his own whisky, placed the glass right in the middle of the coaster in front of him and said, "Tommy, tell me a little about one of your boys, a fella named Jimmy Vale."

"Good man, one of the best the Brotherhood got. Tough, takes no shit from the niggers inside. Why, he do something? This what this sitdown's all about?"

The Lion just looked at him.

"Mr. D," the cocky little shit said, "maybe you ought to tell me what this is about."

The tall muscular man had pulled off the wig as soon as he got the car out of the garage, had pulled into an alley and removed the thing, tossed it on the seat. He pulled a bag off the floor of the passenger side, got jeans and a sweatshirt out of it and pulled them

3

over the fag clothes, leaving on the Air Jordans. He liked those Air Jordans. He shoved the wig into the bag, fought the urge to shove the dog down in there, too. Shit, they'd done a job on it, had put little pink bows on the sucker's ears and one on its little rat tail. He pictured the Chihuahua's picture on a poster, with a line drawn through it. Little rat-looking ugly thing. Even now—you'd think the dog would know better—it was standing up on the stolen Chevy's seat, barking its little ass off when he needed a little privacy. He shushed it—it was too little to hurt—put the car in gear and drove slowly out of the alley, heading for home.

Manny Aeilo stood on the front terrace of the Winnetka mansion his boss owned, surveying the grounds and the surrounding estates with a pair of 10×50 power binoculars, the kind with the wide-angle lenses. Slowly, he'd pan right, then left, looking for signs from New York. He did this three or four times every day, never at the same time, staggering the hours to throw off anyone who might be watching him.

Like the guys late this past summer. They'd been slick, he'd give them that, but he was slicker. You didn't last thirty-seven years in his business being second best.

Those guys had been thorough. At any given time, day and night, there were four guards on duty, protecting Mad Mike Tile from his enemies. Thirty-two guys in Manny's crew, none of them weak, although lately, some of them were going soft. He'd call one of them to him, late last August, early September, hand them the binocs, say to them: "Take a look, tell me what you see," and none of them ever saw anything.

The guys doing the surveillance work had been that good.

They'd dress like typical Winnetka residents, in jogging clothes or bathing suits, all the time wearing the radios attached to their heads, but Manny could tell from the look in their eyes, the way they looked a little too closely at the mansion, hung around the park across the street trying to look casual, that they were checking the place out.

He'd go to the boss, to Mike, tell him his suspicions and what

4

would the man say? Manny's paranoid, seeing dragons in his old age. Mike would tell him that his underlings in the Chicago outfit loved him, revered him, the great Mike Tile who'd brought dope into the city after years of stringent rules against the white powders. Everyone was making money, tons of the stuff, Mike would tell him. Why would anyone want Mike Tile dead? Manny didn't know, didn't have an answer for him. Sometimes it would take him an hour just to get in and talk to the man, having to wait until Mike was through with the young girls he'd taken such a shine to since his wife's death.

Mike would talk to him and be rubbing his nose, shaking his full head of long white hair, running his fingers through it. Sniffing. Mike—what, sixty-four or -five now—and in the last two years he'd started with the young chicks and the sampling of his own wares. Rich enough to snort all he wanted and never even tap the main source.

Manny remembered the good old days, when it was gambling and broads that brought in the money. Plenty to go around, too, with the old man in charge, the Swordfish, ready to go to war and chop the hands off anyone who dared to venture into drug dealing.

Manny had been good, rising through the ranks of Mike's crew until he was the chief, second in command. They would sit down and between the two of them devise a way to defeat their enemies, those who wanted what Mike Tile had.

They'd done that recently, too, three years back when Mike had taken over and decided to give the dying outfit a cash transfusion, drugs being their plasma. It had been fun, the three of them— Mike, Manny, and Manny's right hand, Louis Bamonti—putting their heads together to find a way to destroy the black and Hispanic gangs that had total control of the drug dealing in the city back then. Louis had claimed it was impossible, and Manny had just looked at him.

These gangs, these young, stupid kids who'd filled their heads with dumb ideas, running around wearing gold chains as heavy as hemp, driving their black muscle-cars, had been easy. The ones who wouldn't negotiate had been killed in the style they themselves had immortalized; the cops had gone looking for other

5

gangs, when all the time it was the Tile outfit that had done the killings, using the unfamiliar Uzis and MAC-10s to do the job, throwing the cops off their scent.

What it came down to, in Manny's mind, was leadership, generalship. Now that his own wife had died and his three children were grown, he had taken a room in the mansion, the walls filled with bookcases, every book having to do with war, with warriors, with killing. Manny could name every shogun who ever existed, every Roman emperor. Early on, he'd known that it wasn't in him to lead, to be the head of his own family. But he could be the best mob crew chief who'd ever lived, the greatest gladiator. He had no patience for the politics involved in being on top, the ass-kissing and speaking in riddles. He said what he had to say, the only way he knew how, straight and to the point, without bullshit or any extra words. Patton was the best general who'd ever lived, in Manny's opinion, but he would have made a terrible President.

He believed that he was Mike Tile's Patton.

A bunch of disorganized blacks and Hispanics, punks who worshiped money, were no match for him. He'd taken them over and had been greatly rewarded for doing so.

As had Mike Tile. The millions poured in, tens of millions, and Tile's national esteem with it. Everyone loved him, Mike would say. Men, women, children, even his own bodyguards, see how they admired him, partied with him? Found him new untouched young girls who wanted to go somewhere in life?

If everyone loved Mike Tile, Manny wondered, looking out over the lush green lawn with his binoculars, then why was somebody setting him up?

Frank Vale was pushing thirty-five and had never done a day in the penitentiary, though he'd spent a night or two in the can over the years, usually for some bullshit in a bar late at night, having to teach some wise guy a lesson. He figured by his own count that he'd pulled maybe three hundred burglaries, so the fact that he'd never been pinched for one carried a lot of weight.

He saw himself as a perfectionist with a tight lip, and that made him maybe the best thief in the city. Only one man had ever done time because of a score Frank had set up, and that made him one of the most sought-after thieves in the city. But he was careful, chose only the best he could find to work with, guys he knew he could trust and who would die before giving him up if for some reason they got put in the trick bag. He didn't deal in egos, never had a problem giving orders and could take them, too, if the guy giving them knew what he was talking about.

He figured it beat punching a time clock.

He'd been married once, briefly, to a girl who'd changed in days from a sweet young kid into a nag, bringing her entire zoo into his house the day after the wedding. Two fifty-five-gallon glass tanks filled with freshwater fish, a mixed-breed mutt dog, a calico cat, and a parrot. The bird's name was Gonzo, which she thought was cute, and the ugly green son of a bitch would actually take seed out of her mouth, then coo at her, peck gently at her nose. He'd try to touch it, stick his finger in the cage to pet its head and it would bite him, drawing blood a couple of times before he decided that it would never like him. His wife would bill and coo at the bird: "Gonzo loves only his mommy, isn't that right little baby?" like he was supposed to be jealous of it or something. When he started thinking about making soup out of the thing or pissing in the fish tanks, he figured the marriage was in trouble. He'd gotten a no-fault divorce and had bought her off with a hundred grand cash for six months of her time, and packed her off with his best wishes. He'd kept the dog, and found that he liked it better than he ever had the wife.

He stood six feet three inches tall and in the summer got down to two-ten, would bloat up to maybe two-twenty in the winter but would never lose his hardness, the well-defined muscles kept tight and strong through daily workouts. He didn't do it because he was vain, but because he thought of his body as a machine that had to be kept tuned. He wasn't just playing with his own life here; there were other men to consider. He had to be in top shape, sharp and ready with good reflexes, and they would all get out alive and prosper after a score. He demanded this of himself, and of the men he worked with. Behind his back, he knew, they called him the Iceman.

He kind of liked it, being called that, because it fit his image of himself. There was only one man alive he would ever really open up to, tell things to, and that man was his brother, who was now in the joint, wrapping up a nine-year sentence for home invasion. Thinking of his brother made him smile. Christ, he missed that kid. It would be good to see him.

He pulled the car to the curb about two blocks from his house, shoved the dog under his sweatshirt, the little mutt nipping at him and fidgeting, shit, and jogged home, where the two men he'd picked for the job would be waiting in his basement, studying the floor plans and the alarm systems for tonight's score, the big mansion at 5258 Astor Street. He would be happy to tell them that it looked like a go.

Turning the corner onto Sheridan, he spotted the two cops at the same time they saw him, knew they spotted him and so fought the urge to just turn around and walk away. He walked, casually, toward them, bending down and letting Foo-foo loose, holding the leash, putting a curious look on his face as he pretended to spot the guys. The first one he knew—it was that prick Gunon. The second one was new, probably just came into the unit, was learning the ropes. The new kid was holding his own, giving him the insolent stare that was the trademark of the elite Police Reconnaissance and Intelligence for Crime Control unit, called PRICC by the thieves of Chicago.

"There a problem, officers?"

Gunon answered, grinning. "Problem, Frank? Now when did we ever have a problem with you, huh?" Frank said nothing. This was a part of the life he'd chosen and he'd learned to accept it.

"Nice dog you got there," the new kid said, and Gunon smirked. "I read a study once, said all a you tough guys was undercover faggots."

Frank took a deep breath, let it out. He said, "Tell you what, there's a way to check it out. Why don't you kiss my ass, and if I get stiff, you win." He dropped the leash when the young cop started coming at him, put his hands up, then dropped them

8

because Gunon had his hand on his piece there at the front of his waistband, ready.

"Go ahead, badass, add assaulting an officer to the charges."

"What *are* the charges?" Frank said. The kid had stopped advancing, was standing there letting Gunon handle things. He was breathing hard though, and Frank wasn't looking forward to the visit to the basement of the precinct house. Gunon had lightened the grip on his pistol, in control and showing it. He was grinning in the oily way he had, like a pimp does, pretending to be friends with someone he was trying to beat out of some money.

"Planning a score and not telling your partners about it. That's a serious offense in this town, you know." Gunon laughed—he had a habit of cracking himself up—and his partner smirked.

"Gonna bust you up, Mr. big time. Mr. big time thief. And I can't wait."

Gunon said, "Giraldi, cuff this asshole and put him in the car."

Chapter

Two

It was a day like any other, that's all. Jimmy kept telling himself that, because he figured if he did he would live through it. He'd seen other guys, short-timers about to be sprung, act all antsy and talk about it too much, and suddenly everybody who had a real or imagined beef with them would crawl out of the woodwork, looking for revenge, knowing goddamn well that when a man had an out date he would do anything to keep it. Even maybe back off a step and let you get away with something one time. Which was all it took: one time you backed down, and man, you had better never hit the yard again, because someone would remember and from that moment on life would be hell for you.

Other guys, he'd seen offed the last day, which was the final indignity. The whole point of doing time, the only goal, was to get out alive. Do it one day at a time and get out sometime in a distant future that wasn't often thought about and never discussed. He'd seen guys die over candy bars, over bars of soap, over cigarettes (which was the same as getting killed over money on the outside), over sex, over jealousy, over attitude, over gang affiliation and due to simple anger.

Men died here for cheating at cards, for cheating on their boyfriends, for cheating their bookies, and for cheating at chess.

Some caught their lunch over the dinner table, but not often, because there were hacks armed with shotguns standing on cat-walks in the dining room, so only the psychos went to kill over a meal. Most of the time you died in the tunnels, or in the yard, or in your cellblock, or in the shower, or in your house after lights-out if the guy wanting to do you had what it took to pay off enough hacks to get loose after lights-out. Then they'd pour flammable liquids on you while you slept, and toss in a match. The hacks couldn't get to you in time, even if they wanted to.

Jimmy had lived the last nine years of his life in Stateville Penitentiary and was getting out tomorrow, so he figured to play it like it was just another day.

But man, it was hard. Trying to keep your mind on a day's business when you knew all you had to do was get through the day and you were finally free.

He passed Lanny Cifello in the yard between C and D Blocks and they nodded at each other, touched their right fists to their chests in greeting. "Brotherhood," they said softly. He didn't want to say it, not aloud, not today. There had been stirrings the last few weeks, some racial thing was going to come down, and a blatant sign of affiliation with a gang was not a bright thing to show right now, but everyone in the joint knew who he was, so there was no sense trying to act alone now. And not to do what a brother always did when he passed, especially when there was trouble brewing, might be seen as a sign of weakness.

Shit, it got complicated if you let it.

His gaze lingered upon the grass between the two cellblocks as he passed, remembering. He'd been inside two weeks when the two gangbangers had come upon him, right back there, and instead of his three-year bit, out in one, he'd been here an extra eight years because of what had happened. . . .

He tore his eyes away from the spot, forced his mind off it; the remembrance would bring nothing but anger and resentment and he had no use for that today. Negative emotions drove him most of the time, made him strong, but he had to stay cool today of all days, because he wanted to live to breathe free air.

He lived in an environment where the two strongest emotions

were terror and hatred. Sometimes the two would overlap and you didn't know where one began and the other ended. You walked hard and never backed down, kept your attitude right there in front of you, ran a game on the hacks and the other cons as well as you could. You stood ready at all times to fight for your chastity and your life and you never let your guard down. You had to act as if you didn't give a fuck whether you lived or died, and if you could give the illusion of that you might make it. If you could achieve that mental state entirely, you would survive.

Jimmy knew from past experience, though, that it was a tough thing to do.

When a group of studs had you cornered in the shower and they had shanks and you were naked, the temptation was there, up front in your mind: Drop to your knees, do it, and they'll leave you alone. It beat getting the shit kicked out of you and raped up your butt a dozen times. The problem was, if you did that, that one time in the shower would only be the beginning. From then on you would be open game, an anybodys. Unless you found a jailhouse daddy and even then the odds were even that he'd sell you out, get you to suck off his buddies to prove his power over you. Jimmy could retire if he had a dollar for every time he'd seen some young white boy give in that first time, and wind up wearing mascara and lipstick until he hanged himself off a tier post one night or got killed by the rough-sex psychos.

No, it wasn't for him. Or for anyone else in the White Aryan Brotherhood. But you had to prove yourself to become a brother; it wasn't a fraternity you pledged to. You had to be invited and the weak ones never were. The weak ones were left to fend for themselves.

These days, the lines were less clearly drawn. When he'd first come in, the population had been ninety percent minority and you didn't hang with anyone but a member of your own race. Now, white guys were members of black gangs, for Christ's sake, if the white guy was willing to steal and kill on command. And if he was tough enough to prove himself. No one wanted the sissies or the punks talking trash without the balls to back themselves up. They were booty-banged the first week in, guys like that, and either got

13

killed, wound up in protective custody, or destroyed their minds with drugs to take them away from their harsh reality.

Jimmy walked to the corner of the yard, stood next to a dark, evil-looking man with a shaved head. Michael Knox, the number one of their gang. Jimmy's hands were stuffed down the pockets of his denim pants, his shirt collar up around his neck, the collar of his jacket up, too. It was chilly for October.

"Homeboy, how you doing?" Jimmy said.

"Guy come in yesterday," Michael said, "Bill Bender. White kid, big, in for killing a cop. Came in on the bus from JCC and right away we recruit him, cause we know he'll add to the Brotherhood. He tells Jano that they warned him about the gangs during R and I, told him to stay away from them. They'll corrupt him and if he gets caught in one, he'll get extra time tacked on his sentence." Michael grunted. "Guy killed a cop, he's looking forward to his out date."

"He'll learn."

"You smell it, Jimmy?" There was concern in Michael's voice. "In the wind? Man, somebody's gonna die today, you bet your ass. Every other year, bro, got to kick some nigger ass."

Jimmy nodded. "Been coming for some time."

They both knew how many died inside the wall. There was a cemetery outside the wall, on the prison property, Boot Hill, where dead cons without someone to care for them were buried. There was a name and the dates of birth and death chiseled into a small stone, under which were the letters *W* or *C*. White or colored. Jimmy shivered. A lot more died than the public knew about. Once, a few years back, a suspected informer with less than a week to his out date disappeared completely, without a trace. He wasn't listed as a homicide or an escape, but members of a certain gang were seen hanging around the meat house that afternoon, and nobody who had witnessed that had eaten the hamburger that night.

Michael said, "I want the kid to learn now, today. Word gets out we went looking for someone and he turned us down, we'll look weak. Then you got a chastisement to do on Chaney."

"Chaney?"

"Dumb son of a bitch, he was seen talking and laughing with a jig guard, not one of ours."

"Damn. Chaney, huh?"

"Probably nothing, Jimmy, but you know how it is—you got to toe the line."

"Want me to go light on him?"

"No, full treatment. Fuck him. He got to learn, same as we did."

They lit smokes, stood casually, neither of them with work assignments, hanging out in the yard after breakfast waiting for the whistle. They'd have to go back to their own cellblocks for a count when the whistle blew, and as Jimmy was the block leader and the general enforcer for the Brotherhood, he was now getting his daily instructions from the prison boss.

Around the yard groups stood talking out of the side of their mouths or in whispers, segregated again, no whites and blacks together. A bad sign. Jimmy looked at Knox, who was nodding his head, confirming his belief. Something was in the wind.

Jimmy dwarfed Knox, had bigger arms and bigger balls, and when the last leader, Tommy Jacobi, had been released, Jimmy had been given the opportunity to step into his shoes and had turned it down. It was a high-profile job, and Jimmy liked to lay low. Michael had been next in line and had jumped on it, but he knew who carried the weight and never gave Jimmy any trouble.

"Tomorrow's your date, right?" Michael spoke low, his head down. You never knew when someone was reading your lips. Jimmy nodded benignly, as if responding to a comment on the weather.

"Man, we're gonna miss you. You spray fear like a skunk sprays piss."

"Thanks."

"Tommy wants to see you."

"Whatever he needs." Jimmy spoke the words because they were expected, but he had a sinking feeling in his gut. After tomorrow, he didn't intend to spend a lot of time with members of the Brotherhood. Still, besides Frank, they were all he had.

"Says it's a mob thing, some favor for the guidos." Michael

15

looked up, into eyes dead and cold. "Hey, no offense. We're blood, right? Shit, guineas, polacks, micks, we're all brothers in here, right?"

Jimmy said nothing, thinking, looking at the segregated groups in the yard.

It isn't like the ones on TV or in the movies, that was for sure. Stateville has a yard that is all grass and flowers, neatly tended by cons who knew what they were doing. Liberal groups would come in to preach and would eat it up, seeing the brightness and the gardens, never knowing what atrocities were performed behind the walls every day of the year, like clockwork. Men being owned like slaves, the weak bought and sold back and forth at the leisure of the strong; men who had been too proud to work for four dollars an hour back in the world now thinking they were players if they could slick you out of a pack of smokes.

His gaze moved on to the wall, thirty-foot-high concrete running the circuit around the entire joint. From anywhere inside this place, looking up you saw nothing but sky or wall. It would be good to see cars again, and women who weren't all fat and black and wearing blue hack uniforms.

"You got to see the shrink?"

"Evaluation after lunch."

"Like it matters. You got no parole, right?"

Jimmy shook his head. He knew that Michael was wondering if he was offended, and he appreciated the respect the man was showing him, but did nothing to ease his fears. Fuck him. Let a guy call you a guido or a guinea, it was the same as a black letting a guy call him a nigger. Pretty soon it was a part of your jacket, and everyone was doing it. Michael had meant no offense, but there were limits and he'd come close to crossing a line.

"He'll talk shit, ask me about my mother, and stamp my sheet. They got to make room for some other sucker, got his ass caught."

"Hey, there goes Richie."

Richard Speck was crossing the yard, carrying a paint bucket, lumbering, drunk already. "Hey, Richie!" Michael hollered. "Hey, you ugly motherfucker, I'm married to a *Filipino*—you hear me, asshole?"

It was a game he played and Jimmy did not like the attention it was drawing them. Black faces were staring resentfully, some of the men nodding. Jimmy tightened his shoulders, feeling the spot between his shoulder blades where the shiv would go in, the minute he turned his back on one of those faces. Speck kept walking, lurching, the big ugly pizza-faced punk keeping his head down and acting like he couldn't hear them. The word was he was fag, and when he'd applied for membership in the WAB, Tommy had laughed at him. There were some strict rules, and drunks and fags could never get in. He had the run of the prison though, making the rounds painting the walls, and most of the guys messed with him some. He was a woman killer, on the third rung from the bottom in the prison pecking order, just above rapists and child molesters.

"Yeah, Jimmy, we're gonna miss you around here."

"I ain't gonna miss this joint."

"Don't kid yourself. You might be back."

"Never happen, Michael." The conviction in his voice made the other man pause and look at him directly, no more of the prison yard caginess, staring at him now full in the face.

"You're serious, ain't you?"

Jimmy stared back, feeling his hackles rise. Most of these guys had been in and out three or four times in their lives. Jimmy had been busted for a home invasion when he was nineteen and he'd come of age inside these walls, had matured and reached manhood. He'd spent a third of his life staring at a concrete wall and trying not to think of the wonders that lay behind it. There was no year, two-year bit for him. He'd been here so long he'd forgotten any other way of life, had become a jailhouse survivor and was one of the best there was at the game, but he'd made his mind up when his lawyer had come and told him his out date; he'd never be back. If he had to die to stay free, well, so be it.

"If the brohams"—he nodded his head toward the groups of black men who were still staring at them—"don't get me, if I ever get down that road out there, I ain't *never* coming back."

The whistle sounded, cutting off all conversation. It was a train whistle, attached high up on the roof of C Block. Jimmy spit out his cigarette and held out his hand; he didn't plan to be back in the yard again, ever. Michael took it, held it, squeezed while he covered it with his other hand, pressing something into it. Jimmy patted him on the back, nodding his thanks. He was getting something for nothing in an environment where everything had a price. It was a sign of respect, a going-away present. He stuck his hand into his pocket and released the little cardboard box but kept his hand over it so the square wouldn't show through the material of his pocket, to be spotted by a hack they weren't paying. He didn't need a problem his last day in.

He knew what it was and as he walked to his cellblock he kept his face straight but he was smiling inside. He'd been handed the single most valuable possession there was in the joint these days, more precious than cigarettes or clothing or having your own TV or stereo, more important than cash itself. The gift was the most dangerous contraband you could get caught with, though, because it would say things about you that you didn't want known if you were caught with it.

He was locked into his single cell—another symbol of his status—and waited for the hack to count him in, then stepped to the sink and unscrewed the bottom pipe, pulled it out of the wall and quickly stashed the contraband inside the wall, then inserted the pipe, screwed it back in, successfully hiding the three-pack box of Trojan rubbers from sight.

Chapter

THREE

Jimmy's house was in C Block, the five-tier-high round cell-block civilians get to see in the movies all the time. The only thing the movies seem to get right about the place is the sound. Constantly, twenty-four hours a day, there is noise. Not just sound, but *noise*. Convicts hollering and screaming at each other throughout the day and night, threatening, joking, talking in code. The round block had been built with security in mind but that had been a joke; all it did was allow the cons to know at all times where the hacks were.

Noise bounces off and around the stone walls, up to the ceiling and back down, never stopping. Jimmy lay on his bunk, in the single cell he'd had the past six years, since rising to second in command of the Brotherhood, thinking about changes.

Some things never changed. Food in the joint was always bad and usually cold, cooked in vats the size of wading pools. The cons cooked it, watched over by civilian supervisors and dieticians. They had never found a way to make anything that came out of them taste good. Everything always felt clammy to the touch in here, too. Not just the food; the walls, the floors, they were always clammy, slimy. Only the worst hillbilly would step into the shower barefooted; that was the single most rotten spot in the joint, you wanted to talk about filth and decay. He would read the magazines that said the state spent twenty-five grand a year keeping each con inside and he knew that maybe that was what they charged, but it wasn't what was being spent. Someone was making a lot of money off the penal system. If you asked Jimmy, twenty-five hundred would have seemed about right.

The glass in Stateville gets broken only once. A con would break it and it would stay broken for years. Unless it's in a building that can be seen from outside the wall—then it's fixed right way. Light bulbs were high wattage and covered by wire cages, too high up for a man to get to without a problem. You break the light in your cell and you're out of luck for a year or two, would wind up reading by candlelight if you were one of the lucky ones who were literate.

A lot of guys learned how to read inside, took courses for it, because reading broke up the monotony. Chess was big in the joint; even guys who couldn't read often learned chess. Men with time to kill seemed to always find ways to do it. Cards, checkers, these were big. Other guys just ordered magazines and looked at the pictures of the naked girls. Jimmy found that a waste of time, like looking at a picture of a turkey with all the trimmings when you were starving. Neither served a purpose.

Twenty-four hours, ah, God, and he'd get laid. He had to force his mind off it, because it wasn't time and he could not afford to be weak. He had to recruit the fish, Toby, still this morning, then chastise Chaney. After lunch he had the shrink evaluation, which would be fun. Talking to the headshrinker was the one time when he could loosen up, be himself a little without the attitude right up front. Tonight, he promised himself, once they were locked in and the screaming was down to a low roar, then he would allow himself to dream about what he would do tomorrow.

To keep his mind straight, he thought about changes. Nine years' worth.

Well, for one thing, they no longer strip-searched visitors and employees. That long-term practice had ended after a nurse had been forced to remove a tampon that some female hack figured might be stuffed with diamonds or something. The nurse had sued and had won a bundle, but most important had forced the overturning of the regulation that allowed that atrocity. Hell, when Jimmy had first come in, *kids* had been skin-searched.

Which was something he had never been able to figure out. Back then, you visited in a room across a table, separated from your loved one by a sheet of thick glass that had little holes cut into it, through which you spoke. What was there to pass to him and how could you do it? Now, surprisingly enough, since the passing of the new regulation, cons got to meet with their families in a room guarded by a single unarmed hack. If you could afford to pay the hack off, he'd leave, and you could take your lady into the men's room or off into the corner somewhere for a little head.

Jimmy knew that Frank would never come to such a place. He'd write encoded letters, drop a hundred-dollar money order each week into commissary for him, but wouldn't enter the prison grounds. It was his only superstition. Maybe it came from them visiting their father here all those years ago. Frank would swear that the hacks were feeling him and their mother would slap him silly, call him a pervert for thinking such a thing. Tell him he was going to turn out just like his father if he didn't stop lying all the time. The funny thing was, Frank had never done a day inside, and here it was Jimmy, the baby of the family who was supposed to go far, who'd done all the time. . . .

Another thing better left alone. Ma didn't write anymore, and Frank didn't visit her. Jimmy would look her up when he got out, ask her why she'd given up on him the first time he stopped bringing money over. . . .

The birds, the sparrows, they never changed. Dumb bastards would wing inside, not knowing where they were, then forget the way out. The top of C House was now a goddamn aviary, the tile floors covered with bird shit. They added to the noise level too. The broken windows let the snow in, and in the winter drifts would form against the far walls, sometimes swirling around the place when the wind kicked up, giving the illusion of a snowfall.

The joint was always freezing cold or sweltering hot, and it always—all year 'round—stank.

You had no privacy behind these walls. Guys would use hot plates and boil orange peels, use it for dye and stain a white sheet, then hang it over the commode so everybody couldn't just look in and see them taking a crap or jerking off. You got away with it if you could afford to pay the hacks; if not they'd beef you, send you to the adjustment committee, and they'd decide your fate. On a first nonviolent offense you would get off light, have a letter put in your jacket. Multiple offenders and men ticketed for violent acts would be sent to seg—segregation—a jail within a jail, where you got locked down twenty-four hours a day and they'd let you take a ten-minute shower once a week.

That was another change; there was seg now, the Hole was gone.

Shit, he'd done his share of Hole time when he'd first come in and had his trouble. Not only had he had six years added to his sentence, but he'd had to wait for trial in the Hole, on a bread and water diet, a hole in the concrete floor for a toilet. Back then, you never got a chance to shower.

Jimmy, and every con who knew what it was, thanked God every day for the American Civil Liberties Union. It saved them a lot of grief.

He watched the shadows cross the tier, and when he figured it to be about ten he decided to give himself a few more minutes. Every minute in the cell was relatively safe, and safety was his goal for today. He didn't fear death, but the thought of dying inside on his last day terrified him.

What else had changed? Female hacks, they worked here now. Corruption, that hadn't changed. You could still buy the country asshole hacks for a pack of smokes, and the hip, black hacks usually had gang affiliations, worked for the gangsters they were sworn to keep incarcerated, bringing in drugs and booze and cash money and restaurant food and smokes smuggled in from the South. Letters that wouldn't get censored.

God, sex, how about it—had that changed or what? There were still sissies who would put on the makeup and serve man, and gang rape was in your future if you didn't have friends. The first rule of prison was: Accept nothing from no one; everything has its price. And yet these fish would come in and take a free smoke from someone, nod their thanks humbly, then cry into their pillows when the guy who gave them the smoke turned up later in the evening looking for romance. There were marriages here that weren't pretty. Most of the sex these days was involuntary, and Jimmy didn't know if that was a national trend or just a signal of the general downswing in character of the Stateville population.

He knew that on the outside, AIDS patients lasted about two years. Inside, the average life span from diagnosis to Boot Hill was four months, and a third of the population carried the virus. So much for all the special treatment given to convicts.

He sighed, rolled off the cot, and did fifty quick push-ups to pump up his arms and put some color in his cheeks. He had to have a talk with this new kid and wanted him to worry some, be a little afraid, so he wouldn't be a wiseass and get himself hurt.

"So you want to know about Jimmy Vale, eh?" Tommy Jacobi said. He took a deep drag from his cigarette, let the smoke filter through his nose. He was smirking and it was all Tonce the Lion could do to keep from jumping across the desk and plucking out his eyeballs.

The kid said, "Why?"

Shit. It was the new breed, these young punks who'd survived prison then came out and thought they had wisdom. Hell, all they were was lucky. They were ignorant of the way things were done. In his day, when Tonce had been this punk's age, if he'd ever been invited to the house of a real live boss, shit, he'd have spent three days getting dressed and thinking up good lines to greet the man with, prove he was on the ball. Today this punk comes into his house, this small-time hoodlum who fancied himself a gangster because he was the leader of a strong white street gang, and acted like he was doing Tonce a favor.

The trouble was, he mistook kindness for weakness.

Well, there were ways to straighten guys like him out.

Tonce smiled, placed his drink to the side, opened his desk drawer casually, as if looking for another glass, and took out a Smith & Wesson .38 six-shot revolver, with a six-inch barrel. He grunted at its weight, popped it open and checked the load, snapped it back and spun the cylinder, brought it down to his side as he stood, came around the desk.

He had the kid's attention. Tommy's mouth was open, about to shout something but too afraid to do it, scared to holler for his punk out in the hall. Tonce wasn't smiling now, though he wanted to. He got to Tommy, pulled his hair back hard with his left hand and stuffed the gun into his mouth, banging the sight hard on the kid's front teeth. He kept going, until Tommy gagged.

"I ask you a question, you answer me like I'm one of your sissies out there in the street. What's wrong with you. You got no idea of who I am or what I can do so you bring a man with you, to a sitdown with a boss. That ain't done, Tommy, but I let it go because you don't know any better." He let go of Tommy's hair and began to frisk him, found a small black telephone book in the inside jacket pocket. He tossed it onto the desk, enjoying the terror in Tommy's eyes.

"You're stupid, and I understand that. I deal with stupid people every day. Had a lot of them killed over the years too." He began to ease the pistol out of Tommy's mouth, slowly, gently, letting the kid know exactly what he was doing. Stealing away whatever manhood and dignity he might have had left. Tonce walked around the desk, put his gun away, picked up the phone book and began to leaf through it. He was smiling again calmly, buddies now— nothing had happened.

"Mom and Dad," he said, then looked up at Tommy. "It's good for a young man to respect his parents, that's good, Tommy." He opened the drawer, dropped the phone book in there.

Tonce the Lion DiLeonardi said, "Now, I'm gonna ask you some questions, Tommy, and you're gonna answer them. *You're* not gonna ask *me* any questions, and you're not gonna get cute anymore, give me funny looks. You do, just one fucking time, and I swear to God, I'm gonna go through every name in that phone book, starting with your mother, and send someone over to bury an axe into the head of every living soul you know. You under- stand me?"

Tommy's mouth was working, his eyes wild. If Tonce had done anything less than show him mortality, the kid might have screwed up, called for his punk to come save him, and then there would be bloodshed. Tonce looked at him, the kid maybe wondering if this big old mobster behind the desk would really have an axe buried in his mother's head. He worked his mouth for a time, then found his voice.

"Yes, sir, Mr. DiLeonardi."

"You *do* understand me, you ain't got no questions?"

"No, sir."

"All right, that's good, Tommy. Now I want you to do me a favor. Tell me what you know about a guy named Jimmy Vale."

Tina Lime had had a rough morning. Driving to police headquarters, she tried to calm down. She had to keep her wits about her. Think things through, she told herself, get it all out here in the car, so when you walk into headquarters you can be cold as ice, ready to do what you have to. First, that little prick of a judge in the Markham court had declared a mistrial in the case of a child abuser she'd gotten the goods on. That never went over well with her. As a lawyer, her practice was limited to criminal justice for children, and she went after it with a vengeance. Did her homework, hired investigators who searched into the backgrounds of the offenders, often finding other, similar allegations somewhere in the man's past. When she got to court she'd always be prepared, as she'd been this morning.

What she hadn't been prepared for was the judge's attitude, his near indifference to the enormity of the man's crime. The defendant's attorney, a fat, baldheaded little mouse who was making a great living defending these types, had seemed to be the only person who had the judge's attention. After the opening arguments, then the first witness, the defense attorney had called for a sidebar, argued an obscure point of law, citing the "new frontier" of law they were entering, as if child sexual abuse was a brand-new thing. The judge had gone so far as to stroke his chin as he'd listened, and had agreed that Tina's repeated use of the word *victim* before the jury had prejudiced them, because it implied that a crime had been committed.

Tina had said, simply, "There's a three-year-old girl here who's been raped and sodomized, Judge. You better fucking well *believe* a crime's been committed."

He'd warned her, threatened her with contempt, and she'd had to bite her tongue. She had nothing *but* contempt for this man and his court. Next time, when she had her second shot at this guy, she'd make sure she used the term *victim* only in her *closing* remarks. Make sure, too, that she had a couple of reporters in the courtroom, staring at the judge every second.

Sometimes she wondered, at times like this, what a man like the judge did behind closed doors.

She'd had a message waiting for her back in her office, one of the boys she'd fought for two years ago, a sexually abused black youngster who was now fifteen, had killed his father, the abuser. She'd lost that case, too; as happens so often, the boy had been returned to the people who'd harmed him. They had him at police headquarters at 11th and State, had already charged him with first-degree murder. The cop she'd spoken to when she'd called had said they were charging him as an adult, that the assistant state's attorney was talking about trying for the death penalty.

God, when would it all end?

Least important, she hadn't been able to get ahold of her boyfriend for a few days. She wondered if she'd driven him away, had been too demanding, too suffocating. She hadn't meant to be. God, he'd only been her third man; she still didn't seem to know how to act with them. . . .

Tina parked the car on the street, locked it, setting the alarm. She wasn't taking any chances. Her last car had been ripped off ten feet from the Fourth Precinct front doors. She had to step back, jump onto the sidewalk as an unmarked squad pulled to the curb, nearly smashing into the back of her car. She waited angrily until they got out of the car, roughly dragged a suspect out of the back seat.

When she saw who it was, though, all the anger drained out of her.

"Frank?" Tina said softly, then, *"Frank!"*

*   *   *

26

The PRICCs had roughed him up a little in the car but he didn't say anything; he'd seen worse and would see it again real soon. A twisted ear and a slap on the head were nothing.

What bothered him was how they'd got onto him. This was the fourth time in ten years that this had happened; the PRICC crew getting onto him the week of a score and him having to blow off a lot of serious money because of it. They'd take him in, offer him a partnership, and when he refused they'd kick the shit out of him, work him over real good, threaten him, tell him they were going to kill him, and then they'd cut him loose. For a couple of weeks they'd be on him, watching him like a hawk; then they'd find other ways to supplement their incomes and would leave him alone for a few years, until a snitch told them he was scoring big, or he didn't keep a low enough profile. Then they'd come calling again.

His main concern was how bad it would be this time. The first two times he'd had to go to the hospital; it had taken weeks for the swelling on his face and genitals to go away. Those had been the easy times. The last time, he'd fought too hard and one of the cops had lost his head, had leveled his mouth with a six-inch blackjack. He'd knocked almost every tooth out of Frank's mouth. There were a couple in the back that were his; the rest were now false. Remembering it made his gums ache.

Now he wondered how far to go. He'd made a few remarks to them outside the house, just to get their respect, and he wondered if he'd gone too far. If this new kid Giraldi was a psycho, he could be in big trouble. Either way, he was going to take a beating, so why make it easy on them?

The two of them were talking to each other in the front seat, casually, which was frightening. To them it was just another day's work. He was scum who didn't deserve to live unless he coughed up ten percent. Gunon and Giraldi saw themselves as protectors of the city, men on the front lines who risked their lives to save the city from the crooks. Guys like Frank were harmless, hurt only the insurance companies, so got to live as long as they paid. The problem was, Frank never paid.

They parked at the curb and dragged Frank from the car, hitting him when he pulled back. From somewhere he heard a familiar female voice call his name. He tried to look around, but one of them gave him a shot in the kidneys that doubled him over; then they were dragging him by the cuffs into police headquarters, the back way.

They hustled him into their office in the basement of the building—a big dark-haired guy with his hands cuffed behind him: nothing for anyone to be concerned about. They threw him into a chair and he was surprised when they started out differently than they had the last three times.

There were the two who had pinched him, Gunon and Giraldi, standing by either arm of the chair. He was their prisoner and they were responsible for him. Two other officers were in the room with them. A gigantic fat black guy he'd seen before, whose name he forgot, and a shorter white man, looking too old to be a PRICC. They were an elite unit who punched no time clocks and wrote no reports and their officers were the fittest and baddest guys on the street. This man could have been the father of any one of the other men. He was overweight, but not that it showed, just a paunch and some handles Frank could see where the sides of his waist met his beltline. His hair was blondish and thin—he'd be bald in a couple of years. He had gentle eyes, which did not go well with where he was. Frank figured him to be either a visitor learning the ropes or a real psycho, about to get his nut off while beating on him.

"You want us to cuff him to the chair, Commander?" Giraldi was speaking, copying Gunon's olive-oil sleazy style of speech. Pimp-talking.

"Take the cuffs off, Giraldi."

"What?"

The commander did not bother to answer Giraldi. Frank looked at him, wondering, breathing hard now, noticing that the man's eyes no longer looked so kindly. Thank God for that.

Frank was rubbing his wrists, trying to regain circulation, looking right at the commander. As were the other men. Maybe this was his first time out with the crew, a new leader, and they were wondering how he'd play it. For a beginner, Frank figured, the guy did all right.

He waited until Frank put his hands on the arms of the chair and squared his shoulders, then the commander lifted the phone off the desk, brought it over, dragging the cord behind it, and dropped it in Frank's lap.

"Call your lawyer," he said, and Frank didn't move. The other men began to snicker, seeing where it was going. "Go ahead, killer, call your fucking lawyer. And don't tell me you don't have one. All you hard-ass goombahs got someone on retainer, in case of the occasional occupational hazard like this one here." The man waited until he was sure Frank wasn't going to pick up the phone. He took it back to the desk, came back, leaned down into Frank's face, his hands going over Frank's on the chair's arms. He spoke into Frank's face, smelling of Sen-Sen.

"You won't call him because you know better, right Frank? Because you know who we are and you know that if you piss us off, push us, we won't rest until we got you behind bars for the rest of your life. Maybe even whack you out.

"I've been hearing about you. We got us a real *cowboy* here, don't we boys." He stood back and the men laughed, enjoying this. Frank decided that his first impression had been right. This was a relatively new commander, in the plum job on the force, gaining his men's respect.

"They tell me you're a hard-ass, won't pay us or the mob. The difference being, Vale, the mob's a bunch of pussies next to us." This got a howl, the men laughing outright and saying things like Fucking A. Doodie. The commander basked in it some, smiling, showing fine white teeth. He leaned into Frank again.

"You stupid fuck, don't you know you *got* to pay us? It's the way things *are* in this town. You want to take down scores in Chicago, son, you got to pay us. We take care of everyone else, make sure everyone's happy, and you get to go on to retirement or until you get pinched by the government or you get killed. But Vale, for the last time, you got to understand, we're in for ten points, or I swear to God, you are one dead motherfucker." He turned to Gunon.

"You know this guy, right? Gunon, tell me something, we're

gonna give him the benefit of the doubt. Did you express yourself to him properly, let him know the way things are?''

Giraldi held his arms out, palms up, imploring. ''Commander, I did. This asshole, I knocked his teeth out with a sap a few years ago, trying to convince him. Went to see him in the hospital, brought him some magazines, let him know there were no hard feelings. He tells me he's a retired construction worker, to leave him the hell alone.''

''You knocked his fucking teeth out with a blackjack, and he *still* didn't come across?''

''Commander, it wasn't my fault. The guy's fucking dense. I think we got to kill him, get our point across. Round up the rest of his gang and let them know what happened, get them to come across from now on.''

''You hear that, Frank? They want to kill you. Right now, I'm the only thing standing between you and a bullet, and you're still just sitting there looking like a badass, with your jaws shut. Wanna call your lawyer now, maybe?''

Frank had to hand it to him, the guy could work a crowd. Throughout his spiel they'd been spellbound, laughing in all the right places, and when he'd asked Gunon about the teeth deal, the son of a bitch had sounded hurt, had tried to tell the chief that it was Frank's fault that he'd lost his teeth. The knowledge frightened him because he was no longer just dealing with a bunch of guys who wanted money from him; now they were making noises like they wanted his life.

''Giraldi, you want to kill this guy?''

''Is this a vote, Commander? If it's a vote, I say let me have a crack at him. They been too easy on him, you want my opinion.'' The others were looking at the new gun in town, glaring. He was insulting them while trying to curry favor with the new boss.

''And you, Rosie? What do you think?''

The huge black man shook his head. ''Shit, I vote thumbs down. This bastard's whacko, don't pay us, the mob. What right he got to live?''

''You hear that, Frank? Two to one to kill, with the nay vote wanting his crack at your hard head. What do you think?''

Frank took a deep breath and said what he had to say before he could think about it and maybe change his mind.

"I think if you're gonna do it, you better go on ahead, because I ain't gonna pay you or any-fucking-body else—"

He was cut off when the commander turned and drove his fist into Frank's belly. Frank grunted in pain; the guy was making a big production out of it, swinging from the ground and grunting, making sure he got all his weight behind the punch.

Frank lost his breath, gasped, trying to pull oxygen into his lungs. He covered his belly with his hands, put his head down, tried to prepare himself for what he knew would be coming.

"Get the fuck out of here, all of you," the commander grunted. "This asshole's mine."

Chapter

FOUR

"He come into the joint a fish, did his week in Reception and Indoctrination over at the Joliet Correctional Center, like everyone else, and from there they evaluate you, send you out to a state prison they figure out from the severity of your crime. Say a guy boosts cars, never been in trouble before, he goes to maybe Vandalia or Centralia, picks cherries in minimum for a year, gets rehabilitated. Hardly anyone goes to Stateville first time out unless it's a Class X Felony or some violence thing."

Tommy was talking and maybe a little too much, but Tonce let him go. The kid was showing respect and trying hard to impress him, now that they both knew where they stood. Tonce would nod his head from time to time or interrupt to offer him a cigar or another drink. The kid declined both. Good. He was learning.

"Well, what we had there, was this big, young, tough housebreaker, got himself pinched for Home Invasion back when it was still called Breaking and Entering, B & E, lucky for him. Nowadays, it's Class X, and if you go in when someone's home, man, they nail your ass to the wall.

"He said he didn't know they were home, he thought they were out, and the reason he didn't get more than three years was because the people whose house he robbed, they backed him up in court, said all three robbers took off the second they turned on the bedroom light and saw them in there, screwing.

"But see, Mr. DiLeonardi, he got caught and the others got away, and the cops offered him a deal if he ratted out his partners. It was his first pinch—he'd'a got probation. He told them to cram it. So to make things even, to pay him back for turning down their generosity, they made sure he went to Stateville.

"What we got that first day was this young kid hardly knew shit about life and less than nothing about jailing, he's talking to the niggers and calling the hacks 'sir' and shit, trying to fit in. We talk to him, recruit him—he's the type we want—tell him to stay away from the jigs, and he tells us forget about it, he's gonna do his own time and don't need no gang to make it. Less than two weeks, he's in, doing all right, and they've got him cutting the grass between the cellblocks, trimming the flowers—he wants to work to keep busy and he does a good job. He's next to the tunnels, in a cranny away from the screws in the yard—they can't see nothing, he's cutting the grass with this old power mower takes you all day to start, and these two jigs come in after him, gonna turn him out.

"He sees them coming and swings the mower up, catches the first jig on the cheek, cuts most of the guy's face off, and the second jig, he starts running and Jimmy throws the fucking *mower* at him, gets him in the back of his knees, cut his tendons and muscles all to shit. It took a couple of hacks about ten minutes to tear him away from the jig with the busted legs—Jimmy's on his back beating on him, for Christ's sake—and when they do they drag him to the Hole, strip him and in he goes, waiting for trial.

"What you got to understand, Mr. D, is back then, the Hole wasn't supervised—I mean guys were naked, locked in twenty-four hours, in a cell with nothing in it but a hole to go to the john in. See, there was no way they could hurt themselves or anyone else, so the only time a hack came around was to lay out the ice-cold food once a day, change the water bucket. Or if one of the con's buddies paid a hack off to take him some smokes or a blanket or something.

"But we had a guy on the inside, doing time in there like forever, cause he kept killing people. Guy was doing four life terms, he had nothing to lose, went for the tattoos in a big way, swastikas and white power inked on every inch of him. He listens, gets the drift.

"See, the guys Jimmy wrecked—and he did wreck them; one got like eight operations and is still scarred across the face for life; the other one's in a wheelchair and will never walk again—these guys turned out to be high-rankers with the Unknown Mau-Mau Gangster Nation, which was one of the toughest gangs in the country. They had this initiation deal: they had to kill a white man or woman to get into the gang. The Hole was filled with them, because most of them were recruited inside, and they'd shank a white guy, get thrown in the Hole. Well, they're screaming and yelling to Jimmy, what they're gonna do to him when he hits the yard, and shit, he's shouting right *back,* it's a two-way street— what he did to the rapists in the yard was sex next to what he was gonna do to these guys with their big mouths talking shit when they were all locked down. Our guy inside, he loves this, can't wait to smuggle the word out with a friendly hack.

"Jimmy gets his date, draws six more years for aggravated battery, no possibility for parole. Would have been more, but we had guys, swore deps they seen it all: the two shines went at him with their johnson bars in their hands, whatever. Only reason they didn't let him walk and transfer him to another prison was because we just had the riot right before that, and they didn't want another racial problem right away.

"Jimmy hits the yard and we give him his distance, see what he wants to do, and he ain't in the population three hours, three niggers come at him, coming from different spots in the yard, but we see it first and we head it off, start whomping them. The hacks in the tower shoot a few rounds off into the grass, we got to lay facedown, get locked down for two days, and then Jimmy comes to us, wants to join, knows it's the only way he'll ever get out of there alive."

"So he's locked in with your people."

"Mr. D, it's solid. We take an oath right away, in blood. Once you're a brother, you're one for life. We take top shelf over wives, kids, anything. Whatever the Brotherhood needs, it gets."

"That's inside, when your lives depend on one another. What about out here, after they get out?"

"Believe me, I want something from Jimmy Vale, it's done."

"It better be."

"What can I do for you, Mr. D?"

And Tonce told him.

Tommy left and Tonce sat back in his chair, sipping whisky, smoking a cigar. Thinking that these kids might have the right idea after all. Engrain the loyalty right away, make it a life-and-death matter, and it might mean more. It sure wasn't working too well nowadays on the outside, what with every two-bit punk the mob had working for them jumping into the Witness Protection Program the first time they looked long hard time in the face.

The two-bit punks had been bad enough. They didn't know enough to get men of Tonce's stature into much trouble. But a decade ago a top gunner by the name of Angelo Tombstone Paterro had gone with the feds, and that had been the beginning of the end.

They'd almost had their backs broken by that defection, and if that hadn't been bad enough, the underlings that had been left to try and keep things together started taking shots at each other, going for the top position. Some high-rise booster had nailed some tapes Paterro had left behind for insurance, and turned them over to the MCU. *Madrone,* had that caused some trouble. Scum-bags like Tough Tony Tomase had been leapfrogged through the ranks and were turned into bosses by Mad Mike Tile, the new honcho, because the ranks were so thin and men like Tomase had been so far beneath Paterro that he had never bothered to tape a conversation with him. Men like Tomase and Tonce DiLeonardi. Well, now Tomase was dead and Mad Mike was the head man, answering to his own hand-picked crew, to the mini-commission he'd formed in the name of democracy so one man would never be able to bring the house down again. The only man who knew everything was Mad Mike, and he wasn't talking. Everything else, any single detail might be known by one of the commissioners, who

36

handed orders down through their underbosses, but none of them knew the full score.

For instance, Vito Terne handled the drugs, which the mob had recently gotten into, and no one but him knew what was coming in or how much, and he answered only to Mad Mike, after being subjected to a skin search. They used to speak in a lead-lined room in Mad Mike's old South Side house, the room unbuggable. Tomase had handled the gambling, and had gone south with $5 million, which had brought about his death at the hands of some young gambler in Atlantic City, who came home to a hero's welcome and was given Tomase's spot in the gambling department. Since that day, the kid had never placed another bet.

Philly Two-Fist, the ex-fighter, handled all the hookers. He had a couple hundred guys working under him, but they all reported to Philly, who in turn reported to Mad Mike. Others handled other things, no one man knowing anything about the other's business. The old days of cabareting together were gone. If Mike found out that any of his bosses or underbosses were partying together, he would sit them down in his office and give them one warning. Nobody ever got two.

Himself, well, Tonce was the enforcer, the mob killer. He had two dozen men he'd picked himself, men who were loyal to him, who did the leg-busting and the collecting and the occasional hit when called upon, but for this particular job he had to use outsiders.

Which were never any fun. The last time he'd used amateur talent, he'd called in his cousin Petey the pizza maker, a tough kid who was all the time coming to him, looking for work with the outfit. Their problem back then was a gambler who'd been skimming a bit too much and who knew he was about to get caught, so had started to cozy up to the feds. Tonce could not use outfit talent on someone wired by the government. The hard-liners in the White House were doing everything they could to break the mob's back as it was, and the Chicago outfit was still getting back on its feet, could not take any really serious problems with the Justice Department. So he'd sent out some amateurs, had pulled Petey in from the pizzeria and he and his half-brother had gone out to do the job on the mark.

They'd shot the bastard four times in the head at close range and had left the car in an alley to be found as a warning to any others foolish enough to think of defecting.

Where they'd screwed up, was, the hard-headed son of a bitch had *lived,* and had jumped right into the WPP, and was still singing at gambling trials not only in Chicago, but in Indiana, Michigan, and Minnesota.

Poor Petey—he should have stuck with making pizzas, because Tonce had been left with no choice but to whack him and his half-brother both.

This case could not end up that way. Mad Mike had let Tonce off the hook the last time, seeing as it was Mike himself who'd forced him to use less than top-level talent on the job. But when he'd been called in for this one, it had been by the top New York bosses, and they wouldn't sit still for any mistakes. No, the top boys, sent by the commission itself, had told him he had to hit Mad Mike Tile. They'd spent the summer checking him out, Mike there with his bodyguards in the mansion he'd bought after his old lady died. The New York bosses had figured it to be an easy mark, then had learned how wrong they'd been. So they'd come and thrown it in *his* lap, the lames, figuring him to be stupid. He could see them now, laughing behind their hands, because they couldn't lose. If Tile died, wonderful; they'd keep their word and make Tonce a boss. If Tile lived, if his alarms and guards were enough to fight Tonce off, then they could throw up their hands and say, "What are ya gonna do? Those animals in Chicago!" Shaking their heads and blaming it all on him. But Tonce was no dummy, no *strunz,* and he was gonna cover his ass one hundred percent. By using outside talent. Top-notch talent, but still, no made men; no one who could finger him if they fucked up. And he'd check it out all the way down the line with his old boss, Tommy Campo. Just in case *he* was getting set up, too.

Old Mike, after his old lady died, what a goof he'd turned out to be. He'd gone too far into the coke business, had got himself hooked on snow and the young bitches, sold the South Side place and moved to *Winnetka,* for Christ's sake, of all places. Tonce would have him killed, and had been assured that he would get the top spot for himself, for his many years of loyalty.

He had told the New York bosses it would be his pleasure.

The cop was in Frank's face, cursing. He was punching him good ones, roundhouses to the chest, the gut, not marking his face so a good lawyer could maybe have his ass.

Frank shouted, he cursed, he squeezed the arms of the chair and all the time fought to remain in control; if he swung back, the cop might kill him.

The cop stood back, fat out-of-shape bastard, breathing harder than Frank, even, his hands on his hips, glaring.

From somewhere outside the door Frank could hear a female voice raised in violence, shouting, cursing. He didn't look toward the door, stared his hatred at the cop. He fought his fear, the terror that gripped him, holding on to enough of it to keep him from grandstanding, saying something that might cause his death.

The commander had caught his breath, was advancing again, raising his hands, when without warning Frank's girlfriend Tina Lime burst through the door.

Followed by Gunon, who was right behind her, hopping mad.

"Goddamnit, counselor, you can't go *in* there!"

Calmly, only her eyes betraying her rage, Tina said to Gunon: "I'm already here." Then, to the commander: "Let him go, now, mister, and I won't file charges and have your ass."

"Who the fuck is this!"

Frank was getting up out of the chair, carefully, taking advantage of Tina's presence. He began to walk slowly to the door, holding his gut tightly, his elbows tucked close to his sides.

"She's a mouthpiece from the Legal Aid, Commander—"

"The hell I am," Tina said, walking forward to grab Frank, her eyes on the captain. "I'm a lawyer in private practice, and this man is my client. Fuck with me, Commander. Go ahead." She turned then, started to walk Frank through the door. Gunon stood there, staring at her strangely, looking about to explode. Frank looked down, breathing hard.

Tina said, "Out of my way, you toad." The words spoken softly, with malice. Silently, staring still, Gunon stepped aside.

"Go on," the commander yelled after them, "get that thieving piece of shit out of my building."

They walked through the door, Frank regaining his strength, his pace now quickening, wanting to get the hell out while they could, before the commander got over his shock and changed his mind. As they walked down the hallway, Tina's arm around him, the commander's outrage chased them.

"When he robs *you,* you cunt, we'll see how willing you are to help him!"

Then through the door and outside, Frank feeling relief, mixed with sadness. He spotted Tina's car at the curb, walked to it silently, suddenly ashamed to look at her.

Jimmy walked down the third tier with his hands in his pockets because there were a bunch of black guys congregating on the catwalk a couple of cells away from the new kid's house. They knew him and would take his stance to mean he was carrying. To go the long way around now that they'd spotted him would invite them to test him further, and he couldn't let that happen. He told himself that it was just another day. Another twenty-four-hour period to get through. He could start thinking about lessening the risk factor in his life tomorrow, when he was breathing free air for the first time since he was a teenager. Not now, though. He had to live today the way he'd lived the past 3,200 days. Fearlessly and unafraid of consequences. If these guys even *thought* they smelled fear on him—and fear had a smell all its own—they would pounce and he would lose and he'd wind up on Boot Hill with a "W" stamped on his marker.

The five black guys fell silent as he approached, and he made his mind as blank as his face, neither giving away a thing. He passed them, fought the urge to stiffen his shoulders as he waited for the sound of shuffling feet on the catwalk. He'd hear them coming and that would give him time to move before the shank struck. Or so he hoped.

Made it. Into the cell, and there the kid was, looking at him with large round eyes, authentic terror on his face. He was hiding something behind his thigh, sitting on the top bunk. When he saw it was a white man he relaxed, but not so an outsider would notice.

In a forced, flat voice, he said, "They're talking about me. What they're gonna do to me. Loud enough for me to hear them. The ugly one with the pantyhose stocking on his head lives here with me and he got plans." He lifted a piece of metal from behind his leg, hefted it, a good hunk, maybe a two-pounder, about a foot long. "I'm gonna kill them, they come in here." Jimmy liked him already, the kid hiding his terror and making plans, alone. The kid was working his lips, trying to keep from breaking.

Jimmy said, "They won't, you come with us, Bill. We can get you assigned to the fifth tier with me, down in a cell with one of our people. Any of these guys come near you, we kill them."

"I was just out drinking, Christ, celebrating graduation." He was whispering, almost to himself. His voice now far-off and dreamy. His eyes were wet. He was a big kid, muscular, but his downfall was his face. He was too pretty to cut it and even if he whipped this bunch outside someone else would come calling with his gang. This guy had been cursed by his genes, by an accident of birth. What had been a blessing on the outside was a curse in here. The face that won him pussy in the outside world would turn him into one behind the walls.

"The cops, they started chasing me and I thought it was funny, trying to outrace them, and the squad, it comes right next to me and I went to run it off the road, you know, just like in the movies, but shit, it hit a telephone pole and the cop driving dies and *shit*! I don't know what to *do*."

"Keep it down, that's what. And keep it inside. No one in here gives a fuck about you but us. Don't tell anyone that story, ever. Anyone asks, tell them you killed a cop. You'll get by with our help."

"What do we do now?"

"We go out, walk right past them. The first one says something to you, level him with that pipe and keep swinging. They go over the side and we get up to five, you come into my house and throw

41

the piece over the rail. Swear on Bibles we were together talking about women and heard some scuffling, some screaming, and nothing else. You got it?''

Bill nodded.

"Then let's go.''

They walked by them and this time Jimmy was tense, ready. Two of them were leaning on the railing with their arms folded across their chests, glaring. They'd be the first to go, the easiest. The other three were smarter and bigger, standing with their backs to an open cell. He'd worry about them after he took out the two at the railing. He wasn't counting on Bill to do anything but freeze up and watch. He was hoping the kid would hold his own but he wouldn't plan on it.

The black guys let them pass, giving them nothing worse than stares. Whatever was going to happen inside this prison, whatever it was that had been in the air for the past few weeks would be held off until another time. Maybe, if Jimmy got lucky, until tomorrow afternoon.

Chapter

FIVE

"Just play your cards right and do what we tell you and you'll be cool." Jimmy spoke to him and right away Bill nodded his head respectfully, without argument. Good. He liked a guy who knew his place and was willing to learn, because they got the hang of jailing right away instead of having to go the hard route, get raped a few times before coming around, or, like Jimmy himself, get another six years added on your sentence by being hardheaded. He could have avoided the extra time and been out years ago if he'd only listened the way Bill was doing now.

"What we got here is called a chastisement. You break the rules—and there's a lot of them—you got to pay the price."

"What'd this guy do?"

They were strolling the tier, fifth level, which they owned. Everyone who lived here was Brotherhood. Chaney's cell was in the middle, the door open. Sounds of laughter could be heard inside from down the tier, a prolonged laugh, Chaney cracking up as he watched a game show or maybe a soap opera. Here on the top tier they could almost reach out and touch the riot catwalk, installed after the last big one, where the guards could charge in from the roof if another riot broke out. Last time, it had taken three days for the National Guard to get inside, and seven guards had died along with eleven inmates. The catwalk hung from the center of the cellblock ceiling, going to rust. Lately, it had become a perch for the sparrows, slick with white bird shit.

Jimmy said, "You wait outside, or he'll hold it against you later."

"How about you?"

"He can hold it against me all he wants, but there ain't nothing he can do about it."

Jimmy entered the cell, stone-faced. Chaney, tall, muscular, and ugly, looked up, unafraid. On this tier, men rarely showed any fear of violence from outsiders. Jimmy thought this stupid, another illusion. Nobody owned any prison property; there was no real turf. There was not a single place within the walls where he would ever feel completely safe. It was a lesson he had learned early on.

Jimmy stood, waiting. In the joint, you touched nothing in another man's house without permission. Respect is everything, and Jimmy had known more than one man who had died over something as simple as touching a photo of another man's wife without asking, first. Technically, he shouldn't have even entered the cell without checking, but he was Jimmy Vale, the number two of the Brotherhood, and some of the rules just didn't apply to him.

"Vale, shit, sit down." It was a small cell to be shared by two, and Chaney's roommate was nowhere around. He was new and maybe still thought it useful to have a job, to make time pass.

"Turn off the television and stand up."

"Aw, *shit*."

"Brother Chaney, I ain't gonna say it twice."

Chaney's face was twisted into a self-pitying mask, a *Why me?* look, anger there, too. He snapped the set off, slapped his palm against the wall.

"What'd I *do*?"

"Two Brothers, independent of one another, saw you rapping with a nigger guard."

"I get chastised for trying to get *along*? Shit. And what kind of brother are you anyway, putting the hurt on me, huh? Ain't we got enough troubles, the niggers getting ready to jump any time?"

"It's your choice, Chaney. Take the chastisement or face expulsion."

"Fuck, get it over with, tough guy."

It was always the same; men who knew the rules would screw up, then blame him when he came to extract payment. Like little kids. Jimmy drove his fist into Chaney's belly, hard, and brought his knee up as Chaney doubled over, catching him in the chest. As the man bent over and began to fall Jimmy hit him twice, solid shots to the kidneys. He watched coldly as Chaney rolled to the ground, moaning; then he backed out of the cell.

Bill was watching him with a mixture of awe and fear on his face, not knowing how to act or what to say. Jimmy could see the bulge inside the right pantleg where the kid still held the piece of metal. "Come on," Jimmy said, "third cell from the end." He led Bill into his house, calmly, as if the scene down the tier hadn't happened. From Chaney's cell, he could hear the sound of the television once more blaring. But this time without the accompanying laughter.

The shrink was all right as long as you let him think he impressed you. He lived outside and worked here in the administration building, never stepping foot inside the cellblocks or having any real contact with the cons, but he went out of his way to be hip, to show you he knew what was going on behind the wall.

Jimmy listened and played the game because he was relatively safe here. Even if the joint went up in flames, he wouldn't feel the heat in the admin building. Besides, the guy was one of the few people in the environment who acted like he gave a shit about you as an individual. Once you got past his saying "What's going down?" or "What's the haps?" he wasn't such a bad guy.

Jimmy sat in the chair, his back to the wall, facing the window, savoring the rare sight of glass without imbedded bars. The shrink sat in a chair facing him, his legs crossed toward Jimmy, not behind the desk, because he believed sitting behind it created a sense of authority which the inmates might rebel against. This way he was just one of the guys. The afternoon sun reflected off his back, but Jimmy didn't squint. He liked the sight, the young half-bald shrink looking bright and clean, sunshine behind him. It was easier than looking at the guy's checkered shirts with the black knit ties, his corduroy pants and Hush Puppies with argyle socks.

"So, Jimmy, what's to it?" It was the way the guy talked, and Jimmy could live with it. He would speak, ask a question, then sit back with his fingers steepled and stare at you as if he were really listening. Jimmy figured he was probably not paying a lot of attention, thinking about getting laid or something. If he had any talent in his chosen profession he'd have a big office on Michigan Avenue, with a secretary to bang between the forty-minute hours.

"Getting out tomorrow."

"And how do you feel about that?"

"Good, Doc."

"Any fear, by any chance?" Another of his quirks. The guy would listen to you, then throw in a shrink word, then sit there looking at you like he'd read your mind, pulled your thoughts out of your ears. Sometimes, when he wanted to stay awhile, Jimmy would widen his eyes when the guy made a remark and say, "How the fuck you *know* that?" then sit back and daydream while the guy lectured.

Not today.

He decided to be straight, see how much the guy really knew. There was less than nothing the man could do to him; his date was set. Death was the only thing that could stop him from going home tomorrow. Thinking of death, he shook himself, and the goof shrink, he jumped all over it.

"Hit home there, Jimmy?"

Jimmy smiled. "No." He leaned forward in the chair, ready to express himself openly to this man for the first time. The doctor seemed to sense this, sat perfectly still, his steepled fingers lightly tapping each other.

Jimmy said, "But see, if it's there, it's in a place I can't feel. When I was a little kid, my old man was always in the joint, and the old lady, shit, all she did was drink and beat up my brother. Fires and shootings and family arguments were our movie theaters, what we watched for enjoyment.

"Well, one time, the house down the street caught on fire. The lady who lived there got out, but her dog was inside, see, barking, scared shitless. Frank, my brother, he *wor*shiped that dog. It was the only thing on earth that loved him and didn't turn around and kick his ass all the time. He went right up to the flames a couple of times, but the smoke, it was killing him, see, driving him back, he couldn't breathe, and I believe it was self-preservation, some instinct that kept him from leaping into the fire after the dog. I bet if it had just been flames, he'd have burned up going after the thing, but not being able to breathe, it does things to you.

"So now he's crying, screaming for the dog, and in comes the firemen, not even wearing masks, they march into the house with their hoses and squirt around, and the dog comes running out, into Frank's arms, licking his face, and that's all he cares about, the dog's alive.

"But me, Doc, *I'm* watching the firemen.

"When it's all over I'm hanging around, maybe six years old and still trusting older people. I work up the guts and I go up to this fireman and I ask him: 'How come you guys didn't need masks?' And he tells me that there wasn't enough smoke. I tell him: 'My brother almost *choked* to death in that smoke.' And he tells me, he says, 'He ain't been in any *real* smoke, son.' Then he shrugs, tired of talking to me, and he says, 'You get used to it.'

"See, Doc, that's what I'm talking about here. I been living with real terror for so goddamned long, I got used to it. What you or anyone on the outside might think scares me, or what scares you, it's nothing to me. I been scared so bad for so long that nothing about the outside is gonna even come close to really scaring me ever again."

The shrink was staring at him with his mouth open now, this being a major speech for Jimmy. He shut it with a small click, tiny white teeth hitting each other, blinked a couple of times.

"So you *do* admit to fear, though, is that what you're saying?"

He'd missed the entire point. But Jimmy didn't blame him. The guy was a jailhouse shrink. Jimmy blamed himself; he should have known better than to try and level with the man.

He left the shrink's office and walked down the hall, through two sets of electronic gates to the tunnel, down the tunnel to the outside, into the yard during afternoon recreation. He did not want to be here, had planned on spending most of the afternoon bullshitting with the shrink, but the guy was such an asshole. . . He'd go straight for the cellblock, hit the bunk, rack out for a while, rest while he could. He knew he'd never sleep tonight. Walking, though, he noticed everything.

There was a group of black cons standing together, fidgeting nervously against the east wall. The hack in the tower had loaded his weapon, was standing above them telling them something Jimmy could not hear. The yard guards and the other tower hacks were all watching the scene, everyone nervous now. The tension was so thick in the air that it felt like the smoke in the burning house that Jimmy had just spoken of; it choked him, he knew what was coming and searched around him frantically, trying to find some friendly white faces to bunch with because the shit was about to hit the fan big time; he'd seen it before and knew without doubt that a riot was about to commence.

He walked fast toward a group of angry white faces, brothers, vastly outnumbered but it would be better than being alone. Over the loudspeaker an electronic voice began to scream for the crowds to disperse, disperse *now*, or they would be fired upon. The group of blacks was growing now, shouting obscenities at the hack above them, and one of them threw something that spun upward, glinting as it turned over in the sunlight, a hunk of metal or pipe that took a lucky turn and hit the guard square on his forehead and he began to pitch forward, losing his balance, losing his grip on the rifle as he spun his arms for balance. The rifle hit the yard maybe three seconds before the hack did and Jimmy began to run, wanting the safety of numbers as the speaker ordered all the cons to fall face-first onto the grass but the blacks were yelling, in possession of the rifle and the dead guard's baton, the guy with the rifle firing at the other tower guards, and as the machine-gun bullets began to spray the lawn he and his brothers sprinted for the relative safety of the cellblock, and the riot began.

Chapter

SIX

"All right, listen up, goddamnit." Commander Edward Ryan was about to blister the troops and he knew that after today he couldn't go too far. They'd accepted him up to this point with reservations, and he knew it was mostly luck that had brought him through; there were no rule books or regulations directing behavior for this situation. But after he'd busted up the thief, the rest of the crews would now accept him unequivocally as one of their own. It wasn't something he'd enjoyed doing, but it had served its purpose. Still, he had to see to it that it didn't happen again. It had been only luck and good timing that had saved the thief's life; if the new man, Giraldi, hadn't thrown him the bone, given him the opportunity to play tough guy by wanting his own shot at the man, the others might have forced a showdown, kill the guy or show your ass, Ryan. It wasn't a position he wanted to be in in the future. He squared his shoulders and glared at them.

Ed Ryan said, "You guys want to waste your time and risk your pensions on lowlife scum like this Vale character, or you want to keep what we got here?" Mark Gunon, Anthony Giraldi and Cletus Roosevelt were lounging in the basement office, watching him warily. Christ, what a crew they were. Gunon, the greasy pig—the woman lawyer had called it right: He *did* look like a frog.

Stinky puke with Milton Berle lips and a sloping forehead, all the time with the cigars and the sweet-talk.

Roosevelt, now there was a throwback. The last time he'd seen anything that big and dumb it had been stuffed: Bushman at the Museum of Natural History. The difference being, Bushman, the gorilla, had a reputation for being gentle. There was nothing gentle about Roosevelt. The man even *sat* angrily.

Giraldi was the F.N.G., the Fucking New Guy. Three months in the crew and they'd been testing him from the jump, and from what he'd heard from the other men, he was a shoo-in as a PRICC: corrupt beyond hope. A perfect match, which made a lie out of the way he looked, all preppy and cute, dressed to kill all the time, with the round, rimless glasses. George Bush's kid, gone bad.

Ryan tried to show disgust and contempt, but it was hard. These men wore badges, and minutes ago had been ready to commit murder to prove a point and fatten their bank accounts. They scared him.

"The City Council wants you out, don't you get it? They want to disband the unit, and if they can't bust you guys, they want to send you back to patrol. Now tell me, how much you gonna make, riding in a squad car and writing speeding tickets?

"They got you down to six three-man squads already. Used to be a fifty-man unit. The only thing holding you together is some of the guys that pay you give you lower-level outfit competitors to pinch. And the fact that you managed to get jackets on a few politicians.

"But I got to tell you boys something, and I want you to listen close. You could have pictures of the mayor in bed with little boys, and it won't help you if you keep hauling in thieves and trying to roust them. The second you kill one of these punks, the word'll get around, can't you see that? I don't want to see any more of these Frank Vale types in our squad room again, and that's an order. You want to solidify your political base, you want to work the judges, the aldermen, the dope wholesalers and the mob for all they're worth. Playing around with thieves for ten percent of a score is stupid. These guys get busted, you think they're gonna be loyal to you? We don't have enough of these punks, get picked up and start saying they work for us? We got OPS, Internal Affairs, everybody but the damn Justice Department breathing down our necks. This bitch counselor today, she blows the whistle, what're you gonna do, kill her? A lawyer? I got sent in here from upstairs to straighten this unit out, get your minds off the small stuff and on to bigger things, and I'm not about to let personal greed screw up something took us fifteen years to build. Thieves are out, from now on. They can't do us any good.

"But a guy who can protect us, a guy with prestige and power, say, a councilman, he gets pinched by the feds, you think he's gonna want more headaches? Think he wants his kids to see pictures of him in bed with teenage hookers? No, they'll keep their mouths shut and make us all rich if we let them."

He decided he was doing all right. They weren't sitting and listening raptly, but none of them was arguing or staring knives at him. It was time to wrap it up, quit before he stepped overboard and lost ground.

"I got twenty-six years on the job, fellas, and I mean to tell you I'm not gonna go to the joint because of some small-time jewel thief can't do shit for me. That's it."

They wandered out of the office slowly, through the glass door that had his name stenciled on the top half in large black letters. He could hear them mumbling, grumbling among themselves as they went to their desks, a bunch of loose cannons finally being corralled. Giraldi closed the door behind him as he walked through and Ryan let his breath out slowly, then inhaled deeply. He held his hands out in front of him. They were trembling.

He looked around the office, at the green thick brick walls, the wooden chairs. In a new building and he had an office looked like it came from Elliot Ness. And a crew directly under him, working for him, that were worse than anything Ness ever had to deal with in his lifetime. Killers with badges and guns.

"God help me," Ryan said.

Frank had to take a cab home. Tina had made sure he'd gotten out of the station and had then left him standing outside on the sidewalk. He'd walked to the car, stood there as she got in on her side, holding his gut and waiting patiently for her to unlock the door. She'd started the thing, put it in gear, raced off with him half leaning on the roof, holding the door handle. He couldn't blame her.

And didn't have time to worry about her. He was the Iceman, and there were men he was responsible for.

The cab ride gave him a relatively quiet environment in which he could think. The problem being, though, that none of the things he was thinking about were any damn good.

The PRICC unit was on to him again, which was never a good place for a thief to be, the PRICCs being filled with sharks, stone killers who were rumored to have killed more than one drug pusher who'd shown reluctance to share the wealth. It was common knowledge on the street that other police agencies were investigating the unit and had been for some time. A lot of the PRICCs had quit, some to save their jobs, one step ahead of the OPS or the state's attorney, others out of disgust, the guys being idealistic and disgusted by what they'd learned. Every time one of the PRICCs got into a shootout—which was not a rare occurrence—the papers would rehash the past charges, reprint testimony of stoolies who'd worked against them. If this commander was with them, he'd go down with them. If he was a guy on the take, if what Frank read in the paper and heard on the street was true, then he'd go down the tubes with the rest of them. The PRICCs were stirring up too much trouble to last long in a city already rocked to its knees by political controversy.

Either way, it wasn't his problem. Although it was ironic: a crooked cop, in charge of eighteen other crooked cops, looking down his nose and thinking poorly of a guy who had the balls to go out and steal for a living without a badge to hide behind.

As he paid the driver off in front of his house, he knew that what it really came down to was, the score was off. Simple as that. Three weeks' worth of work would have to go down the tubes. The cops had been waiting for him, so they must have suspected something was about to happen. In this whole deal there was only one thing Frank was certain of: He could never allow the PRICCs to catch him cold, out on a score. They hated him enough that they'd put enough lead in him to sink an ore ship. Ditching the score was a shame, too. It had looked to be about the easiest deal he'd ever done in his life. One of the richest, too.

Shit.

He didn't even get his key in the lock. Adam Lebeaux threw it open as Frank mounted the steps, his black face concerned, Wayne Lockhart right behind him, the big dumb hillbilly holding a pistol in his hand. Foo-foo was jumping up and down behind Lockhart, yapping.

"It's off," Frank said, and Adalebo nodded his head once, which Frank appreciated. But there were no nods forthcoming from Lockhart. He watched Frank lock the door and pushed the dog aside with his foot while Frank decided that if the man kicked Foo-foo, he would take the gun away from him and shoot him with it.

Lockhart said, "Bull*shit,* it is," and Frank said, "In the basement," leading the way, trying to calm himself. "We'll talk about it down there."

The basement was paneled, dominated by a long oak wet bar and a professional-size pool table. A huge furnace sat in the far west corner, the only alien sight among the expensive leather and glass furnishings. Frank sent his laundry out; he'd removed the utility sink. The water heater was upstairs, on the second floor, in a closet. This was the room in which he worked and everyday distractions were not tolerated.

They sat on the red leather chairs, Adalebo and Frank, while Lockhart picked up a pool cue, shot the balls around the large red felt table. Adalebo gave Frank a warning glance, telling him things. They would have to talk later in private. Tension between the two men filled the air. Frank wondered what had happened during his absence.

"I studied those plans like I ain't studied since school." Lockhart was sighting in on the eight ball, stroking the cue softly. The cue ball touched the eight, which banked off the cushion and disappeared into the left corner pocket. He squinted around the smoke curling into his eyes, stood and took a drag of the cigarette, put it back in the corner of his mouth. "Any cops see you around the score?"

Frank shook his head.

"They were waiting outside your house, Frank, not following you. It was a shot in the dark, that's all. I say the score stays a go." He leaned down and shot at the seven ball, cool and under control, stroked it into the side pocket using a nice cut. Frank wondered when it was that Lockhart had decided he was in charge.

Frank said, "They take you in, beat your ass, then watch you for a while, because they're pissed off when you turn them down. They got equipment now, makes a James Bond movie look bush. The score's off."

"Maybe for you . . ." Lockhart casually threw the stick down on the table, the tip scratching the felt surface.

"Wait a few weeks, Wayne," Frank said. "When I feel good about it, I'll set it up again."

"Bull*shit*." Lockhart was pulling on his light leather jacket, bunching his prominent neck muscles. Showing off. Frank stared at him. "You go in, get knocked around some, then lose your balls. I got a score I spent weeks working on, an old lady packing for Miami to spend the winter. I ain't giving this up for you or your lackey there." He walked to the basement steps and began to mount them, his right hand inside his jacket. Frank thought that maybe the PRICC unit had done him a favor, then wondered why he'd ever let this punk in on a score in the first place.

"Don't do it, Wayne," he said softly, looking now at Adalebo, who hadn't spoken a word since Frank had entered the house. The man raised a large thin black hand to his face, put a slender finger to his lips and shook his head back and forth.

Over his shoulder, Lockhart said, "Shit, stop me, Vale." Then laughed.

They gave him a minute before they got up and followed him, looked out the living room picture window to see him swaggering down the street, a big man without the brains God had given to plants.

"I thought you said he was solid."

"Frank," Adalebo said, "we gots to talk, man."

It was the way Frank liked it, two men who trusted each other plotting quietly in the shadows of his basement. The only light came from the long hooded fluorescent bulb over the pool table, the tube covered with stained plastic that told them that Budweiser was the King of Beers. In the corner against the wall, the furnace looked like a creature of nightmare, aluminum arms extending toward them.

"He keeps his mouth shut, Frank. No matter what happens, you got to remember he done seventeen years when he could have walked after ten back home, and seventeen years in Attica ain't easy for no one, but especially no white man."

"He picked up a drinking problem, though, didn't he, Ads."

"Without my knowledge. Man come to me, tell me he got this young old lady, showgirl retired from Vegas, used to the good life and he need a caper to get him straight. Beg me. I tooks him on a couple of things, I don't see a sign of weakness. Hell, we was roomies for three years—you do time, you get to know a man. I turn him on to you after I see he all right. For months now he been cool, ready, professional and patient. Today come, he suddenly change his tune, get all nervous and shit. You ain't out the house, going to scope the caper, he come down here, start pounding down the gin, and I tell him no matter what happens, he ain't coming on the caper tonight high. I or you shoot him first. He pull out that pistol, Frank, put it in my face, call me a nigger. Tell me he waste us both I try to stop him or dime him out when you get home. Shit, the PRICCs show up, I felt almost relieved." Adalebo walked behind the bar, opened the cooler and took out a long-neck Miller, popped the top, raised his eyes at Frank, then brought one back for him after Frank nodded.

He walked cool and slow, moving without wasted motion or

effort. A tall hip black man who could let a redneck call him nigger and not resent it. Adam Lebeaux, called Adalebo or Ads by his friends. The son of a voodoo healer across 110th Street in Harlem, New York, who learned about the con at his daddy's knee, then learned about keeping feelings separate from business while serving three years upstate for killing another man in a street fight, the boy having made the error of calling him the same name that Wayne Lockhart had recently called him without eliciting reaction.

You learned things in Attica if you paid strict attention and didn't blame the cops or the judge for your fate.

He spoke slowly with a streetwise rhythm in deep, cultured tones that sounded almost like a parody. James Earl Jones doing Eddie Murphy. To Frank he was solid and to be trusted, and his word was never questioned.

Adalebo took a sip of his beer as he seated himself, swung his leg over the arm of the chair, then set the bottle on his knee, holding it there with his hand, making little patterns on his light khaki pants, and continued.

"The cops come to the door and start peeking inside through the windows, and this ignorant son of a bitch, he trains the piece on the door—he gonna kill them in your crib if they break in. Guess who do life in Stateville for *that* scene?"

Now Frank grunted. Up until this point, it had all been a matter of simply making a bad judgment call. But if the man had killed two police officers in his house and then split . . . He didn't want to think about it.

"I got up behinds him, close. The cops start jimmying the door, I was gonna put him away, give him one on the back of his neck that'd get him a wheelchair for life, try to get out the back door before the coppers shot holes in my ass. But all they did was rattle the knob some, then go out onto the stoop to wait for you." Adalebo took another sip of beer, shook his head, and looked at Frank. "Good thing it a pretty day outside."

"You go get the dog?"

"I knew it was the kid next door's. You said you only 'sposed to have it for the afternoon. Knew it'd break his heart the little ugly sucker got away.''

"Thanks, Ads.''

"Don't mention it. It got me away from that country jagoff for a time.''

"We got two choices, Ads. We can kill the son of a bitch right now, or we can let him go out on the score, get his ass pinched, and hope he doesn't cop us out.''

"They another.'' Ads bobbed his head, listening to his own inner music. He swigged the beer and set the empty bottle on the tiled floor at his feet. "You the safeman, I the electronics whiz. Old Wayne, he good at listening to scanner radios and standing lookout. Ain't no way I see he gonna get past even that cheesecake alarm and if he do, I doubt he can bust the safe. So killing him's plain dumb—it ain't worth the effort just yet only because he called me a nigger and insulted you in your house. And his getting pinched—if it happen, he won't talk. Man ain't built that way. Third option, Frank, is the man somehow get in and do the score and get away. Way I see it, he owes *me* a quarter for putting him together with you, and for showing him how to beat wired systems. He owes *you* a quarter for setting up the score and taking the time to learn him some about safes.'' He stood, stretched, not showing off like Wayne had, just loosening his muscles, and Frank admired his shape, tall and slender with muscles popping as he touched the ceiling. A six-foot-three Sugar Ray Leonard.

"So we make about a third less of the cash we was gonna make in the first place, without taking no risks.''

"And if he doesn't want to give us a fourth?''

"Shit. *Then* we kill his head.''

Frank didn't answer, but it sounded good to him.

He finished his second beer after Adalebo left, and let himself loosen up some, allowed the tension to drain from him. It had been a long, disappointing day.

Adam had been right. You didn't kill a man because he hurt

your pride. That was just his Italian blood calling for revenge. It was his father in him. Stupid and nonproductive. Adam would not see anything morally wrong with killing another man; in his mind the reality was that it was a crime for which you could serve serious time and therefore one to be given long and sober consideration before you went out to perform the act.

Not paying a partner what he had coming, though—that was worth killing over.

Frank did not know how he felt about that. He'd thrown the shot at Adam, about killing the son of a bitch, more out of a sense of responsibility than anything else. It was something that had to be said. He'd known Adam would reject the choice. It had been a subtle manipulation, a statement made for effect. But what if Lockhart pulled it off?

Maybe it could happen. In the weeks he'd shown the man things, he had had time to learn. Still, safe-busting wasn't like riding a bike. It wasn't simple or easy. It had taken Frank years to learn a soft touch and all the angles. Dumb bastard like Lockhart, he'd probably go in with dynamite and blow the house to bits, or with a hammer and chisel, for Christ's sake.

Frank went over to the furnace, looked at the tile behind it and pressed down on the recessed panel hidden underneath. It popped open on oiled hinges, silently. Revealing a sewerlike tunnel just large enough for a big man to fit through, the tunnel appearing filled with dirty water.

He'd done the excavating himself, the concrete work, too. The tunnel went down ten feet then lengthened into a sitting room, stocked with canned food and water. A silent underground generator provided electrical power and fresh air. There was a small chemical toilet in the corner.

It was better than a safe. No one would ever think to look there, and even if it was found, it would be seen as a septic tank or something of that sort. There was a foot of water under the first panel, and Frank hit a switch that evacuated it into a holding tank. When it was drained he stepped down, touched the button on the floor of the second panel, and it dropped down under him. He reached out with his foot in the dark, found the steel ladder, and lowered himself into the tunnel.

He used it as a safe place for his belongings, and it would serve as a hideout if he ever needed one, secure and with enough provisions to last him a week. He felt around in the dark, found the generator switch, and hit it. The small room filled with light and the quiet rush of conditioned air. The concrete walls around him were wet and smooth; he inspected them for cracks, found none. The room was bigger than a jail cell, the size of a small studio apartment. There was a chair and an air mattress, and a shelf filled with paperback books. He reset the wind-up alarm clock, checked it against his watch. Its ticking gave him comfort. When he'd begun he'd envisioned a large sitting room here, with leather furniture and heat, but he hadn't been prepared for the enormity of the task of simply building the tunnel and had been forced to settle for this. Even then, it had taken three years to finish. He was beneath the freeze line and could survive in the winter with blankets if the need arose.

Which was good enough. Some people he knew lived in far worse environments. Like his brother, Jimmy. Tomorrow Jimmy would be home and he would show his brother his hideaway and Jimmy would be the only other person on earth who'd know about it. Two grown men, one fresh from the joint, going down into their clubhouse; their treehouse. Frank wished he had a can of spray paint or a marker so he could paint NO GIRLS ALLOWED on the wall. Jimmy would appreciate that.

Almost as much as he would like the contents of the steel box there under two of the gallon jugs of water. It was filled with money, Jimmy's piece—a full fifty percent—of the action from every score Frank had taken down since the kid had been inside. Seeing as how Jimmy had done the time because of a busted score Frank had set up, he figured it was the least he could do. Sitting on top of the money box was a jewelry case, a velour box a good watch had come in. Frank smiled and hoped all those years in prison hadn't stolen Jimmy's sense of humor. He'd bought a watch for a man who could now begin to count time once more.

Frank checked the supplies, refreshed the chemicals in the toilet, then climbed from the tunnel and secured it. If he ever needed the place as a hideout, the switch on the rim of the tunnel would close the panels and refill the hole with water.

From where he was standing, even he couldn't see the cut in the tiles that lifted up when the panel was touched properly. The cops never would.

He nodded his head, got a beer from the fridge and sat in his leather recliner, resigned to the fact that the score was blown, but not too upset. He was more upset about Tina's finding out he was a thief. He'd worry about her later, though, after Jimmy was home and he had a family again.

He used the remote to flip on the TV on a platform above the bar, wanting to catch the early news, and learned right away that the governor had called out the National Guard to quell the riot in progress at Stateville Penitentiary.

Manny called Louis into his quarters, the area spacious enough to be called an apartment. Manny's home. He'd had it soundproofed so he couldn't hear the mandolin music Mike would blast at all hours of the night. The good stuff he could listen to; the Sinatra, the Dean Martin, operas, but he hated that old guinea mandolin stuff because it reminded him of the garbage his old man used to play on the wind-up Victrola when he'd been a boy, the old man playing that shit then getting drunk on the wine, ordering him around like he was a goddamn bellhop.

Louis sat down, dressed as usual these days: a silk shirt opened three buttons, the wide lapels reaching almost to his shoulders; threads of gold chains hanging around his neck. There were four-hundred-dollar Italian shoes on Louis's feet. The man had come into Tile's crew three, four years after Manny had; you'd think the old ways would count to him. . . .

"You want a drink?" Manny asked.

"Little Amaretto, settle the stomach, you got it, Manny."

Manny poured the drink, wondering who there was left he could talk to. Mike was a freak; the girls were getting younger and younger every month. Man thought everyone loved him, no one would want to hurt him. Had the guys on the payroll as a fucking status symbol more than anything else.

Look at Louis, for God's sake. Manny himself had put on a few pounds with age, sure, everyone does, but Louis, who was younger than Manny, had gone overboard. Gotten fat, wore a wig half the time when they were out, trying to catch the eye of one of Mike's castoff bitches.

Louis said, "Manny? You want something? Boss's waiting for me."

"Going out to dinner again?"

Louis shrugged. "There's some new joint on Orleans he wants to check out, down near the art galleries."

"Take six men with you—get on the horn and call a couple in. That's only a few blocks away from Cabrini-Green, for God's sake."

"We scared of niggers now, Manny?" Said in jest, with just enough sarcasm to make Manny frown at him. Louis quickly amended it, said, "Come on, lighten up, for Christ's sake, will you? Come with us, you ain't been out with us in weeks."

The last time Manny had gone out with them he'd elected to drive the Cadillac limo, just to have something to do and not have to join in the vapid conversations in the back seat. In the restaurant one of the girls had handed him a five-dollar bill and told him to run up front, get her a pack of Merits. He'd smiled, taken the five, and turned to one of the young guys in his crew, ordered the man to eat it. As soon as the man figured out that Manny wasn't kidding, he ate the bill, swallowed, and Manny had turned back to the girl.

"You ever try and tell me what to do again, puss, I'll tell him to eat your heart that same fucking way," he'd said, and the girl had gone white, excused herself, and hadn't come back to the table.

"I don't like those places, the food, none of it. Besides, my ulcer's acting up."

Louis shrugged. "Have it your way. But you're missing out on the action, Manny. A lot of those bimbos think you're really cute.''

Manny had daughters older than most of them. "Have a good time," he said, and waved Louis out of the room. As soon as the man was gone, he got on the phone, ran a few of the boys down and told them to get their asses over to the River North section right away, find the limo and hang out around it, make sure everything stayed cool.

He hung up and sat there, staring at the wall, trying to remember why he'd called Louis into the rooms in the first place.

Chapter

SEVEN

Ed Ryan sat home that Wednesday evening, watching the news and wondering what the world was coming to. He'd done a lot of that lately. A lot of silent introspection too. Wondering if he really needed all this shit in his life.

He knew that cops had the opportunity to see things that civilians never would, and had twisted views of society because of what they'd seen. But still, anyone could just watch the news and see that things were going to hell in a hurry.

The inmates had taken over the prison in Joliet. Seven were already known to be dead, two of them guards. They were reportedly breaking down the barrier to the Protective Custody area, and even a man of limited imagination could figure out what they were planning to do to the stool pigeons and sissies inside PC. Coach Mike Ditka had been felled with a heart attack. If Iron Mike wasn't safe, who the hell was? Some punk robbers had burglarized the Make a Wish Foundation offices and taken off with the coats, shoes, footballs, and toys that were earmarked for the needy. Another judge had been sentenced in the Greylord Corruption probe, bringing the total to twenty judges, seventy-three lawyers.

And Ed Ryan had been put in charge of the most corrupt police unit ever to carry the badge in the city of Chicago.

The job had cost him his marriage, the respect of his only son, and, if he wasn't careful, it would cost him his life.

He thought of the eighteen men he supervised—and had built files on—for the past year of his life, and he felt depressed and a little desperate. He would bet his star that half of them would kill in a second in order to preserve their lifestyle, which was way above their declared income.

The worst part though, was the file he was building on the politicians. It was, in some respects, the easiest part of his assignment. Mostly making copies of papers, statements, duping recordings and videotapes taken while surveilling some of the most famous faces in the City Council, all the way up and into the mayor's office.

The citizens of Chicago were paying the freight for this, and when it went public, when the Justice Department pulled him in and began indicting these people, and the people learned what they were paying for, the pols indicted would play hell finding an impartial jury anywhere in the state. The prosecutions would make Greylord look insignificant.

The aldermen and women would be busted with their hands in the tills, and might get them cut off before ever seeing a courtroom. Ryan had direct evidence of child molestations, of procurers of children being on the city payroll. Videotapes of some of the most famous names in the city in bed with babies. With adult members of the same sex. This was the blackmail material that the PRICC unit was using to their advantage, to stay in business.

Other evidence in his possession was of a different nature. He could prove in court, tomorrow if he had to, that certain aldermen had pushed zoning changes through for gross profits paid to dummy companies, that real estate deals had been struck after certain powerful brokers had greased their way into certain political pockets. That mobsters were allowed a free rein as long as the bag of money came in every week. He could prove that one of the mayor's advisers was collecting thousands a month from certain rich and influential citizens who demanded and received contracting bids from the city and state; that bids were awarded to minority firms who had no minority members on the payroll. He could name dates and places where the payoffs occurred, names of the people accepting them. Collusion and fraud were documented and verified, and would stand up in court.

This was not an investigation of payroll cheats, not a deal where the papers would moan and scream because some greedy politician had padded his payroll with family members. Nor was it as bogus as, say, catching the fire chief doing architect work during his off hours, without a license or degree.

This was the largest corruption probe in history, big enough to tear down and destroy not only an administration but hundreds of lives and careers.

This was Watergate Midwest, and he was the guy doing the legwork.

Until this job, Ryan had always liked undercover work. Now all he wanted was to get called in and get it over with; retire and spend the next ten years testifying in federal and county court.

He wasn't doing it to change the world, nor was he involved for any personal ambition. He didn't care about being a hero and he wasn't in love with the idea of being on the edge. He didn't plan to write books about it or sell his story to the movies, retire to Florida rich and famous.

He was doing it because the PRICCs were giving his department a bad name, and that was more than he could stand.

There had always been corruption in the police department. When you hire a man in his early twenties and pay him twenty grand a year to start, he's going to maybe take a look around him and see what's going on and make some hard decisions.

For instance: Why should his children go to public school when the children he risks his life to protect go to the private joints and get out of eighth grade knowing how to read? Why should he live in Hegewisch when the gambling czars and the pimps live in Lake Shore Drive high-rises? Why should his wife wear cloth coats when the wives of crooks wore fur?

A small percentage of these men would ask these questions and make their choices. They would take the money from the people behind "victimless crime," pimps, coke pushers, kiddy porn dealers, whores and street hustlers, and the line kept getting further and further from where it had originally been drawn. In the old days, drug money and kiddie porn cash weren't taken; today, they were the main source of income for the rogues.

Men would do these things and tell themselves it was in the best interest of their families. Women cops wouldn't. In all his years on the force, Ed had never known a corrupt policewoman or even heard rumors. He wondered what this told him. It was always men, taking the money and hiding it away, and always, always, just a small percentage of the men.

The figures spoke for themselves. On a force of thirteen thousand, there had been three hundred police officers indicted in the past fifteen years. A lot of these indictments were minor things that the media blew out of proportion. Liquor license steering, accepting a few bucks from morticians to have corpses delivered to their parlors, motor pool bullshit. Shakedowns of tavern owners, minor hit-and-run offenders, traffic ticket payoffs. Things that had been going on forever. The feds would spend millions to nail guys who'd collected hundreds; then the U.S. attorney would get his mug on television again, screaming and ranting, pretending to have caught Hitler.

Ten of those indicted were convicted of taking payoffs to allow narcotic rings to operate in their district, and thirteen officers from several South Side districts were convicted of selling drugs themselves.

Twenty-three major corruption indictments in fifteen years. One and a half a year. The percentage of officers convicted was too small to calculate. Even including the other 277 indictments, you were looking at a corruption level of less than two and a half percent.

And the public, still, hated the cops. The three hundred would get indicted, maybe fifty of them would be convicted, in fifteen years, and every citizen above the age of thirteen in the city of Chicago believed that all the cops were on the take.

Ed couldn't figure it out. Even his son, who'd quit the Chicago force to take the chief's job in Tarpon Springs, Florida, thought he and the rest of the cops in the city were dirty. He recalled their last conversation with some anguish.

"Dad," Little Ed had told him, long distance after five to save a few bucks, the kid's voice tinny and small there two thousand miles away, "we got this guy in today, two weeks out of the Dade County Mental Health Center, wanders up here to smell rich air and winds up raping a woman old enough to be his grandmother. I says to him: 'One word out of your mouth, I swear to Christ, I'll just kill you where you sit.' He tells me it's not *his* fault, he didn't *mean* to do it. He's gonna sue the shrinks who found him fit to rejoin society—they fucked up, letting him go when he still wanted to hurt people inside. Three of my guys, they had to pull me off him, then lie to the county Public Defender and say he attacked me first. The point is, Dad, you always taught me we had to take responsibility for our own actions, you always said there was nobody to blame but yourself, the buck stops here, all that horse-shit." Ed had waited, knowing a punch line was coming. His son Ed, Jr., the pride of his heart and the light of his life, had then said, "Daddy, aw, shit, Daddy, why'd you join that unit?" He'd heard Ed, Jr., fight a sob; then he'd heard a click; then he'd heard a dial tone.

That had been two weeks ago.

Maybe he should call him now, drop veiled hints that he was about to come in from the cold. On his testimony alone Ryan could put maybe thirteen of the eighteen PRICC coppers in prison, but along with his documents and proof the entire unit would crumble.

Only the chief of police and the U.S. attorney knew of his undercover involvement. No one else. It had been his only condition a year ago when he'd taken on the job. The chief had passed the word in his own special way that Ed was a rogue, bent, and that he was looking for a place to put him where he wouldn't do too much harm to the department's name in the five years he had until retirement. Ed himself had been given a background, names and dates provided to him by the feds, sums of money that had supposedly been paid to him, and they'd gotten some of their mob snitches to pass the word along in the right police circles: Ed Ryan was a crook.

Naturally, a guy with his reputation and stature was welcomed with open arms in the PRICC unit. He could bring it respectability while also increasing the income of the cops on top who were intimately involved in corruption, and if he got caught, not a word would filter up to taint their sacred names.

Ed had something they could filter, these days.

There were seven command-level officers involved, and they'd go down with all the rest, and then Ed could retire. Quit the force and spend the next ten years in court, testifying. His credibility had been enhanced almost every week, Ed making judgment calls, intuitively doing things that, a year ago, he'd have figured to be unthinkable. Taking the envelopes stuffed with cash; smirking at videotapes of terrified children being raped; beating thieves in basement offices. These things, little by little, had broken him. Now, there was almost nothing left.

He picked up the phone, dialed the area code and number, then listened as the phone rang once before the recorded voice told a grandfather of two that the number he'd been calling had been disconnected at the customer's request.

This called for a drink. Holding everything inside, with no one to talk to, made him tense. He poured some scotch over ice, settled back down in his easy chair in the bachelor apartment he'd rented when he'd moved out of the house. The TV was still blaring, some talking hair-style with makeup melting on his face was in the foreground, the penitentiary at Stateville behind him, telling the world in a frightened voice that the National Guard was storming the prison at that very moment. You could hear gunshots in the background, and the kid on the tube was flinching and ducking down, maybe expecting a stray round from an M-16 to come flying at him from a couple of blocks away, screw up his hairdo. Ed picked up the remote and turned the thing off.

He was smoking again, too. Drinking and eating too much and now smoking after eleven years without a puff. Unmarried with a kid who hated him, sitting in a fake-leather recliner in a near-empty apartment, feeling sorry for himself. He wondered if maybe his moral standards were set a little too high.

It was time now to come in. That's all there was to it. The men respected him and admired him and listened to him, but he was beginning to lose it. He would make a mistake, and they would catch him and kill him if he didn't quit soon. There was enough evidence to bring the house down, and he had to give it up before he had a stroke or a goddamn heart attack, fifty-two years old and playing cloak and dagger, for Christ's sake.

He wasn't cut out for the rough stuff, either. He could gather evidence against the crooks because they enraged him, but he didn't have the heart for the tough stuff. Beating on men in chairs, guys who knew better than even to defend themselves. Like shooting fish in a barrel. Taking their manhood away from them. From what Gunon had told him about the last time Vale had been in, though, the man was probably expecting them to finish him off for sure this time. Under those circumstances, the guy had gotten a break today. Maybe the break had been on one of his ribs, the way Ryan had pounded on him.

No, he was too old and soft for this. Hated what it was doing to him. Today was Wednesday. On Friday, the unit over on the South Side was planning a major blackmail score on a married black female alderman who was reputed to spend part of every Friday afternoon in a no-tell mo-tel with a certain other black female who was the spokesperson and reverend for one of the city's largest black church congregations. A church with a ton of political muscle. The PRICCs would take pictures, make recordings, and have another alderman on their side, and the head of Operation Feed the People at their beck and call. On Monday, Ed would go into the U.S. attorney's office and tell them it was all over.

His mind made up, he finished his drink and poured himself another one to celebrate. He put his feet up on the old wooden chest he used for a coffee table, lit a cigarette and tried to relax, thinking about how good it would be to just be himself again. Oh, he'd have to testify in a hell of a lot of trials, but that was nothing compared to the pressure he was living under now. He'd bet that with competent lawyers, the bad guys would stall their trials for at least a year, maybe longer. Time enough to make things right. The wife, no, she was probably gone for good. But maybe he could make things up with his son. Maybe wait out the year before the trials began down in Tarpon Springs, getting reacquainted.

The booze gave him the courage to pick up the phone, dial his ex-wife. He'd tell her that he was calling about Little Ed.

She was a woman who always answered the phone tentatively, as if every call were to be feared. Her voice would rise on the last syllable of hello, Gwen dragging the word out into about four separate sounds. They would have been married thirty-one years this Valentine's Day, if she'd stayed with him.

"He-el-ll-looo!?" frightened little Gwen said, and Ed said, "It's me," and immediately she stopped sounding afraid.

"What do *you* want?" There was an implied threat in her voice, then suspicion and accusation. "You drunk again, Ed?"

"Just called to get Little Ed's number." Was he slurring his words?

"Eddie doesn't want you to have it. Why do you think he changed it?" He tried to tell himself that she was just bitter, that she would soon understand and maybe take him back, but resentment was strong in the front of his mind too. Hell, she believed everything she read in the papers. He could see her, going to Father Benoin, twisting her rosary beads. Telling the priest that her husband's name was in the paper all the time as the head of a group of police officers everyone knew were crooks. He could see the good father telling her that in God's eyes stealing was a sin. He could see . . .

Enough.

He was about to say something that would drop her in her tracks when she said, "Ed? Don't you call this house again, Ed, or, or . . ." But she couldn't come up with an *or,* so just slammed the phone down in his ear.

Ed Ryan said, "God*damn*it!" and threw the phone away from him, then lumbered into the kitchen to pour himself another drink, this time to ease the pain.

Cletus Roosevelt said, "That shit wasn't bright, Giraldi, talking like that in front of the man." He was behind the wheel of the dark-brown Buick with regular plates, his personal car, staking out Frank Vale's house from a block away. Mark Gunon grunted his approval of the man's opinion. He was holding a pair of binoculars to his eyes, lowering them frequently, just checking them out for the time when he would need them.

"This is a waste of time," Giraldi said, trying to change the subject.

"I was you, Anthony, I'd keep my mouth shut." Gunon had lowered the glasses and was staring at him hard. "You're starting to get a mouth on you, for a rook ain't proved shit to nobody yet."

"Let me have a chance, Mr. Boss man, sir." Roosevelt was making fun of Giraldi, staring at him in the rearview mirror. "Shit, you expect us to take that? Sonny, I was working stiffs like that Vale punk over when you were still in high school, and you better keep that in mind."

Giraldi still wasn't apologizing. The other two had left the office together after the ass-chewing, their heads together, speaking in low voices. They'd cut him out. He'd hung in there, standing right up, trying to listen, and at last Gunon had sighed and stepped to the side a little, accepting him into the unit. From then until now, neither man had mentioned his faux pas in the interrogation room. Maybe Cletus was just bored, sitting there with his fat ass stuck behind the wheel of a big car that was still too small for him.

"You think this is a good idea, Mark?" Giraldi tried to sound as if Gunon's opinion carried weight with him, and he came close. But it was Roosevelt who answered him.

"You don't want to take the chance, son, you can just get the hell out of the car. What are you, doing us a favor, sitting back there acting like a baby? All's you're doing is making us as goddamn nervous as you are."

Gunon said, "Give it a rest, Cletus. He's new."

"Ain't gonna get a chance to become a veteran the way he's going."

"What's that supposed to mean?" Giraldi had to say it. The black man outweighed him by maybe fifty pounds and was four inches taller, but he couldn't back down from him, let him throw veiled threats his way. He had to show he could carry his weight with the big boys.

Cletus Roosevelt turned all the way around in the seat, making a big production out of it. It looked like the earth rotating. He pinned Giraldi with a glare, nodding his head. Giraldi could see Gunon shaking his head, his lips twisted in disgust. Gunon watching Giraldi watch Roosevelt. "It means," Roosevelt said slowly, "that if you fuck up one more time, sonny boy, I'm gonna see to it myself that you're back in a blue suit, working nights at the Cabrini-Green projects." He waited a few beats, nodding, and Giraldi finally understood that the man wasn't dancing to some song in his mind; his head was bobbing in time with the beat of his heart. He'd never seen that happen before, and decided that the man must be very angry for it to happen to him now.

But still, there was face to be saved. There were eighteen men in the unit, six three-man teams. They ate together, drank together, took their wives to dinner together, and vacationed together. To back down to any one of them would mean that the other seventeen would know about it right away, and then he'd never be accepted.

He said, "Look, Rosy, Mark, it came out wrong, all right? What I was trying to do was intimidate the thief, let him think that what had happened to him before was just the tip of the iceberg, not insult you guys."

Roosevelt said, "Don't matter what you *meant,* Tony. What matters is how you *said* it." He was turning back around in his seat, though, as he spoke, and calling him Tony stood for something.

Giraldi looked at Gunon, who was still staring at him. "I got a lot to learn, is all."

Roosevelt's head nodded again, but this time in assent. It was no longer bobbing regularly. The man was calming down. Gunon nodded at him, too, twice. They'd accepted his weak apology.

"Learn this, Tony," Gunon said. He leaned over and stared hard at him, dropped the glasses to his lap and lifted his hand above the seat so he could point his finger at Giraldi for emphasis. "Me and Rosy, we're your best friends in the world. We're the fucking guys, your ass is in the wind, gonna pull it back in and maybe die trying to do it for you. We'll show you the ropes and make you one of us, and if this new commander is true to his word and expands the units, we'll take you under our wing and push to get you the sergeant's stripes so you can command one yourself. Rosy did it for me and I'll do it for you. But there's one thing you can't never forget, bub, and that's the fact that me and Rosy, we're your fucking family, closer to you than your wife and kids. You can't shoot off your mouth, ever, in front of anyone, without first thinking how it'll reflect on us. You understand what I'm saying here?''

Giraldi nodded and Gunon smiled.

"See, Rosy? What'd I tell ya? This kid's all right. He didn't mean nothing.'' He whacked Roosevelt on the arm and picked up the glasses, stared out at the front of the house again.

They'd come here directly from the meeting in the commander's office, in time to see Vale enter the house, someone opening the door for him, too. Too bad they hadn't suspected someone had been home; they could have had some fun earlier. Giraldi had sat silently in the back, feeling the tension, fearing it, too. Wanting to ask questions but afraid to open his mouth, knowing that he'd stepped on it back there in the interrogation room. The two men in the front seat were so paranoid that they ran a wire on the commander's office phone, and Ryan had been leading the unit for a year. With Giraldi having only four months in, how much support could he expect from them? They'd been sitting here only a few minutes when Cletus Roosevelt had made his statement, bringing it out in the open, and he guessed that he'd handled it well because now they were all friends again.

So Giraldi said, "Listen, what I don't understand is, if you thought this guy was going out on a score soon, why not just watch him and catch him in the act, or right after, take it all?''

Gunon said, "Now you're talking, Tony.'' He lifted the glasses to his eyes and said, "Tell him why, Rosy.''

"Ain't no mystery, Tony. We got a guy here, works a few times a year. There's three of us. You want to take on the extra responsibility, watching his house around the clock in eight-hour shifts? When'd we ever get our other work done? These guys, they're sidelines, that's all. Commander happened to come into the room while you were over here, watching for him, asked me where you were and I told him, seeing as I was trying to do all three of our jobs. The man's all right. I figured it'd be better than lying to him. He got all pissed off and ranted some, but you see how it turned into a good thing, because he backed us up right to the hilt once the man was sitting in the chair."

Gunon said, "There's movement," and Roosevelt started the car, lowered his voice to a gentle whisper as he coaxed a big man along, a man who had just walked out of Vale's house. A big man who was trying hard to walk a straight line and swagger at the same time. Giraldi would bet that the man had done time somewhere in his life. Roosevelt eased the car from the curb and followed the man as he turned the corner and got into a black Mercury Sable, squealed away from the curb. Gunon thumbed his lapel radio and called the Department of Motor Vehicles, gave them the plate number and described the car, then sat back to wait for their registration run.

"We don't like to bring the boss into this kind of thing, cause then he don't have to get a cut. See, what you do, Tony, is you make deals; it's the nature of the game. Every other big-time thief in the city knows who we are and arranges to keep us happy. This punk here, he's a badass, though. So now it's a matter of honor."

Giraldi admired the way Rosy drove, effortlessly keeping the Mercury in sight without getting too close. He let other cars cut in front of him, two or three of them at a time, timed the lights so they'd slide through and never get caught staring at receding taillights. He was a pro, handled the car as such, somehow managing to concentrate on the car in front and at the same time keep talking, instructing the new man. A female voice broke in from the speaker, telling them that the car was registered to Wayne Lockhart, a Caucasian male with light-brown hair and green eyes, six three, two hundred and twenty-five pounds, with no outstanding warrants. She gave them his home address.

"But the boss said to blow it off."

"What the boss don't know won't hurt him."

Giraldi laughed as Gunon said, "There, he's going to the curb."

"I see him, Mark, relax." Roosevelt parked and shut the car down before the man in the Sable managed to get his car backed in at the curb. They watched as the man got out, swaggered up to an apartment building and entered. The address matched the one the DMV had given them.

Gunon said, "Well, fellas, we got a couple of choices here. We can go in, find out what this stiff knows, or we can stay here, miss supper while he sleeps it off. I don't see him going out tonight anyway—he looked about half in the bag. Vale sure ain't gonna let him work." He turned to Rosy. "What do you think, want to stay here, go back to Vale's, or blow the thing off for tonight?"

"Man came out looking mad, Mark." Roosevelt looked up, caught Giraldi's eye in the rearview mirror. "What do you think, Tony?" and Tony told him what he thought, feeling all warm inside because the man who earlier had wanted to bust him was now asking his advice on things.

Chapter

EIGHT

During the first year of his sentence, four of them had been sitting in Tommy Jacobi's cell, drinking home-brew that had been distilled from the skins of potatoes. Jimmy, the quiet one who never bothered anybody but never backed down, listened as Tommy waved a magazine around and made fun of a certain article.

"Asshole with an 'ologist' behind his name, saying our problem is 'sensory deprivation.'" He waited, smiling, until someone asked him what sensory deprivation was.

"Means we didn't get *hugged* enough. Man says if someone had hugged on us when we was babies, we wouldn't be slammed in today."

There was some joking, one guy mentioning the fact that since he'd been inside, more than one motherfucker had wanted to hug on him, which set Tommy off on a story about the leader of one of the black gangs, Malcolm Quinones, who he said was so ugly his mother probably couldn't bring herself to hug him. "Poor woman, gave birth to his ass, then had to cover his head with a blanket so sleep could sneak up on him."

Quinones became the topic of conversation for a time, the three other men downing him, trying to top each other with tales of how ugly the man was. Jimmy put an amused look on his face and from time to time would sip his liquor from the jelly glass in his hand, but his mind was far away.

Right away though, he'd suspected that maybe the "ologist" who'd written the report had been correct. He could not remember a time when anyone had ever hugged him.

Sensory deprivation, that's what it was. All along, he'd just thought his parents hated him as much as they hated each other.

He learned about terror and rage early on, generally feeling one or the other for most of his childhood. And guilt, too, until he got old enough to figure out that guilt was a waste of time.

His father had been a drunk, a low-level mob enforcer who collected and paid out gambling money. The old man always dropped veiled hints to Frank and Jimmy that he was a hit man on the side, when the occasion arose. He would tell them these things in the early morning, just having come in, usually drunk, the boys eating breakfast and getting ready to go to school. They'd hear his key in the lock and flinch, never knowing what kind of mood he'd be in. Generally speaking, though, the violence was confined to after school when they'd wake him up making too much noise, or when the old lady would jump in the old man's chest about something. He'd take off on her and then start on them because they'd cry and scream. Frank caught most of that grief, because he was older and would sometimes try to protect their mother. No, usually, when the old man came home early he did so to spend some time with his boys before they gulped down their cereal and ran out the door. It was his idea of quality time.

One morning he was especially proud of himself. The knuckles of his right hand were cut and bleeding, and there was a bruise on the left side of his face. He told them that he'd singlehandedly stomped an FBI special agent. Told them that he'd pistol-whipped the man right in front of his wife outside a restaurant in Hammond, Indiana, and made him beg for mercy.

Such were his claims to fame.

From the beginning, Frank was the teacher. The two of them would spend as much time as they could out of the house, playing catch together in the street in front of whatever apartment they were living in that month. Sometimes the old man would come or go as they played, grab the football from one of them and toss it to the other one, smiling, hollering "Here you go!" but it never lasted for more than one play. Frank would tell him the old man only did it when he knew one of the neighbors was watching, and Jimmy never said anything to Frank, but he resented the words. It took him a while to understand that the only thing the old man really loved was money.

He'd search his mind, trying to remember if either of his parents had ever hugged him. He decided that the old man had come close, once. At the park one sunny Sunday afternoon, after playing boccie ball and drinking wine with his brothers, the old man had come to where Jimmy was sitting on the swing and he'd pushed him, way up in the air, and Jimmy had been thrilled. He started to hum a song and it went all right—at least the old man hadn't told him to shut up—so he sang some of the words right out, swinging high into the air, filled with love for the guy who pushed him maybe ten times and then went back to the party. Jimmy had wanted to follow him, throw his arms around him and tell him he loved him, but it wasn't the sort of thing you did to a hit man who stomped FBI agents.

Frank had been his best and only friend, and years later when Frank would be sent to juvie homes, then had run away to join the marines, Jimmy had been devastated. The old man would go to prison now and again, and it would get in the papers, and the parents of the other kids in the neighborhood wouldn't let their children play with him, seeing that he was the son of a convict.

It wasn't easy for him, growing up.

His earliest memories were of his father charging out of the bedroom, pulling the waist of his pajama bottoms up around his naked hairy stomach, enraged because something had forced him awake, into the world of hangovers. His eyes would bug out and he'd have his tongue folded over, between his teeth, breathing in and out in a frenzied tempo. Pushing thirty, Jimmy still had nightmares about that.

Their father's rage was never controlled or repressed, and he

never had a problem with self-expression. He would grab a door
and hang from it, kicking it, throwing his body out with his legs at
a ninety-degree angle, slamming the door into splinters, or sometimes he'd use his head, holding a door or a wall with his hands
and shattering it with his forehead, all the time with his tongue
between his teeth, folded over. The only time the tongue would
not be there was when he needed it to scream and curse. Once
he'd been drinking a bottle of beer when their mother had started
on him, and he'd held the thing out and squeezed it until it
shattered. He was, to the young Jimmy, the strongest man in the
world.

Their mother had known who and what he was when she'd
married him, but she never did learn to leave him alone when he
was drinking. She'd belly right up into him, screaming into his
face, calling him words that Jimmy couldn't understand, faggot
and cocksucker, and the old man would lose it, start his mean
faces going. Sometimes he'd put his belt around her neck and
choke her with it. But usually it was just fist beatings. He'd hit her
and Jimmy would hide under the bed and Frank would throw
himself at their father, screaming in an inarticulate rage, and then
the man would turn his attention upon Frank. When he was
through with them he would pull Jimmy out from under the bed,
call him a sissy while slapping him open-handed, a coward who
had to hide from the world. He always said, while he was beating
them, that he'd teach them. They'd learned well. Especially Frank.

Sometimes Ma would have to go to the hospital, and then they'd
have to go live with Grandma for a while. Frank caught most of
the beatings there, with the leather barber strop the woman
kept hanging from a nail in the kitchen. She swore she'd used it on
all six of her sons but not on their mother, her only daughter,
Queenie; tell Jimmy that his mother had been the only one to
escape beatings so bad blood would flow. This malevolent old
woman with her hair always pulled back tight in a bun, with
her little potbelly, would talk about how she beat the skin right off
her sons' asses, but not her daughter's, then say: "And look
how *she's* turned out."

Grandma with her bottle of 151 rum always on the table, putting it in her coffee in the morning, drinking it straight at night. Her pack of Camels right there at her elbow, one always lit, burning. Her eyes were small and cold, and she almost never smiled. Jimmy's mother would be in the hospital, and he'd pray every night that she'd come home the next day, before Grandma decided to whip some skin off his backside. He figured she hadn't yet because she was a patient, loving woman. He already was aware, had been told hundreds of times, that he was no good, a bum like his father.

The six brothers, Jimmy's uncles, would come by and drink their grandfather's booze, telling their mother and father that they were going looking for that bastard who'd hospitalized their sister, and at first Jimmy was afraid that they'd catch him, but then they'd leave and his grandmother would tell their grandfather that they were only using Queenie for an excuse to get away from their wives, that they would just go to the tavern and get all liquored up and then go home and tell their wives that they'd searched for Dane all night.

It was Grandma, though, who'd scared him the worst. He was seven that time and Frank was fourteen. Frank would take the bus to high school, giving Jimmy instructions on how to handle the crazy old lady. Don't pay any attention to her and don't talk back. You pissed her off, and the leather came off the nail. Jimmy was quiet by nature and kept his eyes and ears open, so his grandmother usually left him alone, unless she wanted him to do something for her, at which time she'd tell him to "save Grandma some steps," then send him off on an errand. Frank told him she did that just to get rid of him and Jimmy didn't argue with him.

One morning he'd been saving her some steps, running down to the basement to get her something before she walked him to school, and he'd come upstairs sooner than she'd expected him to find her leaning over the kitchen table, spilling black pepper into a white linen handkerchief. There was a long, sharp knife next to the handkerchief on the table. He looked at her, his eyes wide, and she stopped pretending, looked at him with a gleam in her eye, and told him exactly what it was she was doing.

"If that dago bastard father of yours comes near us, I'm gonna throw the pepper in his eyes and"—she picked up the knife, thrust it at Jimmy so that he jumped back, even though the tip hadn't come close—"poke him full of holes!"

All the way to school, holding her hand, he'd prayed to God that his father wouldn't show up. He told her this on the school steps, how God had protected his father, and she'd told him that "the devil takes care of his own," then said, "He don't care enough about you to come looking for you."

Every few years the old man would get pinched for something and go serve some time. Usually just a year or two in prison, or a number of months in the County awaiting trial before beating a case. He always said he was framed, always told the boys that they couldn't believe what the papers said. The first time he went away, Frank got drunk to celebrate and Jimmy felt great relief, followed by deep guilt because he was happy that his father was locked up like an animal. The relief went away when he learned that they would have to go live with Grandma until Ma could get on her feet. The guilt stayed with him.

The honeymoon with Grandma never lasted. After the first week, Jimmy couldn't do enough, save her enough steps, although he tried. She began using the belt on him, her mouth too. At eight he learned that he was a jagoff, and stupid and ugly. Before he was nine he turned into a motherfucker. Frank had gone south after three months, running away and getting caught, then catching it with the leather strop, then running away again. They finally put him in St. Charles Reformatory after he stole a car and tried to head for New York. With Jimmy's best and only friend gone, Grandma could only turn it all over on him.

He slept in the same bedroom with his grandfather, who saved him. The man would come home from a hard day at the factory and see the look on Jimmy's face, and would grab his hand and take him for long walks around Wolf Lake. Explaining things to him. What life was like in the early part of the century, during the Depression, what school was like back then, how he'd supported a family. Jimmy would try and ask the man questions but Grandpa'd avoid them, never wanting to discuss why Grandma was so mean or why Jimmy didn't have any friends or how come Ma drank so much. After a while it dawned on Jimmy that he was as much an escape valve for his grandfather as his grandfather was for him. The old guy needed to get away from the crazy woman he was married to as much as Jimmy did.

Living alone with Ma had taught him a few things, too. She'd get drunk and try to kill herself, always making sure someone was in the room to stop her. She'd get drunk and tell lies, too. Jimmy, at ten, had spent a few anxious months after she'd sworn to him that she had cancer. She never mentioned it again and he wondered if maybe God had sent down a miracle, like he had when Grandma had been robbed of the pleasure of sticking his father full of holes. Ma had framed ceramic pictures of Jesus Christ on the living room wall of one apartment, little black-and-white tiles one of her sisters-in-law had glued together at a park class, and she'd had to throw one of them away because she'd jerked a pistol away from her head at the last second, pulled the trigger, and *blam!* —one of the Christs had shattered into a million pieces. Jimmy would always remember what it looked like, the tiles falling in slow motion in his dreams, landing in a pile on the floor.

After an attempt, she would always tell him that it was his fault, that he'd driven her to it. That if he hadn't been such a bad boy she could be happy and not want to die.

He wept with gratitude when Frank came home, he was so happy to see him. He tried to conjure up the same emotion when the old man got released, but it wouldn't come.

They taught him how to lie, too. The old man would tell Ma that he was taking Jimmy to Comiskey Park to see a Sox game, and they'd wind up in a South Side bar, the old man getting bombed and Jimmy self-consciously sipping one Pepsi after another, watching, fascinated, as his father threw money around like it was nothing, buying round after round for his friends. He'd make Jimmy watch the game on the television mounted on a platform above the bar while he drank and smoked and cursed with his tough-guy friends. On the way home he'd tell Jimmy: "Don't tell your mother nothing." He'd say it quietly, but there was an implied threat in the delivery that Jimmy could never test.

Ma, too, Queenie, she was great at lying and teaching the finer points of deception. At one point she'd been seeing and taking money from two different men, one of them her husband Dane's best friend. Dane had been in the joint at the time and Frank was in the service, and eleven-year-old Jimmy had to suffer alone as he'd come home from school to hear the bedsprings squeaking as Ma and one of her friends took a "nap." One Friday afternoon they'd come out of the bedroom together, Ma in her slip and Ray in his suit pants and undershirt, when the doorbell had rung and Ma had made Jimmy go tell her other suitor that she wasn't home. He'd taken a beating, too, because he hadn't been at all convincing, the boyfriend had known that the kid had been lying, and the cash had stopped flowing from that source.

He never knew it, but Jimmy's entire life had prepared him for survival during a prison riot, because he had a firsthand and long-term knowledge and understanding of rage and terror, and even though as a child he'd learned to use them to his advantage by hiding them, they were always there, just under the surface, controlling his existence and enabling him to be strong. The major differences between then and now were that these days he never prayed to God, ever, and that he had learned to handle his jumbled feelings in different ways. He'd seen what had happened to Frank when Frank had rebelled against his father. He'd watched and learned and he'd been taught. By his father and mother and grandmother. Taught and taught well. He kept it all inside and would channel it out when the need arose, using it only when he had to, and at those moments it would explode with devastating results.

He knew how to use his brains, too. For instance, he was smart enough to know better than to make fun of magazine articles about sensory deprivation, yet also smart enough not to let the other men know that he didn't think such articles were funny. He walked with his head high and his shoulders back, his eyes always searching, and when the riot came down he knew that he'd been right to live just for today, not to look forward to tomorrow—because within these stone walls, there was no such thing as hope.

Chapter

NINE

The first thing they did during the riot was get the female employees the hell out of the prison. In doing so, they lost their edge. If the warden had ordered the guards to storm the cellblock immediately, they would have caught the convicts by surprise, headed the thing off before it got too far out of hand. But while the officials were worrying about gang rape and mutilation, the prisoners had the time to get organized.

There were four of them crammed into a cell built for one but which housed two, Chaney's cell, chosen because it was in the middle of the tier and any gangbangers looking for the two leaders of the White Aryan Brotherhood—Jimmy and Michael Knox— would have to fight their way through a couple of dozen WAB soldiers. Chaney stood at the cell door, looking out and down at the wild hordes of prisoners, three of whom were taking turns anally raping a white guard. On the other side of the floor, several prisoners were gleefully playing soccer with someone's decapitated head. Michael sat on the lower bunk, eyes staring blankly at the opposite wall, deep in thought. Jimmy had turned inward, standing by the barred window, looking out into the yard, trying to forget that he would have been released the next day. From time to time he would look at the fourth man in the cell, Bill Bender, who was standing against the far wall, trying to stay out of Michael's line of sight. The kid was sweating heavily in spite of the October chill, his eyes rolling in their sockets.

"It ain't so bad, Bill," Jimmy said, softly. "They won't come up here, even with the weapons. There's maybe a hundred of us up here. They want to get the hacks, then bust into PC, kill the stoolies and the guys been hit by the sugar truck."

"Sugar truck?"

"The sissies, the fags in Protective Custody. The guys who put themselves in there for protection from everyone else in the joint. They been hit by the sugar truck, run down, turned into sweeties."

Bill began to laugh, almost maniacally. "Sugar truck!" He said the words over and over, giving them meaning in his mind. "Hit by the sugar truck!" Jimmy watched as Chaney turned to face the kid, sneering. He spit at Bill's feet.

"Watch it, Chaney," Michael said. "The guy's a brother."

"He got to prove it to me, Michael."

"No, he don't," Jimmy said. "He already proved it to me."

Chaney turned back to the carnage, silently. He'd already had one bout with Jimmy that day.

Screams and hoots and hollers assaulted them from below, sexual grunts as convicts shot their wads into weaker inmates, louder screams as guys who had paybacks coming caught a shank in the stomach or back. Jimmy kept his eyes open, for this noise when mixed with darkness was the stuff of madness.

Every time the National Guardsmen would try to open the hatch and enter on the riot walkway, they'd be met by the bullets fired from the guard's stolen rifle and by the quiet zing of .22 zip gun bullets. Whoever had the rifle knew what he was doing, never shooting in bursts, saving the precious M-16 rounds in order to prolong the riot.

Jimmy looked out into the yard, where the unfortunate prisoners who hadn't broken for the cellblocks were being manhandled by the guards. They had been made to lie naked in the grass, their hands clasped behind their heads, their ankles crossed. Guards in twos were searching their cavities, getting back at the cons because a couple of their own had fallen. He hadn't lied to Bill. He didn't think the fifth tier was in any danger. At least until the riot ended. But after that, when the guards stormed in, man, the tear gas would flow and the nightsticks would fly and any con unlucky enough to have been seen causing damage would get his ass kicked big-time. The gas would hit the ground and rise, come up here and settle in the top cells . . .

He stripped the sheet off the top bunk and then tore it into strips, ripping it into pieces maybe two feet long by a foot wide. He dunked these in the toilet and handed them around, telling the men to tie them around their heads when the gas came through and then lie down on the cell floor.

Chaney took his without looking back at Jimmy, enjoying the sight of the white guard crawling toward the stairway. "Ain't gonna make it," Chaney said, "some nigger's gonna stick him, you watch, or they'll pull the nightstick out of his ass and fuck on him some more."

"Nightstick?" Jimmy said, then said, "Who's that guard?" Squinting. He turned to Michael Knox. "For shit's sake, Michael, it's Stanley."

"Stanley?" Michael showed concern for the first time since the riot had begun. He jumped off the cot and raced to the cell door, watching, as the guard, his face twisted with terror and pain and shock, crawled hand over hand toward the iron stairway, veins bulging out of his red face as he strained. Cons ran around and over him, some of them taking the time to kick him as they passed, Stanley covering up then immediately uncovering, crawling again toward the steps. His pants had been torn off and a nightstick was protruding from his bleeding backside. Hanks of hair had been torn from his head. He was crying. Michael, though, was smiling.

"Christ, Jimmy, I been sitting there thinking about how the fuck to get you out of here on time tomorrow. Jacobi'd kill me if I didn't get you out of here on time, riot or not. And this is the way." He turned quickly to Chaney, said, "How many rounds you count so far from down below?"

"Fifteen, sixteen."

Michael was excited now, seeing a way out for Jimmy and running with it. "The magazine's got to be empty by now, or almost. Soon as the hacks know there's only zips to worry about, they'll bust through the hatch. Chaney, quick, you and Bill hit the tier, tell everyone to tie pieces of wet sheet around their heads. Jimmy, what you carrying?"

"I got a shank almost razor sharp."

"I got two of them. Get something for your other hand." He snapped his fingers impatiently. "Bender—hey Bill, wake the hell up—give Jimmy that hunk of metal." Bender did, backing immediately to the wall, safe.

Michael said to Jimmy, "You up to it? Down five flights of stairs, grab Stanley, and get him back up here?"

"Just you and me?"

"Man, it's the only way. Those spades see fifty guys coming down the steps, they'll figure it's an assault and attack. You and me, we can slip down almost before they spot us. Shit, the cells are empty except for up here. Everyone's trying to even scores or busting into PC."

From the screams and hollers coming from the far tunnel, it sounded as if they'd made it, too. Cons were racing, laughing and cheering, toward the tunnel that would lead them to PC. Jimmy hadn't heard a rifle shot for a while. Time was running out. As a known leader of one of the prison gangs, it would take something special to get him out of the joint now before maybe the turn of the century. He nodded, tightened his grip on the pipe, grabbed the shank out of his shoe.

"Let's go," he said, and ran out of the cell behind Michael.

Charged up, their adrenaline rushing in their veins, hollering for the other cons to stay put in their cells, neither of them heard Chaney laugh and tell Bill Bender that seeing as how his boyfriend was getting out the next day, he was gonna need a new daddy . . .

They raced down the stairs single file, Michael having to whack a few guys across the face with his knife, but not many because

what few men were in their way were renegades, without affiliations, just punks caught up in the thrill of having some power for a
change, trying to stand in the way and act tough. By the time they
reached Stanley, the cell floor was nearly empty and the hollering
and screaming and crying from PC was deafening.

Stanley had made it to the second floor, pulling himself hand
over hand up the stairs, grunting and crying out with each breath.
"Get him, Jimmy," Michael said, "all by yourself so he'll remember you." Jimmy squatted and pulled Stanley to his knees,
then draped him over his shoulder and stood, his knife between his
teeth and the pipe in his right hand. Stanley's blood flowed
quickly onto Jimmy's shoulder, down to his waist. The man stank
something terrible. He raced up the steps with Michael right
behind him, gasping through his mouth for breath, feeling sick
from the stench, the guard over his left shoulder weighing a ton
and screaming with each step. Jimmy hoped the Guardsmen would
break in soon, the guy must have some internal injuries to be
screaming and bleeding like that and he didn't want the man to die
before he could tell his partners just who it was that had saved his
life.

As he reached Chaney's cell and began to enter, what he saw
made him stagger back almost to the guardrail, and he had to
whirl his arms to keep from going over. Michael got there in time
to steady Stanley before he flipped over the side, then entered the
cell and saw Bill Bender on his knees in front of Chaney, and
Michael began to holler at Chaney just as Jimmy entered the cell
and eased Stanley down on his stomach on the lower bunk. He
heard Michael yell, then he heard Chaney holler and then Jimmy
felt something wet across his back and he turned in time to see
Chaney reaching back, getting ready to shank Michael again,
watched in shock as Michael grabbed his slashed arm and took the
second knife thrust in the middle of his chest.

Jimmy didn't have time to think. He swung the iron pipe and
reached for the knife between his teeth as Michael fell to his knees
in front of him, between the two of them, Bender now curled up
on the floor, sobbing. The pipe missed Chaney but made him back

up, and he tripped over Bender and was on his way down when Jimmy stabbed him hard, aiming for the chest but Chaney was falling and the knife stuck him in the throat. Blood splattered across Jimmy's shirtfront. Jimmy released the shank and fell back, grabbed the top bunk to steady himself and regained his feet, shaking, looking at Michael there at his feet, the blade in deep.

Michael's eyes were open and he wasn't gasping for air. There was only a little blood around the handle of the shank in his chest.

"He made me put it in my mouth!" Bender's cries matched the guard's on the bunk, a duet of agony.

"Shut up!" Jimmy stepped over Bill and reached down, dragged Chaney across the cell and got him to his feet. The man was still alive, both hands at his throat, where a stream of dark arterial blood was shooting into the air with his heartbeat. Below them, on the cellblock floor, the few prisoners still playing soccer with the head ignored them. The rest of the cons were over having fun in Punk City.

"Don't," Chaney said, and Jimmy pushed him hard, once, and turned back to the cell before the man hit the concrete five floors down.

He pulled the nightstick out of Stanley's backside and listened as Bender wailed to him that he had no choice, the man had the knife at his throat and made him do it, told him that he was going to kill Jimmy before he could ever get released. He was crying like a newborn child. At last Jimmy told him to shut up before he took the nightstick to his head. He rolled the guard up in one of the bunk's blankets and looked him close in the face so Stanley could see who he was, and told him over and over that he'd pulled him into the cell, he, Jimmy Vale, his friend, and he told him this again and again until at last the National Guardsmen broke through the riot hatch and, shooting rifles and throwing CS gas canisters, began to take the madhouse back from the inmates.

Captain Stanley remembered them. At first the hacks had thought that it was Jimmy and Bill who'd done the damage to the man, as

Stanley had been clinging to Jimmy as the guardsmen stormed the cell, Jimmy holding a wet piece of bed sheet over the guard captain's face, talking to him still. The hacks had come in and whacked Jimmy in the head a few times, beat him to the floor before they understood what it was that Stanley was saying.

At that point things changed some. Jimmy and Bill had been rushed through the cellblock and ushered into the warden's outer office, as the only thing that Stanley hadn't got right was the fact that it had been Michael Knox who'd come down with Jimmy to save him. He'd told them that it had been the other living man in the cell, Bill Bender, and Jimmy didn't set them straight.

They were told that Captain Stanley said he owed his life to them, and they kept their heads up and their faces blank, still being cons in the presence of the Man, but when they were left alone in the locked outer office they breathed deeply and smiled at each other.

"Don't tell anyone what he did to me, will you, Jimmy?" Bill said. "You're going home but I just got here."

"Keep your mouth shut and play humble, Bill. Tomorrow you'll get transferred. Count on it. Young kid like you, first-time offender, don't be surprised the governor commutes your sentence." That shut Bill up and gave Jimmy time to think.

Michael Knox had died for him. Other members of the WAB would dope out what had happened, would get word to the outside. As for Bill, wherever he went, he would be in PC, because there were guys who would know that he'd been turned out. He hoped the governor did commute the kid's sentence, maybe grant him clemency. Stranger things had happened and Stanley had a lot of pull in the political arena, would probably, with his connections, even get a warden's job out of this to keep him from suing the state and making millions. So Stanley would take care of Bill and the state would take care of Stanley, and the warden, from what he'd been saying, would take care of Jimmy, get him his scheduled release. All that was left was: Who would take care of

Michael Knox? The man had given his life for Jimmy. And even though he'd never felt really close to the man, the code dictated, demanded, that he do something in return.

Who would take care of Michael Knox, who'd died for him? That was a good question, one that kept him thinking until the hacks came and told them that the chief of the Department of Corrections wanted to speak with them personally, express his appreciation.

Chapter

TEN

The house next door to Frank Vale's had once been an exact duplicate of his own, the large homes on Sheridan Road just north of downtown Chicago being at one time showplaces for the rich. They had now fallen on hard times. Frank liked his house and the privacy it afforded him, could afford, too, to keep it in one piece. Most of the neighbors, though, hadn't been so lucky. The house to the right of him had been cut up into apartments, four separate residences and eleven people crammed into what had once been a private home. As the people with money moved farther north, into Evanston or Winnetka or Glencoe, poorer people took over the homes on Sheridan Road and property values tumbled. Now there were only a few of the large old homes left, the rest of them torn down to make room for rental high-rises for students and seniors, or converted into condos. The City Council had enacted a renter's rights ordinance which had made it nearly impossible for a landlord to turn an honest buck in the city, so they'd sold them out, and now the same people who had once rented these places could no longer afford to live in them.

But Frank had never allowed the real estate sharks to seduce him, even though they'd tried, hard. He liked his place and had spent a lot of time and trouble on the basement.

As he walked out of his house—carrying Foo-foo—he almost wished that one or more of the PRICCs were outside, would give him some mouth. He was in the mood for it.

His brother was set to be released tomorrow and now there was a riot in progress at the prison he was in, shit, the news asshole at ten o'clock had said that the National Guard had stormed the prison, that there were at least eleven inmates and three guards dead. . . .

Too, Jimmy had a mouth on him and a way of getting himself into the middle of things. But what could he do? Go down there and demand that he be let in? Into a place he never intended to enter? No, best to sit tight, wait for someone to call, which they would have to do if his brother was a casualty. But sitting still was driving him crazy, so he turned on the recording machine and decided to take Foo-foo back to little Nicky next door before the kid had a stroke, or worse, he kicked the little rat.

Foo-foo had shit on his basement floor, right there on the deep-pile carpet, then had yapped and bitten at him, as if it were Frank's fault. The dog had a lot of guts, he could say that for it. Also, there was the fact that if he hurt it, Nicky would probably cry himself into a stroke.

So he took it to Nicky, knocked too loudly on the door, looking at the door across the hall—Tina's door—and when Nicky's mother opened her own door he handed her the dog, thanked her in a booming voice, told her to give Nicky his love when he got up in the morning, wanting his voice to bounce off the walls, maybe tear down the door to Tina's apartment.

His voice didn't have to tear it down though, because no sooner had Nicky's mother closed the door on him than Tina's door opened and she was standing there, wearing a man's shirt—his shirt—that covered her to mid-thigh, but there was no covering those high breasts, or those slender legs, dancer's legs now positioned shyly, one in front of the other, as if she was wondering if maybe she should run back inside and slam the door.

His eyes saw the legs, the nipples at the shirtfront, and he felt a pang of jealousy, Frank wondering if maybe she was entertaining another man. No, shit, she wasn't that type, for Christ's sake. And when his eyes met hers, he knew she wasn't ready for other men just yet.

Tina had a slender, delicate neck that curved up and out, leading to a strong chin under a set of lips too big to be real but were. Her nose was slender, almost arrogant, the way she held it in the air all the time, looking down at you. He could see her ears, close to her head with her hair drawn back in a ponytail, held by a rubber band. But it was her eyes that grabbed him, pulled at him, tore at his heart, Tina having the deepest and warmest brown eyes he'd ever looked into—got lost in. She stabbed him with those eyes now—they were slightly wet and filled with warmth, compassion, telling him so much that he had to look away, stare back down at her breasts for a second before figuring that she might get the wrong idea.

"I heard about the riot . . ." She spoke tentatively, which was unusual for her, Tina being a strong, smart girl who knew what she wanted in life. He couldn't find his voice and she took his silence personally, stammered, "Have you heard from your brother?"

Frank shook his head. Tina shrugged. "Well, would you like a drink or something, or do you have something to do?" She put a little too much emphasis on the words "something to do," because Frank's things-to-do had obviously broken her heart and their relationship.

Frank said, "No, there's nothing for me to do," softly, though, without emphasis. He didn't want to lose her, as he feared he'd lost Jimmy. Not tonight, he couldn't afford to lose both of them. He said, "I could use a beer, Tina," and she smiled, shyly, holding the collar of his white shirt closed at her throat with her right hand. She stepped inside, held the door open for him, and he entered, trying not to let his racing heart betray his anxiety.

They were stupid, is all it was. Here they were with a piece of cake in-and-out score—even Frank had said it was the sweetest deal he'd seen in years—and they were going to walk away from it because some cops had slapped the dumb dago around a little. And Adalebo, what a coward *he* turned out to be. After doing time with

97

him in a cell in Attica, he'd figured Adalebo to be a hard one, tough as nails, and as soon as the guinea punk with the fancy house shook his head Adalebo rolled over and showed the world his ass, like a jailhouse faggot. Hell, he'd been ready to shoot the black son of a bitch, just out of disgust, turning over and doing tricks for the big white-trash thief. People sure did change on the outside. Some of the things they'd do for money.

Who did the guy think he was, giving orders? Just because he could open a safe. Big deal. Wayne Lockhart had busted more safes than Frank Vale had ever seen, and not just itty-bitty little wall Moslers like the one they had in the Astor Street mansion; some big suckers, down home when he was young, sometimes drilling them and filling the holes with dynamite, sometimes peeling them, sometimes getting lucky and knocking out the dial with a punch then fiddling with the tumblers until the thing came open. Which was what he would do with the little old Mosler on Astor Street. He knew more about alarms than those stiffs gave him credit for, too. Shit, he'd done time—what, twenty-four years of his life—behind burglaries. How could these guys think he was just a lookout who could keep his mouth shut? Well, he'd show them. He'd pull off the score on his own, and if there was anything near what Frank thought there might be inside, he could take Angel to Florida for the winter, keep her in the custom to which she'd grown accustomed the last five months they'd been together.

Speaking of Angel, there she was, at the end of the bed, looking at him, not yet knowing he was awake and looking back at her. The light from the living room was behind her, gave her the look of an angel with a halo. A Madonna. Like a real angel. His angel. That long white hair, falling straight down to her shoulders, past them to her titties. What fine titties they were, too, almost like they were made from Silly Putty, the way they flattened then inflated under his grip like big rubber beach balls. She said they were real, too, when he'd asked her about them after finding her working in Vegas. No fake tits for the Angel, she'd said. He wasn't sure if he believed her. Either way, they were some fine titties.

And Angel's mouth—had any sissy in the joint brought him off the way she could with that mouth? Hell, no. She would tease him, tell him he'd done too much time, didn't like it the usual way anymore after so many years in prison. He'd tell her it was a pain in the ass, all the stuff that went along with the intercourse, the kissing and the fondling and the love words. He liked it quick and easy, her mouth around him, or going in from behind where he could just roll to the side when he was done and be out of her. No sweat all over him and no Angel wanting him to kiss her on the same mouth she'd just had on his pecker. She'd told him once that if he wanted her to, she'd put a carrot on her belly so he could feel the way he had in the joint, and he didn't understand what she was saying and was too embarrassed to ask. He'd got mad, though, when after he'd told her no she'd laughed at him. He didn't like people laughing at him or making fun of him. Killed people who tried.

"What you looking at, Angel?" He said it sweetly, in his hillbilly accent. Lockhart had done hard time in four states and hadn't been home in over twenty years, but his voice, thoughts, and mannerisms were pure backwoods Kentucky.

"Wondering whether to wake my daddy up." She tossed back her hair and those big titties jiggled up and down, back and forth. "Didn't you say you had to go to work tonight?"

"Gonna, too, in just a minute."

"You want me to maybe . . . relax you, Wayne?"

Lockhart knew from experience that it would be a waste of time. After a thieving he could go for days, one pop after another, but before going out, never. He rolled off the bed, not feeling too hung over, and said, "You just hold it inside of you till I get back, sweetie pie. And while I'm gone, you ought to think about what you want to take to Florida with you for this coming winter."

"Florida?" Angel clapped her hands together and he bet she was smiling but he couldn't tell, as he was looking at another part of her anatomy. "When we leaving, Wayne?"

"Maybe in the morning. If I make it." There. Leave her up in the air. Get her good and scared so that when he did come back, with the pillowcase full of loot, she'd be so happy to see him she'd wear all of that bright-red lipstick off, sucking on him.

All right. No more thinking of Angel. The cold night air knocked out whatever hangover he had left, and the fear racing up his spine kept him on his toes. He was getting old and he knew it. Years ago it was never like this, with the fear and having to get a few drinks in him to get through a thieving. Back then he'd been young and strong, a bull of a man, ready to die before he showed anyone he was afraid, killing a couple of men who'd accused him of cowardice just on principle. Time though, doing time had shown him fear. And having Angel now, Angel who told him she loved him. Maybe she did, but he wouldn't bet the farm on her waiting for him if he got busted again.

He knew that the big-shot real estate magnate who owned the mansion on North Astor wasn't home tonight. He was getting a dinner in his honor over to the Chicago Public Library Cultural Center, a big ta-doo with his wife and kids there clapping their hands. And Wednesday was the maid and butler's day off. The chauffeur would be waiting out in the street, double-parked, for the party to get over with. The house was empty, ready to be cracked.

Lockhart climbed the back fence, dropped heavily to the ground, and ran to the back door. He was dressed in black and was carrying a black leather satchel, filled with the tools of his trade. He stopped at the sliding glass door, took a pen flashlight from the bag, shone it upon the frame. There it was, just as Frank said it would be! There was a black vibration sensor alarm on the door, one small square attached to the glass and another to the frame. The simplest and cheapest alarm on the market. Wayne stuck a magnetized Slim Jim between the two units, used another to jimmy the lock, and was inside before he was on the grounds a full minute. He carefully held the slender magnetized tool in place, set the satchel on the floor, reached into it and removed with his free hand first a six-inch piece of wire with alligator clips on either end, which he stuck between his teeth, then a small pair of wire cutters. Still holding the magnetic Slim Jim in place, he clipped one end of the alarm wire, put the cutter on the floor then rapidly reached up, grabbed the piece of wire out of his mouth and clipped one end, then the other, to the loose ends of alarm wire. He held his breath and pulled the Slim Jim away from the door. Nothing. Slowly, he slid the glass door closed, locked it behind him.

He knew where everything was. The floor plans had been provided, and somehow Frank had even come up with Polaroid pictures of the inside of the place, which Lockhart had studied for hours, so now he knew where every stick of furniture was on the first floor of the place, which was all he was supposed to see. It was good enough, because he was supposed to stand here listening to a portable scanner radio tuned to the police band and guarding Frank, who would be popping the safe in the library while Adalebo went through the upper floors, grabbing loose jewelry and the artwork off the walls. Using the penlight, Wayne Lockhart made his move.

He half ran to the laundry room, his bowel wanting to cut loose on him, and he stopped in the doorway, shaking, and crossed his legs, breathed deeply until the spasm passed. When he was younger he would just drop his pants where he was and take him a dump, getting a big laugh from the other guys, but nowadays the cops had so much stuff, like Frank had said, more than in a James Bond movie, so he never took off his gloves or even dumped in a toilet. You never knew what the cops could scrape off the inside of the commode. Probably learn his blood type and hair color and height, weight, and the color of his eyes from his pooper.

When he was all right again, he moved into the laundry room on cat feet supporting legs that felt weak. He moved the washer out of the way, and, right behind it, just like Frank said it would be, was the alarm box. Carefully, he squatted next to it, opened the panel and trained the penlight on the switches inside. The fourth switch to the right was the one he wanted, the emergency cutoff switch that would shut off all the alarms in the house. They were installed by the ADT people back in the old days when the cops got pissed off when they would get a call about a wayward alarm, have to go out and waste their time on bullshit when they could be down in the local gin mill cadging drinks off citizens. After insurance company insiders told too many thieves about them, they'd changed things and put in private codes, where the owner would punch a number in and shut the alarm down. But these old ones were set and shut off with keys, and if you lost your key and the alarm went off, you would have to race to your secret little place and hit the turnoff switch. Dumb rich fuckers. Older houses like these— with the rich fat cats who owned them since forever feeling too safe or being too damn cheap to update the system—were the easiest ones to pop. Flick one switch . . . right . . . there! and all the alarms in the house would be deactivated. Lockhart got to his feet, raced through the house and into the library, went straight to the funny-looking stick-man picture hanging on the wall, and pushed it aside.

The Mosler sat there unprotected and alone, like a new teenage fish on the cellblock, waiting to get a daddy. As he pulled out the portable battery-operated drill and stuck its suction cups to the wall, Lockhart decided that getting into this thing would be just as easy as, or maybe even easier than, turning one of those young chickadees out.

Man, had Frank ever been wrong. Not that Lockhart was complaining. There had been twice as much dough as the man had guessed. Lockhart was feeling downright giddy. Less than a half an hour inside and here he was, the cleaned untraceable tools left behind, the satchel filled to the top with cash and diamonds and emeralds and rubies. He'd tear the jewels out of their settings at home, on the bed, before he let Angel near him. He'd go out and dump the settings down sewer gratings and then the stones would be untraceable. He ran to the back door, knowing he'd scored over a million cash all by himself, which he wouldn't have to split with any cowardly Uncle Tom nigger or for sure not with a damn stupid pushy dago. It was all his and he would sell the gems down south and have maybe two million altogether.

He walked out the same way he came in, pushed the sliding glass door shut behind him, breathing easy now, the fear gone, a rich man with a smile on his face minutes away from being home free, when the big fat nigger and the short greasy fucker stuck their guns in his face and quietly told him to freeze.

Chapter

ELEVEN

"They interviewed Captain Stanley from his hospital bed," Kane said to Jimmy, not smiling. He was the director of the Department of Corrections, in charge of maybe a hundred thousand men throughout the state of Illinois, and this was the first time that Jimmy knew of that the man had spoken directly to a convict. Usually he gave orders to his underlings, the wardens, who relayed his orders to their own employees, the guard captains, who passed the word on down to the sergeants and from there to the screws, and by the time the hacks typed stuff up to relay to the convicts through posting on the bulletin boards, Kane was already coming up with some new shit to lay on them.

Jimmy could tell the guy didn't like this a bit, talking to a con and having to treat him like a man. He was trying to stay above it all, a superior, but Jimmy was staring at him, silently most of the time, not speaking unless he was asked a direct question. He was afraid to begin a personal conversation with the man; he didn't know if he could keep his mouth shut and his instincts under control. This guy Kane was hated passionately throughout the system, from the hacks to the inmates.

"He told us that if it hadn't have been for you, the rioters would have killed him." He looked at the blood on Jimmy's clothes with his eyebrows arched. Jimmy stayed silent. The man hadn't asked him a direct question. Kane picked up a manila folder off the warden's desk—Jimmy's jacket—and began studying it carefully.

Every so often he'd say "Hmm" or "Uh-huh!" his voice rising on the last syllable, as if he'd spotted something that gave him insight. Jimmy stared straight ahead, not getting his hopes up. There were three guards in the room, along with the warden and Kane, proof of just how far he was trusted by these people. Kane, too, had gone out of his way to let him know that he considered this an us-against-you situation. Jimmy didn't appreciate that.

Now Kane and the warden were huddled by the fireplace, conversing in quiet tones, the warden mostly nodding while Kane used a lot of body language as he spoke. The warden—the little ass-kisser—had his elbow cupped in his left hand and was stroking his chin thoughtfully as he listened, his head never ceasing its bobbing. As if he ever had an original opinion in his life, the puke. Jimmy watched, trying to appear nonchalant and uninvolved, trying to blend into the chair. He knew from long experience that when dealing with these people, it was best to appear mindless, because that was the way they saw you anyhow.

At last Kane stopped speaking and twisted his lips at Jimmy. Was he snarling? No, it was a smile. The man was coming toward him with a smile on his face, actually reaching out to shake Jimmy's hand!

"I have to get back to the city—the governor's waiting for me to fill him in on what happened here. But I want to extend my—and the governor's—thanks to you, Mr. Vale, for saving the life of Captain Stanley."

Mr. Vale? Had the man really called him Mr. *Vale*? Kane was closing the door behind himself and Jimmy had twisted in the chair to watch him leave, in shock at the formal, respectful words the man had spoken. He believed that it was probably the first time in his life that anyone had ever called him mister.

The warden said, "We've decided to, er, expedite your release, Jimmy, in light of the fact that you heroically saved the life of one of our guard captains." He sat back with his ass perched on the edge of his desk, a pudgy little man with a Clark Gable mustache, trying to play Santa Claus and not knowing how, as he'd had no previous experience. Jimmy got it then, knew what was coming before the words left the warden's mouth.

"We'll get you out the side entrance, in an official car. A guard is bringing your papers, your suit, and your money to this office. Naturally, we expect you to keep your mouth shut to the press, and to get word back inside that we did this for you." The little man smiled. Now, the Brotherhood owed them one. And, too, there was the fact that they would have to let him out soon anyway, even if he had to wait a couple of weeks for the investigation to be completed, and the press might be waiting for him. Jimmy understood that they wanted Captain Stanley's humiliation kept under wraps as much as they wanted an in with the White Aryan Brotherhood, and he resented neither fact. It was the way the game was played. This was still prison, and something for nothing was suspicious and worthy of scorn.

Jimmy said, "I understand, Warden," saving the *sir*. He hadn't said the word in nine years and didn't intend to break the record now.

When the guard brought his things in the warden left the room without offering to shake hands.

"The problem is, Tina, it's not that *I* don't trust you, it's that I can't give you the trust of guys I'm not sure *will* trust you." Frank spoke the words quickly, wondering if she understood what he was saying, because it hadn't made sense even to him. He knew what he wanted to say, how he felt, but it was a pain in the ass, trying to express himself to her without saying ain't and without cursing. She was a lawyer whose practice was restricted to abused children; she knew all the words and had probably seen more than Frank had, but she didn't cuss often at home, had told him once that she hated it when men talked dirty, figuring she was one of the guys or trying to impress her, or maybe even trying to insult her, put her in her place for daring to be more than a housewife.

She was sitting next to him, looking at him, her legs up under her. The only light in the room was the glow from the television set, which was murmuring against the wall, the sound low, the set tuned to a cable news channel. He wanted to hear if anything came on about the prison riot.

He took a long sip of his beer, set it on the table next to him, and lit a cigarette, knowing she didn't like him to smoke in her apartment but lighting the thing anyway, needing the extra time to think, something to do with his hands. He didn't think she'd care for it if he did what he wanted to do with them.

"It's just that, there're some things I do, Tina, that I can't talk about. You keep some things from me, too."

"Not from necessity. No one will kill me or give me a bad name on the street with other lawyers if I came home and discussed an abused child with you. I keep things away from you because what I see sickens me most of the time. If I live and breathe my work, Frank, I'll burn out, then sell out. I'll wind up on Michigan Avenue billing three hundred an hour and trying to pretend that monsters don't exist.

"What you're saying, Frank, is, you're a crook. All right, I accept that. You go on ahead and keep being a crook. But it'll have to be without me in your life. A relationship with a crook, one that means anything—that's something I can't accept." She spoke softly, without anger. Stating facts in a pained voice but not trying to make him feel guilty. In a near whisper, Tina said, "*Lying* to me."

"I never meant to lead you on, Tina. It's just that you're so godda— I mean you're so pretty, so smart, so educated, I knew that if you had my number up front, you wouldn't go out with me. I wasn't looking just to score; after the first couple of dates, you really mattered to me."

"But not enough to tell me that you weren't what you represented yourself to be."

"By then I was in too deep. Can't you try to understand? I was falling for you, Tina, and finding out what and who you were, how you looked at things, and by the time I figured out that you wouldn't have anything to do with me if you knew what I really was, it was too late, I was already . . ." He paused, not wanting to say he was in love. He had never spoken the words to anyone and wouldn't begin here and now with a woman who was dumping him. "Already in too deep."

"But Frank, you kept the deception going, led me to believe you were hurt in construction and retired and had investments. The last few weeks, when you kept disappearing for a day at a time, then you shut me out when I asked where you were going and what you were doing, my God, I thought you had another woman! You broke my heart, Frank, because even though you won't say it, I will: I love you." She turned her head away, rubbed at her eyes with the palm of her hand. "Now, I wish you *did* have another woman."

"Instead of being a thief? You'd rather I was a dishonest cheat?" He said the words and felt funny saying them, especially when she shot him a withering glance. When she spoke her voice held a cutting edge and it did the job it was intended to do: It cut him right to the quick.

"You can rationalize your behavior and your lifestyle any way you like, to anyone you please, and you can kid yourself that I'm enjoying some sense of petty jealousy about wanting to know your personal business, but don't you ever, ever again insult me by telling me that you're an honest man, Frank."

"You want me to change? Is that it? Be what you want me to be?"

"No, Frank, I don't. What I want you to be is the man you told me you were. That's the man I fell in love with. Not with a thief."

It was on the tip of his tongue—he wanted to say "That's what I get for being honest with you, for telling you the truth." He wanted to say it but he didn't have the guts. He was feeling small enough already. Too small even to try and tell her that the PRICCs had framed him. She knew what he was now, and he couldn't hide from it; the deception had to end.

It was over and he could live with that, but still, he wanted her to understand.

He'd told her right away, in the beginning, about Jimmy being in Stateville, and during the past few weeks he'd shared his excitement over Jimmy's pending release, but never had he even hinted he was maybe involved in the same line of work that had grossed his brother nine years behind bars.

But she'd found out, and now he was against the wall, caring enough to want her to know the truth, knowing that telling her would end it.

And now here they were, rehashing the same thing over and over again. It was getting them nowhere, and he had other things on his mind. But, God, if he ever needed someone to care for him, it was now.

"I'm sorry."

"For what? For lying to me in the first place or for conning me all this time? Or are you just sorry that you're a thief? Or are you sorry that I found out? Or maybe you're sorry for trying to lie to us both right now about what a 'noble thief' you are. Excuse me, Frank, but I hear it all the time. Sexually abusive fathers getting my colleagues and me in a room and nudging one of the men, trying to talk his way out of the rap, saying, about his own daughter, 'Take a look at her, go on, wouldn't *you* want to fuck her?' Or trying to convince me that a ten-year-old child seduced them. Or my personal favorite, crying, trying to work up some sympathy by telling me how rotten their own childhood was, how, if they'd gotten help sooner, none of it would have happened. If only they had another chance, they'd seek help and it would never happen again. No, uh-uh, buddy. Rationalization doesn't go far with me. The fact is you're a thief, and sooner or later you'll take a fall. So what were you looking for, some little madonna to sit up in the kitchen, wringing her hands, crying and waiting for you?"

"Don't you compare me to one of those child molesters!"

"Oh, that's right. Excuse me, I forgot about the pecking order. Thieves are higher up on the prison ladder than baby-rapers. The thing is, though, Frank, they're all in prison together, aren't they?"

He rose to his feet, pushed his cigarettes angrily into his shirt pocket, grabbed his jacket from the arm of the chair. "I got to get out of here."

"It doesn't surprise me. It's a natural reaction people have when they get their masks torn away. They run. Only there's no running inside prison, Frank. When the prison shrink starts to tear down your defenses, you have to listen.''

He walked quickly to the door with his head held high, and Tina said, ''Go ahead, run. I don't blame you. I'm running, too.''

That stopped him. He turned, looked at her with his hand on the knob. She was still sitting on her legs, her knees white at the caps, staring at him through wet eyes. Her lower lip was trembling.

''That's right, Frank, I'm running away, too. I quit my job today, I'm gonna get drunk tonight, and tomorrow I start packing. How the hell can I help kids when I can't tell lies from the truth? When the man I love can so thoroughly convince me he's good and real when all the time it's a . . . it's a . . .'' She gave in, covered her face with her hands and began to sob, her shoulders shaking. He could tell she was making an effort not to, trying to sob silently so he couldn't see how badly he'd hurt her.

He didn't know what to do. He wanted, desperately, to go to her, rip her hands away from her face and holler at her that he wanted her to go ahead and tear the masks down, because he wanted to know exactly how she saw him. But he couldn't. Maybe it was because the way she saw him would be a lot closer to reality than the way he saw himself.

Instead of going to her, he quietly left the apartment.

Chapter

TWELVE

"The problem is, you goof, we already got one hundred percent of the stuff, so what are you trying to pull, offering us ten percent? You got to do better than that, Wayne."

The greasy one, Gunon, was talking. He had a way of talking and smiling at the same time, his mouth reeling words off, talking shit, like a jailhouse barn boss trying to get in your Fruit of the Looms. The big black son of a bitch, Roosevelt, was sitting in the front seat of their car, turned all the way around, staring at him hard. The youngest of the three was driving them around downtown Chicago, giving him the eye in the rearview mirror when they stopped for lights. The kid, he seemed really pleased with himself. The other two, they just scared him.

"I don't know what to give you boys," Wayne Lockhart said. He was trolling, looking for a way out without offending them. "I mean, you can tell me we can negotiate, but hell, you know the score, I talk my head off right here in the car, tell you all about the score, who set it up, why they didn't come along tonight, you still can't prove nothing on them. I'm the one you got, and I'm the one gonna go away. Hell, even if you offered me immunity, there ain't no D.A. here in the car guaranteeing me nothing."

He'd gone too far. Roosevelt grabbed him with two huge hands, by the throat, squeezed it some and shouted, "You want guarantees, you redneck fucker? I'll guarantee you one thing, asshole! You're goin' away for the next twenty years of your life, that's your guarantee!" Without taking his eyes off Lockhart he shouted, "Giraldi, drive this car to the precinct—this piece of shit's going down." He pushed Lockhart away violently and turned to stare out the window.

"Calm down, Rosy," Gunon said. "We turn this guy in like this, the loot gets turned in, too."

Roosevelt grunted. "We can take our cut from the top."

"Listen to reason. We can do that, but what if this guy, owns the mansion, got it down to the exact penny how much was in there? We got enough problems with the press and the public, enough heat from City Hall, without pissing off some stud, over at a party right now in his honor, probably got the mayor sitting on the dais with him."

"Let's kill him and take it all." Lockhart heard the driver speak for the first time and the words chilled him. So far, it had been the greaseball, Gunon, sweet-talking him, even introducing them all to him, like old buddies; or the jig, Roosevelt, being mean and playing Bad Cop. Now the kid piped up and he talked of murder the way Lockhart might tell Adalebo to pull into a White Castle so he could get a couple of burgers on the way home from the movies.

"Sounds good to me," Roosevelt said.

Lockhart didn't know if he was supposed to speak up now, maybe beg for his life. He figured it was some kind of a game they were running, trying to get him to work for them, make them rich. But what if it wasn't?

He knew what they'd done to Frank, the beating he'd taken that afternoon. He'd seen and got a lot worse from the cops in his day, but still, they'd worked Frank over pretty good.

Why hadn't he listened? Frank had told him to lay low, that the heat would be watching them for a few weeks. He had assumed that if they'd known where the score was, they'd have caught them there, and it appeared that he'd been half right. They'd known, but didn't let on that they'd known, waited in case the thieves thought they were stupid and went out anyway. They probably took it the same way they'd take someone spitting on them.

He thought of his options, which were limited. He could take the heat, go inside again—but no, they'd said that was out because, no matter what, they weren't going away empty-handed. All right. He could keep his mouth shut and get himself killed, and then Angel would find some other dude to suck on, probably find him before Lockhart's body was cold in the grave or even put inside the box.

What had the cop said, about having to do better than ten percent? Yeah, he was right, they wanted something from him. Something that was important enough to them to let him live to do, but what could it be?

Well, so far they hadn't laid hands on him, except for the jig grabbing him and pushing him around a couple of times. And Frank, they'd labeled him pretty good. Was it Frank they wanted? Shit, he'd give him to them in a second, to gain his freedom.

Gunon said, "Anthony, drive over to the rocks by the Montrose Harbor. This late on a October night, nobody'll be around, except maybe a couple of fags, and they won't say nothing. We'll ace this stiff, get home, get some fucking sleep."

Giraldi flipped his signal on, turned left, east, at the next corner. Lockhart's mind was racing. If he asked them what they wanted from him, they'd own him, body and soul. But if he offered something that they took as an insult, they'd kill him sure as hell. There was no doubt in his mind now that the smarmy little greaser next to him would be true to his word. He was talking to the other guys, completely ignoring Lockhart now. They were about to kill him and take all the money unless he came up with something, quick.

Trying not to let his voice break and betray his terror, he said, "Tell ya'll what, fellas. How about I set up Frank Vale for you, deliver him with a pretty pink ribbon tied around his neck. Him and his partner, Adam Lebeaux. That and ten percent of the score good enough for you?"

Nobody answered him for a minute and he began to sweat, fought hard to keep from soiling himself. They were planning on killing him now for sure, and nothing he said would change their minds. Just as he was about to try again, try begging this time and to hell with worrying about them owning him, Gunon spoke.

"You're gonna set up Vale for us? Put him right inside for us to grab, out on a major score?"

"You got my word, sir, I promise. He'll work the rest of his life to keep you happy, too, believe me, I heard him talk over and over about his fear of prison life." Lockhart knew he was babbling but couldn't stop himself. "Him and Lebeaux, they got the terror of prison inside them, yes, sir, not like me. I ain't worried about jailing, I know how to—"

"Shut the fuck up," Roosevelt said. They drove in silence and as soon as Lockhart saw the lake, blue and massive, through the windshield in front of them, he began to shiver, and then, involuntarily, he whimpered.

"Frank Vale, inside, on a major score, and forty percent, bubba," Gunon said, "and you got a deal."

Relief flooded him so strongly that he couldn't find his voice. Forty percent was high, but he was not in a position to bargain. They could take it all and he would have to live with it. He nodded his head so Gunon wouldn't take his silence for refusal, and he tried to relax.

"Only one thing," Gunon said, and now Lockhart had enough back to ask, "What?"

"You try and fuck us, head south or tell Vale about the deal, and I swear to Christ we'll not only hunt you down and kill you, but it'll take you about a week to die, you got me?"

"Yes, sir, Officer Gunon, I hear what you're saying."

In the front seat, Roosevelt grunted again, making fun of him.

Jimmy Vale was released from prison at 11:11 P.M. on Wednesday, October 17. It was a time he would remember for the rest of his life.

The brown, plain, official state car drove him through the side gates, two guards in front and one in back with him, and he turned in the seat, watched the gates slowly swing closed behind him, and

as soon as the car ran through the gauntlet of the TV idiots
surrounding the joint, he rolled his window down and took a deep,
deep breath of free air into his lungs, trying not to sob as he
exhaled. His hands were stuck deep in his suit jacket pockets, so
the hacks couldn't tell that they were trembling. There was a roll
of bills in his right front pocket, a total of $730, his outstanding
commissary cash and the $250 a prisoner gets upon his release.

He wished that he could have left something for Bill, his TV or
radio or some other personal items, but everything you bought
through commissary got stamped with your number and it was
turned back in when you got out, to be rebuilt and stamped with
the number of the next sorry con to put up the top bucks for the
stuff. Kane, and guys like him, were getting fat from the escapist
dreams of the prisoners.

"We can take you to the Loop, Vale," the driver told him.
"Warden give us the okay. No further than downtown Chicago,
though." The hack driving was all right—he wasn't on the payroll, but Jimmy had seen him around. He was on midnights this
week and missed the riot, like the other two in the car with him.
"That was a good thing you done for Stanley," the other hack in
the front seat said.

Jimmy said nothing. Now, after his release, they were beneath
him. It was fun to think that. He had more money in his pocket
than these assholes got every two weeks in their paychecks. Stuck
in their dead-end hack jobs, carrying nightsticks and thinking they
were bad because they could fuck over convicts. He reached into
the breast pocket of his starched white shirt and grabbed his pack
of smokes, began to shake one out, when the hack next to him had
to go hard, told him not to smoke in the vehicle.

It was all Jimmy could do to keep himself from saying something. The words Fuck you were in the front of his mind, and his
mouth began to form them, but he bit them back. They were
giving him a ride, that's all. Cabbies who didn't allow smoking in
their car. If he looked at them that way, he could make it.
Otherwise, it was a long walk to Chicago.

Which turned out to be a short ride. In no time he was on the
wide street that was Michigan Avenue, the hack stopping the car

on Michigan and Randolph, in front of the Metra Station steps, right next to what was left of the old Main Library. He got out without saying a word, not even acknowledging the driver who'd wished him luck.

It was cold out here, after midnight. There were about two dozen people lying on the steps of the now-vacant library building, most of them young and black, huddling, shivering in their cheap filthy overcoats, and Jimmy had the urge to walk up to the door and kick it in, let them get in there and at least sleep on carpeting for a change, instead of cold, hard concrete. Hell, the place was empty. But it was his first night out and not a time to create trouble unless there was no other choice. He turned his back on the men, ignoring their callings for his spare change, and walked down Michigan Avenue, heading north.

God Almighty, things had changed. Some things hadn't, though, and it gave him a strange feeling to be seeing things that looked the same way they'd looked ten years ago. The Prudential Building for one thing. When he had been a kid it had been one of the world's tallest buildings. Now it wasn't even one of the city of Chicago's tallest anymore. The sidewalks were still wide, and there were still plywood tunnels everywhere to protect the pedestrians from falling debris that might drop from the constant construction, but outside of that, most everything else was different. Everything seemed bigger than he remembered, the buildings taller, the streets wider. The sensory opulence assaulted him, after all those years of hearing mostly men's voices screaming and electronic noises. Cars and buses and horns and the shouts of the young black kids there across the street. It filled his heart and for a second he thought about not calling Frank tonight, just getting a room somewhere, a bottle of something that hadn't been distilled that day in the back room of a prison kitchen; a glass and some honest to Christ shaved ice and he'd be in heaven, could wait until tomorrow for the other things, the sex, the call to Frank.

He thought about it but knew he wouldn't do it. By now Frank would be insane, worrying that he'd been killed in the prison riot. He had to set things straight, let him know he was all right, and as soon as Frank heard his voice Jimmy knew the night would be over with. Frank would insist on picking him up, would be insulted if Jimmy dared try to get out of it. Frank was different, had always been different, and Jimmy, well, he'd just turned different these past nine years.

Jimmy walked with his hands in his pockets, a big man in a cheap suit, his head up, though, with the faint trace of a smile on his lips. Past Water Tower Place, which had been there when he'd gone away, then a little farther on past Bloomingdale's, which hadn't. At the next corner he turned left, kept walking, and where Wabash met Rush he turned south, on Rush, smiling full-out now at the tons of black and red metal muscle cars touring the street, at the miles of glowing and blinking neon. He'd been too young to drink here before he'd been arrested, although he'd heard about the street. His excitement was growing in him, threatening to overpower him, and he stopped at the corner to catch his breath, to take it all in, what was happening around him, what these other people surrounding him, filling the streets late on a Wednesday night, seemed to take for granted.

Life. The good life. As he'd never known it. He wanted to embrace it, pull it to him, hold it tight in a lover's embrace. Wanted to race into the nearest saloon and grab the first girl he came to and pull her onto the dance floor and see if he could still move. He wanted to do these things, but he couldn't.

There was too much jail in his blood to let anyone know what he was feeling inside.

Still, he wasn't in jail anymore. He was out, free, with money in his pocket and no parole officer to answer to. There was no time like the present to begin tearing down the walls he'd built inside his heart to protect himself emotionally while staring off at the walls society had built to protect him from itself.

He began walking again. Slowly, casually, trying not to attract attention to himself, Jimmy entered the first bar he came to, and the furthest thing from his mind was that evening's death in Chaney's cell, Michael Knox's death, or what Michael's death might wind up costing him.

Chapter

THIRTEEN

H e should have told her the truth up front. Frank knew this
in his heart, but if he had, she wouldn't have allowed the
relationship to go anywhere to begin with. She would
have cut him loose the second she found out. Or would she?

He had to admit, sitting in his basement, staring at the telephone, willing it to ring, that she wasn't like any of the other
women he'd been involved with. For most of his adult life Frank
had stuck with the type that men like him attract; shallow women
looking for cheap thrills. Not necessarily airheads, however. It
amazed him, the number of women who were successful in their
careers, well educated and intelligent, who were attracted to men
of violence. Any mob or wise-guy or thief hangout, on any weekend night, was packed with them, female traders and brokers and
lawyers on the make, trying to get their illegal excitement vicari-
ously. He would take them as they came, being picky after his
own fashion, but never too picky, seeing as he'd never been in the
market for anything long-term.

The problem was, usually he'd give them the line about being a
retired or pensioned construction worker, with investments, and
they'd roll their eyes, check out the Caddy he'd driven up in or the
fine suit on his back, his gold watch, then roll their eyes and say,
"Sure you are." They'd get the hint and never pry. And when he

was done with them they didn't come around and beat on his door, write him love letters threatening suicide. And they damn sure never decided to quit their jobs and leave town, for Christ's sake. They just moved on to somebody else.

Except for Tina. She'd believed him, maybe because she'd wanted to so desperately.

Another problem for Frank was: Over a period of time, growing more accustomed to her and feeling the first time ever the stirrings of love, he began to believe his own lies. Saw himself as retired, because there was nothing out there that interested him at the moment. It didn't matter to him what it was that he was retired from. If he misrepresented himself to Tina, well, wasn't that natural? A man rapidly approaching middle age, at last finding a woman he believed he could love, going out of his way to put himself in the best possible light? Did it matter what he was retired from? He *wasn't* working, he *did* have investments, and once, years ago, he'd tried to go straight, taking a job in the construction trade. It was a little white lie that had been blown all out of proportion.

But the dream score had come up; one of his connections, an appraiser at an insurance company, had told him about this eccentric billionaire who lived on Astor Street, who had just had his premiums pushed through the roof because of his cheap security system. The man who, after the late Arthur Rubloff, had made more money off major real estate deals than anyone in the city, living in a lavish city home, paying extra money to insure his paintings, jewelry, and artwork because he believed, as the astonished insurance adjustor had told Frank, that "God would look after him."

It was too good to be true. The adjustor had raised the rates significantly, had given the magnate ninety days to install a first-rate security system, and had told Frank that he didn't think the guy would do it because he was dependent on a higher power of the universe to deliver him from evil.

Even though it looked like a walk-through, Frank had gone about the deal as if it were the Federal Depository, lining up the right men to work with, guys who could keep their mouths shut.

Adalebo could beat the ADT alarm system blindfolded, and the black hustler had a friend he'd served time with who could keep his mouth shut and who was willing to stand lookout for ten percent. The insurance man got another ten for turning Frank on to the score, and Adalebo, as the wire man, would get thirty. Which would leave Frank with his customary fifty percent. Some people would think that to be high, but Frank's name was strong; top-rated thieves across the country had offered him as much as forty percent of the take for simply flying into town on the day of a score and opening the box. He declined these offers, though, because he couldn't allow his fate ever to be in the hands of anyone but himself.

Working out the details had taken him away from Tina for a while, and she'd gotten upset, asking questions he avoided, then getting it in her head that he was having affairs with other women. In a way he was flattered, because here was this knockout beauty who wasn't like the rest—she could have her pick of the cream of Chicago's young rich bachelors, yet wanted him—feeling insecure because he was cutting her out for a while.

Then today she had painted him into a corner and he had tried to level with her. It was, he knew now, a case of too little too late. He'd gone on the defensive right away, as soon as he'd seen that she wasn't falling for it, telling her that there were other men involved and he didn't have the right to go into details, but she'd been ready, she was a sharp one, pinned him right to the wall and cut through the bullshit—his masks—and pointed out the fact that he was a thief and worse, a liar.

He'd been able to function, though, through all of the upset, because he was the Iceman. Even after the PRICCs had given him a beating; Wayne Lockhart had showed up for the score and proceeded to drink himself out of Frank's life; the score had to be put off and probably abandoned; and then, to top it all off, the prisoners had begun to riot at Stateville—even with all this and losing Tina, he could function.

But now, alone and all of a sudden let down, no longer keyed up with the thought of the score ahead of him, Frank had time to think, and he didn't like where his mind was taking him.

He tried to get his mind off it, tried to put it behind him. Tried to tell himself she was just another broad and she didn't matter, the thing hadn't worked out and it was time to move on, but the more he told himself these things the phonier he felt, the tighter he felt the mask pressing on his face, threatening to suffocate him.

"I loved her," he said to the images flickering on the television set, then tried it another way. "I love her." The second time felt better.

What he couldn't figure out was a way to tell her and to maybe get her to love him again in return.

He'd blown it with his lies. By wearing the fucking mask for too many years and not knowing when it was time to tear the thing off, cast it aside and for once be himself with a woman. He wondered if it was too late to call her, to vow to change his ways. He had enough money—that would never be a problem. He was a millionaire who could indeed live on his investments.

Could he do it, though? Confront her and tell her that she was right, he was a phony mask-wearing son of a bitch but was willing to change? What bothered him more than anything, though, was the thought that even if he did, even if he went to her and told her these things, could he honestly do it, give up his lifelong battle with society and try for the first time in his life to fit in? And even if he could, if he really and truly knew in his heart that it was over for him and he wanted to settle down, would Tina believe him, be willing to take a chance on him and love him for what he was?

A lot of questions there. And the question that was on top of all the others, as Frank got up and began to pace the basement, was: Is Jimmy okay?

He'd stop and check his watch every few minutes, holding it to the side so the glow from the Budweiser sign or the TV would illuminate the thing; then he'd continue pacing, cursing, thinking, saying aloud, "Jimmy, where are you?"

Where Jimmy was, was in a bar on Rush Street called December's Mother, sipping scotch whisky with his head reeling and his pulse pounding. Man, this was something. The place was filled with women, the joint advertising that on Wednesday evening from eleven till closing it was "Women's Night," and females could drink for half price. Jimmy looked at them, dressed to kill, out to impress the males, and tried to differentiate between the females, the women, the ladies, and the plain old girls.

He figured there had to be some new difference, or the bar wouldn't have gone so far out of its way to advertise the fact. There was so much he didn't know, so many things he had to learn.

Already he'd been in sexual discussions with two women, one of whom had turned the conversation immediately intimate, telling him almost without preamble that she didn't worry about the AIDS virus. Gays got the disease, and it was her opinion that it could only be contracted through anal sex, which she wasn't into, and intravenous drug abuse, which she wouldn't even consider. The government and everyone else wanted the public to be terrified to fuck. It was a conspiracy begun by the Republicans in the White House to change the morals of a nation, blown way out of proportion. The redhead spoke her piece and sat back in her chair, shooting him an open, frank stare, and he didn't know what to say. He stared at her sizable breasts, the woman in a silk shirt with no bra, not hiding a lot, wondering if he was supposed to ask her to leave with him now, or maybe turn intellectual, which he could do, quote one of the thousands of magazine articles he had read in the joint, maybe cite statistics for her. He didn't want to change her mind, nor did he want to alienate her, but she was staring at him, Jesus, waiting for him to say something. He wanted to get laid, wanted it bad, but not bad enough to risk death for. He was finally free and he was still young and knew from his prerelease blood tests and physical that he was healthy. But the rules had changed and he could tell right away, from her opening statements, that this woman was in a high-risk category, using her mind to bullshit herself into believing that she was immortal.

She said, "You've been smoking one cigarette after another since you came in here, right?" Leaning toward him again, giving any onlookers the impression that they were long-term lovers, this woman whose name he couldn't remember. She smiled and showed him a mouthful of lovely, clean teeth. "Do you worry about lung cancer, or do you just do what you enjoy doing?'' What was she saying, trying to tell him? He couldn't get it clear.

He kept his mouth shut. One of the many things he'd learned in prison was the value of silence in situations in which you were uncertain. Still, the woman didn't give up. She tore the cover off his book of matches, scribbled something on it, pushed it across the bar at him, then leaned toward him, smiling seductively.

He resented the look she was giving him, the smile. Like he was a rube she didn't have time for. It would be easier now to say something, but suddenly he'd lost interest in saying anything at all.

The woman said, ''Here's my name and number. You ever get over your phobias, give me a call.'' Her breath smelled of Tia Maria and garlic. Her eyes were a little glassy. He figured she'd been there a while, getting her drinks at half price. She giggled and put on her light leather jacket, tossed her head and strolled away from him, stopping to laugh and talk with a small cluster of other women, looking his way a lot and smiling, before walking confidently from the bar.

The bartender came over, wiping a glass with a bar rag. He was a young guy, in his twenties, appearing cocky and confident but Jimmy could smell his insecurity. He was willing to bet all the money in his pocket, though, that the guy scored like a champ in this place, whenever he got the urge.

''Set up another one?'' Jimmy nodded his head. The bartender set the glass he was cleaning in the bar-well, snatched Jimmy's glass and loaded it with ice, freehand poured from the bottle of Grant's and twisted the bottle up as the liquid hit the rim of the glass. He put the bottle back and knocked on the wood twice. ''Third one's on me, pal,'' he said, then leaned over the bar, whispered in Jimmy's face: ''Good move there, man, letting that one go. She gets two drinks in her and fucks everybody in the joint to prove how attractive she is, then cuts their balls off the next time they see her in here, acts like she doesn't know them. Just hang tight and be cool—it's almost closing. You're new here and unknown, big and good-looking and quiet and you got money. You'll get the cream of the crop before two, believe me.''

Jimmy wasn't used to men complimenting him and immediately began to wonder if the man was hitting on him. But no, he'd encouraged him to get laid, was probably only making what he thought to be man-to-man macho conversation. Helping the new guy, looking for a tip or drumming up future business. Still, Jimmy took nothing for granted or for free. He pushed a five at the bartender, said, "Thanks," and turned just as the second woman sat down next to him.

"I'm Vera," she told him, and Jimmy, getting used to it now and with the liquor calming his nerves, said, "Hi," much more softly than he'd wanted to.

She drank two drinks with him, insisting on paying for the second one, discussing things with him, asking him his astrological sign (which he didn't know), his age (which he did), and what he did for a living (here, he lied to her), before getting down to business. It soon became clear that Vera was much more careful than the last one, being into what she called "dual self-erotica." From what Jimmy could figure from the conversation, that meant that you stripped, looked at each other, and jerked off at the same time. There was a jukebox playing something fast, and a bunch of people were on the dance floor, looking as if they were doing with their clothes on what they would do later with them off. Jimmy was unaware of the Dirty Dancing craze. He watched the dancers, sipped his drink, listening to Vera extol the joys of mutual masturbation, of the imagination, of the karmic currency locked in the heavenly bank every time you denied yourself physical contact with a member of the opposite sex when you were dying to have him inside of you.

He guessed the conversation was supposed to turn him on, but that wasn't working. He felt oddly depressed by it all, in a dark, loud, strange place, having women hitting on him and getting right down to things without any hunt involved. He couldn't take his eyes off the dance floor, off of a beautiful young woman whose right leg was stuck between the legs of a short skinny guy with a '50s haircut. They were moving back and forth in that position, his chest stuck to hers. But her eyes were scanning the crowd, and when they met Jimmy's, she smiled at him. The little guy turned to look at what she was smiling at and as he turned, his face twisted with pain. Jimmy wondered if it had been an accident, or if the woman had purposely kneed him.

He killed the drink she'd paid for and turned to Vera. "You want to know something? When I told you I was a lawyer, I lied to you."

"No shit."

"You knew?"

"You don't look like any lawyer I ever met." Her eyes scanned him, up and down. "You don't dress the part."

"And it didn't matter to you? You still wanted to take me home and play with yourself, looking at me? How the hell you know I ain't the Boston Strangler?"

"Who?" Vera was picking up her purse, acting afraid now, getting up off the barstool. "What are you, some kind of freak?" As she walked away, toward the bathrooms, he almost told her that yeah, he was a freak, or at least felt like one in here, but instead he turned to the bartender, who'd been watching the scene and now moved in, pouring another Grant's.

"Wrong move, bud," the bartender said. "Vera's worth it. You get yourself off, yeah, but she poses, you know? Contorts herself, looking at you, like a *Hustler* centerfold, and she got a drawer full of stuff, dildos—"

"Who's the blonde dancing with the skinny guy?" Jimmy cut him off and the bartender didn't seem offended. Five dollars seemed to go a long way with him. He looked over to the dance floor, where the song was just ending and the girl was now pushing the skinny guy back, as if to say that all the physical stuff ended when the music did.

"Oh, that's Joyce." He said it dismissively, eliminating her from contention. "She's a prick teaser. Don't know the geek with her, but he's been buying her drinks since she came in. Watch yourself with that one, buddy. I don't know anyone got lucky with her."

Jimmy picked up his fresh drink and slipped another five toward the bartender, moved away, toward the small tables next to the dance floor. He sat down and as Joyce and her escort passed he

126

said, "Hi, Joyce." And got it right this time, his voice confident and strong.

She sat next to him and he saw the skinny guy's face fall, go through all kinds of changes. He looked disappointed at first, then hurt, then angry; then he stormed off to the bar, alone. Joyce paid him no mind, sitting with her chin propped on the palm of her hand, her elbow on the table, smiling at Jimmy.

"How'd you know my name?"

Jimmy shrugged. "I asked the bartender." Then said, "What about your friend?"

Now Joyce shrugged. Her eyes were green and wet, deep, sexy eyes. "He's no friend. I just met him tonight."

"You don't make friends fast?"

"Sometimes it takes years and years."

"Me, too," Jimmy said.

There was something about her, something in the way she looked at him and the way she acted that let him know she didn't care if he was quiet. Didn't care if he wasn't witty either. God, he hated trying to force conversation. But when he felt that the person to whom he was speaking was interested in him, he could kick back a little bit and talk without examining his words or being careful.

"I haven't seen you here before," she said.

"I've been away."

"Where?" She asked him the question casually, her tone soft and curious, not being nosy. He decided to tell her.

"I just got out of prison tonight. Served nine years."

"Really!?" Joyce said, her eyes lighting up. She didn't seem offended or afraid, just very concerned, curious. "You're kidding me, right?"

"No, really." Jimmy looked up as the skinny guy approached, carrying two drinks. He pulled a chair up from the table behind them, sat down and made himself at home, placing the drinks down.

"I got our drinks." He was acting as if he hadn't been upset, as if the two of them had planned on joining Jimmy all along. Joyce looked at him for a minute, and Jimmy hoped she'd say something. His instinct was to tell the man quietly to fuck off, but he was afraid of what Joyce might think.

"Marty?" Joyce said. "This guy just got out of prison today—isn't that wonderful?"

Marty looked at him, disbelieving. "What prison?"

"Stateville."

"Joyce, come on, let's go back to the bar. Shit, there was a riot at Stateville tonight. They aren't about to parole anybody until the smoke clears, for God's sake."

Jimmy opened his mouth to speak, then shut it right away. He was about to defend himself, then thought about how it would look, trying to convince some asshole in a bar that he was so an ex-con. Instead he looked at the man, and the guy—the bartender had been right: he was a geek all right—took Jimmy's silence for distress, the liar caught in the act.

"Your name Jack Henry Abbott, partner?" Marty was sneering at him now. "Norman Mailer get you out?"

Jimmy looked at Joyce, who was simply looking back with a curious smile, waiting to see how he handled it. He didn't feel as if he'd lost her yet. Maybe she was even smart enough to respect his silence, saw him as a man strong enough to listen to drivel from Marty because Marty wasn't important to him.

"You gonna stab me if I tell you that you can't use the toilet?" Marty was getting into this, enjoying himself. "Well, let me tell you, I ain't no busboy." He snorted a laugh, picked up his drink and sipped it, looking at Joyce as he put it down, to see how she was enjoying the show.

"You're not a busboy?" Jimmy said, his voice soft, almost without tone. "What do you do, Marty?"

The man said, proudly, "I work at the CBOT. The Chicago Board of Trade. I've got a seat there."

"You want to make it in tomorrow?"

"Is that a threat?"

"Marty, I want to tell you something and I'm only gonna say it one time. You get your ass the fuck away from this table, or I'm gonna grab that greasy hair of yours and yank it out by the roots, maybe make you eat it strand by strand.''

Marty stared at him for only a short time, at last seeming to figure out that the game was over, the man wasn't playing. He stood, left his drink and said in a small voice, ''You coming, Joyce?'' And Jimmy looked at Joyce, not about to say anything to her, letting her make her own decision, which didn't take long.

She stood up, her face white, and took Marty's hand in her own, which was trembling. Jimmy lowered his eyes to the table until they were gone, then got up and went back to the bar.

''Can I use your phone?'' he asked the bartender, and the guy pulled the phone from the wall, handed it over the bar.

As Jimmy began to dial Frank's number, the bartender said, ''I told you she was a ballbuster, pal. You should have stuck with Vera. By now she'd be bending back over the couch like a goddamn love slave.'' He chuckled, and Jimmy looked at him and was about to say something when Frank answered the phone.

It was 2:05 and December's Mother was closed for the night. Rush Street, though, was still alive. People passed him, nobody else alone, always couples or three or four young men or women together, having a good time, or seeming to. Jimmy stuck a cigarette in the corner of his mouth, lit it, then shoved his hands into his pockets, leaned his shoulder against the corner of the tavern's alcove, out of the wind, alone, hoping that Frank would get there soon. He was tired of not fitting in. For the first time since the incident happened, though, he figured that Jack Henry Abbott was more than just some jailhouse madman who couldn't make it in society. Now, with sudden clarity, he understood the man and what he'd done.

Chapter

FOURTEEN

The phone was ringing, and Tonce DiLeonardi hadn't had enough sleep, so he tried to ignore it but whoever it was wouldn't give up. He finally grabbed it, mumbled into it, and it was the man he'd told to call at six, to make sure he'd get up in time for the long drive to Wisconsin.

He pushed his legs over the side of the bed, willing himself to awaken. He could not remember the last time he'd gotten out of bed before the sun came up. His dentures were soaking in a glass on the nightstand next to the bed and he picked the glass up, moaning, and made his way to the bathroom.

He slept in the back seat of the car most of the way to Wisconsin, on an unauthorized visit to the man who'd sponsored him into the outfit. Tommy Campo had been the king of Chicago for two decades, and ran the city with an iron hand. He was maybe the smartest man Tonce had ever met in his life. He would know what to do about this situation.

When he opened his eyes they were driving through farmland, flat and filled now with tall cornstalks. The car pulled onto the prison grounds, into the parking lot, and Tonce told the driver to wait there for him.

What surprised him about the place was that it looked more like an army camp than a prison. There were no high walls, no barred windows. The place looked like a college campus with good security. The parking lot was clean, not even half filled. He could see prisoners walking around behind the joint, mostly in pairs. He walked into the administration building and the guard at the table called him sir and was very polite, unlike the hack at the last federal pen he'd visited, down in Atlanta, Georgia, where the country hack's ignorance was pure. He was shown to a sliding glass door that had little thin bars imbedded in the panes, was asked to take a seat in the visiting room while the resident was sought out.

Tommy Campo entered the room wearing khaki pants and a cotton shirt, with a cardigan sweater on top. He had on a billed longshoreman's cap, and heavy boots on his feet. He looked around, spotted Tonce, and smiled quizzically. He looked at the tiny bars embedded in the glass door and chuckled. Tonce stood up as the man approached and they shook hands. Tommy sat down; then Tonce asked, "What's so funny?"

"I come into this room, it's the only time I see bars. I got a bungalow with two other guys I live in. Nothing like the outside, you understand, but it's private, we keep it clean. We got our own kitchen, so we don't have to stand in line. Every week, my man Julie comes down with fresh meat for us, and I cook up a pot of spaghetti gravy and meatballs." He sat back, took the large cigar Tonce offered him, and asked him if he had any more. "For the guys back in the house." He took the three Tonce had with him, then got down to business.

"I got pinched—what, six years ago now? I'm doing more time than my grandkids will live to see. I don't even think about it anymore; just get through today and worry about the seven life sentences when the first one's over. I get five hundred a week from the boys back home, because I keep my mouth shut. Julie comes up and drops it off, leaves the food, whatever else I want from them. Six years I been here and nearly everyone I ever helped, did anything for, forgot about me after six days. Guys like you. So why, suddenly, you come up to see me, Lion?"

Stunned at the anger in the man's voice, Tonce suddenly began to regret the trip. But the man had called him by the nickname he himself had given Tonce back some thirty years ago, so it was, it seemed, just a mild rebuke. He decided it would be best, with a guy like Tommy, not to apologize, try to bullshit him and tell him how much he missed him. Business was business, and when a guy got killed or sent to the joint, someone else took his place—it was as simple as that. The guy just wasn't there anymore.

He said, "I got a visit from some guys in New York." He told Campo their names and the ex-boss pursed his lips and nodded his head. He was impressed. "They tell me I got to do something, something that maybe I don't want to do, you know what I mean? So I decide to get some outsiders, some home invaders, to go in and do the hit on this guy I maybe don't know if it's okay to hit, to keep me in the clear and so the guy who's gonna get *bombalied* don't get word of it. The thing is, I, under your order, hit the home invader's old man. Remember?"

"Vale?"

"Yeah. But his kid, Frank, is the best there is at getting into a place he ain't supposed to be. But he won't talk to any of us, not since the old man got hit and he had the sitdown with you, so I got to go through his brother."

"I gave him the okay to keep operating, free-lance, without paying us, in return for his word that he would forget about his old man's sudden death."

"Didn't break his heart, either, I remember correctly. They didn't get along. So now I got this kid, Vale, Jr., got the okay from you to operate, and the new guys, they come in and honor all your old contracts, no problem. But if I send the guy out, Tommy, he's got to die. You can't hit a guy the stature of the guy we're talking about and live. That's another reason I'm gonna use outsiders. I like my people, and ain't got enough of them as it is."

"Tombstone Paterro put most of the good ones away, put a real dent in the ranks, that cocksucker. May his wife and kids get cancer." Campo spat dryly at the floor.

"The thing I need to know, Tommy, is, you gave the guy the okay to live. I send him out on a mob hit, he or his brother do it, I ain't sure yet which, then they both got to get whacked. Is that violating your orders? Will the bosses get pissed off and take me out for going behind their backs, hitting their boss, then rubbing salt in the wound by violating your contract?''

"What'd these guys from New York tell you?''

"They said I'd get the guy's spot.''

Campo sighed, took a deep puff on the cigar. "I see the problem. We always been the bastard sons for the outfit. They like us because we're brutal and are willing to do favors, but they've always been a little afraid of us, even back in the old days. Now, they're wondering if they can trust us.''

He leaned forward, his small dark eyes on Tonce. "Let me tell you something. I got guys in here, talk to me all the time. They know who I am and what I used to be, what I am today. They know I could be on an air force base in Florida if I was a lame rat fuck like Paterro, wanted to save my ass, playing golf and tennis. Paterro, he fucked up Chicago, but *I* could have brought down half the goddamn *commission,* and the guys in power know it. So I got respect—I'm like the head of the prison outfit in here.

"What I'm saying is, I got a good idea what you're talking about. These guys, under Tile, right?'' He waited until Tonce nodded, confirming the hit, then continued. "You're worried they might want to pick a few nits, not get back at you for hitting the boss, but for trying to take his place over them. And you're worried that they'll use my contract with the Vale guy as their excuse to get away with it, to save a war from starting with the New York bosses.

"Now, Lion, you mentioned two names to me. Both of those guys, and this goes no fucking further than this room, are commission. They got a seat. If they say you got the power after the hit, then you got it. And the first guy, his right arm is doing time right here with me. Good friend of mine, as a matter of fact. I'll talk to him, tell him the problem, and he'll talk to his friend, tell him what I want. You'll be off the hook. If anyone tries anything with you, he's dead. That'll come from New York, as soon as they get word that Tile's dead.''

"And the boys, the Vale kids?''

"Fuck 'em. Kill 'em both. If they're anything like their old man, they're drunken fucks anyway. But before you go, tell me something: What the fuck did Mike Tile do to get in this kind of jackpot?''

Later, driving back in the car, looking out at the farmland, Tonce felt depression. Tommy Campo, who'd once been big and strong and powerful and full of life, was now a broken old man, mostly bald, with bad teeth and a shambling walk. Tonce shivered. He felt depression, not out of pity for Tommy, but because, if he wasn't careful, he might wind up this way himself. It could happen to anyone.

It was almost pathetic, too, the way the old man had listened, gleefully, to the gossip about Tile's philandering, his cocaine use. He'd cackle when Tonce would tell him a juicy story about Mad Mike Tile, one of the things that had led up to his having to go. He'd said, too, that he could figure out why the commission had ordered the hit. After what had happened after Paterro rolled over, they were taking no chances, coming down hard before a real problem developed. Campo said this was a good thing, as it would instill discipline in the troops, who'd been getting away with murder since he'd gotten himself busted.

Tonce had to listen to another hour and a half's worth of bullshit before the guard came and told them that their two hours were up, which made his day; he couldn't wait to get out of there. The old man had stood, stared him in the eye and told him, as he shook his hand, to be careful.

"Hey," Campo had said to him as he was walking back to the door that would lead him out of the visitors' area, "when you get those things straightened out, come back and tell me what happened, all right?"

Tonce had told him that he would, but he didn't plan on seeing Tommy Campo ever again. Maybe at his funeral, when he was finally free, having served only one seventh of his sentence, maybe he'd go to the service.

He was glad, too, that the man hadn't asked him how he'd gotten Vale to work for him. Vale wouldn't talk to them, and that was okay due to his contract with Campo, so he had to go through

Vale's brother, convince him to do the score and get his brother to bust the locks. He knew just the way, too. The thing was complicated, and, to someone who wasn't involved in it, might appear even a little amateurish. Going through the White Aryan Brotherhood to get a brother of a guy they wanted to work for them to convince him that he had to. Then again, the old guy, with his Sicilian love of intrigue, might have enjoyed the story. Though he probably wouldn't have understood who the White Aryan Brotherhood was. Tonce hadn't seen a lot of black people in the federal pen at Oxford, Wisconsin. Maybe the federal government sent them all to Atlanta, Georgia, these days.

At the same time that the Lion was driving back to Chicago, Mad Mike Tile was crawling out of the round motionless waterbed he slept in, retching from the wine he'd drunk the night before, the cocaine he'd snorted.

A young woman's voice said, "You all right, Daddy?"

Daddy? Who the fuck was this? He looked at her, at her perfect young tanned body lying there in stark contrast to the black silk sheets, feeling too sick to be polite.

"How old are you?" It was a groan, Mike pulling up silk pajama bottoms, tightening the string.

"I told you last night, Daddy."

Just what he needed. Some cunt thinking he was a mark, a john, getting wise with him when he asked a question. "Fuck with me, bitch, you'll spend your next birthday in fucking Saudi Arabia, maybe Iran."

"I'm seventeen." She was pouting at him.

Through red eyes Mike stared at her, wondering if he should get into the bathroom, clean up before he tore into her. If she was seventeen, he was forty again. He looked at her, hard, seeing the round soft breasts, not yet sagged but they would be before she was twenty, lined probably, too, the belly the same way because she'd have a couple kids before that time. Fifteen? Maybe sixteen, outside. He wondered if she'd been any good.

He kept his mouth shut, went into the bathroom and relieved

himself, stepped into the shower. Decided that if she came in there with him, he'd whack her head against the gold faucets, show her to do only what she was told.

He washed his body down, drinking in a lot of the water as it poured over him in jets that were set in eight separate spots in the shower. Big enough for four people, he'd learned.

Body going on him, that was for sure. Soft, flabby, with small breasts now that drooped; you could see it when he was naked and standing up. Dressed, he still didn't look too bad. How long did he want to live, anyway? He decided it didn't matter; he didn't need muscle. He bought muscle: All the strength he needed was on the payroll, a lot of it lolling around his fucking house, eating his food, drinking his booze and screwing his bitches. The rest of them a phone call away.

He shut down the shower jets, dried himself off and stepped out into the bathroom, feeling a little better. He brushed his teeth. When he got back into the football stadium they'd named the master bedroom he'd get a cold Pepsi from the little fridge behind the bar, cool off his pipes.

Tile got the shaving kit out from under the vanity, sat there staring at his own reflection in the steam-proof mirror.

"*Infamata*," he said, whispering, his hands searching through the bag. Ah, there it was.

He took the small capsule out of the bag, fitted it firmly into the base of a pipe, held a lighter to it while he sucked, hard, felt that great familiar whoosh drive right up from his lungs into his brain, filling his head with joy. . . .

Nodded for a few seconds, loving this high, this newfound pleasure he'd discovered that was keeping him young. Made him a tiger between the sheets, enough of a man to keep up with fifteen- and sixteen-year-old girls who weren't experienced enough sexually to have caught the AIDS. He opened his eyes, saw himself there in the mirror and smiled. "The king of all he surveys," he said, truly believing it.

He hid his stash and got up, went into the bedroom and got his Pepsi, drank from the can, his eyes never leaving the girl, who was posing for him and acting like she wasn't. Rolling over onto her belly and lifting her butt into the air a little bit, getting comfortable. He must have been a tiger last night; this bitch remembered the way he liked to do it: from the back, hard and wild.

He killed the can, belched loudly, feeling great.

As he crawled up onto the bed he asked her, in a grandfatherly voice, what her name was.

Chapter

FIFTEEN

Jimmy Vale wasn't the only person whose experiences had taught him things. Adam Lebeaux had learned, too, at his parents' knee. Or over it, most of the time. His daddy had been a hard-drinking juju man who would put a curse on your ass in a minute if you crossed him. He could remove curses, too, if someone paid him enough. He was a con man and a hustler, a juker and a jiver who could talk his way out of almost anything and into a lot of things when he had the opportunity, the inclination, and if the money was right.

Adam would watch him, fighting with his momma when she'd jump his ass about the other women in his life; she'd get right there in front of him and scream, "Fucks you!" and he wouldn't give up an inch, he'd stand his ground and scream, "Well fucks you right back!" They could go at it for hours, shouting and fighting, Momma giving almost as good as she got. A neighbor would call the police and the heat would come down, usually two young white motherfuckers who would stand there taking cop attitudes, not saying anything but looking at them in a way to let you know they were making fun of the battling niggers, and Adam would learn about loyalty, because then Momma would turn on them and tell them that they could "just kiss bofe of our asses!"

before throwing them out. Daddy the juju man and Momma the battler, never taking any shit from Whitey.

His daddy would take him on his rounds, young Adam's face marked with paint that was supposed to frighten some superstitious fool his daddy was working on, Adam supposed to be Baron Samedi or somebody else, some other member of the voodoo culture. But the old man always pulled it off and Adam could never remember ever being hungry.

He was staring up at the ceiling now, the morning almost shot, his woman next to him, wondering just how far wrong things had gone last night. At forty, he figured he never would be hungry again, either. Dead maybe, but never hungry. Even if they locked him up again, he'd never had a problem hustling, getting some other fool to hand over his possessions, his money or cigarettes or chocolate. He'd always get by.

As long as he stayed away from the drunkards and the mainline junkies, he'd make out.

Which brought him to Wayne Lockhart, who, suddenly, had undergone a drastic change of heart.

He had come straight home last night, depressed but determined to follow Frank's instructions. If the man said a score was off, then that was it. Frank was the best. He knew what he was talking about. Man probably wouldn't last ten minutes in the yard, with his ways, bossing everybody around and shit, but he was such a stickler for detail it would probably never come to that. Man hadn't done any time yet. There was no reason to think he would in the future.

In fact, Frank was so damn sure he wouldn't put himself in a jackpot, so intent on keeping his freedom, that he might even drop good old Adalebo from the steady work crew, on account of Ads had brought in a guy and vouched for him, and the guy had turned out to be a drunk.

"Shit," Adam said.

"Say something, baby?" There she was, the world's lightest sleeper, his old lady Dee-Dee. He couldn't come or go without her knowing the exact time of his movement. Woman could read his emotions, too, even better than his daddy had. Always knowing when something was wrong with him, no matter how he tried to cover it up. She'd come to him last night, right when he'd dragged on home, Dee-Dee smiling, dancing toward him, her mind set on taking away his blues. . . .

And damn, did she ever. Stripped right in front of him, pulled him by the fingers into the bathroom where she'd hand-bathed him, prepared him for the feast she was planning on having with his johnson bar for the main course. He looked at her fine shapely white ass, the curve of it accentuated by the red satin sheet draped across the left ass cheek, and said, "No, baby, go on back to sleep. It ain't even noon yet."

She reached for him, smiling sleepily, a long hank of straight thick red hair falling down around her right titty, bouncing back. Woman's hair was alive! "Come on, Ads, let's play!" She crooned it, Dee-Dee who was always ready and never tired. He started to cave in—it would be better than laying there staring at the ceiling, worrying about whether he'd lost the best career thing ever happened to him—when the phone rang and that dumb hillbilly son of a bitch Lockhart told him they had to meet.

He'd learned in Harlem about drunks, what they were capable of. He'd been drinking as a young man, back maybe twenty years gone, in a bar that catered to the hustlers, when a drunk who had the reputation for always fighting with his old woman had staggered in, carrying a hatbox. He'd set the box down on the stool next to him and the bartender had kidded him, given him some shit about how'd he get out of the crib, away from the old lady, who'd had the taste as bad as her husband, always matching him drink for drink, which pissed the man off; it always cost twice as much as it would have to tie one on. The old man had spread his money across the bar, ignoring the bartender, then had looked down, fiddled with the box and ordered himself a shot of Red Dog straight, then pulled his wife's head out of the box by the hair, plopped it wetly on the bar, and said, "Better give this bitch one, too, before she starts her bullshit."

Three times, altogether, he'd seen men who'd been drinking

together moments before with their partners lose their lives over dumbass arguments with those same partners. Six or seven times he'd seen men killed by strangers over arguments over ball games or the outcome of pool games; a few times he'd seen suckers get cut or shot over Tonk card games. No, the juice had never had a strong attraction for him; he'd seen enough craziness from sober people.

Which was why he was reluctant to go meet with Lockhart. The man was crazy enough without demon rum fucking with his head. Still, there were things to learn. Maybe even some money to be made. And besides, he had a score to settle with the man.

Adam got to the restaurant early, one that he'd picked, a trendy joint in the heart of the Loop, owned by a guy Frank knew. If there was a problem, he'd have backup in a second, and even if there wasn't, Frank could never accuse him of meeting Lockhart behind his back. Adam believed in covering his ass. The place was jumping now with the lunch trade. He was well known here, and smiled at the little dapper man in the tuxedo with the Clark Gable mustache who was handing out menus and leading folks to their tables, and he pointed at the bar, letting the man know that none of his regulars had to be dispossessed for him; he was only going to be here a short time.

Adam smoked Kool filter kings, and opened them the old-fashioned way that he'd learned in the ghetto: from the bottom. He made his way to a tiny table for two in the middle of the dark room, sat down and lit a smoke, thinking. About Lockhart and what kind of shit he was going to lay on him, when he heard exaggerated coughing coming from the man at the next table.

He turned, spotted a very tall, slender white man with the blondest hair he'd ever seen, a broad-shouldered sucker dressed in a checked shirt under a black velvet sport coat. The man had his hand over his mouth, making a big thing out of how Adam's smoke was bothering him. His companion was his clone in basic bitch. A tall long-haired blond-headed woman who seemed to be enjoying what her boyfriend was doing. The man rattled something off in a foreign singsong kind of language and the woman nodded, watching him as he spoke, then turned to Adam.

"My friend, he does not speak English. He is from Sweden and this is his first trip to America. He wonders if you would not smoke, all right?" The guy, he was sitting there all arrogant, giving Adam a superior look. Viking asshole.

Adam said, "Hey! You sound just like Inger Stevens! Used to play on *The Farmer's Daughter* on the television. Fine-looking woman, Inger was. For a white ho." The woman looked startled, then turned back to the man, spoke for a minute, then listened. Adam sat back, took a deep drag off the Kool, let it out through his nose. This was starting to be fun.

"He says that smoking is dangerous to your lungs, that it causes cancer."

Adam snorted. "Inger, I been to Vietnam, to the Tombs jailhouse, and I did hard time in Attica. You think I worried about cancer? Shit." He lit another cigarette from the butt of the one he'd been smoking, looking at the man, wondering if the woman was getting wet over this. She looked like the cold-hearted type of ho who would want to see them fight, maybe give up the pussy to the winner. Adam saw movement, big movement, at the bar entrance, and turned his head enough to see Lockhart swaggering toward him. It was time to quit playing games.

"He says he does not understand what is this Tombs or Atti—" She started to speak but Adam reached over, grabbed her hand and squeezed, silencing her. Across from her, the guy began to suddenly not look so sure of himself.

Adam said, "You tell that yah-hey motherfucker that if he say one more goddamn word, I'm gonna knock him down and fuck him, make him the mother of my ass-baby. I bet he understand that." He let go and looked at the man long enough to make sure that his intentions weren't violent, then turned and scowled at Lockhart, who was standing behind the second chair, sheepishly, holding two bottles of Heineken in one hand, the glasses in the other.

"This here bulge in my pants don't mean I'm glad to see you either, motherfucker, so put the goddamn beers down and say your piece. I ain't got all day to hang around here waiting on your ass."

Lockhart sat down and Adalebo stared at him, hard, angry, and

143

getting angrier at the hangdog look on this man's face. They were men here, not kids looking for forgiveness. But here was Lockhart, acting sensitive.

"You was way outta line yesterday, motherfucker."

"Don't, Lebeaux. You know I don't like that kind of talk."

Adam spoke softly but harshly. "Fuck what you like, man. You probably cost me the best job I ever had in my life, I'm supposed to worry about you not liking shit. Shit. Put a gun to my head, call me a nigger."

"You should have spoke up then, Adam."

"When? Before you pulled back the hammer? I trusted you, redneck dumb motherfucker, got you in where guys are standing in line to be, stick my neck out for you and you cut it off like I'm Thanksgiving dinner."

"I was drunk."

"What you think I'm saying to you. I didn't know you was drunk? Frank don't work with drunks. Won't work with me no more, probably, count of I trusted a drunk. He won't trust my judgment no more. You know what happens to solid rap partners, start questioning each other's in-teg-rity?"

"They commence killing on each other."

"Yeah. So now I got to maybe worry about both of you gunning for me. Like I ain't got enough problems."

"He tell you that he was cutting you loose?"

"He don't work like that, Lockhart. What he does is, he just don't call no more. I call him up, he tell me he retired, gonna lay low and spend his fortunes. I seen him do it to other dudes he lost faith in."

"Can I get that faith back, Ads?"

"You? Shit, *you* out of the equation. I'm just hoping he don't hold it against *me*. We been pretty tight, but you never know with the Iceman."

"You remember you guys saying what an easy score it was gonna be? A cakewalk?"

"I didn't hear nothing on the radio about you getting your ass shot or caught. So if you didn't go on home, pass out in your bed drunk, I guess you took it down."

"Yeah, and I ain't got to tell Frank or you I did either, do I? Big shot like that, he might be able to even keep it out of the papers. Even if it's on the front page, I could scoot, fade down to Florida, not give either one of you a dime."

"You think we wouldn't come looking?"

"The point is, I'm here, ain't I?"

"Why that is, Wayne?" Adam decided to see what the man had to say for himself. In Wayne's own dumb way, he was beginning to intrigue Adalebo.

Lockhart looked behind him, and Adam saw the Swedish woman turn her head away quickly, toward the man with her, not wanting to get caught staring at them. He turned back, leaned across the table and said, softly, "I took it down, yeah. You guys think I'm stupid. But I ain't. I did it, and I did it alone, and I'm here because I want to make it a three-way split, right down the middle. I ain't gonna take the ten percent you was gonna throw to me, because I did it all alone—I earned a full share. But I'm gonna split it three ways, no problem. You think that'll get Frank's faith back?"

Adam sat back, staring at Lockhart. The man's breath stank something terrible but Adam hadn't moved, because the words he'd been speaking had been riveting. Now he thought, wondered, put things together. They'd been willing to take a fourth apiece and let Wayne live. Frank had estimated the safe would have a quarter million in cash and maybe as much in jewels. Artwork, there was no telling, it depended on what the man catered to. He'd been in some places, the stickman shit on the walls wasn't worth stealing, and in others where folks had signed Picasso lithographs. Would a full third get this dummy back in Frank's good graces? Adam didn't know, but there was one thing he was sure of: It would damn sure get *him* back on the sweet short list of men Frank trusted. Still, there was something important that he had to know.

"How much you get?"

"Remember Frank saying he thought it might be a couple hundred grand?"

Adalebo looked at him skeptically, knowing what was coming. Wayne would hedge his bets, say that there had only been, say, fifty grand in the safe, maybe that again in jewels. Naturally the dumbass wouldn't have taken any artwork. He crossed his arms and grunted.

"How much was in there that Frank, the best thief in the city, was too dumb to figure out, Wayne."

And Wayne smiled. "Six hundred grand, cash, and a whole shitload of diamonds and emeralds and sapphires and rubies." He sat back himself now, crossed his arms. All in a day's work. "I already took the liberty of getting rid of the settings—didn't think ya'll'd mind."

Ads was grinning back. "Why you redneck devil, you." Wayne laughed, slapped the table with his huge palms, knocking out a little drumroll.

"Thought you'd be happy to hear it."

Ads said, "I got to make a call," and got up from the table, looked at his cigarette smoldering in his hand, then at the Swedish man, who was squirming in his chair, knowing he was being stared at and trying hard not to make eye contact. Dumb. Why hadn't they just left? He stepped away from his table and leaned down over theirs, the woman giving a little jump and a squeak as he smiled right there in her beautiful pale face.

"Hey, Inger, Sven, smoke bother you? Shit, why didn't you just *say* so?" Ads stubbed the Kool out in the ashtray in the middle of their table, slapped the woman on the back and winked at the man.

"Welcome to America," he said.

Chapter

SIXTEEN

For the first time in his life Jimmy Vale was worried about his mental health. Life had always, until now, been a state of survival, something to get through. In the early days he'd simply wanted to get through a day with as little contact with his parents as he could manage. Then, still in his teens, he'd gone to the joint. In there, he had achieved a cold mental toughness, but he'd known that it was all an act, the shell of a turtle that he had to wear to make it. Now, out of a clear blue sky, he had time on his hands and nothing to fear.

He always knew that if you toughed it out, somehow you'd get through.

Which is what he did now, although it was hard. He thought about it, lying in bed in a room in his brother's house that first free morning, hung over. He'd had a hard time sleeping; Frank had set him up in a large, airy room, one with a king-size bed. Jimmy was used to a three-by-six cot in a cell smaller than the adjoining bathroom to this place.

One of the problems was, there was no one to discuss it with, no one who would understand. He'd gone from son to student to high school dropout to prisoner so fast that he'd never learned how to act in the outside world, how to be a civilized human being. A civilian could never understand, but the reality of it was that

Jimmy would rather get through a prison riot, feel safer under those conditions, than sit in a bar with some yuppie idiot trying to steal a woman from him, giving him some shit about not having really been in prison. His hands had started to shake and he'd felt the wild urge to reach out, wrap those shaking fingers around the man's throat and squeeze, hard. In prison there would be no doubt in his mind that that would have been the proper thing to do, and he would have done it. But, too, in prison anyone who'd served ten days in the County would have known better than to jump into another man's face like that; would have known that one of them would have to get hurt. Out here, people seemed to believe that they were safe. Maybe making a lot of money gave them the false impression of security.

Or maybe it was the way it really was. Maybe you could go around being an idiot and not run the risk of getting hurt; maybe that was reality. Maybe, too, guys like him didn't belong on the street, were too—what was the word?—institutionalized.

But wasn't what that guy had done in the bar actually the same thing that happened in the joint, only on a much smaller scale? Hadn't he been seeking domination of Jimmy? Power over him, which he'd tried to gain by making him look bad in front of the girl, Joyce?

Sure it was. The difference being: The guy was an amateur. He'd known some of the rules but only a couple, not enough to know that he'd actually been taking his life in his hands.

So what did that make Jimmy, some kind of freak? A guy who knew all the sicko rules and lived by them, walking around in a society filled with people who sought to use those rules only when they fit their agenda. Like late at night, drunk, trying to impress a woman.

Maybe Jimmy should have just slapped the guy. Some women got off on that, men fighting over them. But the kind of woman who would like that wasn't the kind of woman Jimmy wanted. Maybe tonight, out of desperation, he'd just grab the first one that came along, stop being so picky, wanting to meet the Special Woman before he was hip enough to the culture to even know if there was such a thing. The last woman he'd laid had been a jailhouse punk named Antoine. Now here he was, looking for love.

He decided that if he'd had any sense, he would have gone with one of those two who'd tried to pick him up, should have bought some rubbers and said fuck it. Maybe if he had, he wouldn't be feeling so scared and insecure right now.

The night had gone well, although it was a little disappointing. Frank had tried, had put on the show for him, picking him up in a Cadillac and everything, pouring him drink after drink, with beer chasers, but something was in his ass and he wouldn't tell Jimmy what it was, said they'd talk tomorrow—tonight was for drinking.

They'd done some of that, all right. Maybe too much. As they talked, Frank telling him about his marriage and quick divorce, about the hit-and-run death of his dog, about the death of their grandmother—who'd caught a serious case of religion and cleaned up her act when the medics told her there was a tumor on her colon—Jimmy sensed a subtle shift in their relationship.

For as long as he could remember, Frank had been his only friend, the only man he could trust fully, holding back nothing. The big brother whom Jimmy could look up to. Frank always seemed so together, so tough, had all the answers. But now it was Jimmy who knew the score, who'd been around more. Who'd seen firsthand the true horrors of life. Who'd survived them. The relationship had done a slight turn, shifted, and it put him off balance. When at last he'd gone to sleep he'd passed out right away from the effects of the booze, but four hours later he was up, disoriented, frightened and unsure of himself, becoming more afraid when he at last understood where he was and when that knowledge didn't stop his hands from shaking. Lying in the big bed in the large room, Jimmy had known fear, had realized, too, that maybe you *didn't* get used to it.

He'd been terrified many times in his life, had felt primitive rage and the urge to kill often. For nine long years it had always been one extreme or the other, never anything in between. Until now, he'd had no experience with simple anxiety.

He got out of bed, showered, and felt something stir in his chest as he stood before the closet Frank had filled with clothes for him.

Shoes that had been handmade in Italy were on the carpeted closet floor; fancy suits and shirts hung from the clothes bar. In the dresser fresh new cotton shorts and T-shirts were folded neatly, socks that hadn't been boiled in bleach. He'd spent the night between clean sheets that smelled vaguely of flowers, in a room bigger than the dayroom in his cellblock. Through the night there'd been no sounds to awaken him, no sudden screams for help or for mother, nightmares in twisted, tortured minds manifesting themselves as the prisoner slept, to be laughed at by the other cons, the nightmares and screams later to be used against the guy who'd screamed them, because they were signs of weakness. There were no bars on the windows of this large room, no one outside of it who wanted to kill him or force him to have sex with them. He had nothing to fear.

He told himself the words over and over again, ran them through his mind until they lost all meaning and became only disjointed sounds, but he couldn't stop feeling afraid.

"You're up early."

Frank was pouring coffee into a mug, now got another down and filled it for Jimmy. He was smiling. Proud and happy: His baby brother was wearing the new clothes he'd bought for him, decked out real good, under the roof of Frank's house, home and safe. Jimmy smiled at him, keeping his feelings inside for another time. He didn't want to hurt Frank's feelings by telling him that he was terrified. He would appear to be an ingrate.

"This house, it's too quiet," Jimmy said.

"I know what you mean. For two weeks, after I got out of St. Charles last time, I couldn't sleep. I'd been used to hearing guys getting raped all night. I'd wake up in Ma's house, and everything would be quiet, and I'd think I was inside and no one was saying anything because they were all outside my door, waiting to sneak in and take turns on me."

Damn. Maybe Frank *did* understand. Jimmy said, "You got any cream and sugar?" Feeling decent, even a little safe, for the first time since he'd been released.

* * *

"I got something to show you." Frank spoke and as Jimmy's
guard was down, he just nodded. The pancakes had come from a
box, but they'd been delicious. Smothered with real butter and
maple syrup. The first hot breakfast he'd had in ten years, counting County time awaiting trial. Jimmy was full, smoking content-
edly and sipping coffee, when Frank said the words and he looked
up, saw the serious look on Frank's face.

He was feeling light, almost happy. So he said, "You start
unzipping your pants, I'm out of here," getting a laugh from his
brother. That was better. He wanted the situation light and non-
threatening. He figured he could maybe even get used to this.

"Come on downstairs."

They went to the corner, by the furnace, past the bar, which was
littered with last night's empty beer cans, the large ashtray on the
leather cover overflowing with butts. Jimmy decided that it had
been a good night, would be a good day. All he had to do was
regain his confidence. The only difference between the outside and
the joint was, out here there were more places to hide.

Frank showed him how to pop the hinge and drain the water
from the hiding place, and Jimmy began to get excited, feeling
like a little kid again, in wonder because it felt so good. Maybe
because he'd never had a chance to be a kid back when he really
was one.

They went down into the tunnel. Frank turned the light on,
turned around, and beamed at him. "How about this shit here?"
he said, and Jimmy grinned right back at him.

The box was gift-wrapped and square, small. Frank handed it to
him and he didn't know what to say, could only mumble his
thanks as he tore at the paper. He opened it, saw a large, round-
faced watch inside.

"That's a Rolex," Frank said. "My gift to you, now that you
can start counting time again." Jimmy looked from the watch to
Frank, his mouth working, not knowing what to say. Frank was
staring at him, nodding slightly, wanting his approval but not

pushing him. He felt a strange sensation, the tightness that had been in his chest when he'd looked at the closetful of clothing right there, but something else, too: a lump in his throat that was totally foreign, but which he recognized.

"I don't know . . ." He couldn't finish the words, just sat there on the indoor-outdoor carpeting wanting to reach out and pull his brother to him, squeeze him tight.

"Don't say anything." Frank was holding his hand up, looking solemn. "Just put it on your wrist, all right?" It appeared to Jimmy that Frank was hiding some feelings too.

"And there's something else, too, that's yours." Frank was handing him the steel strongbox, and a tiny key that fit in the lock.

Jimmy held out his wrist, said, "I got a new watch," then touched his chest, "new clothes," and kicked out his right foot, "new kicks on my feet. What the hell else can you do for me, Frank?"

"Open the box and see."

So he did, put the key in the lock and turned it, doing the ceremony for Frank's benefit. The little tin thing, all you had to do was twist the top and it would come off in your hands. He had the box on his lap, his legs folded beneath him, and he lifted the lid and stared down at tightly bundled stacks of hundred-dollar bills, filling the box from end to end.

"That's yours," Frank said. "Your end, fifty percent of everything I made the last nine years."

"Frank . . . Jesus Christ, Frank. How much is it?"

Now Frank shrugged, nonchalant. "Enough so I had to sit on the damn thing to get it locked. Maybe a million and a half, a little more . . ." He shrugged again. "You earned it, so you're gonna take it. You did nine years for that money when you could have given me up, got probation because you didn't have a record yet. You got to take it."

"Frank, you're my brother. Man, you don't owe me anything. I'd never give you up to the Man."

"I know. And loyalty gets rewarded. It's yours, Jimmy, and that's all there is to it. You take it and invest it, I know a guy, turn it into twenty million for you before you're my age. You did nine years for me, on account of I fucked up, and you kept your mouth shut. And I want you to know something else. There're guys, lined up around the block, wanting to work with me. They'd ever heard a rumor that you did time, my own brother, because of a busted score of mine, that would have been it, I wouldn't have been able to find a wino to go out with me. So you deserve it for not even bitching about me in jail, Jimmy. Word never reached anyone about my having set that score up.''

"I would never bad-mouth you, Frank. Shit, you're my only brother.''

"Yeah, and you're mine. So take the money, will you? It's enough, you invest it, Jimmy, you'll never have to do time again in your life. You've done enough of that for both of us.''

Jimmy didn't trust himself to speak, just sat there staring at all that money, nodding his head.

But, suddenly and with great awareness, he felt almost free.

He had time to dwell on that a little back in the basement, after Frank went up to shower and shave. While Frank was gone Jimmy heard the phone ring and started at the strange noise, went to answer it, but Frank must have gotten it on an extension because it didn't ring twice. He sat back down, drinking coffee, smoking, trying to sort things out.

Earlier, he'd been worried because he felt so bad, so insecure and afraid. Now he knew why. He'd done nine years inside, one day at a time, never looking ahead or behind. He didn't play the game a lot of cons played, talking shit and bragging about how big they'd been on the street, what they were going to do upon their release. Jimmy had narrowed his entire existence to the time he was in, had lived totally in the realm of Now, had pinpointed life down to the second in which he was living. Nothing else mattered but getting through that second, to the next minute, to the next hour, surviving through that day. It was the way he dealt with it.

But this morning there had been things niggling at him, things he hadn't had to worry about in a long time. Simple things, a lot of them being things Jimmy wasn't even aware of on a conscious level. Insecurities. Would he be attractive, be able to interest a woman if it wasn't after midnight and she didn't have a bunch of drinks in her? Would he be able to fit into society, or would he go through the rest of his life feeling as if there was a sign around his neck, marking him as an ex-con? What would he do for a living?

That had probably been the one that had made him shake. He hadn't even thought about it before, existing in the joint. Would he have to do things that, if he was caught, would send him back to prison? That had caused him grief, thinking of a future back inside before he'd even been out a day. But what else was there for him? A seat at the Chicago Board of Trade, working side by side with the asshole from last night? Maybe bartending. That always seemed like a job where a man could get ahead.

These things had eaten at him, awakened him, the reality of being outside of a structured environment with no prospects for his future now a real and known terror, worse than anything he'd experienced inside.

What had he told the shrink? You got used to it. What he hadn't known then was that there were different levels of fear, depending on what it was you had to be afraid of.

What did Jimmy have to fear now, though? Not a goddamn thing. Frank had set aside fifty percent of his earnings for Jimmy, as a coming-home present. He had a place to stay for as long as he wanted, a closetful of clothes, and more money than he had ever dreamed of.

He heard the doorbell ring, heard Frank holler out that he'd get it, and as the sounds of approaching footsteps entered his mind, coming toward the kitchen, he smiled, because now he was absolutely certain he had it made, knew it and rolled with it, being a man who, just yesterday, was only a number, but who was, today, rich, young, free, and basking in it all. He wanted to laugh aloud and sing the old Dinah Washington number "What a Difference a Day Makes," and he was grinning like a fool, a full-out hundred-watter, when Frank came into the kitchen followed by a tall, solidly built black man who was smiling right back at Jimmy.

Chapter

SEVENTEEN

"My man, how you making it?" Adam Lebeaux said. He was shaking Jimmy's hand, pumping it, and this made Jimmy feel even better because a stranger respected him enough to ask how he was doing. It felt strange, too, to be shaking a black man's hand and not having to worry about getting chastised for the act if somebody happened to see it.

"Doing good, man. It's good to meet you. I heard about you."

"Two-way street, Jimmy. The man here ain't hardly breathed in the last month without your name coming out on the exhale. Now seeing as you family, and we all know each other, come on down into the basement with us—there's something you might get a kick out of hearing."

He followed them, Jimmy's face blank and solemn but his spirits high because he knew goddamn well that you never discussed business with anyone alive who wasn't directly involved in that business, and here they were, accepting him as a silent partner already.

"See, I did time for Uncle Sam in the Viet, and it fucked me up for civilian life so bad, all I had left to do was steal shit. Last time I was inside I tried to bring suit against the government, collect some Social Security behind what the war did to my mind, but they shot me down."

Frank said, "Adalebo, you're full of shit," but he was grinning, and so was Jimmy. The black man was seated in one of the leather chairs, his leg draped over the arm, slouched down, a beer in his hand. He was making no secret of the fact that he was jiving, pulling their legs.

"No, for real, man, I know a dude got away with it. My man Dan, Danjohn Blandane. He sued the government from a padded cell in Bellevue, got the government to pay his benefits on account of he was nuts because of the Viet. Me, I smoked my mind *out* over there, on the weed, got so that the killing intrigued me. I'd kill something and say, 'Ain't that a bitch!' go up and groove on intestines for a while, watch them ooze out the gook I killed.

"But I didn't interrupt old home week to tell lies about the war. Fact is, that redneck homeboy of mine done pulled off the score last night all by his lonesome."

Frank quit smiling. "You tell him about the fifty percent you and me're in for?"

Lebeaux wore an ear-to-ear grin now, drank half his beer before saying, "Didn't get a chance to. The man called *me*, set up a meet, and before I could get three words out my mouth, he told me we was in for a full third apiece."

"What?!"

Adam nodded. "Wants to make up for his mouthing off to you yesterday. Get back on your good side. Guess how much he scored, Frank?" He saw the look on Frank's face and hurriedly added, "Six hundred sweet thousand fucking dollar. And a bunch of gems already been stripped—all you got to do is fence them if you want. Either way—you do it, he do it, I do it—we're in for a third on that, too, the both of us."

"Do me a favor," Frank said, beginning to smile again. "Don't tell that drunken hillbilly he's too crazy for me to work with until *after* he settles up with us, all right?"

There were three men sitting around the office, shooting the shit, all of them with short hair and jailhouse tattoos. Recruiting was restricted to behind prison walls, to keep out the undercover lawmen. Tommy Jacobi liked it that way, although there were some guys out on the street he'd like to make an exception for, get them in the back door.

Like those boys down on the East Side who'd burned the nigger's garage down. He'd want them on his side. The way it looked, they were going to gross about seven years apiece state time and maybe even more federal if the Gee decided that they'd violated the jig's rights. So it looked like they'd get them anyway. The two men in the office with him were telling fuck stories, Jacobi not paying them a lot of attention. He was lost in his own thoughts, worried because there was a mob guy who had shoved a gun down his throat and was going to kill his entire family if what Jacobi did displeased him.

Even as scared as he was, there were a few things he'd had the presence of mind to keep from the big mobster. For instance, he wasn't anywhere near as sure of Jimmy Vale's loyalty as he'd acted.

The man was different—that was all you could say about him. Big and quiet and he did what he was supposed to do without the usual complaining, but you could tell when you looked in his eyes, he didn't see things the way you were supposed to. Went about his business in his own way, blazing his own trails, never asking anyone for any help.

For instance, Jacobi had served a few years with the man, had personally recruited him and made him his right arm, but in all the time he'd known him he'd never heard him bad-mouth, gossip with the boys. Tommy would tell him somebody named Tyrell Jefferson Rasheed was trying to cut in on the Brotherhood's business or something and Jimmy would look at him blankly for a time, then say something like, "Is that that jig in C House?" Tommy would tell him yeah, that's him, and Jimmy would nod, all thoughtful-like, and the next thing you knew, old Rasheed would have himself an accident, break a leg or an arm or something. No one ever heard the true story, no rumors ever spread about Jimmy doing it, but Tommy knew.

Knew by the way the man would look at him the next time they met. The first time it had happened he'd sidled up to Jimmy in the yard, told him that he shouldn't be doing things without help, and Jimmy had just looked at him blankly. The second time it had happened he'd played it differently, had just said to the man, "Good work," and when Jimmy had said "What?" he'd whispered the name of the guy with the broken arm. Jimmy had said, all deadpan, "Oh, that must have just been a coincidence."

It seemed to Tommy that Jimmy didn't trust anyone with his business, if he could help it. And that, for the Brotherhood's purposes, wasn't good. There were other things, too, that gave Tommy pause for thought.

They'd be talking and drinking, shooting the shit, laughing it up, Jimmy right there in the cell with the rest of them but not a part of them, out in his own little world, like he lived in his mind and didn't pay attention to anything that wasn't a direct threat to his existence, or something he had to do to get by.

He was solid, though. There was no doubt about that. The man had balls bigger than an elephant's, and nobody could ever tell if he was scared or enjoying himself when trouble fell down around him. He'd fight full-out, had fast hands for a big man, a good head on his shoulders, too, always making the right moves. He never made fun of Richie Speck or any of the other fags or drunks. In fact, when the I-57 nigger—what the hell was his name? Jacobi searched his mind but couldn't come up with it, the guy who'd pulled white people off the road on the expressway and blasted them with a shotgun just to kill Whitey—when he was in Stateville, he'd caught hell from every white guy in the joint except for Jimmy.

What Jacobi couldn't figure out was if the man was worried about paybacks, or if he just didn't give a shit about things that didn't directly involve him.

Well, he'd have to find a way to get Jimmy on his side, and quick. The riot yesterday hadn't done anyone any good, either. Half the Brotherhood was inside, the other half free, either on parole or having walked after serving straight time. If there was a race riot going on, though, Jacobi could bet on one fact: Jimmy Vale would survive the thing. He'd gotten through others already in his nine years, and another one wouldn't be that big a thing unless the spades just set it up with the express intent of hitting Jimmy or Michael Knox. The guy would have the headquarters' phone number, as all of their released brothers did, and he, like everyone else, was expected to call within forty-eight hours of his release. The problem being that only about half of the guys in the Brotherhood ever called after their release. If they were paroled they usually did, because they would have to stay in Illinois and they'd need help. But most of the guys who served straight time, like Jimmy, never bothered to call. They either moved out of state or set something up on their own, not needing a support group to get them through, to grease the corrupt probation department officers for them. When guys like that got pinched and went back to the joint, though, they were quickly taken back into the fold. The Brotherhood needed all the solid help it could get on the inside.

He couldn't tell DiLeonardi any of that. If he had, the guy would maybe put the gun in another part of Tommy's anatomy, pull the trigger, too, if the mood struck him. What they'd have to do was stick it out, maybe send a scout over to the brother's house, keep an eye out for Jimmy there, although Frank couldn't be approached directly. Jacobi'd tried that once, and all this time later he still got scared just thinking about it.

Jacobi, like every other thief in the city who knew what was happening, was aware of who Frank Vale was. So when he'd first got out himself he'd called Frank, tried a little subtle manipulation, telling the man over the phone that Jimmy's future prison survival was directly tied to the hands of the Brotherhood, and maybe it would be a good idea if a little part of every score Frank went out on from then on went to the cause. Frank had agreed to meet him, told him to come up to the observation deck of Sears Tower at midnight, they could talk things over.

Jacobi had arrived early, had spotted no backups, and when Frank had shown up at twelve Jacobi had been feeling his oats, was cocky, sure that Frank was going to cave in to his demands.

What Frank did, was, he'd walked Jacobi over to a tall southern window, looked around to make sure no one was watching them, then pulled a great big gun out of his coat, had held Jacobi by the scruff of his neck with one hand, massaging him roughly, the gun between them, standing side by side, the barrel pointing at Jacobi's side.

"I'm gonna tell you something, asshole." Vale had said the words softly, almost with amusement, and it had frightened Jacobi worse than anything ever had before in his life, the calmness in the man's voice. "All I got to do is shoot out this window and give you a push. One hundred and three stories down, punk, and I don't see any wings on you. I'll splatter your brains all over Wacker Drive, go home and eat a nice meal, get a good night's sleep. You believe me?" All Jacobi could do was nod his head. He had no doubt in his mind that Vale was stone serious.

"That's good. Now, to stop me from doing that, what do you got to offer me?"

"Your brother's safe. No problem—no one in the Brotherhood would ever mess with him. I promise."

"I need more than that, tough-ass. I want your guarantee, right here and now, that your boys inside will protect him, because you got to understand something. If a black man or a Mexican or anyone else hurts my brother, I'm gonna figure you're behind it, and I'm gonna pay you a visit, all by myself, and I'm gonna get you back up here and throw your living ass out this fucking window. You believe me?"

"I believe you."

"Give me your word, Jacobi."

"I swear."

And that had been that. The pressure had gone off his neck and he'd stood staring out the window for a long time, until he heard the elevator begin its descent. When he'd turned around, Frank had been gone, but what he'd said, what he'd done, had stayed with Jacobi ever since. In fact, the only time he'd ever felt more terrified was just yesterday, in the mob guy's house, when he was sure the guy was going to kill him and then go out and bury hatchets in the heads of every member of the Jacobi family.

Christ, what a bollix-up.

All he could do for now, though, was to wait by the phone, wait patiently, and pray that Jimmy showed up, called him before

DiLeonardi did, because there was no way, after yesterday, that he could ever lie to *that* man, no, uh-uh—

He was staring at the telephone when it finally rang, making him jump. He reached a tentative hand out, grabbed it, and said hello in a weak voice, sure it was the Lion calling, reading his thoughts and calling just to mess with his head.

When he heard the voice of Peters, one of the prison guards heavy on the Brotherhood's payroll, he almost died, he was so relieved.

The problem with being dishonest, was, there were so many lies you had to tell, so much bullshit you had to remember. Anthony Giraldi thought about this as he watched his two partners, his squadmates, working on a small-time mob case, talking between themselves and mostly ignoring him. These bastards, even after three fucking months together, didn't fully trust him.

Which didn't set too well with Giraldi. He'd been the one who'd suggested they stay at the hillbilly's house the night before, when the two of them had wanted to go on home. He'd told them straight out that if there was going to be a score that night, this would be the guy who would lead them to it; Vale was already aware that they were on to him and would spot them in a minute. He'd asked them what was more important to them, a hot dinner at home or maybe splitting the proceeds of a score?

At that point, though, they hadn't been planning on splitting any score. Their only thought was to nab Vale in the act, blow his ass away, and in doing so send a message to the rest of the renegades out there: Pay or die.

Thank God the hillbilly had gone out alone.

These guys, though, they killed him, they really did. They'd split $400,000, the biggest score of any of their careers—the two of them had admitted to him that it was more than they'd ever pulled down at one time since they'd been on the force—and what had they done? They'd cut up the money and made him promise that he didn't tell anyone else about it, even though everyone, all eighteen working PRICCs and the commander, were supposed to get their end. It was going to be hard, especially when he was around the rest of them. He would want to brag, say something to the other fifteen guys, show them what he'd come up with, and now he couldn't; that avenue was closed to him. At least, he figured, the commander should get his share. Hell, he was their boss. But no, the two men had made it clear, the commander had ordered them to lay off, so now he was only getting what he deserved, which was nothing.

There was now a safe deposit box at Citibank that held Giraldi's piece of four hundred grand, which came out to $133,333. Four years' gross pay all in one bunch sitting there waiting for him to spend it. All that his two partners had told him about the money, thankfully, was to be careful spending it. The rich dude the hillbilly stole it from might have had the sense to record the serial numbers.

If not for him they'd have nothing, and still, there they were, whispering between themselves, cutting him out of the conversation again. Giraldi wondered what he'd have to do to win their trust, wondered if he ever would.

"Anthony, hey champ, pay attention, will you?" Mark Gunon was breaking his balls. "Jesus, you act like you're rich enough, you can afford to sit back and daydream all day, not worry about getting fired." This cracked Gunon and Roosevelt up. They gave each other slaps on the arm and laughed in knowing rolling tones, until the commander, who'd been locked in his office with three other team members, came to the door and told them to knock it off, they were busy in there, and the two men shut up but snickered together as soon as the door closed behind the boss.

Jesus, Ryan looked terrible. Giraldi, as he put his head together with the other two men—who were in their glory; Giraldi had never seen them in such high spirits—and worked on the best way to surveil the mobster, wondered what the hell the commander had been drinking last night.

Too much, Ed Ryan thought. This is getting to be too much. He listened to the men in his office, one of the South Side units,

coordinating efforts that would, if all went well, result in nice
videotapes of a female alderman and a female preacher making
love. Two black women doing what turned them on, nothing
illegal, but they were in the public eye and for that they would
have to pay.

The men were all black, inconspicuous in the neighborhood in
which they worked. Not cutthroats, though, like the crew on the
West Side, who mostly worked on the drug scene. These men
were simple businessmen, going about their business the way they
saw fit.

Charles Osgood, the sergeant of the squad, was speaking now.
He was the biggest of the three and the oldest, with the most
seniority, a twenty-nine-year man with a wife in the department,
two sons, the entire family on the city payroll. He was bald,
except for a pure white fringe around his ears which was clipped
close. There was fat on him, but plenty of muscle under that fat.
Osgood sat far back in his chair, leaning, a coffee cup almost
disappearing in a huge right hand, his deep voice filling the room,
the rhythm of his voice lulling, his tone gentle. There was nothing
gentle or lulling about his words.

"We gots the motherfucker what run the counter by the dick,
and we squeezin', C'mander. He sell out his momma to us, we
wants. We gots the camera ready, inside a clock, lens so small I
finds it hard to b'lieve it see anything, but it work."

"You sure they'll be there this Friday?"

Wesley Parnell answered for Osgood. He was the slick one of
the three, tall and razor-thin, with a tiny mustache trimmed to a
line just above his lip. The player of the group, he was the best
dresser, the smoothest talker, the sweetheart the women loved to
open up to: Mr. Sensitivity.

"They'll be there, Commander. Shit, ain't missed a Friday
there in four weeks now. Must be *their* place." He said it and
Osgood laughed along with him, while Ryan chuckled. The other
man in the room, Taylor Blevins, didn't even crack a grin.

Which didn't surprise Ryan. Blevins was a psycho, certifiable.
The rumor was that he'd chopped his own brother into little
pieces, then burned the pieces in his furnace, for becoming a
junkie, dishonoring the family name.

Blevins sat without movement, eyes on his hands, which were on his lap, folded. He wore an old-fashioned felt hat, the brim pushed far back on his high forehead, the skin of his face baby-smooth and very light.

If Ryan was to die, he knew, it would probably be Blevins who got the job. Killing, it was said, was the only way he ever got to have any fun.

Ryan looked around him, at the three men in the room, listening with half an ear as Osgood continued the step-by-step recitation of their surveillance.

It made him sick. Literally. All day long he'd been belching, pouring the Pepto-Bismol into his gut, wondering if all the booze was finally catching up with him or if he was just sick of who he was, what he was doing. It didn't matter. All he would do now, really, was go through the motions. He'd pack up all his evidence, get it together in one safe place for Monday. Tomorrow, the men in this room would tape the sexual encounter, they would edit it over the weekend, figure out its worth, and have a figure ready for his approval by Monday morning. He would get the tape, the last piece of evidence he would ever get from these men, and would take it with him to the U.S. attorney's office, pile it all up on the man's desk and tell him he was through, dare the man to tell him that he wasn't.

It was over. It had to be. Ed couldn't take any more of this, not one more week.

He decided, though, as he listened to Osgood, nodding his head, that on the way to the U.S. attorney's office he would make one quick stop, at his apartment, to burn the videotape of the women in the hotel room. He wouldn't turn that over. The women weren't corrupt, weren't stealing from the city. What they did behind closed doors in a room bought and paid for was their own business.

He made this decision expecting it to lift him up, but wasn't surprised when it didn't. In fact, the more he listened to these men, the dirtier he felt, and no little acts of compassion he performed would have the power to cleanse him.

How could they be this corrupt, this terrible? These were policemen here, his brothers. Pick out any cop on the street, anywhere, and tell Ed Ryan that he had a chance to jump in front of a bullet for the man, and Ed wouldn't have to think twice. They were bound together in a way civilians couldn't understand, strong men who lived and breathed for their jobs and for one another. They kept the job after the wife left, taking the kids, kept it when they got TB and alcoholism, kept it sometimes until they finished a bottle late at night and swallowed the barrel of their pistol. And a lot of guys ate their guns after retiring, too, after giving up the badge. Unable to face life without the excitement, having the time now to look back and thoroughly examine just how little they'd really accomplished in their lives; all that they'd given up for that shallow accomplishment.

Cops didn't take money; it wasn't right, and these guys would deserve everything that happened to them.

Worse than a cop that took money, though, was a cop who snitched on other cops. It was with sudden clarity that that thought struck home with Ed. He was about to turn on his brothers, rat them out, and there was nothing he could say or do that would change that fact. He was a fink, which, in the eyes of law enforcement officers everywhere, even in Tarpon Springs, Florida, was worse than being crooked.

Oh, God, Ed Ryan thought, just let Monday get here.

EIGHTEEN

Lebeaux left and Jimmy put on his new leather coat, took Frank's car and went to explore the city. Frank was alone again, with time to think.

Adalebo had been full of piss and vinegar, in a good mood because his old cellmate had come through better than expected. Jimmy was high on himself, with new clothes and a ton of money of his own. Frank knew the gestures had gone far, as he'd intended.

Which left him. He'd made a lot of no-risk money and had lost Tina and he had to ask himself if it was worth it. The answer to that one was easy.

Who was he kidding, thinking he could go on like this forever? Eventually, it would have to end: He'd get pinched, or, if he was lucky, killed. Which was a great philosophy to have, seeing death as a break, the lesser of two evils. It was all well and good when he was young, in his twenties and not giving a shit either way, but these days he wanted more.

It would be nice, settling down, sitting in front of a fireplace in the winter, sipping wine, making it with a wife on a bearskin rug. These were things he'd rejected all his life, these symbols of the square world, but the older he got the more attraction these things held for him.

It wasn't the thought of these things that bothered him; it was the idea of playing society's game to get them. Getting up and working for some fool who got his nut off telling you what to do, not promoting you if you didn't suck on his backside night and day. Frank knew nothing about politics or diplomacy and wanted to know even less than he did; had no desire to butter anyone up to achieve advancement. He'd decided early on to get ahead in his own way, by his own means.

His trouble with Tina made him look at himself differently, appraising honestly. Here was a woman who'd put herself through school, who had goals, who didn't sell out when the opportunity arose, go to work for some Michigan Avenue corporation and make the fast buck, turning her head on the problems of the city. She'd gotten her degree and had thrown herself into helping the people she figured to be the last hope for America's survival, the young. She'd worked her way into a partnership with a firm on her own terms, making a fraction of what she could have if she'd gone the route most of the others in her class had taken, defending the piece-of-trash crooks who everybody knew were guilty but who had just as much right to a fair trial as anyone else. She'd told him more than once that she hated lawyers who did that, who rationalized their greed, hid behind the noble idea of Justice and grabbed all that they could, defending scum and truly believing that none of it would rub off on them.

She'd stood up and done what she'd known was right, and now he'd dashed her dreams, her middle-class desires for love and hope, for safety in a world that frightened her. Selfishly, he'd taken away her faith, walked in and done what he could to make her fall in love with a man who, a lifetime ago, had rejected all of the values she held so close to her heart. She'd learned the truth and had cut him out of her life, and now she was going to quit her job and move away, start over in her mid-thirties somewhere else.

What would he have done, in her place? If someone had lied to him and used him, hurt him so badly that he couldn't go on? He would probably kill that person, cold-bloodedly, in the belief that they had it coming.

Good Christ, what *was* he?

It was easy to wear the mask Tina talked about, he saw that

now. The thing was, he could see through it in everyone else while thinking that he himself was too smart for the rationalizations. He would look at a loser, some piece of scum crying late at night in a bar about how the cops were out to get him, how the judge had set him up, talking all that trash, and Frank would feel disgust and anger, seeing himself as above that sort of thing, on a level of reality in which he would never allow himself to blame others for his own shortcomings.

Tina had made him see things differently. Was he any better than the guy whining and crying in the bar? When he would look back and blame his vicious childhood for what he'd become? He did that all the time—he could see it now. Jimmy had asked him about their mother the night before, asking as if he really wanted to know, and Frank had told him that the last time she'd called him she'd whined and cried about how broke she was, and he'd told her to find a sugar daddy to take care of her the way she used to. She hadn't needed him back in the days when he'd needed her, so now it was his turn to not need her. She'd called again, a couple of days later, drunk, and he'd hung up on her, changed his phone number that day and hadn't spoken to her since. That had been six years ago. The Iceman strikes again. He'd told Jimmy the story and Jimmy had stared at him blankly, no emotion showing on his face, but Frank wondered, even through the alcohol fog, what was going on behind those mannequin eyes.

Jimmy had always been the baby, the one who seemed to escape the worst of the brutality. Oh, the old man had given him his share of ass-kickings, but they were nothing compared to what Frank had been forced to endure.

At seven he'd gotten over his fear of the dark because the old man had tied him to a post in the basement, left him there from dusk until daylight. Frank had never cried out for help in the night, ever again.

When he was eleven the old man had caught him sneaking in through a window late at night, had confronted him, asked him if he was a man. Frank had shouted, "Yes!" defiantly. The old man had dragged him through the house by his hair, into his bedroom. Had grabbed one of his pistols, then dragged Frank right back down into that goddamn basement, where, with the lights shut off, he'd thrown Frank to one side and the gun to the floor.

"You're a fucking man!" he'd shouted. "Whoever gets to the gun first kills the other one, you hear me?"

Frank had fallen to his knees, had scrambled madly for the gun, hands frantically searching. He was crying, sobbing, sniveling, doggedly determined to get the gun, to win. There was no doubt in his mind that if he did, he would shoot the old man, just as there was no doubt that if the old man got it first, he'd shoot Frank.

The light came on and there was the old man, gun in his hand, grinning, coming toward him.

Still on the floor, Frank had scrambled backwards, shrieking in terror, until he hit the concrete wall. He'd stared, transfixed, as the old man had walked toward him, slowly, madly grinning, his eyes wide and wild. He'd pointed the gun at Frank, pulled the trigger.

The gun had been empty.

"See?" the old man had said. "You ain't no fucking *man*. *Men* don't piss their pants." He'd chuckled, shaking his head, had turned and walked away, leaving Frank to sit staring at his back, wishing for a knife.

He thought of Jimmy, seven years younger, mostly ignored by the old man, who held out his fiercest assaults for Frank. They'd had the same data, but had interpreted it in different ways.

Frank had always been the loner, an outsider, a man who went his own way, thinking that emotional gratification could be granted him if he had enough things. Until meeting Tina, he'd substituted material things for emotional needs. Jimmy, on the other hand, had always sought emotional safety, a place where he could fit in.

Even at home. In the violent world in which they'd been raised, Jimmy had always argued and sometimes even fought with Frank when Frank would try to tell him the truth about their home life. Always hiding, not wanting to believe the evidence at hand.

The old man was always under a lot of pressure; Ma, always "tired." Jimmy would rationalize away their cruelty, their evil natures. To Frank, they were weasels, people to run from; to Jimmy, they were people to love and someday protect. People from whom he would always seek approval.

Frank always figured Jimmy to be a kid with a hungry heart, while he, as he grew older, decided that he no longer had one.

Until Tina.

Jimmy had always had tunnel vision. Whereas Frank now saw his problem to be that his lens was too wide. So wide, in fact, that he almost missed what was there right in front of him, waiting and loving.

Tina.

He saw it, painfully, now: his entire life being a way of getting back at a brutal father, then a drunken mother who'd done to Frank only what she'd seen work for her husband—beat the kids into submission and make them do your bidding.

Grandma, too, the same thing. The woman had been dying of cancer seven years back and his mother, Queenie, had called him, asked him to go and see the old woman, she was calling out to Frank from her deathbed, and he'd ignored the plea, had skipped the funeral. He'd see his uncles sometimes, in a store or in a bar, and he'd ignore them. They never had the guts to approach him, give him any opinions about his life's choices.

From the beginning, he'd blamed his parents. Later on it had been the system, which had locked him away first in the Audy Home, then in the St. Charles reformatory. Neither place had done anything to change his frame of mind, the way he looked at things.

Three things had happened this week that had forced him to look soberly at his life, and if any of them had happened alone he could have told himself that although the event caused him grief he was still basically all right, that the other people involved were maybe assholes who didn't deserve his time and trouble. But what he'd seen, experienced, in the last two days had made him reflect, negatively, on his life and its motives.

First the cops had come, some jealous sucker having probably dropped a dime and told the cops Frank was rolling in dough, and they'd come to claim their piece of it. They'd discussed killing him, had wanted to do him, and his mind had raced for ways out, had found none. These guys were corrupt animals, would steal the jewelry from their mother's corpse in the casket, but they hadn't come after him because he was a pillar of society. He didn't read a lot in the newspapers about any brain surgeons or dentists getting dragged from in front of their homes and being worked over in the basement of precinct houses.

Then Tina had dumped him, telling him, with clear logic, using her analytical mind, that he was a liar, a mask-wearing, deceiving, rationalizing, no-good bum.

Then Jimmy had sat in the chair Frank was in now, looking at Frank with dead eyes that had seen far too much. A young man physically but ancient in his mind and heart. People would read in the papers about someone sentenced to nine years in prison and they'd harumph and shake the pages, bitch to their spouses over coffee about the light time the crook had received, never thinking about what nine years would do to a man, or about the fact that at the end of those years, society would have to deal with that man again. Nine years, even if you lived according to the charts, was one eighth of your life expectancy. People never took the time to think about what that kind of thing could do to you psychologically, living in a cage worse than any animal's at the Lincoln Park Zoo, for that long a period of time.

Frank had seen firsthand what it could do to a man, because his brother just wasn't the same and never would be again. He'd sat right there across from him and they'd drunk together and laughed and told stories, but Jimmy was changed. Much quieter and more solemn than before, maybe even burned out. Frank knew prison wasn't something you shed like a snakeskin; the damage that serving nine years in a prison environment caused just wasn't discarded cavalierly when your time was up. Jimmy was never going to be the same man again, the carefree, eager-to-please kid he'd been at nineteen. The kid was now a man, and the man just didn't care anymore.

It had been good to see the look on his face when he'd opened the strongbox. Jimmy had shown some emotion then, and Frank hoped that he would take the money and give it up, start over and try to put the past behind him. He hoped this at the same time that he doubted its happening. The little brother, the one who was supposed to grow up and make something out of his life, was now

an ex-con who'd spent a third of his life behind bars. Time like
that had a way of killing a man's spirit.

It was almost funny, like seeing his life in that movie with
George C. Scott that played at Christmastime, the Scrooge thing.
Tina was what could have been, if his past had been different. A
woman who loved him and wanted him and who was willing to
spend her life with him. What he could have had if he'd gone
another route. The cops, the beatings and the threats, that was his
present, his reality, what he deserved, if you wanted to get right
down to it. And Jimmy was his future. The first time the PRICCs
nailed him, it would be the joint for him. They might not want to
kill him, might much rather see him in the joint, physically alive,
but in a place where his spirit and soul would die. Jimmy's
reptilian eyes gave Frank a look into his own future, the Frank of
Yet-to-Come, and when he thought of that, he didn't feel much
like the Iceman anymore.

He shoved himself out of his chair and grabbed a light jacket,
stormed from the house and gave the street a once-over, spotted no
cops lying in wait. He ran next door and then stopped on the
stairway. What could he say to her, what words could he speak
that would make things the way he wanted them to be, the way
they might have been if he hadn't been dishonest? Slowly, he
walked up the steps, entered the vestibule. He pulled open the
broken security door, walked down to Tina's door, knocked lightly,
twice. She asked who it was and he said his name, softly, and she
opened the door, looked out at him.

She was wearing a jogging suit now, and there was a sweat stain
between her breasts. Her hair was disheveled, fell in curling
tendrils around her cheeks. A stray wisp dangled between her
eyes, making her look like a kid.

She didn't look angry or resentful. She didn't look glad to see
him, either. She just looked out at him, as if he was just there,
someone to be dealt with.

Frank said, "It's over, Tina. I'm sorry if I hurt you and I can't
take that back. I would if I could. But that other part of my life is
over, forever. I just wanted you to know that, and that you were
the one responsible for it. And one other thing. I'll put the house

up for sale. I'll move. You should get your job back and keep doing what you do best. The kids need you.'' He wanted to say more, but she was looking at him directly, staring through his eyes and into his soul, and he turned his eyes downward, stared at the floor, and as he began to shuffle away he said, again, ''I'm sorry . . .'' He was almost to the door when Tina, in a wee voice, called his name.

She almost didn't. It was in her mind to let him go, make him suffer, but that was no way to deal with things, either, was it? What had Betty, the analyst, always said? The key to every relationship is understanding, then communicating. Betty who, years ago, had saved her.

She called to him, asked him to come back, and she sat on the couch, the packed boxes surrounding them. The apartment was a mess, things everywhere, in piles to be packed or discarded. The question now was, did she want to communicate with this man, have a relationship with him? He had never shown himself to be guileful; one of the things she most admired about him was his straightforwardness, his ability to cut through the games and bull-shit and get to the point. Until yesterday, she'd seen him as the most honest man she'd ever known.

Was she blaming him for all her problems, her mental regres-sion which, in fact, wasn't his fault? She'd made her choices and would have to live with them, and she could not hold him respon-sible even if his lies had brought back the terrible anxiety, the loss of the self-worth she so cherished.

Tina looked at Frank and thought back, to the nights when her father had come visiting her room, drunk, crying on her shoulder about how her mother didn't understand him, didn't love him, would rather play bingo or go to some other function at the church than be with him. The first time, he'd forced himself on her. After, he'd called her a slut, a whore who'd seduced him, and threatened to kill her if she breathed one word of what had happened to her mother. He'd left the room and she'd cried tears of shame, had hated herself and what she'd done.

But there had been a feeling of power there, too. She'd made him weak, made him need her. Mixed with the shame, and maybe even worse, was a sick pleasure, her sexuality awakened.

She'd been thirteen years old.

Two years later, after the late-night visits had become a regular thing, she'd been arrested at a teenage drinking party where she'd been trading oral sex for beer. The arresting officer, after having gotten the story straight from the other kids, had not done much for her. He'd bragged the story around the station house, saying again and again that she'd probably said to herself, "Tastes great, less filling." The other cops looked at her and snickered, except for one.

His name had been Michael McNamara, and he was the youth officer for the precinct. He got her alone in a little office and he'd closed the door. She'd right away begun removing her clothes, having figured the deal to be a piece of ass for her release. She couldn't have been more wrong.

He was hip to her from the start.

"Father, stepfather, or brother?" he'd asked, and the words had knocked her out.

"I ain't got to tell you nothing." She'd pulled the blouse closed, held the material at her throat, a habit she still had today when she was nervous or afraid.

"No, that's true. All you have to do is sit here and wait for the guy who did this to you to come down here with your mother, then listen to them both call you filthy names after they find out what happened at the party. Now, let's cut the shit. You and I both know the kind of hypocrite he is, what he does to you. Why cover up for him? The way it stands, you have four roads to travel. Insanity, drug addiction, prostitution, and prison. Come straight with me now, and there are ways out."

"I'm no good." Her voice was small and frightened, Tina saying what she'd come to believe after having it told to her over and over again.

"That's bullshit," Mac had told her. "*He's* no good—not you. Honey, you're fifteen years old. You can be anything you want.

175

And you can start right now, by talking to me. I'll put that son of a bitch away if I can, and you can start another life.''

''I made him do it. I paraded around in front of him all the time in my nightgown.''

He'd slammed his hand down on the desk hard, making her tremble. ''They all say that. Every one of them. You can't believe it, Tina. You got to change your way of thinking, starting right now.''

It had taken her some time, with Mac cajoling and pleading, mixing it with toughness, before she finally broke down and told him everything.

It hadn't worked out the way they'd hoped. He'd prepared her, as had the officer from the Department of Children and Family Services, for the worst, and it happened, the way it did in seventy percent of such cases.

The mother had sided with her husband.

Tina had gone away to a home for girls, and had met Betty, and the work had begun.

Now, over twenty years later, she was feeling the same way she had that first day in the home: terrified, hating herself, wishing she would just turn invisible so nobody could see her. The major difference being, she was no longer an insecure little girl.

She knew how to handle herself, had learned to deal with life and all of its ugliness on life's terms. She'd made mistakes, terrible mistakes along the way, but nothing had ever come close to making her feel as full of self-hatred as she had that night at the party, on her knees, trying to be loved, knowing how wrong it all was but powerless to stop.

When she'd learned the truth about Frank on Monday, all her reason had fled. She'd been there again, right on the edge, feeling betrayed and loathing herself, wanting only to run and hide, no special place in mind but just away from here, where the pain was. As early as yesterday afternoon she'd seen that she was overreacting, but once more she was powerless. She had to get away where no one would see her, get to know her, ever again.

Frank had been only the third man she'd been intimate with as an adult, and the only one for whom she'd felt anything. The other two had been pawing, drooling idiots, almost stereotypes of lounge lizards, acting as if she were getting a treat. Frank had been gentle, kind, passionate but loving, the only one of the three who didn't remind her of her father, who didn't make her feel dirty in bed. What she'd learned about him, though, what he'd finally told her last night, had made her feel just as dirty—worse even, because she'd allowed herself to fall in love. Had given herself totally to a man who had used her mind the way her father had her body, which, in a way, was an even worse invasion.

She looked at Frank now, seeing a person who was, just maybe, feeling the same way she once had. Sometimes, she knew, it took years of self-seeking to see yourself as you truly are. Most folks never even get there.

"Frank?" Tina said, softly. "Talk to me."

Chapter

NINETEEN

It had been a rough afternoon for Tommy Jacobi. First, that crazy man DiLeonardi had called. At least Tommy had some good news for him. Not that the old man saw it that way. When he'd told him that Jimmy Vale had been released in the middle of the night, the son of a bitch had demanded that Tommy get Jimmy to sit down that very day, lay things out for him without mentioning DiLeonardi's name. He gave him some information, though, with which to persuade Jimmy, and it was the kind of stuff that fascinated Tommy. After he hung up, he decided that he would indeed use the stuff the man had told him, and then also tell Jimmy whatever else he wanted. If he ever showed up. This deal, though, would put him in real good with the mob. The Lion had been bossy, but otherwise friendly enough. Tommy could see himself maybe working his way in with the outfit through the guy, someday taking over. He was learning, through the Lion, a hell of a lot more than he ever knew about the politics of fear and violence.

He'd sent people out, around one, looking for Jimmy, and had found out a little later that his top moneymaker, Rocco Armstrong, had been killed, and his second in command, Bobby Fratello, had been arrested and charged with murder.

Rocco had a good thing going that was fattening the Brotherhood's war chest. One of the guys would take to hanging around one of the neighborhood bars that still cashed paychecks for the Chicago steelworkers and autoworkers. The plants were almost all shut down now, the Japs and the Germans having kicked the shit out of the bigwigs in Pittsburgh who thought they were so smart, breaking the unions (one of which Tommy's father had been a member of for forty-two years) under Reagan, and then learning that the new stiffs they hired didn't know shit from steel. Still, there were enough of the places around so that Rocco could make a good score every few weeks.

The inside man would hang around the bar for a couple of weeks, always wearing a hat, buying rounds and shooting pool as well as the shit, getting to know the bartenders and the workers. When he got their check-cashing times down, he'd call Rocco, who would come around the outside of the bar and look in the window. The second the cash box was under the bar, the guy inside would take off his hat, which was Rocco's signal.

Rocco had it down to a science. He would enter the bar wearing a ski mask and carrying a .44 Magnum—which had a way of instilling fear and garnering respect—and announce a holdup, then order that the door be locked. The inside man would race to the door, lock it while everyone was going facedown on the floor, and Rocco would turn the gun on the hatless guy, curse him and threaten him for not moving fast enough, drawing suspicion from him. He'd then order the partner to get the strongbox and bring it to him. Then he'd slap him upside the head with the Mag, and the guy would make a big production out of being hurt, dropping to the floor and groaning, while Rocco made good his escape.

This scenario had worked seventeen times in the last year. Last night would have been the eighteenth, except that Rocco had smoked some reefer to calm his nerves before going into the bar, and the inside man, Bobby, had not been the first to move to the door, the order having been nearly carried out by an old-timer who had been aiming to please. Rocco had thought the guy was making a break for it and had shot him, the bullet going through the guy, then through the door, and out into the street, where it had struck a passing squad car. The two officers inside, heading back to the precinct to end their shift, had got it into their heads that terrorists were inside the bar, attacking them, and had covered both doors, waiting for backup. Rocco was unaware of this. After shooting the old man he'd just stared at him for a while, his lip trembling under the ski mask, then had grabbed the cash box and had run out the back door, where the cop watching it had shot him four times before hollering for him to halt. Bobby had been right behind him and the cop had at first thought that he was just another customer, trying to get away from the violence, but Bobby's shortcoming had always been his unflagging loyalty—he'd seen Rocco on the ground, dead, and had gone to him, had cradled him in his arms.

It hadn't taken long for the cops to put things together. Bobby had gotten his head right and had refused to speak a single word to the cops, but they had enough to charge him. Although, Tommy knew, a confession would have been better for them. Bobby might well beat the case, plead that he was just a bleeding-heart liberal who'd been overcome at the sight of the dead holdup man. Tommy hung on to that thought, because he and the Brotherhood would be in enough trouble now without Rocco's organizing and money-making skills. They couldn't afford to lose Bobby, too.

But maybe it would turn out to be a good thing. Now he could plead with Jimmy, tell him how the Brotherhood needed him, work on his guilt. Jimmy was a cagey one, but he seemed to have feelings. He would have to help the Brotherhood, especially seeing as how they had saved his ass when the niggers had put a hit on him all those years ago, and now Michael had died for him. Yeah, that's what he'd do. He'd tell him that it was time now to pay the piper. And if Jimmy told him to go fuck himself, then Tommy had another plan to fall back on.

He'd take the score down himself. The old mob goof had told him that they needed Jimmy to get at Frank, and that Jimmy was to be promised that every dime they found inside went to him and his brother after they wasted Mad Mike Tile. With Rocco gone, money would soon become a problem, and Tommy knew, as did everyone on the street, that Tile was dragging down zillions in the coke trade. Tommy smiled, wondering how many of those zillions would be inside the guy's mansion. Eventually, it would all end up in Tommy's pocket anyway, so maybe going in wasn't such a good idea. No, what he'd do, was, he'd work on Jimmy, on his guilt, make the man understand that the Brotherhood, his only real family, needed him.

But first, he had to find Jimmy.

Who was now pulling Frank's car to the curb in front of his mother's house. It had been a dilapidated neighborhood before, but now it was nearly a ghetto, the far South Side having gone downhill with the closing of the steel plants. Brown faces peered out of windows that had no curtains, black eyes staring at him.

He liked the Caddy, though, was amazed at how quickly driving came back to him. He enjoyed it so much that he decided to get a driver's license in a week or so.

All he'd have to do was talk to Frank. After the shock of seeing all that money in the box that morning, his brother had shown him his other emergency provisions. The three false driver's licenses and passports in different names, with matching Social Security cards, the licenses and passports with Frank's smiling face on them. Frank had told him that all of his money was either in interest-bearing saving or money market accounts, some of it even invested in the stock market. The days of the safety deposit boxes were long past for the new wave of thieves. As long as you dropped less than ten grand inside any account at any one time, the IRS wouldn't start bothering you, and if you paid taxes under the assumed names, you had it made.

Jimmy thought of these things because he didn't want to think about going into his mother's house. He would come to grips with his feelings only after they were sitting together face to face, wouldn't allow himself to think about it sooner because he would then think of possible scenes, act them out in his head, situations that never came true anyway. Nothing was ever as bad or as good as he thought it would be, except for prison. The joint had been worse than he had ever imagined.

He put his mind on other things, and suddenly realized that he'd walked to the side door and knocked without knowing that he'd performed either act. Anticipation, mixed with dread, charged through him. He thought about running, but the door was opening and she'd spot him, see him running like a sissy, and her suspicions from years ago would be confirmed. She'd always said that he'd grow up a woman-beating coward, like his father.

He tried to smile, wanted to, but couldn't manage it. He wondered, as she stepped back in shock, seeing him for the first time in a decade, what his face looked like to her.

"Jesus Christ, oh, my God, I thought it was your father."

"It's me, Ma, Jimmy." There was a cigarette dangling from her fingers, the smoke curling up and around her face. Her other hand held a glass filled with golden liquid that foamed. "Can I come in?"

She stood in the doorway, staring at him, tears filling her eyes, then stepped toward him, touched his chest. The ash fell off her cigarette, spilled down the front of his new gray leather jacket.

"Come on in, son," Queenie said.

There was a can of beer in front of him and he was smoking, trying to make sense of what she was saying. Shit, two in the afternoon and she was bombed already.

"And work and shit, I'm sick today, took the day off, I been too busy to even sit down and relax thinking about the riot at the prison and everything, worried about you and to think that you were already home and nobody told me." There was a break in her prattle and he jumped on it.

"You'd have written to me, I'd have told you my out date."

"Write to you? What about? About my mother's dying of

183

cancer? You and Grandma were so close, you were always her favorite. You'd have broken out and then where would you be?''

Close? To his grandmother? He wondered about what she was saying, then got it. Ma was rearranging history. It was, for her, business as usual. He had an idea about what was coming next, some plea for sympathy, some kind of self-pitying statement. It had been her pattern, after he'd grown too big to simply whip and make sit still and listen.

"I cried so many tears over you, Jimmy. Lost a job, too, when I couldn't go in, my stomach in knots all the time from worry and nerves because of you. I called your brother and that son of a bitch, he insulted me. I should have aborted him!''

"Ma, Frank just—''

"Don't mention that name in my house!'' She pounded her fist on the table for emphasis—little weak Ma always believing she was tough, strong—and her wrist hit the ashtray and spilled butts all over the table. As she got up and wet a paper towel, began cleaning them, he had time to try to reconcile what he was seeing with his memories.

When he'd gone away she'd been nearly ten years younger, and the years hadn't been kind. Always slender, Ma had been a strangely pretty woman a decade ago—although she was ten years older than Jimmy's father—her hard-lined face carrying the remnants of what must have been, at one time, beauty. No longer, though. Her face and arms were fleshy, and there was a roll of fat under her chin. Her hair was still dyed but it was very thin; he could see the roots clearly. She was wearing a robe, probably hadn't been up long. He wondered what she did for money, if she really did have a job.

When his father had been found shot to death in the trunk of his car, she had acted as if she hadn't always cursed him, wished the man dead a thousand times. On the first night of his wake she'd dragged him out of the box twice, screaming, "What will I do without him?!'' What she wound up doing, was, the same thing she'd done before he'd been murdered. Drink. And bring strange men home, though then she didn't have to worry about the word filtering back to the old man in some joint somewhere.

It was a mistake, coming here. He was feeling the resentment building as she cursed Frank, never using his name, always saying "my firstborn son" or "your brother." He wondered how long it would take before she started in on him. He told himself to get out, now, before the real trouble began, then cursed himself for coming there in the first place. But he'd had to find out. See if there was anything left.

She was sitting again, her left arm down on the table, cradling her right elbow. Her chin was in her hand, another smoke burning between her fingers. She was staring at him in a way that didn't make him feel very good.

"You come here looking for a place to stay? Not a word in nine years and now you're gonna come back? Well, go stay with your brother! None of you ever cared. Never gave a *fuck* about the sacrifices I made for you, raising two boys all alone." Jimmy rose to leave and she raised her voice, hollered after him. "Don't think I didn't have opportunities! I had plenty of offers, if I'd dump you kids in a home! I turned them all down and now I'm old and WHERE THE FUCK ARE MY KIDS NOW!"

He shut the door behind him, carefully, on the way out, got in Frank's car and stopped at the first pay phone he came to, dialed the number he'd called collect for six or seven years.

"Tommy?" Jimmy said, and didn't get a chance to say another word for about two minutes, as Tommy Jacobi gave him the kind of shouting welcome his mother would never have the heart to equal or the desire to convey. It was, Jimmy realized, the ex-con equivalent of a hug.

He walked into the back room of the seedy motel, into Jacobi's office, getting a hero's welcome all the way back. Guys shaking his hand and patting his back, welcoming him back into the world.

Tommy came around the desk, his hand out, wearing a short-sleeve Ban-Lon shirt so everyone could see his muscles. He grabbed Jimmy's hand and pumped hard, holding it with his free hand, his face beaming.

"Broham! God Almighty, you give us a scare. I thought you had caught your lunch in the riot, thought the boo-boos had set up a hit on you on your last day. Man, it's good to see you."

Jimmy, too, was smiling. Filled with a warmth he couldn't understand or comprehend. He was just glad that he felt this way.

"Sit down, sit down." There was a leather chair across the desk from Tommy, and Jimmy took it, accepted, too, the beer one of the guys brought him. The other men left them alone, closed the door behind them.

"So," Tommy said, "you get laid?"

"Not yet. I only got out around midnight."

"Shit, first night I got out, man, I was so horny for a broad, I wound up with the first one looked at me sideways. Woke up in a fog, didn't remember nothing, and there was this sort of dead-ass weight pulling the other side of the bed down. I remember thinking: First night out, and I wind up with a man. I opened my eyes and looked at her, and man, it was a woman, but barely. She looked like one of them *Night of the Living Dead* bitches, all decayed and shit." Tommy took a long pull on his beer, slapped it down on the table with a chuckle. "I done a little better for myself since. You want, I can call up to one of the rooms, get you a bitch could suck the cream out of a Twinkie and never touch the cake."

"I had enough of that to last me. I want to get laid, man, with a real woman."

"We can get her to go up on her knees, make you feel right at home."

Tommy Jacobi loved the way it was going. It was nothing like he thought it would be. Michael Knox had often told him on the phone that Jimmy seemed to be sinking deeper and deeper into himself, and here the guy was, falling all over himself to make conversation. Getting out did that to some guys. He decided, after the business was talked over and Jimmy was locked in with them,

186

he would send up and tell Chynna to get rid of whoever she was with, clean herself out and get ready for a guy who hadn't had any real stuff in nine years. She'd probably get a kick out of it, see herself as Florence Nightingale.

He said to Jimmy: "You want to hear one? I'm in the Jewel on a Hundred-and-sixth last night—man, you wouldn't recognize the neighborhood, half niggers now and spics, too—getting a frozen shrimp dinner to take home? There's this shine broad in front of me, wearing a muumuu, paying for maybe five bucks' worth of shit with food stamps. The thing I noticed, she's about a hundred and ten pounds soaking wet, but the front of her muumuu, it looks like she got about size ninety tits. I smell her, just wanting her to get out of there, and she leans over to take a pack of baloney out of the basket when out of her right tit falls this five-pound ham. *Ba-bing,* right into the basket. She don't miss a beat, though, she ducks down, looks around, and yells, 'Who be throwin' hams at me!' all pissed off. I walked right away from it, went into the next line while the security guy wrestles with her."

Tommy noticed the smile on Jimmy's face, was about to begin another story when the man stopped smiling and said to him, "I understand the Brotherhood needs me," and all of a sudden Tommy Jacobi didn't love the way it was going anymore.

In the first place, the guy had said, "The Brotherhood," not, "I understand that *you* need me." There was a big difference there. Was Jimmy telling him that he might help the group, but not Tommy? No, not when they were one and the same.

Tommy said, "I got some good news for you, from inside. They got that new kid—Fender, Gender, whatever his name is—in seg; they're gonna let him out. Man inside said the warden looked at his record, couldn't understand what he was doing in there in the first place. Says he should have got work release, would have, too, if anyone else but a cop had died." Jimmy was looking at him, blankly.

"Michael Knox, too, Jimmy—that's one you owe. Taking a shank for you. Oh, yeah, I heard all about it."

"He said, last time we talked in the yard, that there was something the Brotherhood needed from me."

There he went again with that "Brotherhood needs" shit. All right, fuck it. Time to get down to business. "We got something for you to do for us, as one of us. There's a guy who's gotta go, and you got to do it for us."

"You want me to kill someone?" Jimmy didn't seem too worried about murder, which Tommy appreciated. It showed he had the heart inside him, hadn't lost a step on the outside.

"That's right. Problem is, the guy, he lives in a pretty well protected crib. Got some bodyguards, too."

"They got to die too, Tommy?"

"If they get in the way."

"Tommy? I want to ask you something. Michael died for me. I owe him a life. And the Brotherhood, too—I owe them. I do this for you, take out this guy, and we're even, right? I go my own way, not have to look over my shoulder all the time."

"Is that the way you want it, Jimmy? You want out from us, after all we done for you?"

"I want to start over, Tommy."

"That's the way you want it, that's the way it is." He was going to add that if Jimmy wanted to start over that bad, he wouldn't even have to go out on the hit, see what the guy thought of that, but he wasn't any too sure of how much guilt Jimmy was carrying over Michael. Best to leave it alone.

"You want to start over?" Tommy said. "Well, that's up to you. The guy you got to do, he's probably got a couple million bucks in the house, cash, diamond rings and dope and shit. It's yours, man, all of it, you do this for us. I want the dope to sell, so you don't get yourself in a jackpot, and I'll split it down the middle with you. But everything else, you get to keep."

"Michael said the mob was involved. That who I got to hit, some mob guy?"

"That's right. Mike Tile. He's gotta go down, Jimmy."

"Mike Tile?" Jimmy said. "Forget about it."

"There some incentive in it for you, Jimmy, and your brother, too."

Jimmy scowled at him. He paused, thinking, then said, "That's what it was all about all along, wasn't it, Tommy? You just wanted Frank to do it and he wouldn't if I didn't ask him. You want us to hit the biggest outfit guy in town, in his house. Why? He burn you on a drug deal? You got any idea what kind of heat this'll bring down on me? Shit, they'll skin us alive when they catch us, and they *will* catch us, Tommy."

"Nobody'll be looking, Jimmy." Tommy played his ace in the hole. "We got the okay from up top, from way above Mad Mike. We hit him and take over his spot. That's why you guys get to keep all the money from the caper for yourselves, if that's the way you want it, instead of staying with us. By the way, you want to hear your incentive or not?"

"What incentive?"

"Mike Tile," Tommy Jacobi said, "killed your father."

Chapter

TWENTY

I t took some persuading, Tommy using all of his prison charm and personality, but at last he got Jimmy out of there without a problem. He'd told him about DiLeonardi, how he was behind it and would back them up, and he swore Jimmy to secrecy, made him promise that he wouldn't even tell his brother Frank the man's name, before he mentioned the Lion. DiLeonardi still had Tommy's phone book. He told him that the word had come from New York, that this score would put the White Aryan Brotherhood in the truly big leagues, that it was Jimmy's responsibility to get his brother to pull the home invasion. He worked his magic on the man and when it was done Jimmy had again demanded his release from the Brotherhood, no strings attached, if he pulled off the hit. Tommy had reassured him, smiling. No one was made to stay in the Brotherhood if they wanted out, it was as simple as that. But Jimmy owed this to them, and he could tell by the look in the man's eyes as he said the word that Jimmy agreed with him.

Tommy could tell, too, that Jimmy was impressed by the professional way things had been set up. There were floor plans and copies of the original blueprints, along with a detailed analysis of Tile's alarm system. There were typed single-spaced reports, profiles of the three bodyguards who were with Tile on a twenty-four-hour basis: shift workers who spent eight hours apiece with the man. The reports also stated clearly that the man partied with his troops; the bodyguards would have their defenses down. There was a list of the women Tile preferred, the young airheads he was screwing almost daily since the death of his wife and his decline into mob disfavor. Jimmy read them, stuffed everything back into the briefcase, and left without shaking hands. That was all right with Tommy. As long as the man agreed to do the job quickly, letting Tommy know when it was going to happen, it didn't matter if they were kissing cousins.

He watched Jimmy leave, thinking. Should he send someone to do the other piece of work for him, the second part of his deal with the Lion? No, if he did that, the men he sent would want a piece of the action for themselves. This was his baby, his deal with DiLeonardi, the one that would finally drag him out of the minors and into the big time. It had to be all his, because when he moved up, he wouldn't be taking any of these tattooed retards with him. They couldn't make it in the fast lane.

No, there would be a certain level of risk, but he would have to do the job himself. In order to ensure his initiation into the outfit ranks, it would have to be he alone who carried out the second part of the Lion's instructions. He would whack out Frank and Jimmy Vale all by himself.

The first stop for all state prisoners in Illinois is the castle out at the Joliet Correctional Center. There, they receive a week of R&I—Reception and Indoctrination. During that time they are lectured as to the evils of homosexuality and gangs, given physical and psychological evaluations, and assigned to one of the penitentiaries according to their age, severity of their crime, and the amount of time they had to serve. After going to Stateville, Jimmy had gotten a look at his psyche evaluation.

The doctor had written that he was a sociopath. This word was unfamiliar to Jimmy. It intrigued him. He looked it up in the dictionary and found out that the doctor thought he was a psychopathic personality whose behavior is devoid of guilt. He even went to the prison library and got books, case studies of sociopaths. He learned about people who fit in anywhere, lied constantly, and would, while smiling, cut your heart out if they thought no one was looking. They figured, from what Jimmy read, that everyone else was like that, too.

Until that time, he had always figured shrinks to be pretty smart, almost magicians. After reading this, though, he decided that they were idiots.

No one who had ever known him would understand, because he hid it so well, but Jimmy's motivating emotion was guilt.

Which was why he had to leave his mother's house. He knew it was a waste of time, knew that if he let someone make him feel that way, then that person had power over him. And no one, ever, could be allowed power over him. But that didn't mean he didn't carry the stuff inside him.

It was always there, deep in the back of his mind but not so far back that he wasn't aware of it: If he'd been a better boy, his father wouldn't have gone to prison to escape the family life and his mother wouldn't have become a drunk. Closer in time, if he had been on guard, hadn't been shocked to see Bill Bender on his knees in front of Chaney, had reacted immediately and violently, Michael Knox might still be alive.

Frank, too—there was him to consider. Frank's own sense of guilt had driven him to put aside half of all the money he'd stolen in the past nine years for Jimmy. Frank had squirreled the money out of his accounts, a little at a time, over a period of months, so Jimmy could see it all at once, be overcome with emotion. Then do whatever he wanted to with the cash. It was Frank's way of paying him off. The clothes, too—there were a few grand tied up in the threads Frank had bought for him.

All because Frank had tossed him and a couple of his buddies a bone; had sent them out on a score that he himself wouldn't waste his time with. They'd gone out and the couple had been home and ba-boom, right to the joint for Jimmy.

The shrink had asked him, nine years ago: "Why do you steal?" And Jimmy had told him: "For money." The shrink had written his report based on the information he'd received. But he should have been smart enough to know that a man like Jimmy would never tell him the truth, would never say, "I stole to be like my father and brother." He felt that inside, was not aware that when he was stealing, he was really trying to win their approval.

It seemed to him now that there were several different kinds of guilt, lesser guilts that grew off and branched out from the main and powerful source. For instance, he felt guilty taking Frank's money and clothing. No sociopath would feel that way. After reading the reports, books, and case studies, Jimmy concluded that there were a hell of a lot of people of his acquaintance who were afflicted with that particular mental illness. The prisons were filled with them. Guys who would rip off their partners, kill them for their share of the take. Jimmy looked at these people, all these wise guys doing time thinking they were hustlers and winners, and he put up his emotional wall, allowed nothing that he did inside to breach the bricks. He saw young men who didn't build that wall, who trusted other cons and tried to play the game in accordance with their outside values, wind up being somebody's butt-bitch, wearing mascara and lipstick, most of the time winding up hanging from a shower pipe. No, the strong survived in prison, not the weak, not those who tried to make it with outside moral standards.

Now, released, though, it was a new ball game. Originally he'd planned to go see his mother, ask her why she hadn't written. That scenario had been formulated in his mind, behind the walls. Once outside, though, it had changed. If she'd been sober, if she hadn't been so goddamn hateful, he knew he would have helped her. But she had been the same old Ma, wanting to know before she did anything what was in it for her. And now a guilt feeling, lessened in intensity, was there inside him. No matter what she was, she was still his mother.

And his father—how did he feel about that? It was obvious to him, the fact that Tile had murdered their father was the hook that had been used to bring Frank and Jimmy into the score. The other mob guys and Jacobi would believe that the two of them would jump at the opportunity to even the score, to reap revenge.

Their father would be a part of it. A small part, maybe. But Jimmy would be doing it for another reason, too. To free himself from the chains that had wrapped his soul. It was all well and good that Frank had given him the money and the clothes, for whatever reasons. But Jimmy had to do things for himself. No matter what their mother might be, she had still raised them. Then Frank had always been there for him, when he was free. Right after that the state had taken over, feeding and clothing him, putting a roof over his head. He didn't know how much damage his mother and the state had done to him, or which, in fact, had been worse. But he knew he couldn't go through life taking everything Frank had to give.

He had the blueprints, the floor plans, the alarm system, and the profiles of the bodyguards in the briefcase on the car seat next to him. He left them there as he ran into Frank's house—which was blessedly empty—and down into the basement. He went into the hiding hole, opened the cash box and removed two stacks of hundreds, fifty thousand dollars' worth. He locked the hiding place back up, left the house, and drove to his mother's house.

She answered the door on the first ring as if she'd been awaiting his return. He handed her the money and she took it without hesitation.

"We're even now," Jimmy said, with his mother looking down at the money, not hearing him. "I owe you nothing." Jimmy spoke the words and turned on his heel, leaving her forever, hearing the slamming of the door as his feet touched the sidewalk.

The leaves on the branches of guilt pulled themselves in some, dying on the vine. Killing Mike Tile would square things with his father. Taking down the score would even things up with the Brotherhood, put him at rest with them. That left Frank. He would leave Frank his money, less the fifty grand, and the clothing, too, would stay. The only way he could feel right in his mind about leaving behind the city, the guilt, and the emotional ties that were choking him was to perform the score, from inception to conclusion, entirely alone. Do it and then everyone who had ever done anything for him—his father, his mother, his brother, and his gang—would have been paid back, and he could go away somewhere and learn how to live. The state, he figured, could kiss his ass. He'd paid his debt to them.

At six that Thursday evening he drove to the North Side, parked the Caddy in a manned lot and, with his pocket full of money and new threads on his back, made his way to December's Mother. He could have a few inside him, be feeling warm and relaxed, before he would ask the bartender whether he thought Vera would be stopping in that night.

Chapter

TWENTY-ONE

The appealing thing about being a thief, in Frank's mind, was the fact that he was getting over on the whole, entire world. All of his life, for as long as he could remember, there had been a sense of retaliation after robbing some fat rich happy bastard who'd had it all handed to him on a silver platter. He would read the papers after a caper, listen to the radio and TV newscasts, reveling in it when there was mention of the "ingenious" robbery, or when the victim was portrayed as an "heir" to something. He loved stealing from heirs, from people who'd been given their possessions.

He had once told Tina that his father had never given him anything except a bad name, and he'd meant it, had said it without rancor or self-pity. She told him that the coldness in his voice frightened her, and he'd changed the subject, went back to something safe, putting the Iceman on hold until he was needed.

He would take from the heirs, from the rich, loving every second of it, from the first germ of an idea; when one of the insurance men called him and told him about some idiot who was overinsured and underprotected; when he would read in the paper about some other rich stiff who had acquired a priceless piece of art, and he decided to look into the man's affairs; when Adalebo or one of the rare other men he trusted came to him with a score that looked good, until the very end, gloating over society's concern over his work, the media announcing the fact of his theft to millions of people, he loved it all and felt no remorse.

Instead, there was a bitter glee, *I told you so* imprinted in his mind. Frank was somebody, and was telling the world through his anonymous vehicle, thievery. How good it made him feel, taking from them, from the people who had taken so much from him. Robbing the sort of people who were on the board of directors at the reformatories he'd spent much of his youth inside of, the falsely gruff, hearty liberal types, with their soft fat bodies stuffed into expensive suits, rubbing his head on Sunday and letting their own children play basketball with the "residents," trying to show their kids how good they had it, maybe even trying to make them street-smart by allowing them to rub elbows with the lower classes. Self-important goofs. These men always had the same attitude, snotty and superior and condescending, always telling him things. Letting him know how lucky he was to have their attention all the time, telling him constantly who they were, how important.

Frank played their game, lapped it up like a puppy dog, because here were adults actually paying attention to him; he took it and loved it until he was old enough to see it for what it was, until the day he *did* compare himself to a puppy dog that would take all the kickings and beatings the master handed out, because now and again the master would scratch the dog's ears.

Now he stole from them, showed them what he thought of them and their values, their beliefs in a system that Frank had known to be corrupt and phony since he was old enough to run. He did it, and it had made him a rich man, but his greatest joy came from the knowledge that he'd scared them; that, for maybe even only an hour or two, until they could get a new, tougher alarm system installed, he had shaken them up, violated them, left them trembling and asking themselves the question: What if we'd been home? He was putting them on notice, telling them that the little boy they used to talk down to was now here and someone to be dealt with, someone who had the power of life and death over them and who had no qualms about using it. He wanted them uneasy, wanted them to have a moment of cold fear in their stomach every time they went to put their key in the lock, wondering if he'd returned. Wanted them, also, to stay up a little later at night, making sure they'd set all their alarms properly, thinking about it, with maybe a slight queasiness at the thought of his coming back, this time as they slept. He wanted them to know that they were his for the taking, at the moment he chose to take them. Wanted them fearing him, because it was the next best thing to respect, a respect a man like him could never earn in their world.

He'd spent his life instilling that fear, becoming the Iceman, the man who was a mystery to even his closest associates. He was a man with no friends, who thought he didn't need them. A man to whom love was just a word. A man who admitted to caring about no one except his younger brother, who'd been just as scarred, had suffered maybe even more, because Frank, at least, had gotten out of the home environment and into one in which the strong, like him, survived and prospered.

But now there was Tina, and everything else was changing.

He lay in his bed with his hands behind his head, a cigarette smoldering in the corner of his mouth. From time to time he would suck some smoke into his lungs and exhale it through his nose, moving his hand only to tap some ash off the tip of the thing. He was squinting at the ceiling, wondering.

"Do you hate your mother?" Tina had asked, and he'd told her no. To Frank, she just wasn't there anymore. "But think, Frank, really think about it. Maybe you're just trying to get her attention."

Just like Tina, to cut through all the bullshit. It was the only thing she had said that even hinted of psychoanalysis, but it had struck home. Maybe he *was* trying to get her attention, hers and the old man's and that of everyone else who had told him he wasn't good enough. There were things he blocked out, put a wall around and never thought about because if he did think about them he might have to go out and hurt somebody.

Like: Ma always saying that they'd had such a good loving home life, how she'd done all the right things and they'd just turned out bad on their own. Frank had asked her once if it had been by osmosis and she'd told him not to be a smartass, that their father's influence had probably done the damage. He couldn't argue that one, but when he thought of his childhood it was never with bitterness toward his father's being in prison, or because of the beatings. He would have to shake his head and clear his thoughts at such times, because the image that always came to him was of lying in bed, crying and biting his blanket, listening to the bedsprings getting a workout through the paper-thin walls, Ma entertaining some guy who'd usually be having a beer at the kitchen table in his shorts when Frank got up for school. The bastard would be introduced as their "uncle." Frank would bite his tongue, until, when he was fourteen, he had asked her if she was in the habit of fucking her brothers. He'd had to beat the shit out of his latest uncle, and it had been fun, Frank putting into his fists and feet all the rage that had been building inside of him through all of the years. Ma had put him out for the first time then, throwing his clothes out his bedroom window.

Like: His grandmother and the beatings she so self-righteously handed out, straightening them out, as she said. It was always that, or else, "I'll fix your clock." He'd take the beatings, stoically, never giving her the satisfaction of hearing him scream or cry. She was a real lover of attention, though, Grandma was. She'd once told one of his real uncles that Frank had talked back to her, and the uncle had taken Frank down into the basement, kicked the shit out of him and told him he would spill Frank's blood all over the walls if he ever talked back to his grandmother again. The problem was, Frank had never even thought about talking back. His frustration had overwhelmed him, and he had run away, stolen a car with some crazy idea in his mind about getting to New York. He had tried, often, to turn to his grandfather for help, but the old man seemed cowed by him, maybe even afraid. The geezer seemed so close to Jimmy, though. He really loved that kid.

To deal with it he'd blocked it out, put it in his mind that it hadn't happened. But he hadn't gone to his grandmother's funeral, he wouldn't even talk to his mother, and the only thing about his father's death that had affected him was the fact that the outfit had given him a free hand with his thieving; he didn't have to pay them a percentage. They must have figured it would be easier than trying to whack out the Iceman, who had become much more of a man than his father had ever been.

But in whose eyes? He could walk into any player's bar in the city, and the hoodlums, thieves, and fences would stare at him as he passed; he'd hear his nickname mentioned in whispers. He had the respect and fear of some of the toughest crooks in the city. But in Tina's eyes, what he did for a living didn't make him a man. It made him less than a man.

He had to ask himself: Whose opinion did he value more?

There was no contest.

He felt like a man who'd been blind from birth, never knowing colors, suddenly getting his sight back and seeing for the first time. As long as he kept his sight, everything would be all right. He could learn and watch and gaze at life in astonishment and wonder, maybe even getting used to it, as long as it stayed with him. Losing that sight, though, would devastate the man. Frank related to that idea, hung on to it, because he really had no idea what he was feeling. All he knew was he was feeling something he'd never felt before, and therefore had never missed. Now that it was here, the thought of losing it was beyond comprehension. The last day of his life had been hell on earth. Tina had decided for some reason to forgive him, to love him, as long as he was sure it was over; as long as he was no longer a thief. He didn't know why, any more than he knew what this thing was that had hold of him, but he was absolutely certain that he would do nothing to jeopardize this thing, to make her turn her back on him again.

Frank lit another cigarette off the butt of the last, crushed the stub out in the ashtray sitting on his chest. He was chain-smoking but the thought of taking a drink didn't enter his mind. Maybe it was because he didn't think anything he could drink would match the high he was feeling now.

Once the decision was made, to stop stealing, something had happened. He'd felt, suddenly, like a different man, like Jimmy must have felt last night when he'd walked through the prison gates. There was a lightness there, a giddiness. A sense of joy and well-being. He'd felt fifty pounds lighter. He let his mind run over the possibilities, over what he was losing. No more beatings in the basements of jailhouses. No more sleepless nights, wondering if he'd left some tiny bit of evidence behind that could put him away. No more wondering if some guy he'd made rich was going to turn him over to the police for some consideration in the future, or that one of the insurance men would get caught and turn state's evidence. No more looking over his shoulder. Christ, no more suffering.

Getting Ma's attention? Maybe. But suddenly he didn't want it anymore.

As the Iceman melted, it was with the realization that there was someone else in his life whose attention meant more to him than his mother's ever could. Tina, who was worth anything. Who was worth changing for. He didn't have any idea what he would do in the future, nor did he care.

He'd even kidded her about it, telling her that maybe he'd open a day-care center, play with little kids all day, and she'd told him that was a good idea, she'd bet he'd be good at it, and something else had happened then that hadn't happened in years. He'd felt a lump in his throat. "Really?" he'd said. And even though he'd said it in a wiseass way, that's about all that he could bring himself to say at the moment.

Frank snuffed out the cigarette and smiled, wondering if Jimmy was getting laid. He was glad that he'd been able to do his brother a good turn, set him up financially so he wouldn't have to go out, pull some cowboy shit that would land him right back in prison. He was a great kid and Frank loved him, but he just didn't have the heart for stealing; the talent wasn't there. He rolled over, snuggled his head into the pillow, thinking of Tina.

Frank Vale would never sleep the sleep of the innocent, but that night he came close.

Chapter

TWENTY-TWO

Giraldi sat in the basement of police headquarters, listening intently. He was the young cop, the new guy on the beat who had been checked out and allowed in, where he'd been tested and, he hoped, had passed. He was worried because it almost hadn't happened; his poor choice of words when he'd wanted his crack at a thief had nearly gotten him thrown out of the unit. He knew better now, and was paying attention as Roosevelt spoke, trying to learn something.

"So what this guy got, see, is this alarm system with the outside ringer, but it's also hooked up to a private surveillance system. Can you picture that? The guy's a piece of trash, a mob pusher, but his house is protected. What he didn't know was that the people who watch those screens for blips are usually kids, can't pass the intelligence test to work at the K-Mart. They sit there and sleep and shit, collect their paychecks and go home. Even when they notice a break-in, they got to call the house a couple of times, see if they can get ahold of the party lives there, before calling in the police.

"Well, this mob cat, this Colloto, he dumb about this but smart about other shit. He beat me and Gunon here in court last month, walked out of the courtroom on account of a bullshit procedural error. Man walks down the aisle with his lawyer, smiling, tells us

on the way out: 'Better luck next time.' Forgot who he was
playing with. Now usually, we leave the mob boys alone behind
the cash they give us every month. But we had to send a message,
see, to Mike Tile, who suddenly lives in a mansion in Winnetka
and don't give audiences to the law no more. We had to tell him if
they was gonna get into drugs like they been doing, then they had
to up the ante. There's a lot of heat involved, you understand—
feds wanting to know why we ain't stopped these guys. A couple
of his top guys wind up in the state joint, instead of one of the
federal country clubs where they usually go, he'll maybe take the
hint.

"Just for the hell of it, last night, I'm passing by Colloto's
house and just happen to have a couple of kilos of highly watered-
down smack in the trunk, a big plastic bag of it inside of a plastic
evidence bag. Shit so stepped on, it's barely illegal. I notice no
lights on inside, so I drive to the Seven-Eleven on a Hundred-and-
seventh, give him a call, get an answering machine. I go back,
knock on the door, nothing.''

Roosevelt paused to sip his coffee and Giraldi looked at Gunon,
whose eyes were wide with excitement. Gunon stared back at him,
pointing his finger and grinning—Look at this guy—making sure
the rook was paying attention to the game that had been going on
since the beginning of organized police departments. The old-timer
bragging on himself and teaching the new guy the tricks of the
trade.

"I got to figure one thing. With the lawyer this man got, I can't
be calling Gunon or yourself. They say we set him up on account
of losing his ass in court last month. It'll look better, you understand, if I do it alone. I don't live two blocks from this guido—I
got reasonable cause to be in the neighborhood. I take the dope out
of the evidence bag, the portable radio out of the glove box, and I
go out back, smash a window, and as soon as the siren goes off I
call it in to the precinct, demand backup, then kick down the door
and make my lawful entrance.

"But see, I don't just stand there with the smack in my hand,
waiting for the squaddies. I do that, it'll look funny. What I do,
see, I go over to the bedroom, throw the bag under the bed, let the

bluesuits find it in their reasonable search of places burglars may be hiding. When they pull up I'm back in the kitchen, my badge out and above my head, the pistol in my other hand. We make a sweep of the house, one of the guys finds the dope, and that's it. They decide someone's gonna have to sit there and wait for Mr. Colloto, ask him what the heroin was doing under his bed."

"They got a case?"

Gunon shrugged. "Depends how they play it. Colloto comes in, he'll go apeshit—what are the cops doing in his house, why are his window and door busted. Investigating officer will have to play it cool, tell the man they responded to a burglary-in-progress call, without mentioning Rosy's name. The dope, all the man had to do is say that the bed it was found under is his. Then we can reasonably assume that anything found under the bed is his, too. It's up to the judge now."

"But they got enough to bust him?"

"Class X," Rosy said. "Man's looking at fifteen in Stateville. Feds talking to him right now, trying to get him to roll over."

"He won't talk," Gunon said.

"Don't matter," Rosy said. "The man gonna be in-con-ven-ienced. Gonna cost him a lot of money for his fancy lawyers, and if we get a break and he don't win this one for a change, can you imagine one of these guys in the state joint, locked up with the brothers and the meskins they made junkies out of? They'll have his tough ass wearing Barbie-doll clothes inside a week, pass him around as a two-smoke blow job."

"Jesus," Giraldi said.

"Live and learn, kid."

"So what do we got up for today?"

"We got to go down to the South Side, bring in some of the Insane Unknown Nation. Mayor wants to look tough on gangs before the February primary."

"What are we gonna charge them with?"

Gunon said, "We'll think of something."

They walked past the commander's office on their way out, Giraldi noticing that the man was deep into a telephone conversation, huddled over his desk. Looked bad again, today. A drunken commander, and corrupt co-workers who didn't think twice about entrapping suspects or killing thieves. He wondered what he had gotten himself into.

Which was the same thing Ed Ryan was thinking. His head was killing him, the cigarettes were making him nauseous, but he kept lighting one after the other, trying to get back to his normal state of feeling: numbness. He was speaking to the group leader of the units on the West Side, a tough black man who had led his totally black units with complete autonomy. They were in a different world out there, a different culture that played by its own rules. The PRICCs all *had* to be black, because there were no white faces in its target area. This was where the action really was, on streets where lawlessness was the norm. Jackson's units would bust heads, kick ass, do as they pleased and get away with it because it was expected. The criminals were for the most part the only people in that part of town who could afford telephones, and they weren't calling OPS to complain. It was a section plagued by almost total unemployment and a terribly high drug-addiction rate, a place where they settled traffic disputes at gunpoint. Jackson was technically one of Ryan's subordinates, but that fact was mostly ignored by the men. What Jackson and his five men really were, in Ryan's opinion, were psychos with badges. He listened to Jackson's report, sadly, because if any of the eighteen men in the PRICC units were to beat the case, it would be these six, because although Ryan had evidence on them it was, with the exception of their political blackmail, mostly circumstantial. Even if they did get convicted, it would be for relatively small-potato stuff, and the men would do their time, having literally gotten away with murder.

He could hear someone screaming in pain in the background, and gruff black voices shouting angrily, mixed in with the sounds of crying children. Jackson had found seven pounds of crack and wanted to know if they should bring it in or sell it. The commander's decision had to be made in accordance with the number of PRICC arrests made that month.

Ryan watched the local unit file out, saw Giraldi stare in at him for a second. There was something funny about that kid. In the three months that he'd been there, he didn't seem to fit in. He frightened Ryan, with his eagerness to step in and do damage to that thief the other day—what was his name?

Ryan didn't have time to think about it. He'd stalled Jackson long enough that the man would believe he'd shuffled through reports, looking for answers. He told Jackson to bring the dealers in, all seven pounds of the crack, too. Told him he would make his units look good on the report.

He hung up and checked his watch, saw that it was almost noon. The South Side unit should be in place by now, about to film the two lesbians. Jesus Christ, what a job this was.

Adam Lebeaux awoke early on Friday afternoon, feeling good. Frank had given Lockhart the go-ahead to sell the jewels himself— the man being paranoid again, still not trusting good ol' boy Wayne. And today, in less than an hour, the hillbilly was bringing two thirds of the sale to Adam's house.

Ads sat up in bed and smiled, watching Dee-Dee clean the apartment, amused because his woman cared about what a ridge runner like Wayne and his whore old lady Angel thought of them. Dee-Dee was wiping down the mirror in the bedroom, giving it a good cleaning, her ass shaking fine and pretty there in the tight white shorts she was wearing.

He watched her, proud because she wasn't with him for what he could give her, although he gave her a lot. Nor was she there as an act of rebellion against her family. The fact was, she wasn't a brother-lover at all; she just loved him.

He shifted and she turned, smiled at him guiltily. "I wake you up, honey?"

"Why you cleanin' the bedroom? You figure Angel want to maybe turn a few tricks while she here?"

Dee-Dee laughed the way a woman will when making fun of someone who's not around to hear it. "You better get in the john now, Ads. I'm gonna hop in the shower in about two minutes."

Adam got out of bed and put on a floor-length wine-colored

heavy robe, slipped a thick gold chain over his head. Twenty-four carat, it spelled his name—ADAM—in heavy lettering.

When he got out of the bathroom he went straight to the second bedroom, where they kept the television.

He was happy now, almost high from the videotape he'd paid ten grand for the previous night. A little steep maybe, especially seeing as how the print quality wasn't that hot, grainy and shaky, but still, it was worth it for what the tape held.

In his robe, Adam sat down and poured coffee into a cup, from a carafe Dee-Dee had placed on the end table—his fine white woman knowing damn well what he'd want to do while waiting for Wayne—then lit a Kool and sat back, hit the buttons on the remote.

The screen came to life and it was obvious from the first frame that this was an amateur shoot. Whoever had shot it had done it from a concealed camera hidden inside a purse, a witness the state had allowed in to view the scene as it occurred. Adam would have loved to know how much the woman had been paid. He wondered if she got a flat fee or if she was in for a piece of all the action. Probably not, though. What had probably happened was her man had made her do it, then had taken the tape from her and either paid her off with a good fucking or a slap, whichever he'd felt she had coming to her. He took a deep drag from his cigarette. The camera focused on a great big chair with something attached to the top of it that made it look, from a distance, like a beautician deal, the thing on top of beauty-parlor chairs that dried a head full of rollers.

There was movement now, coming from the left, and now the screen showed a man walking hesitantly toward the big chair. There was a man on either side of the guy, dressed in some kind of uniform. Adam wished this part of the film was in color. The man in the middle walked as if drugged, his head down, his shoulders shaking as he sobbed his way toward the chair. His head was shaved, and his right pantleg was slit to the thigh. The man turned and slowly allowed the other two men to lower him into the chair, looking at them with a pleading expression on his dog-ass face. Handsome guy but scared shitless. The guards ducked down and even with their backs blocking the camera from recording what they were doing, the viewers could tell they were fastening something around the man's legs. They stood, buckled leather straps around the man's arms.

The man's eyes were huge now, bugging out of his head as his lips moved soundlessly. Adam would pay another ten grand for a tape of just the soundtrack; the way it was, all he had was the picture.

Last night, when he'd viewed the tape the first time, he'd rerun this scene maybe a hundred times, moving closer to the screen to try to read the man's lips, see if he was praying or what. What he'd do, he'd ask Frank for the name of a lip-reading ex-con could be trusted, get him to tell him if the man was praying or cursing. He was crying, that was for sure.

Engrossed, Adam leaned forward, the cigarette ash growing long between his fingers, falling off onto the carpet. He watched, enthralled, as the guards stepped back and another man came into the picture, some white stiff in a suit, the man saying something to the dude in the chair. The guy in the chair spoke for a time, his head down—even a lip-reader couldn't help Adam here—then lifted his head, the tears streaming now, forming little puddles on his shirtfront.

The stiff in the suit stepped behind the chair and put a leather eyeless mask over the dude's head, with a little bare patch through which you could see the top of the dude's skull. Then the guards came forth again, this time attaching little electrodes first to the top of the mask, on top of the man's skull, then to his exposed right leg. The big thing that was attached to the top of the chair was placed on top of the dude's head, then screwed on.

The guards stepped back, the sucker in the suit gave a signal, and the fun began.

The body in the chair was lifted up again and again, like he was coming and trying to stand up and shout about it, his hands clenching the chair's wooden arms, so hard Adam thought the arms might crack. Again and again the man was lifted and thrown back down, the cords in his neck sticking out looking ready to burst out of the skin, over and over for maybe two full minutes.

Smoke began to come from the top of his skull and from the leg, where the electrodes were attached, not billowing, just kind of wafting up, as if the man's skull and leg had a cigarette attached to them.

Suddenly the dude collapsed in the chair, deader than shit.

Another guy came into the picture, this one with a stethoscope around his ears. He opened the dead man's shirt, checked his heartbeat, then stepped back and checked his pulse. He nodded his head, put his equipment in a little black bag, then wrote something down on a note pad.

The screen went blank for a few seconds while the director did some splicing and editing. When the picture came back on it was in color this time, with sound, obviously recorded from a much better camera.

The scene was outside a Florida prison, the time early morning, the mood of the large assembled crowd festive. There were cheers and hillbilly bellowing as the ignorant sons of bitches saw the camera pass them, people waving and yelling at the camera, shaking their handmade signs at the cameraman. BURN BUNDY BURN! a lot of them said. Real original. One of them was pretty good, though, some college-age kid holding up a sign that said BUNDY'S LAST MEAL? TOAST! Adam kind of liked that one.

The camera panned to the hearse that took the dead body of Ted Bundy away, and the crowd cheered as the vehicle exited the prison. Adam hit REWIND, and watched the crowds cheering again and again, waving their hands and placards.

This grouping of society was where the real show was.

As a kid, he'd instinctively known enough to respect the law. His daddy, who took no shit from man nor beast, always lowered his voice when the Man was around, and that was enough to teach the young Adam what he needed to know.

They would stop him on the street for no good reason and he would call them sir and officer, not yet a teenager and getting hassled because he was black, not yet old enough to resent it. He figured the po-lice treated everyone that way. They'd call him

Wilbur and he'd try to tell them his name and they'd laugh at him, see him as stupid, tell him that to them, all niggers were Wilbur. It wasn't long before he was told that Wilbur was their Officer Friendly way of calling him Willy.

In the winter, for a laugh, the task force guys would make him take his shoes and socks off, make him stand there freezing on cold city concrete while they casually searched his stockings for drugs. He would hide his resentment, acting afraid and bowing down for them, knowing the pain they could cause him if he in any way balked at their treatment.

But he began to hate them.

By the time he was in his mid-teens, still without a police record, Adam had become totally sensitive to humiliation, his own and that of others. When he saw on the news the story about the man who'd murdered the bus driver because the man had "got into my face," he could understand it totally. When you go through life with nothing, the little you have means everything.

Which was why he'd beaten the man to death, the one who'd called him a nigger. Adam had killed in passion, with rage blinding him to any vision of a bleak future due to his actions. He'd killed in passion once, then less passionately two other times in prison, when the situation arose where it was do them or have them do you.

The first time he'd seen a dead body inside, it had been his roommate's, the sucker having hanged himself off metal bars surrounding the high window of the cells in Attica. The dude had swung there, back and forth, his tongue out, his face purple, eyes bulging, and Adam had played with his dead flesh, pushed his finger into it, marveled as the white spot stayed there instead of going away. He'd smoked cigarettes, looking at the dead white man hanging, pushing him back and forth with his foot, watching him sway, then, bored with it, had rolled over and gone to sleep. He'd told the hacks later that he'd heard nothing and seen nothing, and did not even try to explain the cigarette burns on the man's legs.

For a time after that, they'd had him in a padded room in the psycho bin at Ward's Island, where he had a good time messing with the minds of the other "residents." The shrinks, though, they'd seen through his rap, although he'd been mostly honest.

"Why do you hate society?" they'd ask him, and he'd tell them it was because society had slapped his brain in the face.

He liked Ward's Island better than Attica, but had no choice other than to go back when he'd been judged sociopathic but clinically sane.

But he'd never go back again. No, fuck a whole big bunch of that. Prison was not in his future.

In Attica he'd grown quiet and thoughtful, become a predator rather than the reactionary he'd been all his life. Letting white motherfuckers push his buttons. He'd got out and come home to what, to society? A society that cheered when one of its members got fried in the electric chair? Was this a society he wanted to be a part of, or owe a debt to?

Fuck a whole bunch of that, too.

He saw the citizens every day, and knew that guys like him and Frank and Wayne would die broke and starving without them. The hypocrites who built the prisons they threw the outsiders into. The same people who never asked questions when they bought a hot watch or color television. Who never felt anguish or remorse when they cheated on their wives or husbands, who rationalized their behavior away behind the idea that everybody does it.

The citizens who party while a man fries. Or the types he'd overheard bragging in a bar not a week back, two white working stiffs who fancied themselves players, going on about buying two caps of crack and trading it for coke whore pussy. One man laughing, telling his partner they didn't make enough money to buy that kind of desperate pussy. From young, hooked, drug-addicted black children who were trying to escape, maybe from cops who called them all Claricia. Victims of society in general and their unloving parents in particular.

These days Adam didn't care much for the society guys, like the old man he'd read about in the paper recently, the one who'd caught AIDS from going down on hookers all the time. High society, all right.

No, nowadays Adam was thoughtful; he watched and listened,

paid attention even to the bullshitters and the whoofers. He watched their actions, and made the appropriate adjustments in his attitude toward them.

He didn't have any use for society, and knew that the feeling was mutual—which was why he liked Frank so much, and now his brother Jimmy, a stand-up guy who'd done his time like a man. Even Wayne—he kind of liked that redneck asshole, after a fashion. As long as he didn't call him nigger anymore.

He heard the doorbell ring and rewound the tape all the way to the beginning, lit another smoke and eased back in his chair, putting his feet up. He made sure his robe was open wide enough so Wayne could see the gold chain around his neck, wanting to know if the man had learned enough not to comment on the thing. Probably Angel would want one for her own self.

There was a tap on the door and Wayne opened it. In the background, he could hear Dee-Dee gushing over the dress Angel was wearing, and he tried not to smile, wondering what it looked like, knowing it would show a whole big bunch of her whore's titties.

"Come on in, Wayne," Adam Lebeaux said, losing the battle and smiling. "There's something here I want you to see."

He'd show the tape to this hick before they got down to their business, see if the man could see the same things he did in it, although he doubted that he would. Society had never done much to this big dumb hunk of humanity; he'd brought it all upon his own damn self by being stupid.

TWENTY-THREE

Frank knew someone strange was in the house the second he opened his eyes. He rolled out of bed, fear gripping his spine, and lay on the floor, his hand tearing through the resewn fabric of the box spring, searching for the concealed pistol that he'd long ago holstered between the bedsprings. Found it, got to his knees and aimed the weapon at the doorway.

What was it that had wakened him? He tried to clear the cobwebs from his brain, fighting panic. He'd been dragged from a pleasant dream, where he'd been safe, thrust suddenly into a world that had PRICC coppers maybe racing up his stairs, coming to kill him.

No, there was no sound from the stairway. Cautiously, he got to his feet, the pistol pointing up, held next to his right cheek. He sniffed, then got it.

Perfume. He was smelling perfume, or bubble bath or something, a smell that was alien in this house. Would Jimmy be using bubble bath . . . ?

Frank dropped on the bed, relieved, smiling at his paranoia while at the same time grateful for it. If it had been the PRICCs, though . . .

He forced the thought from his mind, got back down next to the bed and put the pistol back, looking at the torn fabric, wondering if he should get a needle and thread, sew the torn ends together right now, then decided not to, not until he'd had his coffee, relaxed some. His heart had been jump-started and there was no way he could sew a straight line just yet. The cops would never find the seam, the tear he'd put in the box spring and had sewn over to hide the pistol, unless they came in the next half-hour or so. He figured they wouldn't be around today.

He dressed, sniffing the air: bubble bath, no doubt about it now, the scent hanging in the air heavily, with the heat from the shower giving it a muskiness that aroused him.

If he could get Tina to marry him, it was a smell he could get used to.

The woman was blond, naturally so—he could tell that because she was naked, standing in Jimmy's bedroom drying herself, checking herself out in the dresser mirror. The smell was stronger here, as he watched her, turning this way and that as she rubbed, probably looking for cellulite or dimples in her ass.

There wasn't much chance of that. She was put together, solid and stacked; no Tina, but for a bar pickup, prime stuff. She'd taken a bath in the john that had connecting doors to both upstairs bedrooms, and the smell of her bubble bath mixed in with the steam had been enough to wake him up, scare the hell out of him.

He didn't hold it against her, though, standing in the doorway admiring her. He was glad she'd decided to take that bath. This was a fine way to come to his senses.

"Oh!" The woman caught sight of him in the mirror and dropped the towel, stood awkwardly, her back to him, trying to cover herself in front, forgetting that he was getting an eyeful in the rear. On the dresser, next to her open suitcase-size purse, Frank could see an array of perfumes and—yes, there it was, Jean Naté Bath Bubbles—standing at attention, the woman attending to her morning toilette, using the drugstore she carried with her. There was a folded nightgown on the bed. She was obviously a woman who came prepared.

" 'Scuse me, honey," Frank said, pulling the door shut, grinning, wondering where the hell Jimmy had gotten off to. His second night home, he had no business leaving something this fine all alone, not even for a minute.

Jimmy was in the basement, passed out in Frank's leather chair. The plans to Tile's house were laid out on the pool table, the light left on above them. Page after page of detail were scattered around the plans, equally as important but for the moment taking a back seat to the designs themselves.

He'd picked up the woman Beth in the bar and had brought her home, done his business with her, but could not sleep afterward, his mind racing, wanting to get the job done and everyone paid off, no dues left owing. He'd come down here, a man alone, drunk and planning. He'd totally forgotten about Beth as he plotted, drinking beer from the refrigerator, studying the designs until the beer made him see two of everything, so he'd gone over to the chair and had settled down to close his eyes for just a few minutes, and the next thing he knew Frank was kicking at his feet, and he was opening his eyes, and Frank was staring down at him, angry.

"What the fuck is that," Frank said, pointing at the pool table, and Jimmy knew his brother wasn't referring to Beth.

The alderwoman, Janeese Tyler, always wore slacks, big wide trousers that covered her ever-green backside. She was light-skinned and grossly overweight, wore her hair in a big afro fifteen years after that hairstyle had gone out of fashion. It was her tribute to Angela Davis, who'd been her hero when she'd been in college. She was outspoken and loud, never a woman to hide her emotions, one who, due to those defects, hadn't been expected to go far in politics.

Her detractors had been wrong. She'd been right there in front, doing battle for underdog Harold Washington, who pulled the upset and was elected mayor against the odds, the machine, and most of the white politicians in the state of Illinois. And she'd been rewarded. When Washington had died, they'd had to drag her from the City Council chambers, cursing the Judases who hadn't waited for Harold to get cold in the grave before plotting to destroy his coalition. Even though the next two mayors disliked her, there wasn't much either man could do. One was white, and therefore gravely distrusted by her constituents, and the other one had been the next best thing to white, a black man who did the white man's bidding. In the four and a half years that Harold had been in power, she'd grown into her own, and planned to hold the seat until she either gave it up voluntarily or, like Harold, died in power. In her mind there were worse ways to go. Black Power was her battle cry and the word around City Hall was that she was a cunt with teeth. She loved to hear that, as she saw herself as having more balls behind those teeth than any of those white motherfuckers who'd got the power back and were now trying to whine their way into the hearts of the black community with their "time for healing" bullshit. She'd give them something to heal. To her, it wasn't about politics or power. To her, it was a matter of pride and honor, of race, and there wasn't enough money in the Cook County Democratic fund to make her vote for or against something she felt wasn't in the best interest of her people.

Her lover for the past seven years had been Hattie Grace, a preacher woman whose husband had been worse than evil, a good-for-nothing philanderer who drank and gambled, chased women until Hattie's old man had gone down the way of Washington, dying of a massive heart attack, but without Harold's dignity. Instead of dying in his office, Hattie's husband had died in a cheap motel room in the arms of a young prostitute who'd climbed out from under his no-good ass, emptied his wallet and stolen his watch and car and headed for God knew where. Janeese had pulled all the strings she could, stopping the scandal before it started, helping a friend of the people, one who fed the young black babies and the aged. It was the least she could do, and when the friendship became a little more intimate, well, was she supposed to turn it away?

At first it had been easy, when Harold had been alive and a week didn't go by where either Janeese's or Hattie's picture wasn't in the paper with either Harold or Jesse, but now that he was gone and the white devil was back in power, things were a little bit harder.

For instance, the press no longer turned their backs on the private lives of black politicians, now that they knew that the man on the fifth floor wouldn't have their ass if they wrote things they weren't supposed to. First, they'd started on Janeese because she wouldn't repudiate Minister Louis Farrakhan, whom she adored, and to a lesser degree because she was still a dear and loyal friend to Reverend Al Sampson and several other of Harold's close friends who were now treated like pariahs in city government. All they needed, all they had to do was get a breath of the truth, that she and Hattie met in motel rooms several times a week to physically express their love for each other, and God alone only knew what would happen.

At the very least, the homophobic black community would castigate her, and Hattie's church would either have to find a new leader or fall apart. It wasn't like some Southern honky television ministry, where you could fuck around on your spouse and get forgiven by telling other white fools that God said you had been. On the South Side and the West Side, once you were a black icon revered, you had no business stepping off the pedestal, unless of course you were a black man cheating on his wife; then they would maybe turn their heads. But to be a lesbian? No, Chicago wasn't ready for that yet.

So it had become Janeese's habit to make all the plans, the reservations, always in places where her trusted gay male secretary could pick up the key in advance and turn it over to her. She always called Hattie from a pay phone, to Hattie's secure line at the church, not trusting that her political enemies wouldn't tap her own phone. A church phone, though—wouldn't it be nice if their white Irish asses tried it one time? She could topple the entire administration if she could prove one of them had tapped Hattie's line.

What she'd do was: get there early, park as close to the room as she could, and, with a shower cap on her head and dressed in old clothes, wearing shades, would check out the room, waiting for up to an hour, sometimes more if she could get away. Give her time to take a nice hot bath, soak and get ready for her Hattie.

Today she'd come in, and had immediately sensed something amiss. She didn't let it show, didn't act afraid or cautious, but she let her eyes wander the room as she turned on the TV and sat on the bed, forcing herself to smile.

There was a clock on the wall. One of the big black round ones they used to have on the school walls when she was a little girl. A Seth Thomas, hanging there looking out of place, above the TV where you could see it from anywhere on the bed.

She got up casually, adjusted the volume on the set, then stood and looked at the clock, checked it against her watch. She tapped her watch, shook her wrist, looked at the clock again.

The second 1 of the number 11 was opaque black glass.

Oh, goddamn.

There was a camera in there, she was sure of it. The question now was, what should she do about it?

To give herself some time, she went into the bathroom, tore the San-a-Strip from the commode seat and sat down.

Okay. Someone was watching her. As of now, they had nothing. She could get up and walk out of the room, get into her car and drive away, and no one would come calling, looking for money or favors.

That was some shit she couldn't let happen.

Hattie wasn't here, so she was safe. If it came down to giving in or letting them expose Hattie, there was no contest. She would resign and find someone to take a contract out on the motherfuckers, get the film and burn it. But Hattie would be all right, so now it was decision time.

She sat on the toilet, her face in her hands, thinking.

Had she marched in Selma to back down, ride and hide the first time some cheap peeping Tom put his shit in her room? Had she gone against the machine, fought them all to help put together a coalition that swept Harold Washington into power not once but twice in her lifetime, just to back down now that they were trying for some paybacks? Had she stood up as a woman and a black and

222

spit in their faces all these years just to put her tail between her legs and run because some pervert put a camera on her? On the floor of the City Council she would have given an eloquent answer to these questions, one befitting her status and authority, one conveying her sense of dignity and self-worth, her pride. But here and now, sitting on the commode in the toilet of a South Side motel room, she answered herself in a less articulate but no less expressive way.

Fuck no, she told herself. She sure as hell hadn't.

Janeese flushed the toilet and washed her hands, watching her face in the mirror, determined not to give herself away before the proper time was at hand. She smoothed her clothing, patted her shower cap, and left the bathroom, not even glancing toward the clock.

She walked to the bed and sat down, checked her watch again, said, "Shit!" with feeling, then grabbed the ice bucket off the dresser and began to walk away from the bed. She stopped and picked up her purse, almost as an afterthought, then casually left the room.

As soon as she was out in the hall she began to run, down to the lobby and to the pay phones against the far wall. She took quarters out of her purse, racking her mind for the numbers of loyal black supporters within the state police. City police would be no good in this case. Hell, she'd give up her seat if those bastards watching her weren't on the city force. She made contact with one, then called in a favor owed by a man in the United States attorney's office. She looked at the last quarter in her hand thoughtfully, then slammed it into the slot. This was no time for equivocation; it was a time for war, and all wars needed generals. A man's voice answered on the other line and Janeese put all the strength she could muster into her voice and said, "This is Alderwoman Tyler. I need Jesse, now, mister, so don't fuck around with me."

"You ever hear the expression, 'We're twenty-four and seven,'" Frank?" Jimmy spoke the words through the haze of hangover, desperately wanting a glass of water, or better yet a Pepsi. Too, he had to move. He could feel the leather under him, his ass stuck to it from his sour sleep-sweat, could smell his staleness. He stared at Frank hard, then made his move, got up and walked to the fridge, took out a bottle of Coke and downed it in one pull. He got another one out, opened it, and walked back to the chair feeling better. On level ground again.

"It means you don't walk the fence. You're behind someone twenty-four hours a day, seven days a week. You don't talk about them when their backs are turned, and you don't listen to anyone *else* talk about them."

Frank wasn't hearing him. "Don't lay your jailhouse bullshit on me, Jimmy. The smart guys don't go to the joint."

"Only dummies like me, right?"

"That's right. It's where you wound up, and where you'll be again, real soon, you go after someone like Tile. Jesus Christ, where's your brains, in your ass? I come down here and there're timetables on my pool table, the guy's name everywhere, you got some bimbo upstairs probably seen Tile's name on these things, wondering how much coke she can score if she turns you in to the fucker."

"I never said shit to her."

"You were bombed—you said so yourself. How the hell you know what you said or didn't? What if she came down here right now, or worse yet, what if some *cops* came, with a warrant? Don't you listen? I told you what happened. Those guys'd come in here and shoot me as soon as look at me. You know how much they could get from Tile, selling you to them?"

"I fell asleep."

"Tile'll *put* you to sleep, you fuck with him."

"It's all covered, Frank, every base. I do the score, get no heat. Jacobi's in tight with Tonce DiLeonardi."

Frank slapped the Coke bottle from Jimmy's hand and the two men stared at each other, Frank standing right over Jimmy, holding the better hand. If Jimmy tried to stand up, Frank would have him. When Frank spoke, his voice boomed off the walls, but his eyes never left Jimmy's own.

"You tell me there's no heat. Who says so, Tommy fucking

Jacobi? That little Nazi piece of scum? You think he's tied in with the mob, for Christ's sake? He lied to you, you asshole! Get that through your head! DiLeonardi would no more tell that kid what was going down than he'd tell J. Edgar Hoover. Jacobi, good Christ. The same guy wanted me to give him a piece of my scores to protect your ass inside.''

"I'm doing it, Frank.''

"I got news for you, Jimmy,'' Frank said, breathing hard. "I ain't gonna let you.''

"You want to know why I'm gonna do it, Frank? Because this bastard, this Mad Mike Tile, he killed our father.''

Jimmy said it and stared triumphantly at Frank, the cat now out of the bag, the hole card up.

He was amazed when Frank looked right back and said, "So fucking what.''

Chapter

TWENTY-FOUR

J immy couldn't speak at first, stunned by Frank's words.

"What'd that old man ever give either one of us but an ass-kicking! What! I got scars on my ass *still* from him, the son of a bitch! The old lady too." He stalked away and kicked at the Coke bottle, punting it off the floor, hard. The heavy glass broke into tiny fragments as it shattered against the wall. "Shit!"

Jimmy's mouth was open, his lips moving without sound. He was suddenly acutely aware of everything happening around him: could hear the fizzing of the Coke as it formed a puddle on the tile floor; the light from the Budweiser sign above the pool table searing into his eyes.

And Frank, Frank there in vivid color, his face expressing his rage, beet-red and wide-eyed. The veins in his neck the size of pencils, sticking out clearly from his chest to his chin. Frank was breathing in gasps, trying to control himself, getting there by inches; in degrees.

Slowly, Jimmy got up out of the chair, staring hard at Frank. It was only with an effort that he convinced himself that he was not back on the yard, that this was his brother here, a man he owed.

But Frank wasn't going to make it easy on him. He spun on him as Jimmy walked toward him, fists balled and ready.

"What the hell have you done since you got home, huh? What!

You got drunk and you got laid. Did you stop at a restaurant, get a decent meal? Enjoy a good steak or a fucking spaghetti dinner with cheese? Did you? You've been out not forty-eight hours and you've got money, clothes, a place to stay and a goddamn Cadillac to drive. You're gonna throw it all away, go to the wall for some jagweed son of a bitch who'll dime your ass out in a second and put you right back behind those fucking walls! What, you turn into one of those guys who likes it in there, who can't wait to get back?''

Jimmy was advancing and Frank was holding his ground, moving now a little to his right so he could plant his feet and throw the haymaker when Jimmy got close enough. Jimmy could see this, watching Frank move in near slow motion, hearing it all with a buzzing sound following the words, like in the tin tunnel you would hear things from when you were tripping on mescaline.

"There some guy in there you can't live without, Jimmy?" Frank spoke the words softly, sarcastically, begging for the fight, and Jimmy stopped, staring at him, not feeling the hate anymore, now just wanting to get his papers, his plans, get the fuck out before he had to kill this civilian who didn't know shit about him or anything else.

"I just want to get the fuck out of your house, fuck the clothes, the money, man, fuck everything. And fuck you, Frank. I don't want nothing from you."

"Except for me to get my ass killed, saving your ass by pulling the score down for you and your goddamn tattooed asshole-buddies."

"Move on me, Frank, and I'll kill you." Jimmy spoke the words and turned to walk around him, his left hand stiff at his side, ready to strike it hard into Frank's gut if the man moved one inch toward him.

Frank swiveled, his fist going back, when they heard "Hey!" Both of them spinning toward the steps, where Beth was standing, her face puzzled, wearing the see-through silk blouse and the French jeans she'd had on in the bar the night before.

"One of you guys want to knock that shit off and give me a ride out of here? Christ Almighty . . .''

"Go ahead, Jimmy, give your girl a ride home. While you're gone, think about what I said."

The tension was broken and Jimmy was grateful. He didn't know how to fight except full-out, with intent to kill if he could, with maim for life being his only other option. He felt empty inside, his strongest emotion grief, because this man in his outsider's arrogance would never understand. He walked toward Beth, the puzzled girl shaking her head, another ignoramus, walking down into a pit with two lions, thinking she was safe because she knew she was a good person, figured life would give her a pass from harm because of it.

He put his arm around her shoulders, surprised because when it touched her body he could feel her calmness beneath it; the knowledge abruptly revealed to him that he was trembling.

"Family squabbles, huh?" Beth said, with an insider's knowledge. They were almost to the front door when she asked him, seriously, if there really was some guy in prison he wanted to get back to.

Ed Ryan snatched the phone up on the first ring, anxious, barking a sharp hello into the thing.

"You recognize my voice?" It was United States Attorney Drumwald on the line, playing spy.

"What the hell are you doing calling me here . . . ?"

"Shut up and listen. Everything's going up in smoke. Alderman Tyler just had three of your men pinched, in front of a South Side motel. And the pinch will stick. I just got off the phone with Jesse Jackson—he wants them charged federally for violating her rights. You're in as of *now,* mister. Now listen to me carefully. Get everything you've got, even the stuff you've dropped already, and bring it home."

"It's not here . . ." Ryan couldn't think. Everything was happening so fast. The boys on the lesbian blackmail stakeout had been caught, that was obvious, but God in heaven, why was this asshole telling him about it on a nonsecured line?

"Wherever it is, you get it, and you bring it to me right now, Ryan, before this becomes a fuckin' national news case. I've got to call a press conference, and you have to be here, or the credibility of the entire goddamn operation might go down the tubes. You hear me?''

''Give me two hours.''

''I needed your ass here two hours *ago*!'' Drumwald snapped the words and slammed down the phone.

With shaking fingers Ryan hung up, his mind racing. He could see the fix the man was in: Even after the press conference Tyler could claim that the white-racist U.S. attorney's office had been aware of such goings-on and had allowed them to continue while they investigated a case. He could see her, ranting that it was a plot against the black so-called Washington 21. He had to get the stuff, quick, and get it into Drumwald's hands, then help the man figure out a strategy to keep the integrity of their operation intact. Ryan hadn't spent this past year in terror to let it go down the tubes now.

There was also one other thing of considerable importance, a fact Drumwald hadn't mentioned. Without Ryan's testimony, none of the documents were proof of anything except the fact that the PRICC unit was bent. If the other PRICC cops found out what he was doing, they would kill him. Without him there to testify, to run down every phase of the operation before the jury, to convince them with his words and actions that he had indeed been working undercover, then the case would go up in smoke. Then someone like Tyler could easily argue—and maybe even prove to a jury— that the entire so-called operation was just a cover-up thought up by the feds and the white racists in the department after the fact. Ryan would be dead, and his name would be besmirched, and everyone would believe he was just another corrupt, crooked copper.

He couldn't allow that to happen.

The evidence was in the nonworking coal furnace in his apartment building's basement, the door shut tight and padlocked. He'd only gotten a little of the stuff out to Drumwald before he got paranoid and made him give up the cloak-and-dagger stuff the man had wanted to do from the beginning. That was okay if you were a sworn and safe member of the government bureaucracy, a politician. It didn't play so well if you were the undercover cop sweating out your every move. It was dangerous enough, getting the evidence. It had been just too much for him to try and turn it over every month.

He pushed himself away from the desk, lit a cigarette, tried to calm himself down before walking out into the squadroom. He was afraid to think of what the men would do if they even had suspicions of what he was about to do to them. The downtown crew was back, laughing it up in the back as they processed a bunch of gang-bangers, giving the punks a hard time. He could walk out of the office, go right past them in a hurry, and they might not even see him. He'd smoke his cigarette, first, give the nicotine a little time to steady his nerves.

Gunon took Giraldi on the side and showed him a blank sheet of typing paper, put the sheet on the desk and used his fingernail to carve the word LIE into the paper. He winked at Giraldi, walked back to the happy little group of sullen blacks who were hand-cuffed to rings set into the walls, guarded by Cletus Roosevelt. He handed the paper to Roosevelt, who took it with a grunt.

None of the blacks had mentioned civil rights or police brutal-ity, not when they'd been rousted off the street corner and not now. They were from the street, and knew how far sweet words like that would get them. Into the hospital or the morgue one, with a throwaway piece one of the coppers planted on them still in their hand. They knew the rules and knew how to play the game, never calling Roosevelt brother, hoping for racial compassion. In their minds, Roosevelt was as white as the other two coppers who'd pinched them. Knowing the rules, none of them said anything when Roosevelt told the tallest of the four of them to rise up on his feet.

The man did so, lifting his ass as far up as he could, the handcuffs that shackled his hands behind him restricting his move-ments. Roosevelt put the paper on the seat then told the man to sit back down. Gunon was smoking a cigar, blowing on the ash to make it grow longer, faster. Giraldi just stood there, trying not to look stupid. He was puzzled.

231

The black man sat down softly, as if trying not to crinkle the paper. Giraldi understood this. None of them sitting there helpless could know what would set the policemen off, make them go wild and beat them. To Giraldi, they looked the way he figured the slaves must have looked on ships three hundred years ago. Except these captives were dressed in Troop jackets with large red letters on the back of them, spelling out the initials of their gang, with cocked Fila hats perched on their heads, the bills facing their right sides.

Roosevelt said, "Are you with the Unknowns, Blood?" and right away the man shook his head.

"Lie detector can't measure your head, nigger. Answer me yes or no. You with the Unknowns?"

"No."

"Stand up."

He did and Roosevelt took the sheet of paper, handed it to Gunon, who was smirking. Gunon knocked the ash from his cigar onto the paper, rubbed it in with his finger, the paper facing the four black men. Clearly, the word LIE appeared, and the four men showed some emotion. Shock was what they showed.

"You lied to me, nigger!" Roosevelt's face was inches from the man's, his eyes wide and glaring.

"How the fuck you do that!" the man asked, shaken, and Roosevelt slapped him once, hard, across the left side of his face.

"You know what I do to niggers lie to me, boy?"

The phone in the commander's office rang, the extension hookup Gunon had rigged in their own office sounding off at the same time, and the black man was saved from finding out just what it was that Sergeant Roosevelt did to niggers who lied to him because Gunon said to him, "Your turn, Rosy, shit it's probably Blevins, wanting to know if he can make a copy of the lesbo niggers for himself, enhance his love life with the old lady."

It was about thirty seconds later that Roosevelt, his face showing terror for the first time since Giraldi had been in the unit, reappeared and said to him, "Let 'em go, Tony, all of 'em, right now, then get lost, take the fuckers back home, whatever you want, but disappear, you fucking hear me?" Then said to Gunon, "Get in here, man, right away, we got trouble."

*   *   *

Ed Ryan came out of his office calmly, another cigarette dangling between his lips. He needed to go to the bathroom, decided
to wait until he got home. Maybe even then he'd wait, go and crap
on the earth-tone carpet in Drumwald's office, that bastard, worrying more about the operation than about Ryan's ass. Hell, if the
man wanted to make a thing out of it for the cameras he could
mobilize some FBI agents, get them down here and protect him all
the way out.

He told himself there was nothing to worry about, he was the
boss, carrying a piece and in charge. There was nothing to worry
about right there in the basement of police headquarters, for
Christ's sake.

Then found out there was, when he saw Gunon and Roosevelt
standing in front of the stairway, blocking his path, their weapons
drawn and pointing at him.

"Commander," Gunon said to him, smiling, "don't make a
scene, you understand? If you make me kill you, believe me, then
you're dead; I ain't got nothing to lose. It's up to you how you get
out of the building. I ain't got *shit* to lose."

Looking at the drawn pistol, Ryan believed him.

Chapter

TWENTY-FIVE

Frank forced himself calm, angrier with himself than with Jimmy. What could he expect? The kid just finished nine years inside, goddamnit, he wasn't *supposed* to think straight. He went over to the refrigerator, got himself a beer, drinking on an empty stomach before breakfast. A day for firsts. He'd never argued with Jimmy before, either. They had always been united, standing together against a common enemy. He looked at the puddle of Coke on the floor, staining the tile. Fuck it.

It had always been the two of them, Frank feeling more like a father to Jimmy than a brother, the one who would jump into the old man's chest and divert his anger, take the ass-kicking rather than allow Jimmy to get hurt.

Jimmy, who'd gone from a sensitive, devil-may-care kid into the thing that prison had made him.

It sure wasn't going the way Frank thought it would.

He walked over to the pool table, cursing as his heel stepped down in the spilled Coke, leaving track marks as he walked. Thank God the little airhead had come down when she had, there was no telling where they might have gone if Jimmy had taken one more step. Frank had been prepared to strike out, level him one time, maybe knock some sense into his head. Dumb kid, listening to a zero like that asshole Jacobi. Taking the chance of either death or a return to prison if he listened to him too long, because there was no way on earth that Jimmy could take this score down alone.

Frank pulled some papers toward him, studying the layout as well as the written reports, the reports obviously professionally done.

Jesus Christ, look at this. Wireless infrared alarm systems on every door and window, even on the upper floors. A strong wind would bring the bodyguards running, Uzis blazing.

Prison was out of the question. If Jimmy tried to take this place down, he would die. My God, the carriage house out front had been converted into a fucking arsenal, the bodyguards sleeping and eating there when they were off duty. The on-duty guys ate in the house. There were four day servants in the joint, a small number for such a big house. Frank looked hard at the many pictures of the place, front and back, from both sides, marveling at the professionalism of the surveillant. Typed single-spaced reports told him what the pictures couldn't.

The pictures, though, told him plenty.

The place looked like a giant Taco Bell, with the red pipe roof, the white brick. The awnings over the windows were of the same material as the roof, right down to the color. Thirty-five rooms, with the back door leading right to Lake Michigan. The estate could not be breached from that side.

Or from the front, from what Frank could see.

What was Jimmy thinking of? He was looking to die, that had to be it, sitting down here drunk, figuring a way in. Shit, even for him, for the Iceman, this would be the score of a lifetime—if he could get in and out without getting killed.

He thought of a younger Jimmy, a tall skinny kid with acne, a boy who idolized his big brother, who wrote letters every night when Frank was in the reformatory.

Then saw the front of the estate, the cameras right out there in front of either side of the curved driveway, the only way in and out of the place. The drive made of staggered brick instead of pavement, circling from the ten-foot iron gate to the front of the house, then back out to Sheridan Road, so the big man could come and go as he pleased without ever having to put his car in reverse.

There were about four hundred feet of frontage, no trees or shrubbery, no place to hide if you made it over the fence. Unless you could hunker down and hide behind a blade of grass, there was plenty of that. In the picture there were ugly little trees on either side of the double-doored main entrance. But how would you get there?

There were cameras at both the entrance and exit gates, panning left, then right, never at the same time, never moving at the same rate of speed twice. There was no way to trick them.

He pictured it in his mind: Jimmy climbing the fence, maybe in a black sweat suit, seeing himself as a man on a mission, trying to flee his oppression. He'd said he didn't want the money, the clothes, the car, the place to stay. Wanted to make it on his own. Did he think those things were bribes, for Christ's sake? They were matters of honor, not payment for keeping his mouth shut.

The surveillance team that'd checked out the house had written in the report that one of them had approached the estate and had stood there staring at it, gaping, playing tourist. Within two minutes two men wearing sidearms had come to the fence and told him to move out, now. The man had told them that as far as he knew, it was a free country, giving them some lip so they'd know he was anything but what he really was. He'd wanted them to see him as ignorant, a man flirting with death and not knowing it.

They'd told him he had two minutes, or his free ass was going to get stomped all over Winnetka.

And Jimmy was going to go in there, was he?

In his mind's eye he wasn't seeing Jimmy as he was, the ex-con with the attitude, filled with hate. He was seeing the young guy, little Jimmy, getting shot down on the lawn by these guys. Twitching in his death throes.

The gate went all around the estate, down far into the lake, past the tiny private beach property in back. This area was overgrown with shrubbery, uncut. Through the shrubs Frank could see a small powerboat moored to the fence, looking new and well tended. That made sense. Even if Tile had degenerated half as bad as the street said he had, he'd be smart enough to have a getaway set up somewhere. The Chicago police wouldn't touch him; he paid too much for that. But if the feds got on to him and he didn't get the word from a friend in the Justice Department—and the mob had a lot of friends in the Justice Department—then he'd want a way to get out fast, as they were trying to beat their way past that massive fucking iron gate, with bodyguards shooting at them.

He saw the young Jimmy lying on the grass, his life draining from him, his body filled with bullet holes, his eyes filled with grief, passion, because at least he'd had the balls to try for his freedom.

The pictures of the rear of the estate had obviously been taken from a boat, from a great distance with a special lens. The close-ups showed him everything, but they were grainy, like the pictures you saw in the Italian porno books of famous American actresses, shot from the same kind of distance: the movie star naked, sunbathing by her pool at her villa near the Mediterranean; they'd shown Jackie Kennedy's breasts once. The old wooden steps leading down to the beach were overgrown with foliage, not used lately. From the color of the shrubbery he could guess that the pictures had to have been taken not long back, maybe September. A few weeks old. Current enough.

Someone had put a lot of effort into this score, wanting Tile dead bad. There was work here that would have taken Frank maybe three good months, right here in front of him, ready to be put to use. And someone had persuaded Jimmy to do it, and that would be easy enough; he could see how Jimmy had been convinced—they made it look so easy, all the setup work done. Just get in and do it.

Only Frank knew from vast experience it was never that simple.

He kept staring at the pictures, the floor plans already locked into his brain, ready to be taken out and looked at, at any time. Absently, he gathered all the typed pages together, a light beginning to shine in his mind, dim but glowing. Something about that shrubbery in the back of the house, the boat. The great expanse of blue lake between the boat and the house . . .

He pictured Jimmy lying dead on the lawn, cars whizzing by on Sheridan Road without noticing. The guards had their feet on his neck, as if standing there waiting for someone to shoot their picture. He pictured Tile coming out of the Spanish style house, smirking as he approached, brutally kicking Jimmy in the head.

Frank sat in his chair, chain-smoking, reading the pages again and again. The last page always grabbed him. From what Tile was paying out and from other sources, the report stated that it was a good estimate that at any time there was in excess of five million dollars in cash locked in the walk-in vault in the basement of the estate. And God only knew how much cocaine. It stood to reason. The place was virtually impregnable; Tile would feel safe, especially with his gangster's arrogance. He would want a huge amount of cash nearby, though, just in case the feds came calling. He'd have plenty of time to get his stash and split in the boat, never to be seen again, like one of the Miami Colombians, who'd post million-dollar cash bonds and take off in the night. Frank bet that Tile, in spite of his rumored insanity, had made some strong connections south of the border.

Five million cash, maybe twice that in powder. Jimmy would see it as his ticket to freedom. Or maybe just the spoils of war, the battle really being over their dead father. Jailhouse paybacks.

He had one last image of Jimmy, this time on the speedboat, his corpse weighted with chains. Two thugs were heaving him over the side, into the cold waters of Lake Michigan in October. His body went in with a splash, sinking down into the blackness, while the thugs laughed, with Tile looking on from his private beach through binoculars.

Frank set the papers aside and got up to call Adam Lebeaux.

"What're we gonna do with him now?" As Gunon spoke, Ryan felt a cold shiver race up his spine. They were in a safe house, one of the many places the PRICCs could hide out in, in times of emergency. It would have been just such a house that they would have brought the thief for killing, if Ryan hadn't intervened.

His hands were cuffed behind him, the links of the device threaded through the wooden rungs of the straight-back chair. His sweat-smell was making him sick, was at least one of the things contributing to it. These men were discussing his murder, but not in the greedy, passionless tones they had used when discussing the thief. No, they were scared, in a position they had never before encountered: stuck with the choice of letting him go with the knowledge that doing so would seal their doom, or killing him and taking that risk, too. Murdering a cop who was in the performance of his duties was a capital offense in Illinois, could get them the chair.

Roosevelt said, "I think whatever we do, we got to bring Giraldi in on it."

"He's too fucking new. We don't know if we can trust him."

"His phone's been nothing but social calls, or work calls to us. You think he's undercover? The fuck would the feds run *two* of them in on us? Besides, he give us the idea the other night, about staying with the hillbilly, didn't he? Wasn't it his idea? And didn't he want to beat on the thief? Take his turn with him? The boy was gonna try and take us down, he'd'a done it when we grabbed the four hundred K. Shit, he was ready to put the redneck in the river, wasn't he?"

"Who you trying to convince," Gunon said, "me or yourself?" He paused, reflected, then said, "It *does* make sense." Gunon looked at Ryan, his face showing his hatred. "You rotten cocksucker," Gunon said, softly.

Ryan shivered again.

Gunon said, "We bring Giraldi in, do this guy, then no matter what happens, he's in it with us, won't be turning over later. Nobody gets immunity when a cop gets killed."

Roosevelt said, "It'll bring him closer to us. Be one less thing to worry about. Maybe we should get him to pull the trigger."

"Get him on the phone," Gunon told Roosevelt.

Chapter

TWENTY-SIX

It was a bitch, walking the field all day with nothing to do. Tommy Campo strolled the prison grounds, wearing a cowled sweater with a pair of Minnesota 30 boots on his feet. The guy who'd sent them to him said the company guaranteed them to thirty below zero, no problem, money back if your feet get cold. It got that cold out here a lot, in the middle of nowhere.

He walked the field, ten circuits every afternoon, unless there was a yard of snow on the ground, which was the way it was half the year. A man who'd spent his life in a state of high excitement now with nothing to do for the rest of that life.

At the edge of the field there were yellow lines painted into the grass. Cross it, and you were an escaped federal prisoner. That was it, no barbed wire, no guard towers with armed hillbillys in them. A good place to do time, if you had an out date somewhere down that lonely paved Wisconsin road.

He would die in here. He knew and accepted that fact. The only thing that kept him going was the respect he still commanded, inside and outside of the joint. He could cross that yellow line, like a football player stepping out of bounds, and where would he be? Nowhere, that's where. An old man on the run who'd get caught then shipped to Atlanta, or, if the cops really wanted to get tough, to Marion, Illinois, the new Alcatraz.

No, this was how he'd spend his life, eating the good outside food smuggled in by the hacks on the take, stirring his simmering spaghetti gravy and filling their small cottage with good cooking smells, playing gin for cigarettes. And to think, at one time he'd been bigger than Mike Tile would ever be. Brought down by the one man he'd trusted with his life.

May that prick's grandchildren get cancer and die horribly.

It had been good to see the Lion, though. Good kid, even if he hadn't ever come visiting before. It had been a pleasure for Tommy, taking care of the small problem for him with the New York wise guy's second. Hell, they were brothers now, doing time together.

Tommy Campo kicked a rock out of his way, stopped and watched as the thing bounced across the line, into free country.

He started walking again.

He should be retired now, playing with his grandchildren, enjoying the fruits of his lifelong labors instead of in here, getting his nut kicking rocks like a kid, bored to death.

The visits broke up the monotony, the phone calls, too. He'd make them collect, talk for a time to people who suddenly got awe in their voices because he'd decided to call them.

He began to walk rapidly toward the administration building, his mind on calling Tonce DiLeonardi. See what was up with the Tile problem, give him his assurances that there would be no problem from the East Coast. Maybe make the kid's day for him, hearing from the old boss. There wasn't much that could be discussed over the prison wires, but if you knew how to talk the right way you could say enough, get your point across. He knew the Lion knew how to talk the right talk. Shit, hadn't he himself taught him how?

They were in the basement, two primitive men who were uncomfortable with emotions, trying now to express them. When Frank apologized Jimmy asked him if he'd ever said the words before to any man, ever, and Frank admitted that as far as he could remember, he never had.

The spilled Coke was washed up, the two of them sitting facing each other, Frank in his chair, Jimmy on a barstool. Neither of them was drinking.

"You'll die if you try that, Jimmy," Frank said, and Jimmy's face twisted in disgust.

"Not again, all right? It's gonna happen, Frank, it's as simple as that, and you're out of it. I'll take a few weeks, a month, checking it out, and then I'll do it. All the help I'll need I'll get from the Brotherhood. You weren't even supposed to see those fucking papers, for God's sake."

"The Brotherhood know how to deactivate alarms, do they, Jimmy? Bullets bounce off them, too?"

"Frank . . ." There was a warning implied in Jimmy's tone as he spoke the name. They heard the front door slam and Jimmy started, but Frank just sat there, smoking, unconcerned.

"Down here, Ads," he hollered.

"He got a key?"

"I trust him, Jimmy. He's my brother, too."

Frank was looking at him funny, and Jimmy wondered if Frank was trying to figure out how far he had taken the Brotherhood's line. He felt a small sense of shame, that his brother would consider him hateful toward any friend of his, no matter his race. And jealousy, too, because it was obvious Frank thought Adam a more competent thief than Jimmy. Well, that was probably true.

There was something here that didn't make sense, some unstated words that Jimmy was afraid to ask to hear. There was tension in the air, excitement. Danger? Maybe. Something was happening, and Jimmy was hoping in his heart—he'd long ago learned not to even try to bullshit himself anymore—that Frank was planning on giving him help on the score, maybe advice. At least he'd called Adam.

Who was now bopping down the stairs, a leather satchel in his hand. He walked, grinning, to Frank, unzipping the satchel as he approached, turning it over as he reached him, dropping banded stacks of bills in Frank's lap.

"Gift from Wayne, broham. For the jewelry."

Frank brushed the bills to the side of the chair, smiling.

"See anyone out there?"

"No heat for miles around, 'cept trolling squad cars down the Drive, looking to make some weekend cash from the speeders. Wouldn't have brought in the dough, there was any suspicion in my mind."

"See?" Frank spoke to Jimmy, who raised his eyebrows.

"What I'm saying is, this ain't the yard anymore, Jimmy. Watching your back isn't good enough. You got to watch the back, the front, both sides, above and under you at the same time, or it's all over, brother."

Jimmy didn't speak, resentment stirring because Frank was giving him a lesson in front of another man.

"You take the car, get over to a pay phone nowhere near this house, and call your friend, tell him to call you back from a pay phone. Tell him I'm in, you talked me into it." Frank held up a hand. "No, don't say anything yet. I know the way these guys think, what they'll believe. You don't. Tell him you talked me into it and we're pulling down the score two weeks from tonight. Give him a list of bullshit you'll need, sweet-talk him, convince him it'll happen then. Then get back here. In the meantime, I'll talk to Ads here, see if he wants in."

"Then you *are* in?"

"I won't let you die, Jimmy." Frank's voice trailed off, and Jimmy could have finished the sentence for him, knew what the man had almost said. He'd nearly said: "alone."

Jimmy stood, nodding his head. "All right. So it's set for two weeks then, right? You and me."

"You, me and Adam, if he wants in. But it won't be two Fridays from now, it'll be *next* Friday, if we do it, and none of them will be expecting it, not even Tile."

An hour later Tommy Jacobi was celebrating because the Lion had tossed the telephone book into his lap, letting him know his mother was off the hook. He'd earned it, too.

When he'd come in he'd been respectful, not like that last time, shit, what a mistake that had been. No, this afternoon he'd come in, let the man think he was being disrespectful because he'd dropped by without an appointment, but the news he had was so good it couldn't have been expressed over the phone. And the second he'd told the old man about how he'd hooked Jimmy and Frank into the score, the old man had given him his phone book back.

The Lion smiled at the kid, wanting him to know that he'd done the right thing, was now in favor. He got up, poured them both a drink of Royal Salute, and watched as the kid sipped it slowly, *Madronne,* smelling it first, acting like a don in one of those stupid Hollywood movies. Still, he was showing respect for a change.

It would almost be a shame to have him killed, now that he was coming around, but he had no choice. Everyone who had anything to do with this deal would have to go. They were all civilians, and wouldn't be missed. Best of all, with all the other people involved dead, nothing could ever come back to him, even with New York's approval and blessing.

His problem had been that there were people loyal to Tile, even if he had gone over the edge in his old age. People who might want revenge. So the masterstroke was getting outsiders to do it, scum who, it would seem, had gone about the business on their own, and who'd then been paid their retribution by none other than Tonce DiLeonardi himself. It was almost too good to be true. He'd do the job New York wanted, and make it look as if he'd gone nuts when his good friend Mike had been killed, had murdered everyone involved.

It wasn't unprecedented, thieves going after outfit bigshots. Years ago, the house belonging to one of the biggest mob men in the country had been robbed while the man had been on vacation, tens of thousands stolen from a barrel safe in his bedroom. They'd gotten away, but within weeks bodies started turning up in cars, with their hands cut off at the wrist.

The Lion could make this look like the same kind of thing. Ascend to the throne, with everyone's blessing, the hero who'd saved the city from a bloodbath.

Yes, it was indeed almost too good to be true.

He was pouring them another drink, keeping the banter up so the punk wouldn't get suspicious, when the phone rang. He let it. That's what he paid people for, answering phones when he was having a meet.

There was a knock on the door and one of his boys entered, a look of apology on his face, staring into the Lion's deadpan gaze with trepidation.

"Tommy's on the phone boss, calling collect."

DiLeonardi felt himself wince involuntarily, his visions of grandeur being intruded upon by the very real specter of the cost of making one mistake. The last thing he wanted to do was talk to a guy who was the epitome of failure, serving life without the possibility of parole because he'd fucked up.

He smiled, getting it back, the feeling of being on top of the world, and said to his bodyguard, "Tell him I'm busy. To call me"—he looked at Jacobi—"in two weeks. Yeah, I'll take his call then." The bodyguard hesitated, wanting to tell his boss he was making a mistake, afraid to. DiLeonardi could see it in his eyes, the man caught behind the power that had once been and the power that was, the power that was winning, because the man shrugged, closed the door softly behind him on his way out.

The Lion drank his scotch slowly, savoring it. Power? Wait until they saw the power that was yet to come. No one had ever yet held such power.

He turned his attention to this Jacobi punk, sitting there grinning at him like they were the best of buddies, in on a secret. The Lion said, "You got some time, Tommy? I want to tell you about my plans for you." And the kid got all wild around the eyes, nodding his head like a neglected child finally getting a chance to go to the ball game with the old man.

It was all in the way you played it, the Lion believed.

Tommy Campo stood staring at the phone for a minute before he could speak, holding it away from his ear, disbelieving. The Lion hadn't taken his call? Disregarded his motherfucking phone call? That fat little cocksucker!

He hung it up, the tip of his tongue between his teeth, aching for a fight. He dialed a series of numbers, breathing heavily, waited three rings until the operator came on and he told her that he wanted to call that number, collect. The phone rang on the other end and when the operator told the hood who answered that there was a person-to-person collect call for Mr. Tile from Mr. Campo, and would he accept the charges, Campo smiled because respect came into the hood's voice right away, no more of the bored badass tone he'd answered with, and he assured the operator that the charges would indeed be accepted.

TWENTY-SEVEN

"It's got to be Wayne, Frank, shit, anyone else either sell you out or drop the dime, one. Goddamn, this is Mike *Tile* we talking about here."

"Why you staying in, Ads?"

"You trusted me enough to ask, that's why. You think I don't know this is gonna be either a suicide mission or the pot of gold? But there ain't no other game in town, brother. I die on this or make a couple million. Is there a choice in that? Athletes said if they could take a drug and win the Olympic gold medal, knowing the drug gonna kill them in five years, they take it anyway. That's the exact same way I been doing my business for years. Make the money and hope your crime partner don't have to make a deal with the law a few years from now. Who can you trust anymore? Even Lockhart, last thing I 'spected was him to get drunk the night of the score, and I roomed with the boy for a good piece of time, thought I knew the man.

"Couple million dollars, Frank, what with the dough we made off the deal with that crazy hillbilly for doing nothing, I be able to lay low for a good hunk of time. Maybe forever. You the onliest man I ever met in my life, I ain't got to worry about him later, who he might speak to, not only to deal his way out of a jackpot,

but, shit, just bragging in a bar. Crime business ain't what it used
to be. There too many big mouths."

Frank knew what he meant. There was a handful of men he
would work with, guys he figured would stand up in a jam, but on
something like this, Adam was the first name to come to his mind,
there was never a thought of calling anyone else.

Ads understood things, wasn't afraid of a man because of any
position he might hold in the outfit or anywhere else. Money was
money, and partners were guys you died for if the need arose.

He was right, too, about the other thing. Who could Frank trust
now? There was Jimmy, that was a given, and then there was
Adam himself. Anyone else, on a thing like this, might bring
down more heat than the score itself would. But it would take four
men, minimum, and his back was against the wall.

"Even if Lockhart stays sober, is he safe? Will Tile's name
scare him?"

Adalebo grinned. "Shee-it. For a piece of a million-dollar
score, that redneck go in there and tear Tile limb from limb, smile
for the security camera, make sure they get his good profile. He
ain't scared of no mob. Besides, he was packing for Miami two
days ago. I got to call the boy, else he be on a plane this evening,
want to kill me he find out what he lost out on."

"Not from here, Adam. I haven't seen any PRICCs around, but
that doesn't mean they're not working. Get him away from that
broad, talk to him, give him the chance to turn you down. Don't
tell him any names, just that there's a big one going down soon,
say, half-million for him, working outside only. He might be a
drunk, but I'd bet the farm he's solid. Still, I don't want Tile's
name mentioned after you leave this room.

"He wants in, tell him to go home and wait. Tell him I said if
he drinks even one beer, he's dead. And I mean it, Ads. Jimmy'll
have to do all the other work himself if he can't cut it. Then pick
me up at Randolph and Michigan; I'll be waiting on the steps of
the library for you. There's no way I'm taking this down without
an eyeball inspection."

Adam got up to leave. Frank said, "One thing, Ads." He
stopped, turned, tense but smiling.

"Jimmy says this is the guy killed our old man. Once we're in there, he'll kill Tile."

"Means we don't got to wear masks."

Adam left and Frank breathed in deeply, rubbed his face in his hands, hard. Expelling the air through pursed lips. Okay. He would do the job and end it all, if it looked anywhere near as good in person as it did on paper. Get in and out, half an hour tops. Tina would never even have to know.

It was that, or live with the fact that he had personally allowed his younger brother to get killed. After the kid had done nine years behind the only failed score he'd ever set up.

Frank changed clothes in a hurry, not bothering to shave or shower. He heard Jimmy enter the house, calling his name, as he came out of his bedroom, zipping his trousers. He didn't have much time to shoot the breeze.

"You tell him?"

"Just like you said, Frank."

"Sit tight, get some rest. I got some work to do; then we'll come and get you, talk this thing over."

"Want me to come with you?"

Frank didn't bother to answer him. He grabbed the paper bag with his disguise inside, took his keys from his brother, and left the house, heading out to drive to the North Side and steal a car. There was a man he had to see about some heavy equipment, and it wasn't a man that Adam Lebeaux or even Jimmy had to know about. There were people he trusted, but the Iceman didn't need any of those few men knowing who the others were.

Mad Mike Tile slammed the phone into its cradle so hard it cracked the plastic base in two. He picked the thing up and threw it, watched as it sailed through the air then stopped dead, the cord stretched and not giving in, the phone falling to the floor with a stuttered ring.

"That son of a *bitch!*" Tile picked papers up from his desk, slammed them back down. "That *son* of a bitch!" He bellowed it this time, rising from the chair and turning, slamming his hand into the wall, palm first. He was breathing heavily, snorting air into his lungs as if he'd just run a marathon.

"Oh, that rotten son of a whore cocksucker!" He paced the room, his long white hair flying about his head, in his eyes. He shoved it back with his hand, let the hand slide down to his nose, rubbed his nostrils, hard, breathing in. There was enough dope just in his desk to OD half the North Shore, but as much as he'd like to indulge, he was going to wait. Until after that goddamn DiLeonardi was drawn and quartered, tied to a chair in the wine basement and skinned fucking alive.

"Manny! Louis! Get the fuck in here!" He stood there in his silk pajamas, getting a little bit of control back because his boys were obedient. He could hear their feet pounding down the carpeted hallway, marking double time. All right, he had to be in charge here. Couldn't let them see he was afraid. He'd send them out to pick that bastard up, then he'd sit down and think this through, all alone, without the bitches, the lady, nothing. Then get it all out of DiLeonardi, find out who'd set it up, and send them their boy, the Lion. In little fucking pieces, he'd mail him to them. Get their attention, then demand a sitdown.

His two chief enforcers stuck their heads in the door and he waved them in.

"Get out there, the two of you, to Tonce DiLeonardi's house. You get in there some way, somehow, without drawing too much attention to yourselves. This is sensitive. Get inside, tell him I got a job for him, whatever. Take silenced pistols. Blow those four cheap fucks he calls bodyguards out of their socks, then bring that fat traitorous piece of shit back here, you got me?"

He watched, almost in awe, as the two men looked at each other. Was he that far over the hill? Fear struck him hard as he wondered if they were in on it, too, on the hit that his dear friend Tommy Campo had told him about, encoded words spoken over telephone lines. Well, he knew where the guns were, too. If they didn't come back, he'd go looking for them, and woe be unto their goddamn guinea asses.

"I speak a language you guys don't know?"

"Uh . . . Mike? Tonce is a boss . . ." Louis said. He could have guessed it. This asshole, he'd live the high life, fuck the bitches and drink the booze. But ask him to do something hard and he wants to question you.

"That's right, Louis, and I'm *his* fucking boss. And *your* fucking boss. And that son of a bitch better be in my office before nightfall or I swear to God, I'm gonna take an icepick to both of your fucking eyeballs!" His voice had been rising more with each word, Mike working himself back up into a rage, pacing and winding up right in front of them.

"Fuck you waiting for!"

They left, hurriedly.

Tile stormed from his office out into the hallway, from there into the large dining room. Three men in shirtsleeves were playing cards at the oak table, flipping dollars down into a large pot. Tino, Danny, and—what was the new kid's name?—Kenny, yeah, Kenny, that was it. Having a few laughs around the card table, like at the Polish Democratic Club. God in heaven.

Tile said, "Game's over. Tino, go upstairs and get rid of the bitches. Take them home. Anyone out front, in the guardhouse?"

Tino said, "Just Sleepy, Mike, watching the gate. We was kind of waiting for the Friday night action to start."

"Ain't gonna be no Friday night action, not this Friday night, maybe not ever again. Get those bitches home, they got to be out of here before Louis and Manny get back. We got work to do. Move it. You other guys go get some firepower, Jesus Christ, three guys sitting around and none of you carrying heat. How're you gonna protect me, eh? Then get out there in the street and find a thief named Vale. Two brothers, Frank and Jimmy. Find 'em and don't come back to this house unless you're carrying their brains in a hatbox, you got me?"

Dan and Kenny scrambled as Tino headed up the stairs. Out to the guard shack, which in any other neighborhood would have been a fine, expensive house in its own right. Out here, it was just what they called it, a shack.

They entered, to see Louis and Manny in deep discussion with

253

Sleepy, who was anything but. He was called that because his love of cocaine kept him awake for stretches that lasted up to three days. Sleepy was eyeing his two bosses, the men looking up, tense as the two soldiers entered.

"What's up?" Dan said.

"You want to know what's up?" Manny said. He was the quieter of the two, the elder statesmen. The men were surprised that he was speaking. It was usually Louis who did the talking, with the deadly Manny mostly just staring his disapproval at them from eyes that seemed to be looking up out of a grave. "The jig, Dan, that's what's up. The old man's going hard, wants us to whack out the Lion's bodyguards and bring the Lion here."

He was standing straight up, like an army general, his hands behind his back. There was a belly on him, but on Manny it just made him look stronger, more invincible. Even the usually easy-going Louis was staring at them gravely.

"You're good boys." Manny was speaking to the three soldiers in the room, making what sounded—Christ—like a commencement speech. "But the two years you been on this detail, you been soft. The broads, the booze. We know about the dope, too, Jesus, it's everywhere all of a sudden. Me and Louis, we been trying to hold it together. Now it looks like it's too late.

"I been with Mike thirty-four years. Louis, he been with him, what, just under thirty. We're like the Roman centurions, see. We do what the boss says." He brought his hands out from behind him to display an old army .45, a World War II model. He worked the slide, jacked a bullet into the chamber.

"You guys, you remind me of myself, forty years back, under thirty and ready to try anything. Only then the only drugs around were smoked by nigger musicians. There's gonna be a war, fellas, ain't no way around it. We'll bring the Lion in, do what we're told, and go down with the man. Everyone in the country knows who we are, where our loyalties have been. If there's a hit out on the man, we go with him. It was a thing we knew about from the beginning. You guys, now, it's time to prove what you're made of." Manny pointed the gun around the room. "Anyone want to go AWOL?"

There was a general silent shaking of heads.

"He send you to tell me something?"

"To do something, Manny. We got to load up and go hit a couple of guys, brothers named Vale."

"Then get out there and do it. Then get your asses back here." He turned to Sleepy. "Get loaded, heavy, and get into the house. Wait for me there. I'll come in with the magnetic card. Then we'll call everyone on the payroll, make our plans."

Louis said, "We're gonna get slaughtered, ain't we, Manny?" and Manny didn't answer him, just looked at him hard before putting the .45 back in its holster.

Frank and Adam watched the exodus from the safety of the park a half-block away. They'd done the circuit, up and down the block, the two of them dressed in pastel clothing, Adam holding on to Frank's arm as they strolled down the sidewalk in front of Tile's mansion. Now, sitting on a park bench, only one other couple there sitting three benches over, arguing, they watched and commented, afraid to be hopeful.

"Where they going, I wonder?" Frank said. The couple three benches down looked as if they'd just stepped out of central casting, some director yelling, "Get me a couple of yuppies!" His hair was moussed, wet-looking, the man slim and muscular, waving his arms to make his point. She was wearing some funny kind of pants that had a waist on them that came to just under her breasts, cinched with what looked like a piece of clothesline. She hung her head and shook it back and forth, the tipped ends of her hair swinging in unison.

"Look like rats jumping ship to me."

A man entered the park carrying an easel and palette, set it up and sat down on the bench next to them, began to sketch the couple arguing. Adam leaned into Frank, caressing his forearm, whispering now as he spoke.

"Son of a bitch, got to sit right next to us. Don't get hard now, Frank, it just for show."

"Where the fuck are they going?" Frank saw the last car pull out, a Caddy limo, a couple of years on it but shined up nice and pretty. It was full of women, a man at the wheel.

"Man took off in a hurry, the one with the long hair and the red IROC. Shit, you people drive funny cars."

"You think this is a joke, Ads?" There was just the barest hint of threat in Frank's voice.

"I think, Frank, that we walking into something wet, deep, and smell like fish. Shit, those guys weren't changing guard, man, they was running! You see that tall fat old sucker, yelling at the punk in the limo? Shit, the women were terrified, you could see it all the way over here. I bet they don't come back tonight. I bet we could walk right in there now, take it off."

"We should be so lucky." Frank rose to leave, putting his arm around Adam. It was a good ruse; in liberal rich suburbs, people always turned their heads away when they saw two men being intimate.

"You seen enough?" Adam said, his whisper being drowned out by the young man in angst, who was rising to his feet, shouting now.

"What is it you *want* from me! I've given you everything money can buy!" The woman was sobbing into her hands, still shaking her head. The man on the next bench was looking up, then back at his easel, his hand flying as he charcoal-sketched them.

"Quaint," Frank said, and Adam didn't miss a beat.

"*Every*thing quaint in Winnetka, Frank."

Chapter

TWENTY-EIGHT

It was rough, waiting for them all by himself, Jimmy knowing better than to pace, but wanting to. It was one of the first things you learned in prison if you were to survive. Patience. Jimmy sat, being patient, in Frank's leather armchair in the basement, waiting. The lights were off and he forced himself to breathe easy, to relax. But he couldn't shut off his mind.

Frank was the best there was at what he did, bar none. Jimmy knew that. Knew, too, that there was nothing personal about his decision to leave Jimmy out of the surveillance—an ex-con two days free is as easy for a cop to spot as a veteran cop was for the ex-con. Different sides of the same coin. Two outsiders to the straight world, doing their tribal rituals, most of the time with the con losing the dance, sometimes fatally. No, Frank would want no one but another professional with him on the look-see, and Jimmy was a lot of things, but he was far from a professional thief. As long as he was there when the score went down, to look Tile in the face and make him answer for the old man, get even with him, that was all he needed.

But what if something went wrong? What if security was tighter than the report stated, what if—

Jimmy caught himself up short; this was neurotic thinking. There were no ifs in a thing like this. If he had tits he'd be Frank's sister. Ifs were for losers. Frank had said next Friday, and next Friday it would be.

He wondered what had changed Frank's mind, had made him decide to go to work on the project. The money involved? Professional pride? Or was it the knowledge he held that his only brother would die if he tried it alone?

Maybe Frank had some paybacks of his own to resolve. If not for the old man, then for Jimmy.

Tina sat on the couch, eyeing the boxes, now unpacked, all over the apartment. The apartment, God, it would have been hard to give up the apartment. It would have been worse, though, to quit the job she loved, helping the people who needed it most in the world.

She'd simply taken a couple of days off. Her court calendar was clear, and she never took vacations, she had plenty of time coming to her, so there was no need to feel guilty about just taking a few days.

But she did. There were lives to save, literally. Minds on their way to being destroyed, the minds of the supposedly innocent. She'd seen—rarely, but still, real and frightening—nine-year-olds who had no innocence left, who'd had it stolen from them, little sociopaths who viewed the world as their possession, the people in it their playthings. It was too late to save them. But for every raging preteen killer there were a million abused kids who *could* be saved, turned around. Made to realize that what had happened to them wasn't their fault.

She'd had a raped male child tell her that his worst shame was over the fact that he was now a "gay bird." His uncle had told him that's what the world would call him if he ever told their little secret. He'd been easy. Tina had told him, "If you're slashed with a knife, does that make you a *wound*? If you're shot, does that make you a *bullet*?" The child had understood. He was the victim, not the abuser. She'd made him understand that he had no more reason to feel guilt than he would if a stray rock, thrown by a stranger, had struck him. Today he was fifteen, had a brown belt in Wa do Ka karate, and invited her to tournaments to watch him in action.

When she wasn't doing things like that, she had a tendency to feel guilt over the time she was wasting.

Still, the boy she'd gone to see at Eleventh and State had been charged as an adult, there was nothing she could do for him today. The weekend was right there to be enjoyed.

She checked her watch. Early afternoon on a Friday, there wasn't much she could do even if she *did* go into the office.

Maybe she ought to call Frank, get together with him, begin a weekend of healing. From what she knew, they weren't really much better off than that young child had been. They'd both been victims, and both had spent years believing they were wounds.

She shook her head to clear it of those kinds of thoughts, reached for the phone and punched out his number. She'd keep it light, a little breezy. Not play mother or analyst. Just get him over there and tear his clothes off, one piece at a time. Afterwards, they could get into the other, heavier stuff. It would be a good way to begin the healing.

Jimmy heard them coming into the house through the back door in the kitchen and he waited, knowing where they'd come. He relaxed his face into a blank prison-yard deadpan, and when they came down the stairs he knew what they'd see: a patient professional man who was about to debrief the scouts.

He knew right away though that something was different. Frank and Adam were stone-faced and silent, moving with purpose, into the room to stand before him. The tension in the air was electric, reminding him of the prison yard a couple of days back when he'd come out of the tunnel from the shrink visit, saw the group of blacks forming against the wall, looking up at the guard, the riot about to commence. . . .

Frank said, "It's on, Jimmy, for tonight. Get your shit together and your asshole tight, 'cause we're not gonna get more than one shot at this." Frank turned to Adam.

"Go pick up Lockhart. If he's had even one beer, or you

suspect he has, forget about him. You know where the work car is; the equipment's in the trunk. We'll only need about half of it. Be back here in an hour; come in the same way."

They watched Adam leave, walking up the stairs without the usual bop in his step, a man with a mission too professional to profile or style. When they heard the kitchen door slam shut, they looked at each other.

Frank said, "I want to check the plans again, look them over just one more time." The phone rang and Frank let it. "Go upstairs, into my room. There're some heavy black gym clothes in my bottom drawer. Bring two pairs down here."

Jimmy was looking at Frank, the ringing phone beginning to get on his nerves.

Frank said, "Bring the clothes, then I'll run the rest of it down to you before Adam and Wayne get back here." He turned, walked casually to the bar, behind it, picked up the phone hung under the bar top.

Jimmy listened, not moving as Frank said, "Hello." More of an angry growl than a greeting. Jimmy was wondering if he should express his feelings, his gratitude. Wanting to, but not too sure about how to do it. He knew his brother had nothing to do with egos or pride or pity or sorrow or sensitivity, especially when he was working, but it wasn't as if he were some guy Frank worked with; hell, he was his only brother.

He heard Frank say, "I'm working, Tina," watched as Frank hung up the phone, not slamming it, not being gentle. Just hung the thing up, as if on a wrong number.

When Frank said, "What're you waiting for?" Jimmy decided that he wouldn't try to express his gratitude. The Iceman was back, colder than Jimmy had ever before seen him.

There was no conversation in the car, Manny and Louis in the front seat, sitting straight, Manny driving, obeying the speed laws as Louis checked out the 9 mm pistols, screwed the suppressors in place. Good weapons, fifteen shots apiece, after which the suppressors wouldn't be worth shit, but they'd be throwing the pieces away after using them, and if they couldn't take down four guys with thirty shots then they didn't deserve the silence the suppressors would give them in the first place.

They were professionals about to go forth and labor at their craft for the first time in a long time, anxious and wound up.

Manny would turn and check Louis out from time to time, worried about the man. It had been so fucking long since Louis had had to be trusted. Had there been too many women, too much wine? He'd soon find out.

As for Manny, he had no doubt that he'd done the right thing. A true warrior knew how to motivate his underlings. If he'd had to, he would have killed those boys back there. He would be needing them, and a lot of others, soon. He hoped they wouldn't take forever to find the Vales, kill them and get back to Mike's. Once the Lion was found dead, the war would commence.

He and Louis would have to do the bulk of the work, though. Between them they'd enjoyed over sixty years of the good life attributable to Mike Tile. They owed him loyalty unto death. If the shogun told his samurai to fall on his sword, did he balk? Manny had put three kids through college. Mike had been at all three graduations, had handed all three of Manny's children fat envelopes filled with cash at those graduations, then again when the children married. His daughter was a doctor, for Christ's sake, not some fat dago housewife, wringing her hands because the old man stayed out late drinking and beat her when he came home. Mike Tile had been good to Manny, a true emperor. What other way had there been for him to make that kind of dough, be that kind of provider? Without Tile backing him up, bringing him up through the ranks with him, his kids would have been lucky to get through Catholic high schools.

No, he'd do it, follow the boss's orders down to the wire, die in his service. It was the only way to do it, unless they wanted to whack Mike themselves, put an end to it right there. The New York wise guys, they might pull that off, kill the boss to save themselves, but it wasn't something Manny could live with. Although he had his doubts about Louis. Louis, however, had the knowledge that if he tried anything stupid, Manny would kill him personally, so what it came to, probably, in Louis's mind, was: would he die now or later? Manny had to suppress a smile, wondering if Louis would take a crack at him, trying to get out from under. He kind of wished he would, just to see if he himself still had the reflexes.

He parked the car at the curb in front of the Lion's house, took the weapon that Louis handed him, gave it a quick but thorough check, the pistol held low, under the windshield. He jacked a cartridge up into the barrel, slid off the safety, put the untraceable gun in his waistband, and got out of the car.

The guy who opened the door stood back in respect when he saw who it was, opened the door wide so they could pass through. He said, "Tonce's in his office, he got a guy with him—"

Manny said, "Get the others into the boss's office. Mike wants me to tell you something, then the boss is taking a ride with us, no more than two of you with him. Choose between yourselves who wants to go. But I'll give you a hint: it's party time." He walked past the man as if he were in his own house, down the hall, into the Lion's den, Louis right behind him. He could hear Louis's labored breathing, the guy scared but standing up. The man who'd answered the door was calling out names, gathering the lambs to the slaughter.

They stepped into the office without knocking, DiLeonardi's head coming up, an angry scowl creasing his face, about to speak harsh words. Until he saw who it was. Puzzlement replaced anger. He said, "Manny." Manny kept walking straight toward the young punk stud in the other chair, short-haired boy with Nazi tattoos showing, shit, Manny reaching for the pistol as DiLeonardi said, "Louis?" some fear getting in there, not quite sure what was going on.

Manny stopped three feet short of the kid in the chair and pulled the silenced piece, pointed it so that the end of the suppressor was an inch away from the punk's forehead. The boy's eyes widened, going cross-eyed, trying to look down the barrel, and Manny shot him, once, the kid going over, chair and all. Hitting the heavily carpeted floor, shaking for a second, the boy's nervous system not quite sure it was dead.

Manny held his finger to his mouth, shaking his head at the Lion, a pasty-faced shaking Lion now, out of the jungle and knowing these were not giraffes he was fucking with. Manny walked behind him, took up a position where DiLeonardi was shielding him, and Louis stepped out into the hall, his weapon still hidden, shouting at the four bodyguards to hurry it the fuck up, time was wasting.

They came in at ease, no weapons evident, and Louis stepped to the side and started blasting; Manny could see him getting into it, the light bright in his eyes from the pure pleasure of killing, even as he himself opened up.

When the smoke cleared there were five bodies on the floor of the Lion's den, and DiLeonardi was whimpering, on his knees now, praying.

"How many you use?" Manny asked, curious.

"Seven," Louis said, and Manny grunted.

"I fired six, but remember, that's counting this punk on the floor." To DiLeonardi, he said, "Get the fuck off your knees. This ain't church. Mike wants to see you, tough guy, and guess what? He ain't real fucking happy."

Adam Lebeaux considered himself a professional judge of character as much as anything. He could con, which is about what he'd done in the car, knowing Frank was like mercury, could change with any motion that grabbed him. He wanted to take the score down now and Frank was thinking on next week, so he'd subtly persuaded him with everything he had, trying hard not to go overboard so Frank would suspect something, but still, giving it enough to convince the man that the time was now, they'd never get a better opportunity.

It worked, too. Frank hadn't said anything until they'd got to the house, told them both at the same time that the score would go down tonight. Adam had felt elation, mixed with dread. He wasn't as sure of himself as he'd pretended to be. He'd seen the plans, and even without bodyguards, the house wasn't going to be an easy nut to crack. Still, he'd been mostly honest. He didn't think they'd get a better shot at the place.

Which didn't mean that this shot would be a joy. Might even be the last shot any of them ever took at anything.

Which was why he didn't go directly to Wayne's apartment. Frank had said an hour, and it would take him tops ten minutes to get over to Lockhart's place, another ten to get back to Frank's. Adam and Dee-Dee lived between them. So it was logical that he stop at the crib, say good-bye to Dee-Dee the proper way, just in case.

He entered his house in a hurry, went into the bedroom ignoring his woman's questions. He found the keys to the lockboxes, the bankbooks which he'd had put in her name as well as his, forging her signature to the papers. He shushed Dee-Dee, told her to leave the room, and as soon as she was gone got onto the phone. When Wayne answered, he didn't waste a lot of time.

"The deal's tonight, motherfucker, and if you took or take one goddamn drink, you a dead hillbilly redneck motherfucker. I pick you ass up in forty minutes. Be ready, waiting outside." He hung up the phone and called for Dee-Dee.

He told her that if he didn't come back she was to go to the banks and clean out the accounts, slowly, never taking more than ten grand out at one time, to fool the tax man. He told her that all of it was hers, and thanks for the memories. He told her that if he stacked all the women he'd ever known side by side, she'd be the one standing head and shoulders above the crowd, no bullshit. He told her she was the best piece of ass he'd ever had in his life, white or black. He told her these things and her eyes filled with tears, Dee-Dee wanting to ask questions but having been with him long enough to know better.

"I love you," Dee-Dee said, and Adam told her not to worry about a thing, he'd be back, probably.

"I love you," Dee-Dee said, losing the battle and breaking into tears, hiding her head in her hands, knowing how much he hated any sign of weakness.

Adam took her in his arms, his eyes going to the clock on the nightstand.

If he could calm the ho down, get her to knock off the lovey-dovey bullshit and the waterworks, he could get his rock and pick the redneck up with plenty of time to spare.

Chapter

TWENTY-NINE

Before Roosevelt left to make the phone call he'd made good and damn sure that Ryan wouldn't be going anywhere. He'd checked the bracelets on the man's hands, then had used his own to secure the commander's left leg to the bed frame. He looked funny sitting there, one leg pulled up, a wet stain right there on the front of his pants.

"Thought you undercover motherfuckers were supposed to be tough," he'd said. The commander had done some pleading, trying to tell him that he could make things a lot easier on him if he let him go, now, while Gunon was in the toilet. Sure, he would.

Gunon had come out of the john and Roosevelt had left, and now wasn't a block away when his beeper went off, scaring him in the close confines of the vehicle. He was glad that Gunon wasn't with him, he'd never have heard the end of it, jumping like that. Well, hell, he had good reason to be nervous. He looked at the beeper, at the number digitally displayed. Headquarters. Damn. Shut the thing off? No, not yet. There were other men to think about here, dudes from the unit who might not have been picked up yet, who might have a way out for them. If one of them called, they'd beep him from a pay phone, leave a number and expect him to return the call from a pay phone, too.

He cleared the beeper, pulled over into a gas station, and called

Giraldi, giving him his instructions in as few words as possible, hanging up on the man's questions. Let him sweat. In Roosevelt's mind Giraldi was a long way from being one of them. If he pulled the trigger for them, killed the commander in cold blood with the man handcuffed and defenseless, then he'd be welcomed with open arms as a partner, and not a second before, no matter what Gunon said.

He went into the gas station, bought a twelve-pack of beer, some chips, some frozen burritos to warm up in the old oven when he got back. They'd missed lunch. He drove back to the safe house, his beeper going off just as he entered. He looked at the number. It was not one he recognized. He left the goods with Gunon, got back in the car and drove to a different pay phone, his heart wanting to jump with relief, his head telling him to wait.

He dialed the number and a man with a southern accent answered it, hesitantly. It was not a voice he recognized.

"Who are you and why'd you beep me?"

"Officer Roosevelt?"

"Sergeant Roosevelt."

"Sergeant Roosevelt, this is Wayne, we . . . uh . . . met the other night, remember, on Astor Street?"

"What do you want."

"There's a big score on for tonight, Sergeant. Vale and his nig—uh, his partner, Lebeaux. I just got the call myself or I'd'a called you sooner—"

"You wait right there and keep that fucking line clear. I'll call you back in five minutes."

Roosevelt hung up and went back to his car, sat in it, thinking. A minute, then two, passing as he thought of ways to do it, then rejected them for one reason or the other. After three minutes, he figured he had the way out.

He got out of the car and went back to the phone, flashed the badge at some screwball who was talking on it, putting his thumb down on the depressor, cutting off the dummy's call. The guy started to complain mildly, so Roosevelt grabbed him by his shirt collar and threw him, backing him off a couple of yards. He turned to the phone without glancing back at the guy. He dialed

Lockhart's number, told him exactly what he wanted him to do, assured him that as soon as everything went down he was a free man, could walk away, but he had to be there, at the score, carrying the homing device they would be bringing him, or they wouldn't be able to find him, now, would they? Shit, sometimes, it was like dealing with little kids.

He hung up and found another quarter, dropped it in the slot and called Giraldi again. Told him exactly what he wanted him to do, in detail, made him repeat it, open line or not. When he was sure Giraldi could do what he'd been told, he hung up the phone and turned, the idiot he'd hung up on still standing there, staring up at him, looking ready to say something mean, the look on Roosevelt's face shutting him up, though.

He got in the car, still scowling. He'd bet that that little turd had been about to give him shit about he paid his goddamn salary. Last guy told him that, he'd bopped him hard on top of his head, shut his ass up right quick.

He drove back to the safe house, this time letting his heart jump away, because he believed he'd found a way to save all of their asses.

Anthony Giraldi had driven the Fila-hat gangsters back to their neighborhood, not in the mood for any bullshit. Which, thank God, they hadn't handed out. He knew what this meant. It was, in fact, something to be respected. These were men, gang members maybe, but in their own way stand-up. Now, some punks, they would be expressing their gratitude all the way back, or even worse, talking shit, giving him a hard time. These guys had just sat in the car sullenly, not even thanking him for the ride, which he hadn't had to give them.

Roosevelt and Gunon had wanted him out of the office so bad that they'd even told him to be nice to gangbangers, which meant something big was in the wind. Just what he'd been waiting for all along, the chance to prove himself, and they'd shut him out.

He wondered where he'd lost it, what he'd done to cause them to mistrust him. All he could think of was the problem with the

thief a few days back, and that hadn't been all that damn big a
deal; they'd straightened it out and he'd earned his spurs by
making the decision to stay and watch the hillbilly's house. Goddamnit, he'd earned their trust, had made them rich, and now they
were shutting him out.

He was a single man, one who enjoyed his solitude. He lived
for his work and was seldom lonely and never bored. Now,
though, alone in the North Side studio apartment, he was antsy,
full of excitement, wondering exactly what it was he should do.

He'd called the commander's office and had got nothing but a
steady ring; more of the same at the man's house. This wasn't that
big a surprise to Giraldi. Whatever had happened had been set into
motion by the phone call the commander had received early that
afternoon, which had been overheard, listened to, by Roosevelt.
He knew the commander's office and home phones were tapped.
They'd told him that early on. Told him the commander had been
in the unit only a year, and was not yet fully trusted. They'd told
him this knowing that he was not stupid, or he wouldn't have been
accepted as a member of such an elite unit. Told him knowing full
well that he was to infer that it meant that *his* home phone also
was tapped, that they were watching him. Well, he had nothing to
hide, surely not in this apartment. So goddamn small that he could
walk from one end of it to the other in seven steps. If someone
didn't call soon, he'd wear a hole in the carpet.

When the phone rang he jumped, then ran to answer it.

As soon as he hung up, though, the doubt and fear came
flooding back.

That damn Roosevelt, always being cryptic, always testing.
Asking him if he was with them or against them. When he assured
the man that he was one of the crew, Roosevelt gave him an
address and told him not to come there before dark, and to come
heeled.

Were they planning to kill him, tie up any loose ends that might
hang them later? Jesus, it got scary, if you let your mind wander.
Telling him to come heeled might just be a ruse, said to put him at

ease, make him feel safe, then as he walked through the door, thinking he was one of the boys, bang, two in the back of the head.

Dark still two or three hours away and he had to wait here, walking and thinking. Sweating, too, good God, he stunk. He headed for the bathroom, dropping his clothes behind him as he walked.

He was out of the shower, a towel draped around his waist, sitting in the single chair in the apartment, staring at the blank television screen.

Should he run down a superior, ask for advice, some kind of supervision? No, what if the men just wanted to test him again, that wasn't beneath them. Maybe what it was, the commander had gotten a call that would make them some big money and they'd rushed Giraldi out of the place so they wouldn't have to split it with him.

He was sitting there thinking that he'd go so goddamned heeled he'd make Rambo look like a sissy when the phone rang again.

It was a good thing that there were six units. Headquarters was under siege, he couldn't dare go there now. He called the office number again and some headhunter federal officer had answered it. Giraldi had talked to enough of them in his life to know what they sounded like. This one was trying to be cool, act like one of the boys, but he was federal, Giraldi would bet his pension on it.

There was an office on the West Side, though, not far from the downtown office. Roosevelt had told him that he had less than a half hour, so he drove fast, ignoring the traffic laws, grateful that it was not yet three-thirty and there was little traffic. He ran into the West Side precinct, down toward the PRICC office and back to the working officer's area, past the supervisor's desk.

The room was empty, maybe all of them pinched already, and Giraldi worked fast, wanting to get what he needed and get the fuck out. He found the device, little thing smaller than a pack of nonfiltered cigarettes. The receiver, though, that was the size of an old-fashioned dial radio. Which didn't matter. There would only be cops listening to it, watching the grid beep on the screen. He ran out of the precinct, expecting to be challenged at any time. He wasn't.

Lockhart was waiting for him outside his apartment building, jumping into the vestibule and waving at him frantically, hurrying him on. Giraldi entered, quickly, handing the man the small transmitting unit, then was shoved into the shadows, falling onto the stairs, the powerful southern man tossing him there easily.

He'd been set up. Any second now Gunon or Roosevelt would saunter down the stairs and shoot him in the head.

No, now the hillbilly was apologizing, his voice cracking, telling him that the car turning the corner was Adam Lebeaux's . . . telling him that Lebeaux was eyeing the goddamn unmarked squad, shit.

Giraldi found his voice and told the man to tell his partner that the detective from the unit was upstairs, fucking the neighbor on the top floor, shaking his head when the man said, No, shit, that woman's uglier than a dog, having to tell the dumb bastard that the guy in the car didn't know that.

Giraldi watched, from the shadows, holding his breath as the man ran out of the building, eyeing the unit himself, and jogged to the car. As it pulled from the curb he could see the big man's lips moving, explaining things to the black guy behind the wheel. He prayed that the black guy would believe Lockhart. He waited a full minute before leaving the building.

He entered the safe house not fifteen minutes later, carrying the transmitter. He was greeted like Richard the Lionhearted returning from the Crusades.

"Gimme that." Gunon grabbed the transmitter from him and began to fiddle with it, setting the computer. The commander was in a chair trussed up like a turkey, with a gag in his mouth and a handkerchief over his eyes. God, the man had wet himself.

Roosevelt went to him, began to take the cuffs off his hands and ankle. He made the commander stand up, then cuffed him in front, removed the gag and blindfold, walked him to the door, draping the commander's jacket over his hands so no curious onlookers would see that he was handcuffed. Without another word, the four of them walked quickly to the unmarked squad.

It was amazing, technology. Giraldi was thinking this, trying to keep his mind straight and off what was happening, listening to Gunon discuss the transmitter and receiver in a calm, lecturer's voice.

As long as the transmitter was within three blocks of the receiver, they'd receive an audio signal as well as visual confirmation. The little white dot, see it there in the middle, looking for its little buddy the receiver? It would beep, move in the same direction as the transmitter. He'd keyed in the coordinates, given it Vale's address, and now the grid would lock in, telling them exactly where the transmitter unit was, as soon as it locked on to it, when they got within three blocks of it.

"Amazing little device, look here, all the way down Sheridan Road, you can see it right there on the screen, your eyes are good. Cross streets, everything. They turn, the blinking dot turns, like ghost monsters chasing Pac-Man."

Giraldi let him talk, breathing in slow deep breaths, trying to calm himself down. The commander hadn't said a word since Roosevelt had untied him.

Now Roosevelt was talking, telling him that he'd found a way for all of them to beat any case this asshole here might have set up against them.

All they had to do, Rosy assured him, was wait for the score to go down, shoot the crooks, shoot the commander, tell the bosses that in the running gun battle with the bad guys the commander had died heroically.

"You're the one, Anthony, gonna pull the trigger, you understand."

Understand? Jesus Christ, did he ever.

Still, he had to ask: "What'd he do? Goddamn, Rosy, he's our boss, for Christ's sake."

Roosevelt pulled to the curb two and a half blocks away from Frank's house, a half-block over. Gunon said, "See, lookit, goddamn, there it goes, telling us where Lockhart is. They ain't left yet!"

"Lucky for us," Roosevelt said, then said to Giraldi, "This cocksucker here, he's a stool pigeon. Undercover, wants to send us all away for twenty years. You ready to take a fall like that, Giraldi, tell us now, cause I sure ain't."

Right, tell them now and die along with the commander. He said, "Stool pigeon? The commander? Fuck! Run the scenario down to me on the way, will you, Rosy? I'm not sure what's happening here, with these guys, the thieves. But the thing sounds good to me, I just want to be sure I know what's happening."

"You'll do it, then?" Gunon now, talking from the back seat, right there next to him.

"Do it? To a stool pigeon? Shit, without his testimony, they got nothing, right? We walk?"

"Might be forced to resign, the good of the force, but no papers be turned in, tapes, transcripts, none of it'll stand up without his direct testimony."

"Commander," Giraldi said, looking into Ryan's terrified eyes, "you are one dumb, dead, son of a bitch."

Gunon saw a figure moving toward the house, and he stopped listening to Giraldi, grabbed the binoculars out of the glove compartment.

"What's that!" Roosevelt said, and Gunon told him to shut the fuck up, he was trying to find out.

What it was, was a woman.

"There's a *broad* going over there, for Christ's sake."

"Oh, sweet Lord," Roosevelt said, "this is getting better and better."

Tina had waited the better part of an hour, stewing, wondering just what in the hell it was the man had said to her. He was working. All right. It had actually taken some time for her to catch on. Working on what? He had vowed he'd never steal again, had given his word. If there was one thing this man wasn't, it was a phony. Frank had lied to her, had rationalized it away, using his mind to tell himself it was all right. But to lie to her now, to use her for no other purpose than to be cruel the next day, no, she didn't believe that was in him.

All right, so what the hell could he be working on? All he ever did in his life was steal. He'd been successful at it, had never been caught. Still, it was the only work he knew.

She still wanted to believe differently, to tell herself he was working on the deck, on the basement, working on a goddamn model airplane, but she couldn't. Not after she'd heard the coldness in his voice.

So that's what it had come down to. Frank had had good intentions, but the second he'd laid eyes on his brother, he'd reverted. Did she need that in her life? Bullshit, she did.

That was when she began to get mad, to rage and seethe inside. She walked around the apartment several times, trying to calm down, the pacing not doing much good. There were other, better ways to vent that anger. Like working out, taking a jog. What had Betty told her? Stay calm inside, in control. Think things through before you act. It had worked for years, but was failing her now.

"That *bas*tard!" She shouted the words in her living room, angry at herself as well as Frank. Knowing full well that she would carry this with her for days now that it had begun.

Well, he'd caught her with her pants down once. She'd played her emotions to the breaking point when she'd seen him being dragged into the police station, when her dreams had been shattered. She'd nearly quit her job then, run away. This time, he wouldn't get that close. This time, she knew what he was. This time, she'd stay strong, calm inside, in control. He wasn't worth it. The hell with him and all his posturing, his "Don't move baby, *I'll* move" macho nobility.

Communication. That was the key.

Sure, that was it. She would communicate her ass off to that son of a bitch.

Tina grabbed an army jacket and ran out of the apartment, down the stairs and onto the street. There was a strange car in front of Frank's house, an older, nondescript vehicle. She noticed it because she was used to seeing his Cadillac parked there. It hit her then, what it was.

My God, it was for real. This was a work car, a thief's crew car.

She hesitated, a little scared. Then walked on.

The door opened before she could mount the final cement step, Frank leading the way out of the door, a bunch of male bodies behind him, still inside the house, a bunch of vague, big shapes in the background. He spotted her, and the sight of her broke his concentration.

Frank organized the crew, told them their jobs, and when he was sure they were ready he got up, walked out of the house, stopped in his tracks when he saw Tina standing there, Jesus, right on the top step.

His resolve broke, his determination to get the job over and done with fractured, wanting to do nothing more than take her into his arms and walk away from it all, from Jimmy, Ads, Wayne, everything. It must have showed on his face, because Tina, who'd been standing there looking about ready to pull a pistol out of her jacket pocket and shoot him, now relaxed, her face softening, her eyes filling, not with tears, but with compassion.

"Frank . . ." Tina said softly.

He stared at her, standing on the porch. Inches from her as she slowly mounted the last step. He was about to reach out for her when Adam's voice whispered behind him.

"Ain't got *time* for this, Iceman."

Making him remember who he was. He pushed past Tina, turning so he wouldn't knock her down the steps, then didn't bother to look back at her, got into the front seat, behind the wheel of the work car and stared straight ahead, at the street. The other men filled the car and Frank started it, shot a glance at the front of his house.

Saw her standing there, her hands at her sides, staring at him, her gaze cutting through him.

He put the car in gear and raced from the curb.

Wasn't at the corner when Wayne couldn't help himself, had to stick his two cents in.

"Forget to tell the bitch you wasn't studding tonight, Frank?" There was a man-to-man locker-room tone in his voice, Wayne not meaning to offend, just being one of the boys.

Frank said, "Wayne, shut the fuck up, right now, you hear me?" And, luckily for Wayne, he did.

"The fuck was *that* all about?" Roosevelt said.

Gunon, looking through the glasses, chewing a toothpick, shook his head slowly.

"Let's find out."

Tina stood there, watching them drive away. The second she'd seen him, all her conviction had seeped out of her, she'd lost the desire to knock him flat, lay him out with words.

Actually, after seeing the look on his face, all she really wanted to do was grieve for him.

It was so obvious, the look. Telling her things about him that maybe he himself didn't know. The last thing Frank Vale wanted to do at this moment was to go out with that motley group of losers, risk his life for money.

He'd wanted to come to her, she knew. If the slender black man behind him had kept his mouth shut, she bet he would have, too, blown the thing off and left it be.

Maybe if she'd said something, made a move, a gesture, reached out to him as he'd passed . . .

No, that wasn't her move to make. The ball had been in his court, and he'd purposefully thrown it out of bounds.

In a way, she told herself, she was lucky. She was finding out now, when her faith in him was still broken, instead of six months from now, when she was totally in love with him again.

All right. Life goes on. For the living. From the look on Frank's face when he passed her, she didn't hold much stock in the man's ability to be fully alive. If that's the life he wanted, if he could be suckered into it so easily, then he could have it, it wasn't her business. Or her problem.

So why was she so torn apart inside?

She began to walk down the stairs, was nearly to her own stairway when the car pulled up next to her and the fat, greasy cop jumped out and grabbed her, and before she could punch or kick or even scream he had her in the car, in the front seat, between himself and the large black man who wheeled the car away from the curb before the greaser could even close the door behind him.

Chapter

THIRTY

Manny and Louis dragged the Lion into the house, through the big double doors and into the foyer. He wasn't fighting, but they were rough with him, slapping and cursing him, a man about to die who was beneath respect, deserved no final dignity. A Judas traitor. Mike Tile met them in the hallway.

He surprised Manny; ignored the Lion and came to stand in front of them, in a smoking jacket, for Christ's sake, his hands clasped in front of him, bouncing on his toes.

"You got any of your cigars on you, Manny?"

Manny reached for them and the boss stopped him with the wave of his hand.

"Light one, get it going good. Louis, get this Judas into the cellar, tie him to a chair. Find out when the hit on me is supposed to go down."

"There ain't no hit!" DiLeonardi began to speak and now Tile showed his anger, it broke through the casual façade with brutal quickness. He slapped the Lion once, hard, with the back of his hand, and Tonce staggered backward into Louis.

"Don't you *ever* speak to me, you motherfucker. You got something to say, say it to Manny or Louis." He turned and began to lead the way toward the cellar.

*   *   *

It was maybe a fifteen-mile drive from Frank's Sheridan Road home to Mad Mike Tile's, but it was like going from one entire world into another. They called Frank's neighborhood Uptown. They called Mike Tile's Millionaire's Row.

When he and Adam had first discussed the project, Frank had asked him: What do you know about Winnetka, and Adam had told him he was aware of two things: Rock Hudson came from there, and there were a whole lot of rich motherfuckers lived in that town.

He'd been right on both counts. In the car now, silent, the entire thing laid out and all four men knowing their roles, the possible consequences of them, savoring what might be their last free or living moments, Frank thought about what Adam had said. It was the only way to keep his mind off seeing Tina, standing on his step, staring. . . .

He shook his head, angrily. Then began to maintain. He wasn't alone here, couldn't afford to let the other men see him like this.

What had Adam said? Rock Hudson came from there. It's what Winnetka, to Frank, was all about. The people in their estates all big-timers, liking the glitter, the self-importance, the jealousy evoked in lesser humans, the big mansions being their outward symbols of success, but inside, in their souls, it was all phony and they had to know it. The way Hudson knew he was a homosexual but played the game, reveled in the glamorous straight image, his heartthrob façade that the world got to look at, shaking their heads, women coveting him, men jealous of him. Frank wondered if it ever caused the man grief, telling all those lies for so long. He hoped it had, as then he would be able to at least respect the man. You are what you are, and to deny it or disregard it was the worst form of criminal activity he could think of.

Tina would never understand that. In a million years. Like it or not, he was a thief, an outsider.

Or was he? God almighty, could he, all the time, have been bullshitting himself? Was he really just another Rock Hudson, showing the world one face, the one he wanted them to see, when deep down he wasn't at all what he represented himself to be? It jumped into his mind then, the picture of her, standing staring after him. If he'd gone to her, taken her into his arms, would she have eased into him or resisted?

Later, he would think of it later. After the project was completed and they were all out and safe. The Iceman had to be a stone-froze glacier on this one, or it would be the end of it for all of them.

He drove mechanically, obeying the speed limit, the traffic laws, ignoring, too, the BMWs and the Volvos that swerved around him, the drivers angrily blaring their horns at the man who dared travel the North Shore at the posted speeds. He heard Jimmy say something to Wayne, calming him, the hillbilly cursing under his breath because some thin goof with a short-trimmed beard driving a Beemer had thrust his middle finger at them. Christ, this guy had done time? Still, it reassured him. Wayne was as guileless as Adam had said, a man after money, dumb, and that made him safe, at least for the time being.

Frank parked the car in the lot at the public park, put the master key under the mat. He turned to face Wayne. "You and Jimmy wait here." He held up a hand to cut off Jimmy's protest. "I can't get past the alarm without Adam. The rest of the plan stays in effect, to the letter, got it?"

Jimmy stared at him, hard.

"Hey, you got it, or do we blow the whole thing off right here?"

"I was supposed to come in with you."

"Wayne needs a backup, Jimmy. The front-gate guards, if there are any, have to be neutralized. He'll need your help."

There was a moment of sullen staring, Jimmy's and Frank's eyes locking, and in the silence Frank thought hard: Blow it off, right now. Not knowing if he wanted to give it up for his brother's sake or his own. If Jimmy decided to give it up, though, it would be over, all of it, and he could go back to Tina. . . .

"Yeah, Frank, I got it."

Frank grunted and reached into the glove box, popped the trunk. He and Adam got out and went straight to the trunk, words not needed between them. They each removed a backpack and slung it on, two happy campers strolling the North Shore. If this were Hyde Park, they'd fit right in. The hope was that any police or other suspicious eyes would see them as a couple of elder students from Northwestern University, maybe even teachers, out for a Friday night hike.

As they began to walk away from the park Wayne called to them and they turned, in unison, and Wayne told them the deal had to be over with by nine, because that's when the park closed. Adam told Frank that the man was worried about getting a parking ticket, smiling, and they turned their back on him and walked away.

Down and across the street, less than a block to the public beach. It was full dark now, the black waters stretching. To the right, Frank could see the skyscrapers of the city, to his left, nothing, the high cement wall erected there blocking the public bather's view from the next-door estate's private beach.

"Man paid a lot of money to keep folks from seeing some sand," Frank said as he undressed at the water's edge.

He and Adam were wearing the black sweat suits, over diving outfits. They stripped down to them quickly, covering their feet with black rubber skintight stockings, as thick as the suits. In the backpacks were covers for their heads, which would leave just an oval of their faces exposed to the cold water.

"Maybe he's got an old lady likes to sunbathe naked," Frank said. Adam still didn't answer him.

Frank said, "Shit, all you got to do is swim out past the wall, go over to their side. They got lake rights, too?"

Adam's mask was secured, the end tucked into the neck of the suit. With his dark-brown face, he was nearly invisible. Frank could hear him breathing. Adam said, "You don't got to convince me. I knows you the Iceman."

Frank put on his own mask and lifted the plastic bag with his weapon out of his pack, picked up one of Adam's two plastic bags, the one with Adam's gun. The other, heavier one, with the tools of his trade, Adam would carry himself.

They buried the knapsacks with their clothes in them, and began to wade slowly into Lake Michigan.

*　　*　　*

Jimmy smoked a cigarette then got out of the car, closing the door gently. The park was empty, their car the only one on the lot. Sitting there made him feel exposed. "Pop the trunk," he said to Wayne, then walked to the back of the car, his hand on the trunk's down-curve. It opened and he held it half-closed, looking up and down Sheridan Road, searching for the Mars lights of a passing squad. He let the trunk open, leaned into it and removed the tranquilizer gun and two more legitimate pieces, both revolvers. It was overkill, the trunk filled with guns and extra ammo, Frank fitting them out for a massacre. The house had lights on only in the second story, for shit's sake, and in the basement, the cellar or whatever rich people called the underground part of their house. The main floor and even the guardhouse seemed empty, were, at least, dark.

He hid the weapons, the trank gun in the front of his pants, the two revolvers in his pants pockets, his sport coat covering the butts.

"It's time to go." Jimmy said the words softly, not caring if Wayne heard them or not. It was time for *him* to go, no matter what this fool said.

Wayne came out of the car in a hurry, his face creased with concern, worry, some anger there, too. "They said a half hour, sonny."

"I ain't your sonny, motherfucker, you got that?" Jimmy's hand was in his right pants pocket, holding the butt of a .38 Smith. The only thing that concerned him was if he could whip it out and smack the man with it, shut him up and put him away if he moved on him. He wouldn't shoot him, that would destroy the score and bring heat on his brother.

Wayne backed up, his hands going up, palms out, stopped them at chest level. "Whoa now, pardner, just take her easy, hear? We in this together."

Jimmy spat, answering him without words, then backed away from the car. "Come or split, it's your choice." When he was twenty feet away from the man, he turned his back on him, his eyes scanning Sheridan Road for a break in the traffic. He didn't hear any footsteps behind him.

Gunon had the receiving unit on his lap, watching the dot carefully, taking his eyes away to slap Tina one time, hard, when she opened her mouth to speak. He heard a sharp intake of breath from the back seat.

"You got a problem with that, Anthony?" No answer. Good. After all he'd done for this punk, he should be able to rip this broad's bloomers off, have a go at it without Giraldi opening his mouth.

The slap, though, had straightened her out. Jesus, some broads, thought they were men.

"You his old lady, on the street?" Roosevelt asked.

Silence.

"Lady, I ain't gonna ask you two times." He took one huge hand off the steering wheel, casually, brutally, motioned toward her. She leaned away from him, but Gunon pushed her back. She gasped, but did not answer.

Roosevelt hit her with the back of his hand, his eyes never leaving the road.

"Bitch," he said, "there's something you got to understand here, the rule book's out the window, we ain't got a fucking *thing* to lose." Then, to Gunon, "You getting the picture?"

Gunon said, "Sure."

Giraldi said, "*What* picture."

Stupid kid, you had to spell it all out for him.

Gunon said, "Anthony, sometimes, I just don't know. Don't you get it? Can't you see what we *got* here? Jesus Christ, a way out of it for the three of us and you can't even think on your feet good enough to figure it out."

He paused, waiting, enjoying himself, until at last Giraldi said, "Figure *what* out!"

"Shit, this here counselor's the bitch come into the office to drag Vale out, don't you recognize her?"

"Yeah . . ."

"Today we're waiting for the guy to go out on his caper, and who's there on the stoop to kiss him good-bye?"

"She's *in* on it?!"

"In on it, your ass, she's probably the ringleader. All the rich people these lawyers got for clients, she probably goes over, has high tea with them, then sends Vale out to take the place down." He looked over at Tina, appraising her. "Give him some puss to keep him in line, make sure the split's right, ain't it, doll?"

Tina stayed silent.

"So what we got here," Gunon said, "is a crooked lawyer, on Vale's payroll. Desk sergeant at headquarters seen her ranting and raving, shit, probably twenty, thirty uniforms, too. In cahoots with the thieves. Who, by the way, we been following all fucking day. She's the driver, though, now. We just made her part of the act." Gunon waited, pleased with himself. He fiddled with the dial of the receiver, told Roosevelt to make a left at the next corner, then straight ahead. Behind the wheel, Roosevelt grunted assent, then picked up where Gunon had left off.

"What you're missing, Tony, is right there in front of you. The bitch kills the commander, he gets decorated, post-hum-ous-ly, then *you* kill the bitch who killed our boss."

"*After*," Gunon said, "we use her as bait to get the money from the thieves."

"*Madronne*," Giraldi said.

Roosevelt parked in front of the Scotland Yard Bookstore, less than three blocks from the Tile estate, sitting tensely, waiting.

Giraldi spoke first, breaking the silence. "How long you figure it take them to get in?" As far as Ryan could see, Giraldi was the only one of the three showing outward signs of nervousness. Gunon and Roosevelt just sat there staring ahead, their attitudes telling Giraldi to leave them alone. Strange woman, sitting there between them, silently, maybe praying. Not crying or begging; she seemed to be holding up better than Ryan. Ryan sat in the back seat, next to Giraldi, counting the minutes to his death.

Gunon spoke, but not to Giraldi. "They leave Lockhart outside, you think, Rosy?"

"Ain't no other way. Man ain't a thief, he's a junkyard dog, a guard."

"Think they've had time to make their move?"

In response Roosevelt started the car, put it in drive. "If they haven't, we'll just take them there, blast 'em all, and the snitch, too."

"Yeah, but if they ain't in the house, we can't get at it, at the shit in there, the drugs, the money."

"We'll teach the Mad Dog a lesson about paying according to his capabilities another time, we got to. Right now, we got asses to save. Our own." He raised his voice, spoke to Giraldi now.

"Leave the cuffs on till after he's dead. Do it when you feel the time's best. Either inside the grounds or, if they ain't gone in yet, after we do the thieves. If we got to do it now, if we can't wait quietly for the thieves, then do the bitch second, but use your service revolver. The cold piece goes into her hand, once she's dead."

"We got no jurisdiction out here, Rosy." Ryan heard Giraldi speak, encouraged by the words, even by the crack in the man's voice. And he suddenly knew the truth. *This man did not want to kill him,* was looking for ways out.

"Sure we do. We followed these boys all afternoon on a tip the commander there got, shit. That's why we didn't know about the other crews getting picked up. We been out doing our jobs, and if the performance of our duties take us beyond the city limits, well, hell, don't you read the rule book, Anthony? I mean, does *crime* have boundaries? Shit, then why should we?"

This got a laugh from Gunon, which chilled Ryan. He was breathing in slow, measured breaths, trying to put it out of his mind, telling himself this wasn't happening to him. He wanted to shout at them, scream his rage, but the terror held him in check. Maybe, if he was silent and compliant, Giraldi wouldn't do it, would let him go while the others were blasting away at the thieves. That would leave only the woman for him to look after.

"But the U.S. attorney called him, right? I mean, the guy

knows Ryan was safe at twelve-thirty, in his office, not about to go out following thieves.''

Roosevelt's head began to bob, and Ryan saw Giraldi flinch at the sight. What did that mean? Gunon half-turned in the seat, his smirky smile in place.

"Anthony, calm down, will you? Nervous, huh? First time out? You got to earn your spurs, same as we did. See, thing is, Tony, we don't give a fuck what the U.S. attorney, the FBI, the chief of police, or anyone *else* thinks. We don't even care what they *know*. The only thing that counts right now is what they can prove, and if we stick together, get the story right, there ain't a goddamn thing they'll be able to prove.'' He smiled at Ryan, shook his head.

"Kid got a long way to go, eh, buddy?'' He turned back to Giraldi.

"Just sit there and tell yourself, we was following the thieves all afternoon, over and over again. So when the feds ask you what happened, you got the idea in your mind.''

"Can I ask one more question?''

Roosevelt said, "What!''

"Should I take the gun I kill him with from one of the thieves, should I use one you got extra, or what? You said you had a cold piece. I'm not gonna use my own, have the tests show it was from my service weapon.''

Roosevelt said, "Good thinking, see, Anthony, now you're on the ball. Take one of theirs, shit, they'll be packed to the gills.''

Ryan looked at Giraldi, who ignored him, and lost his momentary and tiny sense of comfort, knew with a supreme certainty that there was absolutely no hope.

Jimmy walked with purpose to the side of the house, looking through the iron gate at the guardhouse, through the window, seeing nothing but the cadmium glow of the television screens in the empty room.

These guys, these so-called pros, they had to make everything so complicated. Okay, Frank needed Adam to get in, but why the *Sea Hunt* bit, when there was no one to challenge them from the front?

He was in dark shadows, on a small patch of lawn that separated the iron gate from the wooden privacy fence of the estate next door. He looked up, then back through the window, then out to the street, waiting for a break in the traffic. When he couldn't see any headlights he squatted down and leaped up, caught the top of the iron bars, did a slow pullup, got one leg between the bars, resting on the square iron crossbar, then balanced himself, brought up the other leg and stood, awkwardly, waving his arms, staring down at razor-sharp tips. He jumped off, hit soft grass at the side of the guardhouse.

He walked around, crouching, to the front of the place, the trank gun in his hand. He wasn't worried about taking any guard's life, but about the noise the weapon might make in the open, how far the explosion would travel on the night air, with the lake right behind them. He came to the front door and threw it open, rolled in with the pistol extended, held in both hands, came to a stop when he hit the wall.

Nothing. He got to his feet and searched the place, moving quickly. The house had looked tiny from the outside, in perspective, with the mansion behind it. From the inside it was every bit as big as Frank's place. There wasn't a living soul inside the building.

Jimmy put the trank gun back down his pants and pulled one of the .38's, walked out the door and along the fence to the side of the house, from there along to the back, taking care as he passed the basement windows. He heard the muffled sound of a man screaming and stopped, terror gripping him. Had they caught Frank? Were they torturing him down there?

He lowered himself to the ground, between two of the windows, inched forward until he could just see into the basement.

There was rack after rack of tall shelving down there, and he could see the corks stuck into the wine bottles that protruded from every square. He squirmed another inch, then could see one man, an old guy, Tile. Standing in front of a man whose legs Jimmy could see. He inched forward, hearing Tile screaming now, so close, Jesus, if Tile looked up . . .

He got a full look at the man in the chair and stopped short, in shock.

They had the guy tied to the chair, three of them, Tile and two other old guys. The guy in the chair had his shirt ripped to his waist. Slabs of fat shook at his sides, in front. On his nipples and all around them there were large red ugly marks. Burn scars.

Tile yelled something, right in the man's face, then waved at the tall old guy, who puffed hard on a cigar, blew the smoke at the tip then stepped forward, casually laid the glowing ash against the man's left nipple. As the guy screamed and struggled, Tile motioned to the other old man, a fat guy with a bald head, and this man stepped forward, in Jimmy's way but he could tell what the man was doing.

He was cutting the man's pants away from his body.

Jimmy blinked his eyes and began to back away. He told himself that the guy in the chair probably deserved it, told himself he had seen worse, trying to calm himself down. This was nothing compared to the sight of Captain Stanley, getting gang-raped, then crawling around pathetically with the nightstick in his backside. He'd watched that with a casual detachment, used it as his way out of the joint.

The difference was, back in the joint, stuff like that was commonplace, was expected. Not here, in this town, with all these mansions, this kind of thing happening in the basement of a house had to cost ten million . . .

He was easing back, his head out of sight of the window now, trying to control his terror, shaking, then moving fast, digging his feet in for a purchase to stand and run around back, when his right foot slipped, tapped hard against the glass of the window behind him, and all hell broke loose.

The unmarked squad pulled up right next to the only other car in the parking lot. Ryan could see a tall broad-shouldered man leaning over the seat, staring at them. The man started to get out of the car and Roosevelt hit him with the spot, making sure his hands were empty. The man in the car got it and raised his hands as he eased out, chest high, like he was used to doing it.

He had felon written all over him, from the cut of his Elvis haircut to the scars on his right cheek, the belly hanging over his

belt, even the stance, the attitude, his eyebrows raised innocently—
There some problem here, officer? Ryan noted these things with
heightened perception, wishing he could change places with the
man. He would get hassled, maybe even beaten, but he'd get to
live.

The man smiled tentatively as he saw Roosevelt, came closer,
bending at the waist and speaking from four feet away, as if he
was afraid to come within grabbing distance.

"They inside, all of them by now."

Ryan looked across the street, at the silent mansion, the piped
roof. It was hard for him to believe that violence was occurring
behind those ivied walls.

"How long they been gone?"

"Twenty minutes, sir." Good touch, calling Roosevelt sir.
Redneck asshole Elvis impersonator, probably wanted to say *nigger*
instead.

Gunon spoke loudly, leaning over Roosevelt, Tina stuck between them, her hands up, trying now to push him back.

"Good job, Wayne, that's real good." Gunon was smiling,
ignoring Tina but getting back on his side of the car, getting out of
the car; look, see? How could a friendly guy like me hurt anyone?

The man Gunon had called Wayne stood up, stepped back
cautiously, as Roosevelt, too, got out of the car. Ryan watched
them, the two of them coming slowly at Wayne, who was backing
up, fighting hard to keep the smile on his face.

Ryan felt something touch his hand and jumped, a high squeal
forcing its way past his lips. He saw the woman moving swiftly,
silently, toward the open door. . . . Softly, Giraldi shushed him,
dropped something cold and small into his hands, something steely,
something . . .

Jesus Christ, the key to the handcuffs.

Giraldi whispered to the woman, "Get down, under the dash-
board, *now*, lady!"

Roosevelt and Gunon were closing on Wayne now, whose back
was against the car, Gunon's hand going into his back pocket,
coming out with a long slim blackjack. The smile had vanished
from Wayne's face, and he began to drop his hands.

Ryan worked the key, his hands shaking so hard he dropped it into his lap, twice, working there in the dark, his eyes going from the key to the scene outside the vehicle, his terror enhanced because now he had a way out, there was hope, he could live if he could get just these goddamn cuffs off his hands before one of them turned, spotted him there working at it.

He noticed the interior light going on, could not see the woman. She had obviously followed orders. He was vaguely aware that Giraldi had opened his door and was getting out of the vehicle, weapon drawn—there! The left hand was free!

Ryan moved to slide over, away from the three men out there on his side of the car, wanting the vehicle between him and them when he made his break, but Giraldi was in the way, standing behind the open door, half in a crouch, his weapon obviously on the car's roof, taking aim.

Ryan turned frantically, looked through the window in time to see the sap come up and heard Giraldi yell "FREEZE!" at the top of his lungs just as Gunon brought the blackjack down with a terrible thunking sound on the top of the hillbilly's head, sounding like an axe going into a tree. The man went down, dead before he hit the grass, and Roosevelt was turning quickly, going for his gun.

"State's attorney police, asshole, drop it!" Giraldi yelled it and across the street a piercing shriek began and everyone jumped, then Gunon dropped to the ground, tearing at his gun, Roosevelt fired and Giraldi dropped him, fired three quick ones into Roosevelt's massive chest, turned his pistol on Gunon and didn't give him any more warning, just blasted off the other three caps into him. Gunon stopped moving and just lay there, dead.

The siren across the street was incessant, a steady, shrill sound that wouldn't let up. Ryan listened to it, too frightened even to have ducked down out of the line of fire.

He heard Giraldi breathing, gasping for air and letting it out hard, the man's knees weak. Giraldi lowered himself slowly onto the seat, quivering. In the front, the woman's head peeked cautiously over the seat.

Giraldi said, "Jesus, oh, Jesus."

All right, Ryan thought. Put the fear behind you. Work through it. He was a commander, goddamnit, not some punk of a thief. He took charge. "Anthony. That your name? Anthony, get on the horn, call the cops. Anthony?"

Giraldi looked at him, breathing hard, quivering. . . . "All this time, I thought you were dirty."

Ryan was shaking pretty good himself. He said, "Me, too."

"State's attorney told me you *all* were dirty."

"Feds told me the same thing."

Giraldi gave out a little shaky laugh, remembering what had to be done in that moment, getting quickly out of the car and going over to the bodies, kicking the pistols away from them before checking for vital signs.

Ryan got out of the car and went around to the front, sat down in the driver's seat, smiled at the woman, who waited until now to break down. He put his arm around her, told her it was going to be all right, everything was okay. Then he picked up the radio and began to call for help.

Chapter

THIRTY-ONE

They came out of the water together, close, the both of them sweating from more than exertion. They crawled on their hands and knees to the water's edge, moving away from each other, each going to opposite sides of the iron fence to make harder targets. Frank tearing the guns from the bag, holding them one in either hand, ready. He stopped and gave the boat a quick glance—he'd been right, these arrogant bastards even left the key in it; who'd fuck with the great Mike Tile?

Adam paid him no attention, stood and moved quickly toward the growth of bushes, Frank in step with him on the other side of the private beach. Adam stopped, studied the stairs for alarms, traps, saw nothing. He nodded at Frank and they pulled together again, began to slowly mount the stairs, Frank's head swiveling from side to side, the weapons at the ready, held waist-high, barrels pointed out.

Adam stopped at the sliding glass window, began to study it as Frank peered into the house, looking for trouble, seeing nothing.

Adam touched Frank's shoulder, and they moved back, away from the glass. Frank put his ear next to Adam's mouth.

"Top-flight, Frank. Gonna be hard." The whisper was difficult to distinguish, the words spoken with fear. Frank moved back and Adam put his ear in place.

Frank said, "How long?" and they switched again.

"Hour, minimum."

Frank moved away, took up a position on the deck, and Adam opened his bag, removed the tools of his trade, and stepped to the glass door . . .

As the alarm blasted off.

They both dropped into a crouch and Frank looked at Adam and Adam raised his hands—"I didn't do nothing!" He dropped the equipment in his hands as Frank threw him the gun, took a step forward as he waved Adam back, took aim and blew the lock off the sliding glass door, pushed it open and ran into the house, already knowing what had happened.

Frank ripped the mask from his face and when he screamed his voice was an anguished wail.

"Jimmy!" he yelled once, then ran into the darkness of Mike Tile's mansion.

They started shooting at the window, weapons going off rapidly, a couple of them, Jimmy could make that out. He lay between the windows, his hands over his head, the .38 in his right hand ready, the hammer back. As soon as there was a break in the shooting, he made his move.

He leaped to his feet and, shooting at the basement window, began to run around back, to where Frank would be. He got to the edge of the house, stuck his head around slowly, the gun at his right cheek.

No one was there.

Desperately he ran around toward the back porch, the bushes and tree limbs grabbing at him, holding him back, slowing his progress, and when he heard Frank calling his name, he gave a mighty push and was free, ran onto the porch and into the house through the sliding glass doors.

He saw Adam's back, Adam moving slowly, a weapon in his hand, backing Frank up from the rear. Jimmy let his breath out, stepped farther into the house in time to see a figure move from the shadows, gun pointed, the man shooting Adam three times in the back as Jimmy stepped forward, screaming, emptying his own gun into the man. The man went down and Jimmy went to Adam, kneeled quickly and took a fast look. Dead.

How many were in the house? Was it a trap? And where was Frank, had they captured him? Jimmy threw the empty .38 away and reached into his pocket, got the other one.

Stupid move, coming in here. Jimmy ran back through the door, outside and around the house, ignoring the thorns that tore at his face and clothing, running hard but not moving fast enough. He ran to the window he had looked through, got down and saw that at last he'd done something right.

Mike Tile was hiding, his terrified face sneaking out past the shoulder of the guy in the chair, looking at the two other old men, who were advancing on the staircase, firing handguns, their backs to Jimmy.

He shot through the glass, aiming carefully, the first bullet hitting the taller man and spinning him, the second bullet entering his belly, the man falling as Jimmy turned the gun on the shorter guy, began squeezing the trigger, not stopping until the pistol was empty.

He used the butt of the pistol to break the glass, slid through feet first, went directly to Mike Tile.

"How many are up there!"

"One, just one, I swear to God!"

The man in the chair was screaming at him, giving thanks that they'd shown up, ordering Jimmy to untie him. Jimmy pulled the trank gun and held it at Tile's head, at the temple. At this range, at that spot, pulling the trigger would ice him.

"Frank! That you?"

The guy in the chair was hollering, telling Jimmy he worked for him, goddamnit, untie him. "Shut the fuck up," Jimmy said, watching as Frank ran down the stairs, the gun ready. Jimmy pushed Tile away from him and the man fell to the ground, his hands waving around his head, begging.

"Give me the gun, Frank," Jimmy said.

"We got to get the fuck out. *Now,* Jimmy. Get Adam and split."

Jimmy pulled the gun from Frank's hand. "Adam's dead." He turned to Tile.

"I know what you're doing here, that fucker lied to you, he killed your father!" Tile was cowering, crying. Jimmy walked to him, slowly. "I didn't do it! The order came from Campo and he did it, the Lion did it, I swear to God." Jimmy raised the gun and fired one shot, into the man's head. He turned before Tile's body had stopped seizing.

"Jimmy, *no!*" It was Frank, standing in front of the guy in the chair, the Lion. Protecting him.

"Jimmy, he's our ticket, we can't kill him, listen to me!"

"Frank, get out of my way."

"We need him to square it for us, Jimmy, or won't either of us live till morning."

"Get out of my way, Frank!"

Frank said, "You got to shoot me first, Jimmy. Me, then him, if you're gonna do it. Just kill me now."

Jimmy lowered the gun and stared at Frank. Above the din of the alarm, they could hear the first faint sounds of sirens.

"Untie the fucker, then, while I find the safe."

"No time for that. Get upstairs, out the back, start the boat. I'll be there in a minute."

Jimmy surprised him, he didn't argue. As if in a trance, he turned and began to walk toward the stairway, taking his time.

What saved them was the gate. By the time the cops found one of their own brave enough to find a safe spot to climb over, the powerboat was gone, out in the distance, the motor too far away to be heard from the tiny pier.

Frank steered, Jimmy guarding DiLeonardi. It wasn't the way Frank would have liked it, but the kid hardly knew how to drive, you couldn't expect him to know how to steer a boat at night.

Frank used the skyscrapers as his source for bearings, the lights of the Sears Tower at first, just to get near the city, then the Hancock building when it came into view. If he played it right, he could pull the boat to the lake breakwater less than two blocks from his house. Get them ashore, then sink the thing.

He stood on the rocks, watching the boat sink, hearing DiLeonardi's heavy breathing. Frank had to hand it to the guy, he was patient, knowing Jimmy would kill him if he opened his mouth. He'd wait until he got Frank alone, then offer him a deal, which Frank would take. He couldn't spend his life running from these guys. . . .

"It's under, Frank, what are we waiting for?"

Frank turned to him, to his brother, or the man who had once been his brother. There was no resemblance anymore between the youngster he had once loved and this person in front of him. Iceman? No, that could be turned on and off at will. What he was looking at was an institutionalized creature of the prisons system, a man without conscience or compassion. The way he'd killed Tile, just executed him. Still, Frank knew all along that would be part of the deal.

To his brother he said, "Let's go."

Across the street, Ryan used the car radio to run down Drumwald, after he'd alerted the Winnetka police to what was going down in Tile's mansion. He'd talked to the man, patched through to his home line, watching as the law from three neighboring suburbs stormed the estate, guns drawn, crouching and holding their weapons in one hand. Amateurs. They'd be lucky to get into the house without one of them shooting one of their own.

Drumwald spoke with authority, calmly, probably sipping cognac in front of his fireplace with some cute young secretary who wanted to wind up someday in the governor's mansion. He said, "Quite a night's action, eh, Ed?" And the bastard actually chuckled, as if Ryan had just described the plot of a TV show to him.

Drumwald said, "What I want you to do now, get one of those local yokels to drive you right down to FBI headquarters. Turn yourself in. Get some rest, man, my God, it's been a rough night for you. I'll debrief you in the morning, how's that?''

Ryan listened to the man, the pain in his head getting stronger with every word Drumwald spoke. Giraldi was next to him, smoking, his head down, shaking it from time to time, expelling white smoke that curled up and softly attacked the windshield. Ryan leaned over, reached into Giraldi's shirt pocket and took out his cigarettes, his lighter, saying, Uh-huh, sure, into the mike, but thinking: asshole.

He played the string out, though, knowing what he was going to do before Drumwald even stopped speaking. When the U.S. attorney finally said good night—cheerily—Ryan dropped the mike and turned, waiting a minute to be sure his voice was calm before he spoke.

''Anthony?''

Giraldi looked up, without much interest.

''I need a favor.''

''A favor. Right, you need a favor. Commander, after this, there are no favors. From tonight on, there's owesies due.''

''Then I'm calling it in. I want you to drive me to my apartment, where I'll give you a bunch of papers to deliver to Drumwald tomorrow, after you make copies for your boss. Then I want us to escort this lady home, make sure you alone pick her up tomorrow, get her statement. It can wait till then, on my authority. Then I'll be needing a ride to the airport.''

Tina was in the car, silent again, sometimes dropping her head to her hands, but most of the time bearing up well for someone who'd been so near death.

Had to be tough on her, knowing her boyfriend or client or whatever Vale was to her was inside that mansion, that the cops would not be in a good mood when they stormed the house, would shoot first and ask questions later.

''Going somewhere, Commander? That little prick on the wire say something to upset you?''

''I need a rest, a little vacation. I heard Florida's nice this time of year.'' They both looked around, at the platoons of police officers charging around madly on Mad Mike Tile's lawn. He

298

looked at Tina, and she was looking back at him. He nodded, encouragingly, but she didn't say anything. Well, it might take her awhile. He hoped she'd be all right.

If they left right now, they'd be long gone before any of that crew across the street got organized enough to come looking.

Giraldi started the car, backed out, and turned down Sheridan Road, driving slowly. He said, "Florida's hot, around the southern tip, this time, Commander."

"I was thinking," Ed Ryan said, "more around Tarpon Springs."

On the way, Anthony Giraldi got on the horn and called his boss, who was a lot less casual than Drumwald. After a quick rundown of the night's work, Giraldi told the man he'd be in as soon as he could get back to the city, then gave him the names of the men who had done all the damage at Tile's estate.

"Frank Vale and his brother Jimmy. Guy named Adam Lebeaux, and a hillbilly, Wayne Lockhart. Lockhart's dead. Confirmed. The others are all in the house or escaped some way, I didn't see the local law bringing out any prisoners."

When the state's attorney asked him if he knew any addresses it was in his mind to tell the man, shit, look in the computer, but remembered that state's attorneys had a habit of becoming mayors. He had to think for a minute, remembering back to a couple of hours ago, when they'd grabbed the woman.

There it was, hell, just a few miles down Sheridan Road. He told his boss the address, was embarrassed when the man congratulated him. More embarrassed because Ryan was listening in, and Ryan had damn near been killed tonight and all his boss wanted to do was get a good night's sleep, talk to you on the morrow. Still, it felt good, getting a stroke from the Man.

When the man told him he would send some troops over to the house, just in case, Giraldi signed off and turned to Ryan.

"What the hell's in Tarpon Springs besides sponges, Commander?"

It was cold in the car. This was not something either of them was used to doing, this surveillance bullshit. They wouldn't have been on Manny's crew if they weren't shooters, they'd both been made, but goddamnit, Danny figured if you had a hit, you just went up to the guy, whacked him out, and that was that.

Still, the way Manny had looked at them, his pistol ready. No, it wouldn't be him who would drive them home empty-handed.

It had taken over an hour to find out where the guy lived, which had been a pain in the ass, what with Kenny bitching about how hungry he was in every bar they went into, pouring booze down, too, as they spoke to people. Manny was right: They were getting soft. Drinking on a hit? A couple of years ago, Danny would have shot Kenny himself for even thinking about it.

They sat, one hour, then two, across the street from the son of a bitch's house, Danny's anger overflowing, behind the wheel, smoking and coming up with more and more creative ways to do the guy, teach him about showing up where you're supposed to be on time. Fucking Tino, he got to drive the broads home. Was probably tooting lady and sucking puss right now.

"There they are!" It was Kenny, sitting up, all excited.

They removed their weapons, watching the three men walking up to the house, a fat guy in the middle, staggering.

"Let's do it," Danny said, and they got out of the car, quickly.

Frank heard running footsteps as he turned the key in the lock, turned in time to see two men running down the empty street at them, weapons drawn. He pushed the door open, shouted to Jimmy, who turned, spotted the trouble and dropped into a crouch, aiming and shooting the first guy, adjusting and firing at the second, who stopped, raised his hands in surrender as Jimmy fired three more times. The guy joined his partner on the street.

Frank shoved DiLeonardi into the house, began to follow him but stopped because Jimmy was walking away from the house, toward the gunmen.

"Jimmy! Get your ass in here!"

"Where'd they come from, Frank? They were waiting. Not good at what they do, either." He spoke over his shoulder, walking rapidly toward the two bodies, seeming unconcerned.

300

"Jimmy, for Christ's sake, get *in* here!"

Jimmy dropped down to one knee, picked up the men's pistols, gave their bodies a fast search. Frank heard him say, "Shit, no extras." He hefted the two weapons, one in each hand, and began to walk back toward the house.

"My gun was empty, Frank. These goofs, they come out on a hit without any extra clips. Think they're the Lion's?"

Frank was standing there staring at him, in awe. Softly, respectfully, fearfully, he said, "Jimmy, we got to get into the house, right now."

And Jimmy said, "Why, man, any fool can see it's all over." Then he laughed sadly. Stopped only when the first squad car came spinning around the corner, lights blaring.

Chapter

THIRTY-TWO

They were in the basement, the house surrounded. Frank was on the phone, buying time with the negotiator who was promising them the world if they would just put down their weapons and come on out. From time to time, Jimmy would bust a cap loose, out the window, just to keep them on their toes. By now, Frank knew, the SWAT teams would be out there, in charge of the situation. They'd let the negotiator bullshit with him until they were ready to make their charge, then they'd come in blasting.

The negotiator told him things without even knowing he had, though. Useless information, but still, Frank stored it away. Habit, more than anything else.

Like the guy saying, We know you and your brother are in there, and Frank said, You're fucking right we are, with enough dynamite to blow up the whole block. So they knew about Jimmy, somehow, but not about the Lion. Was there anything he could do with that? Get a clear line and let the Lion talk to someone at headquarters, someone who was in his pocket?

No, it was too late for that. The TV crews would be out there by now, newspaper people everywhere, they'd never just walk away from this one.

Yet they'd come so close. Just get into the house and get

DiLeonardi to make a few calls, get the word of honor of some-body high up in the New York mob that they had a free walkaway. These guys, they always kept their word. If those two bastards hadn't come charging up the street.

But they had. And now they were all dead.

Frank let the guy's voice drone in his ear, knowing that as long as the line was open they'd be okay. When the line went dead, they'd be coming in strong. He looked around him frantically, his mind racing, trying to find a way out.

The basement would be defensible, at least until they ran out of ammunition, which wouldn't take long. There was nowhere to go, not even to the crawl space. The cops knew the two of them were in there, would know there was no way they could escape. Still, maybe they should kill DiLeonardi and get down in there, it would at least take them some time to find them.

DiLeonardi cowered in the corner of the basement, this was not his fight. Jimmy had told him if he opened his mouth he would kill him, and now the Lion was staring frantically around him, looking for something to hide under.

The phone went dead in Frank's ear.

A tear gas canister came crashing through the far window, bouncing and exploding at Frank's feet. DiLeonardi screamed in terror and Jimmy turned to the window, fired once to make them move back, then turned to Frank.

Frank could see tears in Jimmy's eyes, then heard his brother apologize.

Little late for that.

"Get down in the hole, Frank."

"Come with me."

"I ain't going back to prison, Frank."

DiLeonardi screamed and Frank turned to him, saw that the man had opened his jaws so wide that his goddamn dentures had fallen out of his mouth. He was crying like a baby, about to die and knowing it, the tough guy who lived his life by a code he wasn't man enough to die with.

"Come on, right now, Jimmy. They'll be coming in a minute."

Jimmy mumbled something that Frank couldn't hear, and Frank

ran to the back of the furnace, opened his hole, then had a thought, and turned back to the mobster, the Lion.

Jimmy muttered again, but a bullhorn was blaring outside the window. Jimmy was sitting under the window, the guns in his hands, his back to the wall.

Frank walked over and picked up the Lion's false teeth as the bullhorn told them they had thirty seconds to come out or the house would be stormed. The second tear gas canister came through the window right above Jimmy's head, coming for Frank, who ducked. The thing landed in the Lion's lap. He bellowed, hitting at it, getting off his lap and curling into the fetal position as Jimmy stood, his head at the window, the bright lights behind him backlighting him. The sight clutched at Frank's heart.

"All I wanted was to find someone to hug me just fucking once." The words soft, whispered. Frank wasn't really sure what Jimmy had said.

Jimmy said, "You killed my father." Then shot Tonce DiLeonardi, over and over, the body jumping on the cold tile floor.

Frank looked up as the top of Jimmy's head came off and then he heard the rifle shot, the bullet passing through Jimmy and ricocheting around the basement.

He ducked, the teeth still in his hand, and, in shock, stared at the corpse of his only brother. Then shook himself alert.

If he hurried, he could do what he had to do before the cops came charging down on him.

Tina Lime had allowed them to take her home, but they couldn't make it past the corner; the block was being evacuated. Through the car windshield she could see Frank's house, brightly burning.

She'd only cried once, in the car, with the danger over and the commander there for a shoulder. She wasn't ashamed of that. She wouldn't do it again, though.

"I'll get out here," she said.

"Ma'am, listen to me, you've been through a lot tonight. Let us take you to a motel, or, hell, use my apartment, I won't be needing it.''

It was a kindly gesture and she appreciated it, but still, this was home. Without answering she got out of the car and stood there, watched as Giraldi waited to see what the commander would have him do. The commander sighed, nodded at her and she nodded back. He turned, waved Giraldi on, and the car glided from the curb.

Tina walked to the wooden yellow police barriers, horses, they called them. Her neighbors were all around her, shouting above the roar of the fire, some yelling curses at the dozen or so cops who were manning the line, some in bedclothes, some of the men in underwear, bitching about the cold.

As she stood there watching, a lone tear fell down her left cheek. Angrily, she wiped at it. Then watched unblinkingly as her lover's house burned to the ground.

They let them go back into their homes as soon as they were sure that Frank's house was in no danger of blowing up from a gas leak. Tina walked in a trance, into her building, with Nicky now beside her. With him there, she had someone to comfort, something to take her mind off what had happened that night.

"They made me leave Foo-foo!" Nicky voiced the complaint for maybe the tenth time, and Tina smiled. With children, her patience was never-ending.

"Foo-foo's going to be fine."

Nicky's mother told Tina that she wanted to talk to her tomorrow; see about a lawsuit. This was America, and these Gestapo bastards had no business pulling them out of their homes in the middle of the night. Tina told her she'd see her then.

She stayed up all night, sitting on her window ledge, watching the police sift through the house next door; watched them drag two body bags out, too.

In the afternoon, Giraldi came, alone, and took her downtown, where she gave a statement. Stayed with her the entire time, looking out for her. She appreciated that, too.

He hadn't been to bed yet either, she could tell. His eyes had dark bags under them, and he was wearing the same suit he'd had on the night before. In the car driving home, it got a little close, but she didn't complain.

At her curb he turned to her, knowing the story now, a decent cop who cared suddenly at a loss for words.

"I'm sorry about your . . . uh, boyfriend."

"No, you're not," Tina said, getting out of the car, then stooping down before closing it, she said, "but it's kind of you to say so."

The house next door was gone, just burnt beams and melted shingles everywhere. The large furnace had somehow survived the fire without blowing up, and she stared at it, waited for Giraldi to drive away before walking toward it, drawn to it.

The police had put their yellow tape up: POLICE LINE NO TRESPASSING printed repeatedly. She could see how much the locals respected it; all the scorched furniture was gone, stolen the second the law pulled away.

What could she expect? This was Uptown.

She held the tape, walked under it. Darkness was beginning to fall, and she walked carefully, stepping down into the basement, where Frank used to love to make love, the stereo playing something romantic. . . .

She didn't know how long she stood there, waiting for his spirit to come to her. She did know that it was full dark, though, when the noises started behind the furnace, making her jump.

The intense heat had made them wait a while before entering the house. Frank could hear them shouting outside, someone hollering that if they had explosives in there, the whole block might go, another voice screaming out, How'd the fucking fire start?

Frank had started it, after shoving his dentures into DiLeonardi's mouth. Poured alcohol on the man and had set his dead ass afire, even through his pain and shock, surprised at how easy it was to do. He'd gone over the bend, seeing Jimmy die. He tried to tell himself this but wasn't buying any.

*　　*　　*

The Iceman had finally lost it, trying to save his own sorry ass. Had turned into a subhuman.

He stayed down there, even after he knew they were gone, not sleeping, some of the time in a corner whimpering silently.

Even if he made it out of there, what would he have? Tina was a goner. She'd call the law on him or shoot him on sight. Jimmy was dead.

He looked at the money there in the strongbox. Jimmy's money. At his false identification. He could get away, hide out for a time and come back. There'd be a few million, altogether, that he could get his hands on.

Aloud, he said, "Big fucking deal."

He didn't want to come out, wanted to stay inside there, safe and warm, forever, slowly wasting away from starvation. Out there, a home invader could get invaded. By feelings, emotions, things a man in his line of work couldn't afford. Still, they came to him, overwhelmed him, and he couldn't deny them.

Jimmy had found a way to bury them, to get rid of the feelings and emotions that had blinded Frank. He'd served nine years in prison to get rid of the garbage, though, and that wasn't an option in Frank's mind.

Frank wondered if he should just lay down and close his eyes, try and will himself dead. How far would he get, a toothless man in a goddamn wet suit? He hadn't even had time to grab any of his clothes, get into something he could walk down the street in.

If only he'd grabbed one of Jimmy's guns on the way down. That'd be a way out. Easy too. It would beat prison.

He waited until his watch said he'd been there twenty-four hours, then collected his possessions, his money, his ID, everything in the strongbox, with the box under his arm. He wondered if there was a guard posted out there. If the door would open at all, or if the rest of the house had collapsed onto his little hatch . . .

The thought filled him with panic. Dying wasn't so bad, if he could do it at his own hand, but to let them win, to let them kill him that way, get the last laugh on him and not even know it. . . .

He ran up the ladder, hit his switches, and shoved his shoulder against the hatch. Slowly, it lifted. Frank stuck his head up until his eyes were clear of the hatch, looked around, saw nothing but scorched property, his property, everywhere. The upstairs walls weren't even standing. From the broken glass of the window Jimmy had been shot through, he could see that it was full dark, his watch hadn't broken. The furnace blocked his view of the rear of the house, but if there had been a cop posted, he'd have come running by now, coming to shoot ghosts.

He silently wormed his way out of the hole and carefully stepped over to the far window, the one nearest the alley. Any police guard would be out front, keeping the curious away, the scavengers, the souvenir hunters, the invaders. . . .

He slithered through the window and stood in what had been his backyard, but was now just a small plot of grass. It was important to him now to get away, far from here, quickly. He wondered if he was losing his mind, if he was really past it, because he felt tears streaming down his face. Some fucking Iceman.

He made it to the alley, stopped in the shadow of a garbage can, looked back over his shoulder, what was left of his heart yearning.

Was that a noise? A footstep?

Tina had waited, watching from behind the furnace, as Frank pulled himself out of some kind of hole. She stepped back, not daring to breathe, not wanting him to see her.

She couldn't reach out to him, not after what he'd done. She was a lawyer, for God's sake. She couldn't harbor fugitives.

Then she suddenly knew he hadn't lied to her. Frank had told her the truth when he'd said he was through, that he loved her. It wasn't in him to be cruel.

So why had he gone back to stealing? What had made him change his mind?

She could remember the sound of his voice as he told her, when she'd called, that he was working. It had sent a shiver up her spine, the coldness there. Frank, whom she'd loved. Casting her aside and going back for . . . what, the last big score?

If it had ended there she could have made it, could have gone on with her life and maybe someday forgotten him. But the police, what had happened, my God.

In her mind she pictured Frank in the basement with Jimmy, dying, being blasted by the thousands of rounds the police had shot into the house as it burned, getting back at them for shooting at the police through the windows. As soon as they'd seen the flames, they'd gone insane, someone had started shooting and then everyone was, emptying their guns into a burning house.

She pictured Frank in terror, dying, maybe his last thought being of her.

Then remembered how she'd felt as she stood there, hours passing, wishing him alive.

She made her way out of the house and walked slowly around the side, through the gangway. Saw him standing in the alley, looking back toward her house. The alley lamp cast enough light for her to see his face, the anguish there. . . .

She stood at the end of the burned-out house, stepping back when Frank stiffened, into the shadows, behind one of the few still mostly standing beams. He turned back and stared at what would be her living room window, the one she'd sat in all night, when she thought he was dead.

She remembered many happy, near-glorious times in this back-yard, barbecues last summer, Frank burning hot dogs while Foo-foo stole food from their plates, little Nicky so happy, Frank his surrogate father.

She stood there in the deep shadows, thinking these things, then watched Frank turn his back on her, begin to shuffle slowly out of the alley.

How far could he get in that rubber suit?

She waited, letting him walk out of her life, knowing this was for the best. Her heart was aching, each step he took a knife thrust deep into her chest. Still, she let him walk.

He stopped, turned one more time, the look on his face, his lips moving.

Softly, he whispered: "Tina . . ." His sense of loss devastating her.

Tina said, "Frank?" Then stepped out of the shadows, moving quickly toward him.

He stopped, startled at the sound of her voice, and she went to him, all business now, grabbed his hand and began to pull him away from the alley, the light hanging there above him.

"Come on," Tina said, her voice filled with conviction, her mind made up, "we've got to get you inside before someone spots us."